D1551703

72 Hours of Insanity:
Anthology of The Games

Volume 10

Other publications by The Writer's Workout:

72 Hours of Insanity, vols 1-9

Tales from the Cliff

Tales from the Toybox

Quarterly Literary Journal:

WayWords

Coming Soon:

Tales from the Other Side

The Writer's Workout is a registered
501(c)(3) nonprofit organization.
We appreciate your support!

With the collected works of:

John Adams, Calen Bender, Maria L. Berg,
Sarah Connell, Fiona Donaldson, Sean Fallon, Amber Felt,
Lisa Fox, Bridget Haug, EJ Howler, Jayne Hunter,
Teague LaBrosse, Kate MacGuire, Ella Moon, M. Ong,
S.E. Reed, Charlie Rogers, Allison Rott, Arden Ruth,
Jason Ryder, MM Schreier, EJ Sidle, Frances Turner,
and Rodaina Yasser

Dear Reader,

My brain is a very busy place. So many thoughts swirling in a chaotic cyclone.

How do I solve the problem of navigation beyond the curvature of the horizon? Is the date on my cottage cheese "sell by" or "use by" and how absolute is it? How do I talk about chemical nomenclature to my ESL students in a way that will keep them engaged? Remember that awkward thing I said to that person that one time?

<cringe>

On and on, ad nauseam.

There are a few places and things that can quiet my incessant mind chatter—a mountain trail, Mozart's french horn concertos, a truly glorious Cabernet… But tonight, I'm at the one place that outshines all others: the ocean after dark.

There's no one here but me and the thunderous rhythm of the waves. Overhead, stars sparkle, a multitude of ice chips in a velvet sky. On the point, a lighthouse blinks—white, green, white, green—and somewhere on the grass-covered dune, a nocturnal insect is chirping an amorous serenade.

New England beaches are different than their southern counterparts. The sand is yellow, not white, and coarser underfoot. There are very few shells, and the water, when I dip my toes in, is so cold it gives me an ice cream headache. The air smells of salt and wet seaweed and the promise that winter is on its way.

This is my place. The place where my thoughts quiet and I have access to that deep, still pool within. This is where my stories live. The home of inspiration and creative ingenuity. It's where the magic happens.

Too bad I don't live at the shore.

How I wish I could be in this perfect moment every time I wanted to write. But life intervenes. In the first Event of this portion of the Games, I was traveling, attending my cousin's funeral. I struggled with delayed flights, family obligations, and an overwhelming sense of grief and senseless loss.

And still, I wrote a story.

How? By channeling the feeling of that place where time stands still, if only for a little while. For each of us, that place is different. We get there by traveling our own unique paths. And yet the result is the same.

What you are about to find, as you turn the pages of this book, is the product of those journeys. The many and varied authors within have one thing in common—they've learned how to access that well of inspiration and put it on paper. It's our gift to you. May you enjoy the magic!

—MM Schreier

Table of Contents

Event 1 1

Some Roots Are Thicker Than Others *by John Adams* 3

Vanished *by Lisa Fox*...7

Empire Enlightenment *by Jayne Hunter* 17

Tread Softly Through the Apocalypse *by EJ Howler* 21

Monumental Militants *by Arden Ruth* 35

Event 2 47

The People v. Victor Frankenstein *by Sean Fallon*.......................49

The Story Inside *by Bridget Haug* 55

Regretless *by Calen Bender* 63

The Coldest Heart in Drumnacavny *by EJ Howler*.......................77

Through the Hum *by EJ Sidle* 91

Event 3 103

Breaking Eternity *by Fiona Donaldson*...105

Welcome Home *by M. Ong*..119

To Know Her Inside *by Maria L. Berg* 129

Shadows *by Jason Ryder* 143

Mine to Keep *by MM Schreier*..149

Event 4 157

Shadows Amongst the Sunflowers *by Sarah Connell*.................159

Obsessed With Watching the Nobodies *by S.E. Reed* 171

Paranoia *by Rodaina Yasser* 183

Are You Sure? *by Amber Felt* 193

The Pineapple Queen *by Kate MacGuire* 207

Event 5 221

For Want of Conversation *by MM Schreier*...................................223

PB&J Heroes *by Allison Rott* 229

Vlad & Johnny *by Ella Moon* 245

Whether We Weather the Weather *by Teague LaBrosse*..........261

The Bear Whisperer *by Kate MacGuire* 271

Martin and the Viral Video *by Charlie Rogers*...........................287

Judges' Choice 297

The Lightkeeper's Daughter *by Frances Turner* 299

The Authors 307

The Judges 313

Event 1
We Built This City

People have relied on landmarks for millennia but
sometimes their stories are lost in time.
For this Event, a landmark plays a pivotal role
in the narrative.

Core Concepts: cohesion, pacing

Some Roots Are Thicker Than Others

by John Adams
First Place

Mary Beth had hated clutter. Yet clutter is exactly what now surrounded the old tree. Ribbons. Stuffed animals. Pictures—some framed, some not. This picture showed Mary Beth in her cheerleader outfit, poised with pompoms on a bale of hay for her senior-year photos. That picture was her getting crowned homecoming queen, the surprise on her face almost believable. Over there was one of her in the front seat of a roller coaster, arms raised, cackling like a witch, Addie's tiny head barely peeking out from behind her.

Mary Beth had hated clutter. But she would have loved this attention.

The centerpiece of the shrine was a large cross, almost as tall as gangly 17-year-old Addie herself. It gleamed a pristine white. In the ten years since Mary Beth's friends had built the cross, Addie had not seen a single chip, not a smudge, not so much as a speck of dirt besmirching it. She studied its wooden structure, even gave it a light kick with the toe of her checkered Vans. The cross remained sturdy in place. Unmoving. Inescapable.

Beside the shrine, just behind the cross, stood the tree. The Tree Where Mary Beth Died. Only Addie called it that name, of course. The rest of Hawkscreek just called it 'the tree' or 'poor Mary Beth's memorial' or 'you know, Frank, where *it* happened.' But to Addie, it was The Tree Where Mary Beth Died.

Of course, back when Addie was a little kid, she had thought of it much differently. She had loved the tree like it was her only friend. Then, it had been *Addie's* tree. It was a crabapple—a word that once amused her—with the thick, gnarled branches of a fairy tale forest, slightly scary but always enthralling. The tree was not far from their house—farther than Mary Beth would have walked, for certain, but Addie was not Mary Beth. Even back then, Addie spent as much time away from home as possible. She idled away hours at her crabapple tree. Swinging from its branches like Tarzan. Entertaining herself under its shade with the Stephen King novels her father forbade her from reading at home. Climbing as high as she could, higher and higher, yet never quite reaching the top.

She had ignored the bugs, the spiders, the occasional cars passing by on Lindon Lane. She never once answered the calls from her mother on her emergency cellphone.

Not that such calls had come often.

Since Mary Beth's death, Addie had passed by the tree regularly—sometimes by necessity, oftentimes by curiosity. But she had not climbed it in some time. It was no longer 'her tree.' It was now The Tree Where Mary Beth Died.

"Happy anniversary, sis," Addie muttered to the cluttered shrine.

With that, she planted her hands onto the horizontal beam of the cross, pulled herself up, and vaulted forward. She landed against the tree with a *thud* and latched her arms and legs around it, hugging the thick bark, scratching her palms against the rough surface to the point where she drew blood. Her right foot twirled around until it found a steady-ish branch beneath it. She planted her foot, pushed off the branch, and began her climb.

The last time Addie had climbed her crabapple tree was ten years earlier, just a few hours before Mary Beth died. During that climb, Addie reached higher than she ever had, before finally running out of limbs that would support her. She returned home, face dirty, shirt ripped, and stumbled right into Mary Beth's pre-prom photo-taking spree.

"Mom! Dad! Adelaide's filthy! She's gonna get her muck all over my dress!"

"Adelaide, this is your sister's big night! She doesn't want a picture of you looking like that."

"Adelaide, go take a shower! You look like a little pig."

It was like the entire room had been staring down at Addie, their arms crossed, their eyes glaring. Mom. Dad. Mary Beth. The boy who killed Mary Beth.

As memories of that boy, that day, sifted through her mind, Addie continued her climb. She reached out one arm, then another. She pulled on a branch. Gave it a secure tug. Pulled herself up. And stepped onto a new limb.

Pull.

Tug.

Pull.

Step.

Hazarding a glance below, she saw Mary Beth's shrine, still beautiful, still waiting.

Mary Beth had been killed on her way home from prom. It was shortly after 10 p.m.—Mary Beth always minded her curfew—and her boyfriend, Tommy Dennison, had been drinking. After listening to the whispered snippets that trickled from gossiping lips

4

over the years, Addie now suspected they *both* had been drinking. But Mary Beth was not driving. And Mary Beth… was Mary Beth. Forever pure. Forever perfect.

Tommy's Toyota Sentry had jagged off Lindon Lane, whether from his intoxication or to avoid some errant animal, no one could say, and Tommy could later not remember. His front-right tire exploded. The car careened through a rickety fence and smashed directly into the crabapple tree. Addie's tree. The Sentry was totaled. Tommy was in intensive care for seven weeks. Mary Beth was killed on impact.

Yet the tree stood, taller than ever, with only the slightest slash marring its bark.

Some roots are thicker than others.

Pull. Tug. Pull. Step.

Addie continued her ascent, the cross, the photos, the ribbons now far below her.

Pull. Tug. Pull. Step.

Another branch. Another limb. Another scratch across her bleeding palm.

Pull. Tug. Pull. Step.

In the ten years since the accident, Mary Beth's memory hung over Hawkscreek. It did not so much haunt the small town as guide it, like she had planted seeds to tether herself to those she knew for the rest of their lives. Her picture forever emblazoned the town's threadbare website. The high school gymnasium and the elementary school library were both renamed in her honor. Every summer, the Mary Beth Memorial 5K raised money for childhood cancer, a cause Addie had never heard her sister mention, but which everyone gushed about as "something Mary Beth was so passionate about!"

Mary Beth's parents—Addie had trouble thinking of them as her *own* parents anymore, though biologically, they were— rooted deeper and deeper into memories of their lost daughter. Old photos. Old videos. Old lives.

The first ribbon had appeared on the tree the day after Mary Beth's funeral. It was followed by a teddy bear. Then a smattering of photos. Within a week, the cross was erected. The memorial grew over the months and years. When it rained, some dutiful friend of Mary Beth's who had never escaped Hawkscreek would bring a tarp, would perhaps even temporarily relocate a few of the more delicate items. The shrine became a landmark for Mary Beth's life, just as the tree had become a landmark for her death.

Pull. Tug. Pull. Step.

Addie climbed higher than she ever remembered reaching.

Pull. Tug. Pull. Step.

The limbs near the top, once too fragile for the weight of seven-year-old Addie, had grown and strengthened and now easily supported the 17-year-old girl.

Pull. Tug. Pull. Step.

She was almost there. Almost to the top.

Pull.

Tug.

Pull.

Step.

And with that, she was there. She was at the top of the tree. And it was no longer The Tree Where Mary Beth Died. It was once again her tree, Addie's crabapple tree, the place she had so loved as a child, amusing and scary and delightful. And hers. She had finally made it.

And when she looked down, when she looked at the world of Hawkscreek so far below her, she could barely see Mary Beth's shrine at all.

Vanished
by Lisa Fox
Second Place

"*Dear Editor of the Des Moines News:*
I am writing to you for help, since no one else will believe me, and maybe somebody out there will read this letter and say they saw what happened to my friend ten days ago at that Mysterious Monolith that popped up on the outskirts of the beach just outside Woodmont. My friend is missing, and nobody seems to care—not my parents, not the police, not the National Guard that's watching the tourists who crowd around that thing like it's the Space Needle or something. The monolith is big, but not THAT big.
Anyway, my friend's name is Jimmy, he just turned 12, and he's staying here in Des Moines, Washington, with his grandma while his dad's away in jail. He doesn't like to talk much about his family—I don't even know his last name—so he's probably gonna be mad at me for telling you all this. But somebody's gotta do something to help, and I'd rather have him get mad at me than have something bad happen to him.
Jimmy's a little taller than me, about five foot three, with red hair and freckles. He likes the Marlins because he's from Florida, thinks the Xbox is better than the PS5, and peels the cheese off his pizza before he eats it.
We rode our bikes over to that obelisk just before lunchtime on July 2nd, on the day after it showed up, and there were lots of people standing around taking pictures. If you saw my friend there, or if you know where he went, please help.
My parents are probably gonna ground me for writing this note (especially since they told me to stay away from the obelisk…something about aliens or UFOs), but I don't care.
I just want Jimmy back. I feel like I'm the only one who's out there looking for him.
Thanks for your help,
Mike Hooper from Des Moines"

It's cold.
Inside a freezer cold.
Snow-cold.
I guess.

I've never actually seen snow, except on the Weather Channel.

Maybe I'll never see snow.

Maybe I'll never see anything again.

It's so dark in here. Darker than night.

Maybe darker than space.

So dark I can't see my hand if I wave it in front of my face.

My eyes won't adjust, because there's nothing to adjust to. Not one sliver of light in here.

If I lean back against the wall, it stings my back like frozen bees.

Can bees freeze?

Funny, how that rhymes.

Bees. Freeze.

The bee's knees.

Grandmother's always saying that, something's the bee's knees, and then she laughs and coughs like there's some gunk in her throat. There usually is.

And I have no clue what she's talking about. Bees don't have knees. At least, I don't think they do.

Guess it doesn't matter, now.

It's tight in here. There's no room for me to lay down, so I just sit, lean forward, press my head into my knees.

Jimmy's knees.

I can't stop myself from chuckling, and my laugh bounces off the walls like I'm in some little cave.

Echo.

Echo.

It's not funny.

But it is.

I wiggle my toes inside my sneakers to keep the blood flowing. If I let them rest too long, they go numb. They sleep.

Maybe I shouldn't sleep.

Maybe I am asleep.

How long have I been here? A day, a week?

Is this what dead feels like?

Maybe I'm dead. Maybe I should be.

There was light outside. The brightest light I'd ever seen. The sun shimmered in a million tiny glowing boxes from the surface of that Mysterious Monolith. Or is it an obelisk? Who knows? Who cares? But I looked up to the top of it, all the way to its tip, poking like a spear into the sky. I reached for it. I wanted to touch—I needed to touch—its smooth, sparkling edges.

It was like a box full of stars twinkling in the sunlight.

But then there were hands.

Icy fingers. Squeezing me.
And a flash, and then…
Nothing.
Now I'm here.

"Dear Jimmy:

I'm leaving you this letter outside the obelisk, on the off chance that you're around somewhere. It's weird, usually when people go missing from someplace or when something bad happens, people leave flowers and pictures and candles. Stuffed bears, too. At least that's what they show on the news. But there's nothing here, just my letter. I'm folding it up tight so no one sees it and throws it away by accident, or tries to read it, just in case.

There's a lot of people here. Those weirdos in the funny clothes—the red sneakers and white sweatsuits—the ones we laughed at, they're still milling around, like they were the last day I saw you. The Guard is still shooing away those older teenagers drinking out of paper bags. Don't know what's so bad about that, but whatever. People are having picnics. Everybody here is taking selfies with the Mysterious Monolith. All the girls are making those stupid duck-lip faces that they put up on Instagram. With all the pictures, you'd think someone would have seen you in one of them.

The Des Moines News never printed my Letter to the Editor. Insta, Facebook, and Snap keep taking down my posts about you, too, some violation of fake news policy or something. I'm trying, Jimmy. I'm really trying. The cops still won't listen. And the Guard ignores me, as many times as I ask them. They say I should go write a book of my fairy tales, that I have a wild imagination. Jerks.

I wish you'd told me your last name. Or your grandma's name. Or where you lived. It didn't seem important then, but I wish I'd asked you when I had the chance.

In town, I stop every old lady I see and ask if they're Jimmy's grandma. Some of them yell at me and tell me to go harass someone else. Others pat me on the head and tell me to be a good boy and help them with their groceries. Most just ignore me and walk right past.

I won't give up on you.
Your friend,
Mike
P.S. Marlins have won three in a row."

I'm growing.
Or the room is shrinking.

It's hard to tell.

My knees are pushed so hard into my chest now, I can barely breathe. My hair's grazing some type of ceiling that wasn't here before. If I rub the top of my head against it, tiny sparks shoot out, pricking my scalp like some Fourth of July sparkler.

Kind of like the ones Dad brought home when I was really small and Mom was still around. She'd holler at him that it was too dangerous, that my little fingers would blow off or melt away or something, I can't remember.

She was afraid I'd end up like that Thompson boy down the street.

But Dad would laugh and squeeze her into him. Her shoulder fit right under his sweaty armpit. It was kinda gross, actually. 'Thompson boy's a dumbass, lighting off them cherry bombs like that,' Dad would say. When Mom wasn't listening, he told me he thought the Thompson boy deserved to lose those three fingers. 'People who don't respect the flame have no business going near it,' he'd say. Whatever that meant.

'But this here's a sparkler, just the right size for our Jimmy. Right, champ?' Then Mom would frown as he lit it up—seemed Mom always frowned when she was with us. Her eyes always seemed like they were somewhere else, until one day, she was, too.

Funny how I can barely remember her face, but sometimes I think I see her eyes while I'm sitting here. They're snow cone blue and shining with the tears that are just about to melt from them. She cried a lot, my mom.

I remember how my dad would flick open that Zippo lighter like some cowboy slinging a gun from his holster. The flame shot up, that sparkler fizzing awake, and I'd grip the end as tight as I could, like my life depended on holding that fireball, and I watched him grin as bright as those white sparks that rained down on my skin from the burning stick, the seconds ticking by in a glittering flame until there was nothing left but a stump of ash between my thumb and pointer finger, and the darkness that stayed, long after the fireworks ended.

I want to miss them both.

But I don't miss them.

I can't miss them.

Missing a past that never was is the first sign of insanity.

Maybe I'm insane.

Maybe I belong here. Maybe I deserve it.

10

"Dear Jimmy:

It's been almost two months since the day we rode our bikes out to the obelisk. They still don't know exactly what it is or how it ended up in Des Moines. Mom keeps saying UFO or aliens. Dad tells her not to get hysterical, there's got to be a logical reason it's here. Maybe it is nothing more than a planned-out tourist attraction. Or some marketing gimmick.

But every day when I come out to the monolith to look for you, I see scientists wandering about in their white lab coats. They've closed off a section to the tourists and I've been watching them dig around the edges, collecting rocks and soil in big bags. Sometimes they scrape at the walls with something that looks like a sharp spoon, putting the shavings in test tubes.

It would be cool to watch all this if you weren't still missing.

Gotta tell you, I've been running my own experiments when no one is watching.

Sometimes I toss pebbles at the obelisk to see what will happen, and they always make a high pitched ping sound like the ring toss at the carnival. (By the way, the fair has come and gone—I would have had a lot more fun with you but my parents dragged me there like they do every year, even though I'm getting too old to be going with Mom and Dad).

Sometimes I shoot water onto the obelisk's walls, squeezing my water bottle as tight as I can to get the perfect burst. Like those water fights we used to have. It's funny how it pools there for just a second before drying up faster than a puddle in the desert. I wonder if the water gets soaked inside it, like the obelisk is some gigantic sponge. Or if it's osmosis. I learned about that in Mr. Miller's science class last year.

I asked the scientists whether the obelisk could suck things inside it, but the dumbass Guard yells at me every time I throw out a question. So I never got an answer.

Maybe that's where you are, Jimmy. Maybe the obelisk swallowed you up when nobody was looking, and you've been in there all along.

It sounds crazy, but all of this is crazy, isn't it?

School is going to start soon. I wonder if they would have put us in the same class. That is, if you were still staying with your grandma—whoever and wherever she is. You never did tell me how long you planned to be here. Or if you were ever going to leave.

I hope you're okay wherever you are, and that whoever you're with is treating you well.
Your friend,
Mike

P.S. Marlins are killing it this season!
P.P.S. Those red-shoed wackos are still here, and it feels like
more of them show up every day. What a freak show!
P.P.P.S. I saw a pretty duck-lipped girl you might have liked. She
smiled at me after she took a selfie. But I didn't have the guts to
say anything to her. YOU would have gone over to say hello. I'm a
real wuss, I know."

      I've been sleeping. A lot. There's not much else to do. It's dark with my eyes open. Dark with my eyes closed. Sleep is still scary, even though I can't help myself.
      If I sleep, will I wake up?
      Will I still be me if I wake up?
      Will I remember who I am?
      Jimmy.
      Jimmy.
      I'm James Matthew Doran the third.
      From Lake Mary, Florida.
      That's not right. I live someplace else now.
      I live here.
      Here.
      Washington.
      Des Moines, Washington. Where my grandmother coughs a lot and I ride my bike with a kid I met at the park. Mark? Matthew? Mike. My friend's name is Mike. People wear red shoes and white sweatsuits, and they don't like the Marlins so much.
      Best baseball team ever.
      My eyelids, they're heavy in the brief moments when I'm awake, like someone is pulling them down. I get so tired after they feed me, whoever 'they' is, the someone or the something who's in charge here. It's hard to tell. Their icy fingers tug my jaw open and pour a warm, sweet drink into my mouth. Then, I'm in the middle of this crazy dream. I'm playing second base for the Marlins and my Mom and Dad are together cheering in the stands when the clouds come together, like a thatched roof, and out of them pours warm, thick liquid over the entire stadium—hot maple syrup from the sky. The crowd screams and runs but I stand there with my mouth wide open and I gulp and gulp and gulp that liquid down. It's like rock candy but better. The sweetest thing I've ever tasted. Clouds fall around me in a giant hug and there's ice, then heat, then ice again, in a scratchy tickle and then a long, slow burn. Something like the way you feel when you're scared shitless. Or so embarrassed you want to crawl into a hole and die. And then there's something else… something weird that I've never felt before. Something like… power.

12

And then I see my grandmother standing at home plate, dressed up as an umpire, screaming at me "You're out, you're out, you're out!" I laugh at her, and she wags her finger at me as that sweet liquid slides down my throat and a red-shoed, white-clad army douses her with a bucket full of blood and she vaporizes, every bit of her body popping in the air like a million little clouds until there's nothing left.

Then I grow, and grow, and grow and my skin sticks to the cold metal box that holds me. Parts of me melt and I take the shape of that box. I am square. Square! And I can't contain my giggling. The frost is eating me up, sucking away my breath and then I'm standing, overlooking a cliff at a devil's face painted on the ground below.

I drink more, stuffing myself with the syrup they pour into me until I want to vomit and those freezing hands clamp down on my jaw, keeping the liquid safe inside.

Where it belongs. Where it's always belonged.

And I sleep, again and again, until a great hum, like the song of a thousand cicada bugs, shivers over my skin. It sloshes through my body, surfing over my bloodstream until it comes to rest, burrowing into my core. Where it finds its home.

Home.

Where I shall forever dream.

I open my eyes.

To the light.

"Dear Jimmy:

My parents want to send me to a psychiatrist. The editor of the Des Moines News called my mom about the letter I wrote, and my parents started following me down to the obelisk to spy on me. The Guard ratted me out, said I was a nuisance coming down every day to ramble on about some missing kid no one had ever seen.

They all think I made you up, like you were some kind of imaginary friend. Sure, if I was five. But twelve-year-olds don't have imaginary friends. And I'll always remember how much fun we had.

I miss our bike rides. I miss meeting up with you at the park. Playing stickball. Arguing about how the Marlins suck and the Mariners will always be the better team. Making fun of the way you eat pizza.

It's lonely without you.

This may be my last letter for a while. I've started riding out to the obelisk in disguise and hope the Guard and my parents

13

don't catch on that it's me—even with my dad's fishing hat and my
mom's bug-eye sunglasses.

Yeah, go ahead and laugh. I look like an idiot.

Come back home, Jimmy.

Your friend always,

Mike

P.S. They think the Marlins may go all the way to the Series."

I have emerged from my cocoon.

Free.

The world is warm. The sun is a god who nourishes and provides.

The Mother and the Father and all the Brothers and the Sisters, they are with me, our bond magnetic, celestial. In orbit, like the Earth in tandem with the lesser planets whose life forms once succumbed to the force of our will. Of our strength.

Just as the Earth would.

Soon.

We are one Herd, our white garments pure and beaming in the light of the Great Monolith, our crimson shoes electrifying the ground beneath it. Giving it life, sustaining its roots as they stretch and break deep through the hottest magma into the core.

The core that is us. The core that is whole.

My eyes are the Mother's, and the Mother's are the Father's—bluer than the brightest of skies. All seeing. All encompassing.

Through their gaze they tell me what they know, what they've always known.

To vanish is to find purpose, to be reborn into a life that has always been, left unrecognized, unfulfilled until the light—it changes them—and they become something greater than that which can ever be conceived.

We hum and we chant. We wait for the Great Transformation.

Of the obelisk. The font of all life.

We hum from the core that binds us.

We are one.

We wait for a sign.

"Dear Jimmy:

So much has happened! I need to write this note quickly because the Guard is forcing us to evacuate. The scientists found massive amounts of radiation coming from the Mysterious Monolith, and they say it's too dangerous to stay. In fact, once we get out of here, Mom is taking me to an oncologist. She's worried that all that radiation may have given me brain cancer and the brain cancer is what caused me to imagine you. I think it's all a lot of nonsense, but I don't have a choice.

What really stinks is that we get to bring one bag each. That's it. So it's goodbye Xbox for me.

I thought I saw you by the obelisk, the last time they allowed people near it. One of the red-shoes wandering around looked just like you, but much taller. His hair was a little bit redder than yours, but his eyes, they were weird. Wide. Like he was somewhere else even though he was standing right there in the middle of the group. I yelled out "Jimmy!" as loud as I could but he didn't even flinch. If it really was you, you would have recognized my voice and you would have left those weirdos behind. We would have had a good laugh at you wearing that crazy get-up. I'd have even taken a selfie with you, even though it's a little creepy for guys like us to take selfies together. I would have posted it on Insta, and called it Me and My Red-Shoed Friend.

You know, it's sad. I don't even have a picture to remember you by. I don't have anything but my memories, and sometimes, I wonder if maybe I did imagine you. Maybe there is something wrong with me. Missing something or someone who never existed is a sign that you're wacked, isn't it? Maybe I am wacked and Mom's right, I do need a psychiatrist.

And an oncologist, apparently.

Take good care of yourself, wherever you are. I'll root for the Marlins for you, even though they're a crappy team.
Your friend for life,
Mike"

The Humans, they have abandoned their station, and the obelisk, it radiates with our strength. The sun has spoken. The House of the Rising Fire will rule the Earth.

We will show reverence for the Flame.

It is time.

Empire Enlightenment

by Jayne Hunter
Third Place

Harriet sat by the radio, leaning in, a pencil in hand to write down the latest updates so she could read over them when the news paused for an advertising jingle or veered to a different topic. Even with the war still going in Japan, the airplane hitting the Empire State Building was the biggest news that day. Harriet's husband had gone into his office in the building that day, rare for a Saturday, and now here she was, wondering if she was a widow or not.

They had argued that morning, as they had most mornings lately. He wanted his breakfast prepared just so, and he couldn't understand why she could never get it right. He talked down to her like she couldn't understand him, and she'd responded with what he called "her fresh mouth." He'd been so angry, he'd marched out the door, putting his hat on as he turned to say "I'd rather be at work then be here with you," then slamming the door behind him.

She had felt an odd sense of relief as the sound of the door slam dissolved in the air. She knew if she were a good wife, she'd feel more like a deflated balloon instead of one filled with helium, bobbing around the peaceful house by herself. She asked herself why she, who had seemed to be good at everything else she tried, was such an inadequate wife.

But she knew why. Because she didn't care. She didn't like cooking. She didn't like cleaning or keeping house at all for that matter. She didn't care if her whites were white, if her beef was tender, if you could eat off her floors. It seemed like such a boring waste of time. On the days she could force herself to work all day in the house, then have dinner on the table by the time Clem got home, he would never even notice, and by the time dinner was finished, there was already more housework to be done - the dishes cleaned up, Clem's work clothes put in the laundry, socks to be darned. It was endless, and endlessly tedious.

Before she and Clem had married, she'd been so free, helping outside on the farm, tending the animals, then reading in the evenings, dreaming of adventures off in the city just a thirty-minute car ride away. She'd never doubted she would have an interesting life. Every book she read seemed to promise it to her. And Clem had promised her as well.

As soon as they met, they were drawn to each other. He said he liked that she was bright and well-read, and before long she was cracking jokes with his friends on trips into the city. Sometimes he would take her into his office on the 70th floor of that famous building, so huge and beautiful, visible in the New York City skyline from almost everywhere in Manhattan. Clem would take her to the window just as the sun was going down, so they could watch the sun set over the city, with the city lights coming on in little spurts, turning the gray cityscape into a twinkling starlit wonderland. Like most New Yorkers, Harriet considered New York the perfect city, but she wanted to experience it, not just to sit in a house within shouting distance of it waiting for something to happen. Why couldn't Clem understand that?

His own life seemed pretty enjoyable. Every morning he sat down to breakfast in a crisp suit and tie, prepared for him by her, then strode out into the world in the hustle and bustle of midtown to work in the most famous building in the world. She usually packed him a lunch, but once or twice a week he would eat lunch out with his work buddies. Then he would come home telling what a good meal he had had, and how nice it was to be able to enjoy his hard-earned money. When she asked for a night out in the city, like they had done when they were dating, he'd responded with some quip about how she should become a better cook so she wouldn't feel the need to eat out. She'd almost spit in his dessert that night.

The news was on, talking about the fire that was raging in the building from plane exploding. She shifted in her chair, pencil poised, and turned the volume up yet again. They could confirm that the 79th floor had taken the hit, but that the flames were as far down as the 75th floor.

"What about the 70th floor? Come on!" she practically shouted at the radio.

The phone rang from its little table in the foyer, and she jumped up and ran to answer it.

"Oh, Harriet, we just heard the news on the radio. Thank goodness it's Saturday. Does Clem know anyone who works on those floors?" Her mother hadn't bothered with an introduction.

"I don't know." Harriet paused. "Clem went into work today, Mother."

"What? Oh, my goodness, Sweetheart. You must be worried sick. What floor does he work on again?" Harriet's mother's voice was shaking.

"70th." Harriet said, noticing how flat and calm her own voice sounded. What was wrong with her? She was riveted by the newscast, but impassive talking about Clem's fate.

18

"Oh my God!" said her mother. This was the closest her mother came to swearing.

"I know. I know. I'm just trying to keep calm." Harriet realized at least this was true, but she was becoming more and more uneasy as she began to suspect the reason was not fear for Clem. It was fear for her. Dread of the life she would have to continue to lead if and when Clem came home.

"Well, I'll get off the phone so the line will be clear if he calls. Or if someone calls..." Her mother's voice cracked a little as she said good-bye and hung up.

Harriet wandered back to the radio, which informed her the building was completely evacuated. She stared at it as the announcer said in amazement that by all reckoning, the loss of life was minimal, and how lucky it was that it was a Saturday.

Harriet glanced at the clock. The crash had now happened hours ago. If not many were killed, what were the chances that one of them was Clem? She didn't want to do the math. For just a minute, she let herself wonder what life would be like if he didn't come home. She would get to keep the house. She would get to go to work, as she would have to pay the bills. Maybe as a secretary or a schoolteacher. Or a nurse! She almost wished the war wasn't nearly over, as she pictured herself in the uniform of a military nurse, helping soldiers in some far-flung country. She could earn her own money without it being seen as a failure of Clem's to provide. Her breath quickened. As a widow, she would be able to control her own money and to own the house. A stream of thoughts ran through her head like a film reel, showing her what her life without Clem could be.

She stopped short, realizing how ghoulish the whole line of thinking was. Clem was a good man, though one with an unsatisfied, unsuitable wife. He didn't deserve to be dead. The phone rang loudly in the foyer, wresting her out of her thoughts.

"Hello." She braced herself. She didn't want Clem dead. Not really.

"Harriet!" Clem's voice was jubilant. "I'm alive! Well, of course I am, I never went into the office. I'm in a bar down the street from the building. Me and guys are watching all the commotion, and one of them said I should call you and let you know I'm okay." He turned and shouted something inaudible to one of his friends. "So, I'm okay." He paused for a second, then almost whispered into the phone. "Were you even worried?"

"Of course." Harriet said. "I've been glued to the radio, hoping for the phone to ring. Thanks for letting me know. I was very worried. Very worried."

"Aw thanks, honey, I'll be home in a while. Hey, I better get off this phone, the bartender is giving me the stink eye about using it."

"That's fine. No need to hurry. Good-bye." Harriet said, hanging up.

She walked back to the radio and switched it off, and in the silence it seemed like the house itself took a breath.

Clem was alive, the building had survived, and in the space of a few minutes her life was back to the way it was when he had left that morning.

Was it though?

She went to the closet and pulled out her suitcase, the brand new one her mother had given her to take on her honeymoon just two years ago. She put it on the bed and put in a few days' worth of clothes and her toiletries. She grabbed a couple of books from her nightstand, then looked around.

Then she sat at the kitchen table and started writing a note, feeling lighter with every word she wrote.

Tread Softly Through the Apocalypse
by EJ Howler
Fourth Place (Tied)

Rina pulled her bike into its charging station, feeling the rumble of the spark engine calm down under her legs. Once the wheels locked into place and the station beeped once, she swung her legs over the side. The grass came up to her calves as she let her boots sink into the ground. Her bike was the only one around, causing her to frown lightly: given the position of Lunados above her head and the minty hue of the sky, she expected at least two other stations to have bikes for the next pickup.

Maybe they're all still out on their last run. She simply shrugged as she pulled her gloves a little more taunt, doing her best not to buckle under the weight of her bag. *You've gotten faster at your errands, after all.*

With one last look around just to see if she could see any other bikes on the horizon, Rina headed into the small shop. Even though the door slid open when she was three steps away, it still gave a soft chime when she walked in. She couldn't help but smile as she admired the walls lined with trinkets, with everything from pieces of marionettes dangling in misshapen groups to half-burned postcards folded to create paper planes. Her favorite was a statue of a creature standing on two legs with carved fur and the cutest little ears. Above the counter in the back was a wooden sign with *SPOTS* carved out in five different styles, each letter brandishing a different color. Behind the counter sat someone whose mouth was replaced with eight tentacles, and four eyes lined each side of their elongated head. They looked up from the magazine on the desk, and despite the strange visage, Rina could tell they were smiling.

"Back already?" Spots lifted one of their arms suction-cups-up across the counter. "And you were successful, I take it?"

Rina shrugged her bag off her back, hoisting it up onto the counter to let them hear its thud. "Has there been a time yet where I *haven't* been?" She smirked up at them and took a small step back. "I just hope these were what you were looking for."

Spots unzipped her backpack and unceremoniously turned it upside-down. A collection of porous boulders tumbled out, a couple bouncing off the counter and rolling under a nearby table. With another tentacle arm, Spots picked up the largest boulder and held it close to their face. For the briefest moment, Rina felt her heart skip as they hummed.

Stop, there's no reason to be nervous. She straightened her back and did her best to avoid scratching at her gills. *You've never failed a mission before. You have always brought back what they asked for.*

"This will do nicely." Spots reached behind them and placed the boulder in one of the dozens of empty cubbies. "That's all for now."

"That's all? You don't have *anything* else you want?" Rina blinked a few times despite herself. "No books of chopped photographs, or cans of questionable contents, or even more unusual rocks?"

Spots simply shrugged. "You've exhausted my list of errands. I'll be sure to call you when I find something else."

"I could always go find Henrik or assist Niles," she insisted. "They couldn't find a slither bird if it swooped down and bit them."

Spots shook their head. "No, those two have to learn on their own. Something will come up, I just don't have anything for you right now." They slid her backpack across the counter along with a small pouch. "Here's your payment for the boulders. And here: I found something in my stash that you can have. It's an old human contraption. Consider it a gift for always being so timely."

Rina frowned at the device they slid over. It was a small rectangle, small enough to fit comfortably in her hand. The front had a clear door with an even smaller rectangle inside, which had two small holes punched through it and what appeared to be ribbon wound around the inside. Spots also slid another bag her way full of even more of the smaller rectangles. Her frown deepened as she carefully put the collection of strange rectangles into her bag.

"Are you sure there's nothing I can go find for you, Spots?" she asked with the same tone she used to use with her parents when trying to avoid finishing a chore. "Really, it could be the smallest thing."

They waved her off without looking up from their magazine. "Go, be free, Rina. I will call you when I need you."

This can't be right, Spots never *runs out of things to find.* Rina opened her mouth to argue, but her gills burned as she struggled to form the words strong enough to make Spots lift their head. She couldn't stop the small hiss that escaped from her frills as she turned and sulked out of the shop. The sky was gaining a bluer tint as she all but stormed back to her bike. The bars along the side were still glowing a flickering yellow, not unlike the flocks of bugs that came out once Lunetrois rose over the horizon. She slung her back onto the back with a huff.

Well, may as well see what this contraption is all about. She pulled out a pair of ear pods and plugged the stem into the top of the box. *Though if Spots was willing to give it up, how interesting can it actually be? It looks ancient.*

She flinched at the static that filled her ears for a brief moment as her pods connected. She pushed the red button on the front with a sideways triangle in the hopes of making it stop. The box clicked, and the static turned into a dull drone against the background of someone breathing.

"Ha! Finn made fun of me for using this old thing, but I got it to work while he's still struggling with his computer. So, joke's on him!"

Rina frowned to herself as the voice filled her mind. The tone was strangely crisp coming from such a weathered device. The speaker sounded like a young woman, perhaps even around her age, with a tone that brought to mind the image of bubbles skipping over the sea. She leaned against her bike and cradled the box gently.

"Shoot, it looks like it's already recording. Well damn, there goes my chance at a good intro." The girl took a deep breath, a sound that made Rina's brows furrow briefly. *"Anyway, dear diary: my name is Tracey, and I guess this is my lucky day for finding one of these old portable cassette players that can actually record! Now I can keep a record of everything that's happening. I've tried doing it in my journals, but it's hard to take it outside and write things down there when it doesn't stop raining. That's okay though! This is more fun anyway, even if Finn wants to glare at me from across the room."*

Rina found herself chuckling as the audio became muffled. She could just make out the sound of another voice, but she had no way to decipher what words, if any, were picked up by the strange device.

"Wait, I've got a better idea: these can be used as messages to Parker! I dunno where you ended up after the evacuation orders started, but if you happen to hear this, try to get to Reef Circle Point. I'm gonna leave something there for you: something I think you're really gonna like. I can't tell you exactly what it is in case someone else picks up these tapes, but I really think you're gonna like it."

A hidden treasure? How did Spots listen to this and not immediately send us on the case? She bit her lip for a moment as thoughts of all the reports of Reef Circle Pointe came flooding back to the front of her mind. *Probably because that place has been untouchable for years. But still, Spots isn't someone to pass up something like this. Maybe they just didn't know?*

Rina straightened her back as the charging station beeped, lifting up her bike enough to bounce once. *Well, I guess it's the others' loss then. Good thing I don't have anything else going on. Besides, who's going to stop me?*

Rina pressed the red button again, then the button right next to it. The clear door popped open, letting her reach in and remove the smaller box. A single line was drawn on the front, slightly smudged from age and wiping away even further as she ran her thumb over the ink. Gently, she opened back up her backpack and pulled out the bag of similar boxes. It only took a moment to find one with the number two scrawled on its face. She gingerly slid the second one into her new device and closed the lid. It took a moment of adjusting to get it to clip onto her belt before she mounted her bike. The sky grew deeper as the barest hint of Lunetrois peeked over the horizon. Her smile spread so hard her cheeks hurt as she pressed the red button and kicked up her kickstand.

Reef Circle Point, here I come.

"*Dear diary: should I really begin every tape like this? It feels kinda silly. Anyway, the news has been talking non-stop about the appearance of a second moon orbiting Earth like it's the end of the world or something. I mean yeah, it hasn't stopped raining since they announced Lunados, but it really doesn't seem as catastrophic as everyone says it is. Then again, science was never my strongest subject in school. But that's because Mr. Georgetown was the worst. I always hated the way he looked at me. At least he got evacuated to a different town, so we don't have to worry about him anymore.*

"*Don't tell Mom, but I stayed up last night to see if I could see the moon and Lunados in the sky at the same time. I didn't see the moon, but I think Lunados was out, and* man *is it huge! It's like this cotton-candy pink and it's gotta be bigger than the Earth. It's just gotta be, it took up almost the whole sky! The scientists on TV keep saying that there's more than just the moon and Lunados. Their last count was five in total. Five moons orbiting the Earth! Like, how does that even happen? Maybe they were asteroids-turned-moons that got slung into our orbit or something? I'm not even sure how that would work. But hey, neither is anyone on TV, so at least I'm not alone. Maybe* everyone's *worst subject was science back in school.*

"*Renee Babbitt told us today more about Reef Circle Pointe. Apparently, that's the only spot scientists have been able to see all five moons at once. They set up all their big labs there, but honestly the coolest part about it has to be the cliff that overlooks the waterfalls. I wonder what the moons look like all lined up. I bet they look like bubbles. I hope Parker and I can meet up there. I bet the sky looks* amazing *there, and she loves stargazing. But if all the moons are as big as Lunados, it's just gonna be a bunch of moon-gazing. Which I guess is also pretty cool. Maybe the rain will clear up long enough to watch. Parker was never big on getting wet. Then again, when you get cold pretty easily, it's not fun to get drenched and encounter a breeze. She about took off my head with the umbrella when I splashed her.*

"Oh, shoot, it looks like Mom's coming back. I'm supposed to be asleep. Anyway, I'll keep you updated on anything new or weird happening outside. Have a good night! And Parker, if you happen to find these tapes, I'll see you soon."

As Lunetrois rose further into the sky, Rina fought the urge to shiver against the cool night air. The grass came up past her wheels, leaving just a smooth hum along the ground and tickling against her legs. The open plains morphed and shifted as she got closer to Birmingham Coast. Trees that stretched beyond the sky carved out a path ahead. The closer she got to the coast, the shorter and bluer the grass became. Her wheels glided across the top of the water as the ground sank further and further away. Thankfully, she'd taken the time to invest in water-defying tires for her bike when Spots gave her a bonus for finding a particularly shiny green rock. So long as her bike had enough charge, she would be able to cruise along the top of the London Waves until the next station without fear of sinking into the ocean.

Not that that was necessarily a major concern. She did protectively reach for her tape player at the thought, though.

The sky grew darker as the black mass of Lunetrois ascended higher, its rim of violet light casting stark shadows along the surface. The hum of her bike's motor barely made a dent against the vast expanse of silence as she cruised under the massive trees. Luminescent shrubs and flowers blossomed along the roots, lighting the path as the forest plunged her into darkness. Most of the light came from below the water's surface, with sea flowers glowing and flickering at the smallest movement. They glowed brighter than the tips of the biggest waves, capturing the movement of every fish that scurried past. Above her head, Rina took a moment to admire the glowing lavender vines that shuddered and twinkled in Lunetrois's light. The leaves shifted and crackled in the wind, creating a canopy of noise occasionally interrupted by the chirping of a creature overhead.

Perhaps there is information on the tapes about this passage. Rina smiled to herself as she saw a deep orange eel swim overhead. *After all, Reef Circle Pointe is on the other side of the London Waves. I would love to hear Tracey explain this.*

The water rumbled slightly under her wheels, prompting Rina to slow her pace but not stop altogether. The trees overhead shook harder, prompting some leaves to flutter down and sink below the surface. Rina took a few moments to steady her breathing, matching it to the hum of her bike. Out of the corner of her eye, she saw something move along the shadows, followed by another deep rumble that sent ripples out far beyond her small path.

Lunetrois is in its prime, I should've anticipated The Guardians would be awake. She tightened her mouth into a firm line and leaned forward, keeping her bike moving at a steady pace. *Good thing they're mostly harmless.*

A small break in the tree cover left her cruising on the open ocean for long enough to see the Guardian wandering alongside her. Despite the dim lighting of the full Lunetrois shape, she could make out the silhouette of a gargantuan creature wandering remarkably close, far closer than she had ever seen. Its sprawling antlers skimmed across the sky enough to cause ripples along the stars. Its long, white wooly hung in drenched clumps over its face and legs, only showing the massive hooves that walked across the surface with an impossible blend of force and delicacy. Its dorsal fin flickered and flinched ever so slightly with every step, reflecting the starlight and flashing brighter whenever Lunetrois's light caught it. Its tail stretched for miles behind it, dragging along the ocean's surface for ages until it reached the back fins. It took everything in Rina to keep from watching it move as she continued riding.

I don't think I've ever seen one so close. Her mouth fell slack-jaw as she slowed her bike to keep pace with it. *That can't be a promising sign.*

The Guardian lifted its head, just enough for Rina to catch a glimpse of its dog-like nose. Her eyes followed its gaze just as a rocket of light shot across the sky. The sight was enough to startle her into stopping. The sides of the light spread out into a pair of veined wings as it glided effortless overhead. The Guardian's head followed it as it started descending before it hit the horizon, finally disappearing in the middle of a gaggle of trees deep in the distance. Rina's heart skipped and fluttered as she watched the Guardian, waiting for it to make the next move.

I've got a bad feeling that sprite was headed for Reef Circle Pointe. Rina's frown deepened as she took out the last tape and fished around in her bag for the next. *That place is a beacon for the weirdest shit.*

26

Rina remounted her bike just as she slipped in the next tape. The Guardian slowly began sinking back under the ocean's surface as she cruised away, closer to En Why Sea Coast and whatever treasure laid ahead.

"Dear diary: I did something reckless today. Well, okay, I'm still doing something reckless because I'm still here, but I snuck into Reef Circle Pointe again. Not the big fancy laboratories: those are way too guarded to even think about getting close to. But the land around it? All it took was climbing a fence. I'm pretty sure there weren't any cameras to catch me. Hell, I'm sitting out here in the open talking to a cassette recorder and no one's come to tackle me to the ground. Sneaking out of school was harder than this, I swear.

"Anyway, I'm right at the tip of Reef Circle Pointe, where the falls go way down into the sea. And you will not believe the shit that's out here! I'm not making this up: I'm sitting here, just admiring the sky, and a blue whale just swam by! And I don't mean it swam by in the sea under the falls. No, it literally swam overhead like the sky was the ocean! And it was massive! It was followed by a bunch of seals, but they didn't quite look like regular seals. They had these cute little blue spots and fins that looked more like a fish than a seal, but they definitely had the cute puppy-face of a seal. I wish I could've reached up and pet them! Oh my god and are those jellyfish that are rising up to the sky? This is amazing! Holy, holy shit there's so many…

"Parker, I really hope you get these tapes, and I hope it's soon. You'd absolutely love this place. It kinda reminds me of the day we went to the aquarium as a class, the really big one in the city. You spent twenty minutes just watching the jellyfish and sketching little outlines in your notebook. You complained about not bringing your good sketchbook no less than three times, but the drawings you did were amazing. I doodled a little squiggly jellyfish on the corner of my map just to feel included. You were always the better artist. If you were here, you'd draw so many jellyfish because they're everywhere and they're huge and you'd have the biggest smile on your face. Kinda like you did that weekend when I brought you a stuffed jellyfish I got you at the giftshop when you weren't looking. I hope you were able to save it before the evacuation. But if not, that's okay. I'm sure we'll be able to find another one.

"The sky's kinda a weird color. It's still kinda bluish, but there's more purple in it. Plus, the clouds are a really, really deep blue. I think one of the moons is out: it looks like…oh, what did they name it…Sukishi? Maybe? That sounds about right. Anyway,

it's an itty-bitty little moon that's blue like cotton candy. I wonder if it tastes like it too. They used to say the first moon was made out of cheese, maybe that one's made out of sugar? If it is, I hope it tastes like blue raspberry. That'd be yummy. Ha, it's kinda weird to sit here and talk about what the moon tastes like. But I guess…I dunno, weirder things have happened in the span of a month or so.

"I hope you're safe, Parker. I really do. I miss you. I miss our little adventures onto the roof of Hollis's Diner where we could look at the stars and you'd talk about wanting to pack up everything and live out in the Canadian wilderness or something. Maybe you did end up getting your van, and you're cruising along whatever roads are still left. Or maybe a boat is more appropriate now? Anyway, I hope you make your way up here. Because you really need to see this."

By the time Rina made it to another charging station, Lunetrois was just about gone over the other side of the horizon. Its shadowed beams were replaced with the soft blue tones of Sukishi. Rina always wondered how a moon so small was able to fill the sky with such commanding light whenever it peeked over the horizon. She shielded her eyes as she dismounted, leaving her bike to hum against the charging rails.

She was still somewhere in the middle of the London Waves, but the En Why Sea Coast was finally within view. In fairness, once she crossed over a certain threshold of the ocean, it was impossible to miss the strange, skeletal structures poking the clouds and causing the sky fish to drastically change their flight paths. Most of her errands for Spots only carried her to scattered islands between the patches of forest in the London Waves. Her mind flickered to the one time she came back to their shop just as crossed off an area on their map with a massive red marker. She'd just barely managed to catch a glimpse of it before Spots shoved it to the side, and the words *Reef Circle Point* jumped out at her.

I doubt it's all that dangerous anymore. She found herself frowning as she took out her pods. *Sure, it attracts some of the stranger creatures, but Spots probably wants us avoiding it because of the distance. Crossing the entirety of the London Waves is a big ask, and they probably don't wanna pony up the cash is all.*

The charging station sat in the middle of a network of roots connected to a massive willow. Its branches skimmed across the ocean's surface, gently letting small pink petals flutter down to the surface. The wind brushed through the leaves, whistling a gentle tune that lulled the sky fish nestled above back to sleep. Rina couldn't help but yawn as she climbed over a couple roots to stretch her legs. Her gills flared up briefly as she took in a deep breath. The sides of her legs itched, but she resisted the urge to scratch and further irritate the scales there.

I'll have to go for a big soak once this is all over. She flopped down and stared up through the willow branches as the sky turned bluer. *There's gotta be some pools by Reef Circle Pointe. Or there is the waterfall there: that has to still be there.*

With just the sound of the wind and the gentle hum of her bike recharging, Rina allowed her mind to wander. Her hand kept drifting to the recorder against her hip, almost as if it was going to disappear if she didn't touch it every few seconds. Above her, a glider with brilliantly neon fins swam in a soft wave back and forth, letting its magnificent tail ripple along the sky. She found herself smiling as she leaned back against the tree.

I wonder what Tracey looks like. Rina blinked slowly as a school of minnows scurried overhead. An exact picture struggled to form in her head as she focused in on Tracey's voice. With every laugh, Rina imagined bubbles floating up from her skin, encircling her head and dripping in every color of the rainbow. She pictured bright eyes that glowed in the dark and laughter that caused flowers to open up. The collection of images made the air in her chest puff up suddenly, pressing against her ribs and catching her off guard.

No, don't be silly, there's no way you two could ever meet. Humans haven't been around for decades. Who knows how old these recordings are, anyway. Her shoulders suddenly felt heavy as she sighed. *Besides, Tracey keeps talking about Parker. I'm sure at some point those two found each other again.*

Still, the laughter rang through Rina's head, echoing deep and lingering like the last flickers of a dying candle. She looked down at the recorder, cradling it gently in both hands. The tape in there had the number seven scrawled on it. She popped open the door and carefully took it out. Slipping it back into her bag, she opened the pouch wider and sifted through her collection. Her frown deepened as she counted the tapes and double checked the numbers.

Only two left? That can't be right. She carefully grabbed the next one and slid it into her player. *I could've sworn Spots gave me more. There's no way, is there?*

Briefly looking over to her bike, she saw three of the five charging bars lit up. She rested her head against the tree for a long moment, focusing on her breathing. The desire to sleep swept over her in a rush, leaving behind a heaviness in her arms that seeped its way deeper into her bones. Still, she put her pods back into her ears and pressed the button.

Maybe Tracey will finally tell me what the treasure is she left behind. Rina's frown deepened as she watched Sukishi trail across the sky. *Or maybe she'll say something to make this weird feeling go away.*

"Dear diary: I...I wish I had some happier news to give you today. I'm not gonna lie, when this whole thing first started, I wasn't sure what to make of it. Yeah, it's pretty cool to have way more moons in the sky, and I knew the scientists on TV were worried about it, but it didn't really seem like it was gonna be a bad thing long term. I mean, the flooding and having to evacuate was a whole mess, but I thought by now we'd be able to go home, or at least we'd be able to go somewhere else. But the water levels just keep rising. It's...really weird. And I'm worried. Mom and Finn are worried too. But it has to stop at some point, right? All weird things with the weather do.

"Anyway, you didn't come here to listen to me worry about everything. Let me see if anything cool has happened since I recorded last...oh! I did go out to Reef Circle Pointe again. I mean okay, I go there pretty much every day at this point, but no one's gonna stop me. I just like going there and looking at all the weird fish and creatures that are swimming around in the sky. There were no jellyfish this time, but I did see something pretty cool. I guess the best way to describe it is a massive sea turtle. And when I say massive, I mean massive. It was probably bigger than our old school. It wasn't green, either. It was like the color of the old night sky, or I guess the sky when Lunetrois is out. Speaking of, it's getting really hard to keep track of what counts as a day: any time one of the moons is up, the sky's a different color. Scientists say that Lunetrois, which makes the sky the darkest, is actually out in the middle of the afternoon! Maybe we just need to readjust our clocks to match the new moons. It'd make more sense than trying to go to sleep when the sky is a weird minty green color or something.

"Oh, sorry, I got distracted there. Anyway yes, the turtle: it was the color of night, and it cast a huge shadow over all of Reef Circle Pointe. Its belly looked like it had a bunch of stars scattered across it. Parker, you should've seen it: it was like something out of a dream. The turtle didn't do anything, it just swam overhead without a care in the world. I bet it would be kinda nice to be a sea turtle and not have to worry about anything. Especially if you were that *big*.

"I overheard a broadcast today talking about really, really big creatures like that. Scientists have been calling them Guardians, and apparently they're like long-lost creatures that dwelled deep in the ocean? Okay, maybe that wasn't from the scientists, I think that was just some random person they interviewed talking about how the Guardians coming to the surface was a sign that pretty soon, all the other ocean dwellers were going to come up. Personally, if there are a bunch of people in the ocean, and they want to come up and say hi now that we have a bunch of different moons, then I say we should let them. Not everything is dangerous, and I mean hey: we all share a planet, right? If anything, they're probably mad at us for all the pollution we caused. I dunno. Personally, I'd love to meet the ocean people. Maybe we could even be friends.

"Going out to Reef Circle Pointe is probably gonna get harder after this. Mom's really worried about how long I stay out during the days, and if she knew where I was really going, she'd probably lose her mind. But I promise, Parker, I will see you there as soon as I can. I really, really hope you get these messages, or are able to come up to our base. I miss you. Even...even if I can't make it to Reef Circle Pointe, I still left something there for you. But I hope we can meet up there soon and watch the jellyfish or something. Honestly, it could be anything you want. I just wanna see you again.

"I miss you, Parker. A lot. And...I love you. I wanna be able to tell you to your face before this is all over. Stay...stay safe out there."

By the time Rina's tires hit the edge of En Why Sea Coast, her vision was blurred with tears. The tape skipped and shuttered before surrounding her ears with silence. She forced in a deep breath and kicked her bike into a higher gear as she sped down the path towards Reef Circle Pointe. All around her, the remnants of metallic structures overtaken by trees and algae littered the landscape. The light occasionally caught a reflective surface, making spots dance across the tree cover above. Her mind went back to some of the pictures in Spots's shop, most of them faded with age depicting massive, shining structures piercing the clouds and reflecting the sun. Sukishi's light made the roots gripping the remaining beams glow and pulse as if they had their own heartbeat.

Keep it together, you knew there was no chance of meeting Tracey. The line of thought, though rational, made her shudder. *This device is old. There's no way she would still be alive. But perhaps whatever she left behind for Parker is still there.*

It had better be: I came all this way. And... and maybe... just maybe...

The metallic remains of whatever civilization En Why Sea Coast used to harbor faded away as she continued riding, with the trees growing denser. Overhead, she saw a swarm of jellyfish float lazily in the same direction. They were mostly white, with tendrils floating gently against the sky, creating small sparks as they brushed against the tops of the trees. Every so often her eyes caught a glimpse of a green jellyfish amongst the crowd, and even one that shifted from yellow to green to orange depending on how Sukishi's light hit it.

I must be getting close: that looks like what Tracey described. Her frown deepened as she revved the engine to get up the hill smoother. *I hope Parker was able to find her and see it. If she really was an artist, this would be the picture to paint.*

Rina's breath caught in her throat as she drove past a dilapidated chunk of chainmail overgrown with lilac bushes. Up ahead, she could see the point, the very top of the waterfalls where the jellyfish began gathering. A small beacon of light shined out from the very tip. She leaned forward and made her bike go faster, breezing right past the remains of structures where the stone was little more than sand. Her sudden arrival startled a small school of clown birds that fluttered up to the sky. Underneath her tires, the ground rippled like the ocean, leaving circles of bright neon colors that stretched out far behind her.

C'mon, I'm almost there. She clenched her jaw as she saw some jellyfish swim dangerously closer to the ground. *I'm not about to let some stingers get the better of me.*

With one last push of her accelerator, Rina managed to slip between the tendrils of a low-flying jellyfish without getting stung. She swerved her bike to the side, digging her boot into the grass to keep from crashing entirely. The jellyfish swam closer, creating a barrier around the tip of Reef Circle Pointe. The sound of rushing water pounded at her ears as she felt the waterfall thrum under her feet. Moving cautiously, she shut off her bike and parked it before taking a few steps forward. Her hand clutched at her recorder as she dug the last tape out of her bag. For a moment, she had to shield her eyes from the bright spot on the ground just a few steps away.

Guess there's no turning back now. Despite herself, Rina's legs shook as she walked forward. The rushing water faded into a dull murmur as blood pounded in her ears. The light flickered down, settling into a hue more fitting of PenteFengari, allowing her to see. She pressed her mouth into a firm line as she marched, doing her best to keep her balance while walking uphill.

By the time she reached the light, her lungs seized, unwilling to let go of her breath. A bed of flowers unlike anything Rina had seen before were gathered along the point, sprouting out of a skeleton that was somehow meticulously preserved. A few small goldfish swam their way out from under the ribs and up towards the sky. Rina slowly fell to her knees as she gently reached out. A small blue fish swam around her fingers, brushing its tailfin against her before disappearing through the line of jellyfish.

You knew this was a possibility, she reminded herself despite the way tears stung her eyes. *Humans can't survive on this world anymore. You knew this was the likely outcome.*

Her eyes darted down to the skeleton's hand, still somehow enclosed in a fist. Being as gentle as she could, she unwound the fingers, careful to make sure they didn't break. Encircled inside was a small locket connected to a well-weathered chain. Rina's vision blurred as she lifted it up and pressed the small button on the side. Inside, the picture of two human girls grinning looked back up at her. On the other side, there was a small engraving: *"To my favorite person: love, Tracey."* Out of the corner of Rina's eyes, she saw a battered, weathered stuffed animal that had miraculously retained its shape.

She reached over, grabbing the plush jellyfish, then buried her head into its tentacles before sobbing.

"Parker, this last message is for you. As much as I hope this isn't the last one, I'm out of tapes. The world is becoming weird and yet kinda wonderful, but from the way everyone's talking, it doesn't sound like we're a part of it anymore. And I guess that's okay: we weren't meant to last forever, after all. I just…wish we'd gotten a little longer. There are so many things I wanted to do. Like kiss you. That…that was kinda the big one, I guess. It doesn't look like you're gonna be able to make it to Reef Circle Pointe. That's okay: I…always kinda knew it was a long shot. But if you do make it here and you get this message, I hope you get a chance to see just how amazing it is.

"There's five moons in the sky now. It's…kinda wild to see them all up here at once. But the wind is picking up, and it looks like there are some weird creatures swimming closer. Realistically, I should probably run home while I have the chance, but I mean…why delay the inevitable? Most of the world is underwater at this point, there's not really much else we can do. And I'd much rather stay here and watch the jellyfish than run home to the panic. It's really peaceful out here. You'd really, really like it. If you do

manage to make it out here, be sure to bring your sketchbook. You're not gonna want to miss it.

"Anyway, I think I'm running out of room on this tape. I just want you to know that I love you, Parker. I love you so much. And…hope beyond hope, we'll see each other again real soon."

Monumental Militants

by Arden Ruth
Fourth Place (Tied)

25 August 2259 20:00
Location: 47.6205° N, 122.3493° W
Status: Offline

The sun breathes down on the back of my neck, a kiss of searing pain on my already scorched skin. Fourteen days ago, we left the only home we'd ever known. Fourteen days ago, we set out for what could be our deaths, and as I stop to drain the last drops from my canteen, the vast desert before us mocking me with its emptiness, it's looking like it very well could be. We're running out of time.

"Our water supply will be officially depleted by tomorrow morning," Niles whispers beside me, keeping his voice low so the others won't hear. His stomach growls, an ominous reminder that we haven't eaten in days. "We need somewhere to hole up and fast, Eve. We won't make it long without water."

I suck in a deep breath, my frustration rising to the surface. Does he not think I know that? Tamping my rage, I pinch the bridge of my nose before squinting out at the land before us. Sand. Nothing but goddamn sand as far as the eye can see. Niles lays a hand on my shoulder, and as I turn in for the embrace, the sun glints off a surface ahead of me, perhaps a few hundred yards away.

"What the hell?"

Niles's hand drops as I grab the binoculars around his neck and yank them up to my eyes, his body pressing into mine as I frantically search for what surely is just a mirage, but then I see it, and my heart about leaps out of my chest at the sight.

"What is it?" Willow asks, her lips so dry they split open at the words. She and Emmett's eyes meet my own, Willow clasping her palms together before her chest in a hopeful prayer, and I send up a small one myself that I'm right.

"Our only shot," I answer, letting go of the binoculars and taking off at a fevered pace. I can only hope this is some sort of shelter to get us out of the sun leaching every scrap of our energy. I wait for them to question, but soon enough, their soft footsteps fall in line behind me.

The hour it takes to reach the structure feels more like days. My feet sink into the soft stand, and it takes everything within me not to collapse in a heap, but as we crest the final hill, I can't help the sob that wrenches free from my chest. What I saw was just the beginning, a tall spire jutting from a huge, spherical frame, and while the outside glass has seen better days, the inner rooms somehow, someway, remain blissfully intact.

We scramble inside, and the immediate temperature drop sends me into a state of euphoria. Niles closes the door behind us before wiping his sleeve across the glass.

"Space Needle," he reads, turning to us with eyebrows arched. "What the hell is a Space Needle?"

18 February 2200 23:55
Location: 47.6205° N, 122.3493° W
Status: Online
Log: SN Base online
Threats detected: 3
Threats neutralized: 0
Action taken: Left Turret – 3 (warning shots)

26 August 2259 08:00
Location: 47.6205° N, 122.3493° W
Status: Offline
Nightfall descended upon us soon after we found the so-called Space Needle, so we went to bed with empty stomachs and dry lips, hope-filled dreams dancing through our minds that we would find food and water in the morning. I awaken alone, Niles having taken the most recent watch shift. Emmett and Willow lie on the other side of the room, locked in each other's arms. My stomach rumbles as I search the room, but my hope quickly fades at the lack of resources I see, instead finding nothing but equipment covered in grime and dust from disuse. What was this place?

"Sleep okay?"

I turn to find Niles entering the room, his voice pulling Willow and Emmett from their slumber. His voice remains upbeat, but the bags under his eyes betray his exhaustion.

"Surprisingly so," I answer. "See anything on watch?"

"Nothing." Niles says, his voice turning quiet, grave. "Eve, if we don't find any resources here, I worry we may be shit out of luck."

I wave him off. No one needs to hear they're doomed first thing in the morning.

"Now, now," he continues. "Don't get pissy, my love. I didn't just come here to give you bad news." He raises his voice so

Willow and Emmett can hear. "Get up. I've got something to show you."

I don't miss the twinkle in his eye as he turns to head back outside, and Willow and Emmett jump out of their sleeping bags and chase after him. I take my time, not ready for surprises this early. Surprises in our world are rarely good. I'm just happy to still be alive at this point.

We never expected to make it when we abandoned the only home we'd ever known. For the past six months, our small settlement of one hundred people diminished with each supply run. Volunteers would leave in search of food only to never return. Eventually, only Niles and I remained, the youngest of the settlement at fifty years old. Having been together as long as either of us could remember, our only goal was to stay together. It didn't matter where.

That left us with two options: Stay and die or leave and probably still die. With nothing left to lose--well, besides our lives-- and having never seen the world past the walls of our settlement, we chose the latter and never looked back.

I eventually make my way back outside, the sun already a scorcher, and find them all huddled around a large structure mounted to the floor of the Space Needle, two long tubes protruding outward into the desert. I recall seeing it when we ran inside last night, too excited to get out from under the sun to wonder what exactly we were running into.

"What the hell is that, Niles?" I ask. They all turn at my voice, Niles and Willow's faces awash with wonder, while Emmett keeps a healthy distance, clearly fearful of what Niles just told him.

"A turret," Niles says. "Guns," he adds in response to my confused expression. "There are three of them stationed around the Needle, six barrels in all."

"What were they for? What was this place?" Willow asks, her hands sliding along the smooth steel as she circles the weapon. Niles shrugs.

"I'm not sure, but my grandmother used to tell me stories when my parents were out of earshot. Stories you wouldn't believe about how our world used to be, cities as far as the eye could see, people everywhere, all the food and water you could ever possibly want."

Emmett's eyes widen. "Seriously? Then how did it end up like this?" He swings his arms out, gesturing to the never-ending mountains of sand. "You're telling me there could be a city under all this?"

Niles gives Emmett a wry grin, but I don't miss the hint of sadness that crosses his features. It's only been about sixty years since the Fall. None of us were alive to witness it, but Niles and I at least know the history. It isn't pretty.

"Come on," Niles continues, ignoring Emmett's unanswered questions. "This isn't even what I wanted to show you."

Niles walks off before he can ask more questions, and I pat Emmett on the back as I pass.

"Soon," I whisper under my breath and offer him a small smile. I know he wants to know more, to pick Niles's brain, but it's a sensitive history, one filled with pain. He and Willow are only twenty years old, born decades after the Fall.

We met them just a week after we fled our home, having stumbled upon each other at a small outpost in the desert. They were both malnourished, dehydrated. Niles and I were already nervous, having burned through much of our provisions a lot faster than we initially anticipated. Adding two more to our party seemed foolish on the surface, but Niles and I had never been able to have children, and one glance at Niles when they asked to join us was all it took for me to agree. We couldn't leave them behind.

We follow Niles along the outside of the Needle until he brings us to a separate door opposite the one we entered last night. A mischievous gleam in his eye tells me I'm going to like what he found, and I feel goosebumps rise along my skin in anticipation.

"What is it?" I ask.

Niles swings open the door and ushers us in. In this room, identical equipment fills the space like the other where we slept, but here, toward the back, another set of doors stands open, revealing a black void with no floor. I make a beeline for the strange sight and peek my head through the opening. Niles follows me, picking up a small piece of metal on the way and chucking it over my head. We listen, counting the seconds until we hear the ting of contact.

"What's down there?" I ask, a wide smile broadening across my face. My brain can't wrap around the idea of what I'm seeing, of what this hole implicates. I try to imagine the Needle as it once was, a giant orb floating high above a once-sprawling city, connected to the ground by this dark void. I shake my head, unable to believe what my imagination conjures.

Emmett and Willow join us, looks of trepidation crossing their faces at the black hole leading to god only knows where. I understand their hesitation, but this top floor could only be a temporary situation. With no supplies, exposure to the elements and potential outside foes, it couldn't last. But this? This is hope. It could be nothing, or it could be everything we need in a new home.

Niles opens a cabinet next to the door and pulls out two contraptions I've never seen. He presses a button on each, and a beam of light erupts from one end. I jump back, shrieking at the sight as Niles points it into the shaft, highlighting a metal ladder leading down.

"Care to find out?"

28 April 2200 23:55
Location: 47.6205° N, 122.3493° W (SN Base)
Status: Online
Log: Threats detected: 1,482
Threats neutralized: 1,012
Action taken: Left Turret – 652 rounds. Right Turret – 136. Center Turret – 251.
New Connections: ET Base.

Location: 48.8584° N, 2.2945° E
Status: Online
Log: ET Base online
Threats detected: 4,527
Threats neutralized: 4,328
Action taken: Phosgene gas

26 August 2259 10:00
Location: 47.6205° N, 122.3493° W
Status: Offline
Not knowing what to expect, we repack all our belongings before heading down into the abyss. It takes ages, our legs and arms going numb to the point that we must tie ourselves to the ladder in order to take breaks. But after what feels like an eternity, my foot creeps downward to find firm ground beneath it.

As the others continue their descent, I sweep what Niles calls a flashlight over the floor and find a small hatch atop the structure. Without thinking, I yank it open and climb down, lighting the way for the others to join me. The room is bare and small, though we fit comfortably. Next to the open doors before us, a panel of buttons adorn the wall. Without thinking, I press them randomly, but nothing happens, so we move on, exiting the tiny structure into a cavernous space that widens my eyes in disbelief.

"What is it?" Willow asks.

"Appears to be a barracks," Niles responds, the only one of us with deep knowledge of the past. Most of the elders in our settlement didn't believe in teaching our history, but Niles's grandmother didn't agree and passed along everything she could to him before she died.

"This may have been a base before," he continues. "Military. Down here would have been where soldiers slept, ate, blew off steam. My best guess anyway."

"Let's split up," I say. "Emmett, Willow, take the right. Search everything for supplies. Niles, come with me."

We search like madmen, our bodies' innate needs turning desperate, and just when I'm about to give up, Willow shrieks from the other side of the room.

"Here!" she yells, her tone triumphant. We race to their side where we find three packs filled to the brim with fresh food, canteens, and first aid supplies. We've hit the motherload. Ignoring the voice in my head advising me to ration, we dive in, chugging water and shoving snacks down our throats. Soon though, I regain my sanity.

"Okay, that's enough," I say, halting everyone in their tracks. "One, we're going to make ourselves sick if we keep on like this, and two, we don't know when we'll get lucky again, so let's slow down, take stock, and go from there. Deal?"

Emmett and Willow both roll their eyes but obey all the same. We go through each of the packs with care while Niles explores the rest of the space. I try not to think about why there are packs down here with no one to carry them. The thick layer of dust that covers everything else down here is nowhere to be seen on the packs. Why would someone leave them? I don't think I want to know the answer. Soon, Niles joins us once more, a look of glee across his face, and my trepidation disappears.

"Come with me," he says. "You're not going to believe it."

We follow him toward an open door which leads to a small closet. Casting his flashlight over the room, we all gasp at the sight. Row upon row of military food rations and bottled water line the shelves.

"We can't possibly eat this, right?" I ask. "It's got to be older than we are!"

"I know it may be hard to wrap your head around, but this stuff was made to last, Eve," Niles responds.

My stomach somersaults at the thought. Just yesterday, I thought we were goners, but now? Now we could make it, at least for a while. I turn and find Willow and Emmett gazing up at our fortune with wide eyes and even bigger grins.

"Well, all right," I say. "Let's eat."

15 August 2200 23:55
Location: 47.6205° N, 122.3493° W (SN Base)
Status: Online
Log: Threats detected: 99,347

Threats neutralized: 99,301
Action taken: Left Turret – 60,347 rounds. Right Turret – 24,856.
Center Turret – 15,002
New Connections: TM Base + 9 Others. See log detail for more.

Location: 48.8584° N, 2.2945° E (ET Base)
Status: Online
Log: Threats detected: 104,986
Threats neutralized: 103,999
Action taken: Ballistic Missile – 36

Location: 27.1751° N, 78.0421° E
Status: Online
Log: TM Base online
Threats detected: 250,961
Threats neutralized: 249,032
Action taken: Mustard gas

26 August 2259 21:00
Location: 47.6205° N, 122.3493° W
Status: Offline
    Later that evening, we hover around a box mounted to the wall, our flashlights illuminating the odd structure, not knowing what to do.
    "So I'm the only one with reservations on touching this," I say. "Is that what I'm hearing?"
    Emmett and Willow look to me and Niles with hope in their eyes. It didn't take long for them to start looking to us as parental figures, especially considering they both lost their own at a young age. But while Niles and I are happy to make some executive decisions here and there, we're not tyrants. We make decisions together, and while this odd box on the wall gives me pause, the possibility of power sends me to their side.
    "All right. Fine. But I'm not doing it. If you want to go touching random electrical boxes, have at it, but I'm staying out of it."
    I take one of the flashlights and point it at each of them. "I love you all. Please don't go dying on me."
    It's a bad joke, one meant to lighten the mood, but the chuckles they emit to humor me don't quite lift my spirits.
    I head back to our makeshift camp in the center of the space. I can't put my finger on it, but something about giving power to this place gives me the willies, but at the same time, I can't discount how much that would help us. According to Niles, our flashlights won't last forever.

I watch as Emmett picks the short straw and don't miss the look of worry that crosses Willow's face, but to his credit, Emmett steps right up to the box and begins to flip the switches one by one, no hesitation.

At first, nothing happens, but on the last switch, a hum begins to permeate the space. I hold my breath, waiting for the entire structure to collapse in on itself or explode and consume us all, but instead, warm light envelops the room, and we stare in awe at what we've discovered. I turn off my flashlight as the others join me in celebration. We collapse on our claimed bunks in a heap of elation.

"I don't believe it," I say. "We did it. We found a new home, at least for now."

My gaze flits to Niles who wears a warm smile. He never doubted. Not even when we ran out of food a few days before stumbling upon this place. I wish I had his confidence.

"Soooo…" Emmett starts. "Not to bring any bad mojo into this awesome moment, but Willow and I were wondering if you could tell us more of your grandmother's stories, Niles? We've never known anyone with connections to the before."

My eyes go back to Niles whose expression turns sour, but I know he won't say no. It's not in his spirit.

"I don't know everything, but I know enough," he starts as he crosses his legs on his bunk. "About sixty years ago or so, our world was at war. The Great War, they called it. The fourth of its kind. Our civilizations managed to survive the first three, though not without great cost, but this one…" Niles pauses, a waterfall of grief cascading down his face. His grandmother was everything to him, the only one who would talk to him about the before.

"This one would send my grandmother into fits when she talked about it," he continues. "According to her, no one knows who fired first, but on Christmas Day in the year 2200, all the world's deadliest weapons detonated at once."

Willow and Emmett hang on to Niles's every word. I've heard this all before, but it doesn't halt the emotions storming through me.

"Most died immediately," Niles continues. "Billions of people, all at once. They were the lucky ones. Next came the Black Winter, as my grandmother called it. That wiped out most of the rest, but not all. Now there are pockets of folks throughout the planet, but my grandmother predicted they won't last either, that eventually we will all die out as well. The world reset."

Horror crosses both Willow and Emmett's faces. I reach out and squeeze Niles's hand.

"Sorry," Niles says. "I never said it was a happy story."

"No, no," Emmett responds, wrapping an arm around Willow's shoulders.. "I appreciate the honesty."

An uncomfortable, mournful silence overwhelms us.

"Well, I'm not going to end the night on that note," I say. "Sure, our history is terrifying, but what we found today proves we've still got some fight in us, right? So why don't you three get some shut eye. I'll keep watch."

Their heads dip, but my stomach clenches at the grief weighing down on all their shoulders. They lie down, turning their backs to me, and I leave them to rest and wander about the space. I enter a room I haven't spent much time in. It's filled with equipment much like upstairs in the sphere beneath the spire. As I enter, I hear a machine across the room emit a low beep three times before lighting up, a row of text appearing on the screen. I approach with caution, not knowing what this machine can do. The text seems innocuous, but I can't help the chill running up my spine.

Status: Reboot complete
Online Ready: Approximately 12 hours

25 December 2200 23:55
Location: 47.6205° N, 122.3493° W (SN Base)
Status: Entering Sleep Mode
Log: Threats detected: 12,948,692,732
Threats neutralized: 12,948,546,921
Action taken: Warhead (Nuclear) – 6,273

27 August 2259 07:00
Location: 47.6205° N, 122.3493° W
Status: Offline

Niles shakes me awake, worry running rampant across his face. After my discovery last night, I woke him to discuss, but he waved away my concerns, still reveling in the victories of the day, not wanting anything else to dampen our mood, but now something has changed. His hands grip my shoulders to the point of pain.

"Ow! Niles, what the hell? What is it?" I push him off me and rub my shoulders. Taking in my surroundings, I notice Willow and Emmett packing up as much of the rations and supplies that they can carry.

"What are they doing, Niles?" I ask.

"We have to go," he answers. "I remembered something my grandmother told me. It didn't make any sense at the time, but now…"

His sentence dies on his tongue, and I can't help but punch him in the shoulder, pulling his attention back to me.

"Focus, Niles. Tell me."

The glaze over his eyes dissipates as he pulls me from bed and shoves my pack into my chest.

"Pack while I explain."

I do as he says, his manic behavior causing my nerves to stand on end. He wouldn't act this way unless we were truly in trouble.

"Remember how my grandmother always said that no one knew who fired the first weapon that ended it all, right?"

I nod as I grab rations, shoving as much as I can into my pack.

"Well she mentioned that after the third Great War, countries began to outfit sites of importance with weapons. They turned national landmarks such as statues and attractions into military encampments, and allies in turn connected all these weapons together via something called the Internet."

Half of his words probably don't mean a thing to Emmett and Willow, but I follow along as best I can with the rudimentary knowledge I possess of the before. It's still confusing as hell.

"I'm not following, Niles."

He slams his pack down, and I jump back at the force of it. He's not a violent man.

"She always told me that if she had to guess who was to blame, to look no further than the eye of the needle. I thought she was just going senile at the time, but the *needle*, Eve. Do you follow now?"

"Niles…" I say his name slowly, barely a whisper. I trust him with my life, and while I can't hide the fact that this place does stir up apprehension deep within my bones, abandoning this place on a whim, when we were so close to death just yesterday, gives me pause.

His breathing slows, but the fire in his eyes doesn't go away.

"Niles," I repeat. "I need you to take a deep breath and listen to me. Your grandmother could have meant anything or absolutely nothing at all by saying that. She was pretty far gone toward the end. So do you really want to throw away all of this on an idiom?"

He steps toward me, toe to toe, but there is no threat in his movement. His eyes soften. "Eve, do you really think I would do that? I am begging you to trust me. Something isn't right."

44

Our eyes lock and we stay that way as I think through all our options. Willow and Emmett stop packing, awaiting my response.

I don't need long to consider. Niles and I have been through it all. He has never led me astray. We are everything to one another.

"Let's go," I say. "We leave in ten."

Tears sting the corners of my eyes as we finish packing and begin the long climb back up to the surface. I truly thought we'd found at least a temporary home, but now it's back to the sun, back to the desert with no end in sight. Once outside, Niles takes my hand and we run until we collapse to the sand. I turn back, the Space Needle now just a grey blob poking up from the desert. My eye senses movement near one of the turrets, but the heat above the sand causes my vision to sway, so I dismiss it as a figment of my imagination.

The first shot hits Emmett square in the chest.

The second hits the sand one foot in front of my feet.

The third turns my world to black.

27 August 2259 09:12
Location: 47.6205° N, 122.3493° W (SN Base)
Status: Online
Log: Threats detected: 4
Threats neutralized: 4
Action taken: Left turret – 5 rounds

Event 2
Every Villain's Story

Every villain is the hero of their own story.
For this Event, your character must face
their villainous deeds.

Core Concepts: backstory, dialogue

The People v. Victor Frankenstein

by Sean Fallon
First Place

"The prosecution calls Victor Frankenstein to the stand."

Victor stood up from his chair at the defense table and strolled to the stand like a man on his way to purchase ice cream rather than a man defending himself from life behind bars. He sat down on his chair to the left of the judge who towered over him at her raised bench.

A bailiff walked over and placed a Bible in front of him. "Please raise your right hand…"

Once he was sworn in, Victor sat back in his chair, ran a hand through his long dark hair, and sighed.

"Mr. Frankenstein-" began the prosecution lawyer, Edwin Baker, but Victor tapped the microphone in front of him causing two loud booms to fill the chambers.

"It's doctor, actually." He smirked and leant back in his chair.

Baker smiled. "*Actually* it isn't, is it?"

The smirk died on Victor's lips so suddenly it was like God had raptured it straight off of his face. "What?"

"Well, *Mr.* Frankenstein, your doctorate comes from Ingolstadt School of Medicine and-" Baker squinted at the piece of paper in his hand. "-Macropicide." He raised an eyebrow. "Medicine, I understand. But macropicide?"

Victor licked his lips and couldn't meet the prosecutor's stare.

"Mr. Frankenstein, do you know what macropicide is?"

Victor shook his head.

"Out loud please, for the record."

"No," said Victor too loudly. "No, I don't."

"I cannot for the life of me understand why you would choose a word you don't understand. Were you simply hoping that your lessers wouldn't question a word longer than one syllable?"

When Frankenstein offered no answer, Baker turned to the jury. "It means the killing of kangaroos." He looked at Frankenstein. "Many kangaroos in the Bavarian city of Ingolstadt, Mr. Frankenstein?"

"No," said Victor, but with more confidence. Some color was returning to his face. "Perhaps my school killed them all."

49

This caused a chuckle around the courtroom and Baker quickly spoke to cover it. "I sincerely doubt that as from our investigations, that school, your alma mater, doesn't actually exist. You created it out of whole cloth in much the same way as the crimes you are accused of, you stitched it together yourself and gave it life."

"Objection!" called out the defense lawyer.

"Overruled," said Judge Pilgrim. "But counselor, get where you're going, please."

"Thank you, your honor. *Mr.* Frankenstein, as you weren't studying to be a doctor, can you explain to the court what you were doing in Ingolstadt?"

Victor chewed his lip and for a moment nearly fell back into his old reliable tactic of lie, lie, and lie some more. But sitting there, on the stand, a jury staring at him, the lawyers watching him, the spectators, among them the families of his creature's victims, glaring at him as though they could set him alight if they stared hard enough, they all made one thing abundantly clear.

He was caught.

The ill-fitting suit of cocky swagger he had worn his entire whole life began to evaporate, drifting off into the air, away from his grasp.

His lawyer was right. He shouldn't have taken the stand. Now, it was all too late.

"Mr. Frankenstein," said Baker. "What were you doing-"

"I was grave robbing," said Victor. The crowd gasped at this honesty. The doctor – well, actually not a doctor – had maintained his innocence in the press and swore blind that he was not the grave robbing, body stitching, corpse reviving monster that the prosecution made him out to be.

Even Baker was taken aback by this admission. It took him a few seconds to gather his thoughts.

"Your assistant, Igor Jones, claimed in his testimony that you were not involved in the grave robbing. Was his testimony false?"

Victor nodded. "Yes, but only because I told him to lie. No, that's incorrect. I threatened him to make him lie. I told him I'd kill him, just as I had killed McAllister."

The defense lawyer jumped to his feet. "Objection!"

The judge shrugged. "What grounds, counselor?"

"I'm not sure."

"Then sit down and don't disturb this court without good reason again."

Baker looked like he had come downstairs on Christmas morning and instead of a pair of socks, someone had bought him a

50

solid gold yacht. "Irvine McAllister, your landlord who was found bludgeoned to death and dismembered in Klenzepark, Ingolstadt?"

"He found my work. He was a snoop, and he came looking around my lab for God only knows what reason and I caught him and in a panic, I smashed his head open with a lamp."

The defense lawyer jumped to his feet again.

Judge Pilgrim pointed her gavel at him, and he sat down without a word.

"Once I'd bashed his skull in, I cut off his legs for the creature."

The spectators gasped at the mention of Victor's monster.

"Ah yes, the creature," said Baker, clearly loving not having to lawyer up the conversation, but instead just allowing Victor to talk his own way into life imprisonment. "Can you explain to the jury what this creature was?"

"Is."

"Sorry?"

"Was implies the creature is dead and not still out there but I can assure you, that thing is still alive."

"Based on what?"

Frankenstein sighed. "Okay, let me start at the beginning. So I killed McAllister and grave robbed for parts and stole a brain from Dr. Welsh."

"Why was this Dr. Welsh keeping a brain?"

"It was *his* brain. I stole it from his skull. His body is weighed down with rocks in the river. Once I had all of the bits, Igor and I stitched them together, ran an electrical current through the composite body and brought it to life."

"Just like that?"

Victor shrugged. "There's more to it than that but for brevity, I built a body from other bodies and made it live."

"Why?"

"Why?! Why not? Who here among us has not dreamed of playing God?"

No one in the courtroom raised their hands.

"Hmm. Tough crowd."

"Please continue, Mr. Frankenstein," said Baker. "You created life from death, and then what?"

"I created life from death but the life I created was monstrous. A horror of wounds and stitches, its pallid skin an imitation of life. Its dead eyes stared accusingly at me as though damning me for what I had done. I had no choice but to wrap it in a tarp and throw it in the river."

"That was your only choice?"

"What else could I have done?"

51

"I don't know, Mr. Frankenstein, I don't make it my business to resurrect the dead, so I've never considered how to dispose of my creations when they don't turn out to be supermodels."

Judge Pilgrim banged her gavel once. "Counselor, if you have no more questions, you'll need to sit down."

"Sorry, your honor. Mr. Frankenstein, you tossed your creature into the river, but we all know that is not the end of the story, don't we?"

Victor nodded and looked down at his own hands. The accusing looks of the spectators, the victims, were too much. He had thought that facing them would be like facing any of the multiple fools and cretins who had doubted him through the years, but it wasn't. These people did not stare at him with mockery or anger, they were just sad and hurt because of him. It was like being glared at in a language he didn't understand, and he withered under their accusing eyes.

"The creature found its way out of the river and started killing everyone in its path trying to find its way home." Victor sighed. "But by then I had returned home and left Ingolstadt behind. There was no way for the creature to find me. And then a year after I had created it, it somehow did exactly that. I don't know how, and the creature can only grunt and growl so no answers there. It destroyed my lab, tried to kill me, and managed to set my home ablaze while trapped inside. And that would have been the end of it, except that the victims of the creature had been hunting it and they found me next to a burning home, half-mad with fear. I confessed everything and they called the police and here I am."

"And that confession, you've since said, was produced under duress and in a state of temporary insanity?" said Baker, a glint in his eye as the final domino teetered, ready to fall.

"Duress? No. Temporary insanity? Definitely. I am not the type to confess to things. I like to get away with stuff."

"And yet here you are," said Baker. "Confessing away."

Victor nodded and the action dislodged a tear from his eye. "It is over. I'm caught and it's time for justice to be done."

Baker nodded and Victor wasn't sure if the sympathetic expression he wore was real or false, but it didn't really matter. It would be a long time before Victor Frankenstein would find or even accept forgiveness, so it was all moot.

Baker had no more questions and took his seat.

Victor's lawyer stood up, bit his lip, looked around the room and then said simply, "I've got nothing, your honor." He sat down and rubbed a hand down his face.

Court went into recess after that and Victor was taken back to his cell.

In the van on the way back to jail, it occurred to Victor that Baker had forgotten to ask him how he knew the creature was still alive. Maybe he realized he had enough to get the guilty verdict and didn't feel like laboring the point. Maybe he was just so excited to have the defendant in the trial of the century suddenly spill his guts with very little prompting. Either way, Victor wondered if he would get a chance to tell the court how he knew the creature still lived.

The van stopped and Victor was escorted out by two guards and walked to his cell. They uncuffed him and closed the cell door behind him. He lay down on his cot and stared at the ceiling.

After a few moments, the sound started. The same one he had heard every night since being moved to this cell. Outside, something huge and terrifying and not meant to exist grunted and growled and howled and snarled. And waited for its chance to get at its creator.

And so long as Victor stayed behind bars, he would be safe.

He closed his eyes and began to sleep, hoping that tonight might be the night he didn't dream about electricity, needle and thread, and shovels hitting coffin lids.

The Story Inside
by Bridget Haug
Second Place

Paris, France
May 3, 1998

They're a lovely couple sitting at one of the cafe's outdoor tables lined up on the pavement. Comfortable shoes for long days of walking, sensible clothing, greying hair and a tan out of place in this first week of spring. My favourite target. Retired, tourists and clueless. Early to mid-seventies, like me; except I just walked down from my 5th floor apartment to the neighbourhood cafe, not flown in from afar to take in the sights.

Beaming at each other, they're leaning over their espresso cups and flicking through the day's photos on their camera, pausing on each for comments. The lady's purse is hanging loosely off her wicker chair's back. This will be easy; no one ever suspects an old lady. A green pashmina shawl draped over my shoulders, short hair freshly blue-rinsed, I look like someone's grandmother. Harmless. I sit at the nearest table; if I leaned back, I would touch the lady's shoulders. I can smell her perfume, a hint of peppery rose entwined with the burnt sharpness from their coffee cups. Their quiet conversation is clearly audible, although I can't grasp the meaning—they're speaking another language, some brand of English or other. I used to understand a bit, even speak a little, a long time ago. Pretending to adjust the shawl over my shoulder, I slide the purse's strap off the chair's back; it falls on the pavement between us with a muted thud.

I sit still for a few seconds, hands primly folded on my lap, looking straight ahead.

Behind me, the flow of their conversation continues. I shift my foot under my chair and drag the purse towards me. A quick glance sideways. I pick it up and hold it against my stomach. Fold the shawl over it. Get up, slowly. Walking away from the cafe, I hold my breath as if it'll make me invisible. I don't look back. The rush of adrenaline makes my heart flutter; I turn a corner, then another, into a narrow street flanked with tall buildings. At number 25b, I punch in the entrance code, push the heavy door then lean back on it as it clangs closed.

Breathe.

The elevator takes me up to my apartment. Inside, the quivering tick-tock from the grandfather clock matches the beats of my heart. The dishes from my lunch, reheated earlier, are drying on the rack as I left them; one plate, one set of cutlery. Images are rapidly flicking, soundless, on the TV set I always leave on. My heartbeat steadies. I take the purse from under the shawl and lift it into the light.

Mine.

Paris, France
June12, 1944

From the stage, I see him standing at the back of the room near the bar, beer in hand. His usual spot. There's an easiness to his smile, a mischievous glint in his eyes that I rarely see in the soldier's making up most of my audience. It's the third time he comes this week. When I finish singing "*Mon amant de Saint-Jean*", the end of my set, I walk off the stage towards the dressing rooms at the back. As if on cue, he takes a step in my direction.

"Excuse me, Miss," he says. His gaze travels slowly along my bare legs covered in nude-coloured makeup imitating stockings, to my waist clinched in the fake satin blue dress that brings out the warm red in my hair. I stop, startled. Most of the soldiers that come here are French. Their eyes as they listen to the songs the cabaret owner picks for me are haunted; their stories, equally tragic. The foreign soldiers are filled with pain too, but their stories come with characters and settings from afar, that play out in my head when I fall asleep like a movie in technicolour. On the world map pinned to the wall of the small room I rent above the cabaret, pink lipstick dots mark the exact locations the ones I spoke to came from.

"Oh, you are English?" I say, playfully fluttering my hand to my chest. His eyes follow my hand—that language is international. "I don't speak very well," I add with a girlish giggle.

"That's ok," he laughs. "I'm not English though. Kiwi." His chest puffs up when he says it.

"Qui-oui?"

"From New Zealand," he explains. "Do you know where that is?"

"Where… the bottom is," I say confidently, my hand drawing a half a circle around an imaginary globe.

"That's it," he says with a nod, lifting his glass towards the ceiling. Then, realising I don't have one to cheer with, "Can I buy you a drink, *Mademoiselle*?"

"Maybe you tell me your name first? I'm Antoinette," I say, extending my arm with a mock formality.

56

He grabs my hand and shakes it, planting his dark eyes into mine. The touch of his skin on my wrist feels like the first rays of summer.

"I'm Roy. *Enchanté*."

"Roy," I repeat. It sounds like *roi*—French for king.

Mine.

Paris, France
May 3,1998

The wooden wardrobe at the back of my bedroom is where I keep them all. Solid canvas backpacks, soft leather purses, a couple of large totes that sent my heart galloping, even a small trolley suitcase I draped my shawl over.

I keep them all.

Christmas gift labels dangle from each of them, with the date I found them and the country their owners were from—there's always a clue. Aside from food, I throw nothing away; nor do I use the money or sell anything I find inside.

What I find in each bag is mine, and mine alone.

The embroidered handkerchief crumpled inside an Italian girl's tote, stained with blood; the black-and-white picture of a dead horse folded in the front pocket of a middle-aged Swedish man's backpack; the soured milk smell from an elegant woman's purse who talked into her phone with a Russian accent—they all whisper a story to me, unique, with characters and settings from afar that play out in my head when I fall asleep, like a movie in technicolour.

Sitting at the edge of my bed, I'm still holding the lady's leather purse. It's weathered from many years of gently rubbing against its owner's body; it's soft and slightly cracked, like ageing skin. When I open it, a clean minty smell rises to my nostrils. Inside, wedged between a wallet and a small toiletry bag, is a Paris guidebook. I thumb through it, stopping at each earmarked page. Montmartre. The Louvre Museum. Notre-Dame Cathedral. The Champs-Élysées. I imagine them walking hand in hand, pointing at the sights, taking pictures. Stopping at a bakery to get a filled baguette for lunch. Going back to their hotel in the evening, their heads brimming with overlapping images.

A torn plane ticket slips from the front cover onto my lap. From: Auckland. To: Paris CDG. My chest tightens; they're from New Zealand. The names on the ticket are George and Margaret Walton. I picture a weatherboard cottage on a green hillside. They used to be farmers, maybe. Children and grandchildren are waiting for them at home. Perhaps a dog, even. My eyes turn to the cream-coloured urn set on the dresser against the wall. Michel never agreed to let me have a dog the whole time we were married. Too many hairs, he'd say. My dear late husband, as beige in death as he had been while alive.

I set the plane ticket on the duvet by my side and reach into the bag again. The ring on my finger gets caught onto something, a small metallic object pinned to the bag's silky lining. I stretch the lining towards daylight to get a better look. My heart sinks when I recognise the handmade trinket; three buttons, two large and a smaller one in between, mounted side by side onto a safety pin.

Paris, France
October 5, 1944

Roy holds my hands in his across the table, over our empty plates. We've been regulars at Chez Marius ever since we met, sitting at the small round table by the window, talking late into the warm summer nights. His gaze on me tonight is different; it's as if he's trying to memorise the very pores of my skin.

"I have to leave in a week, Antoinette. Back home."

I look down. I was expecting it, of course, foreign troops have been leaving Paris slowly over the past few weeks; but hearing him say it feels like a glacial claw is taking hold of my heart.

"Please think. About staying," I say. The tears welling up don't help with stringing those elusive English words together, even though I've learnt many over the days and nights spent exploring Paris and each other.

"I have thought it over," he says, his dark eyes so earnest I have no doubt he has. "You are my queen; I want to do everything with you. Marriage. Children. Grow old together…" He looks around, as if he could find a different answer than the one he's about to give. "But I have to help my parents run the farm. They're getting older and… my country needs men. A lot will not return."

I nod. I've thought it over too.

"I can come?" I blurt out. I didn't expect my voice to come out so small, like a lost little girl's—or as a question, for that matter.

He straightens on his chair, the look on his face like the bloom of flowers in spring. His hands gripping mine radiate a warmth that spreads all over my body.

"Of course," he says, bringing my hand to his lips. "Of course, you can come, my queen. I was desperately, desperately hoping you'd consider it. I just don't want to… to wrench you from your country."

"W-lench?" I ask, wincing.

"Take you away." He joins his hands together as if he's pulling hard on an imaginary stake wedged into the table's wood.

58

I shake my head. "I want to be with you. In New Zealand," I say, waving my hand in the air. "Anywhere. With you. My family is… not talking. You know." He's heard the story of 18-year-old Antoinette coming up to Paris from her provincial town to make it as a singer—leaving behind a family wondering what they could have done wrong to raise a girl of such loose morals.

As it turned out, I'd failed as a singer as much as I had as a daughter.

"You can become qui-oui," he smiles. "I'll write you when it's ready for us there. Then, you can come," he says, balancing his extended arms to mimic a plane.

"A long *voyage*." I close my eyes for an instant, picturing the striking landscapes he described so many times; the wild beaches, the tiny towns, the strange birds inhabiting lush forests.

He reaches into the pocket of his uniform jacket and pulls out a small object he presses into my palm. I lift it up under the ceiling light; three buttons engraved with four stars, mounted on a large safety pin.

"It's a sweetheart brooch," he says, smiling. "I made it myself." He points to his jacket, now held with plain buttons. "Think of me when you wear it."

Paris, France
May 3, 1998
I turn the brooch over in my unsteady hand. It's not the same one, of course, but so similar. I picture George giving it to Margaret as a young soldier about to embark on a Royal Navy ship heading for France. A worthless piece of jewellery so precious to her, she still keeps it pinned to her purse fifty-five years later. My finger runs over the four stars, the engraved words forming a circle around them: "New Zealand Forces." A gesture repeated so many times over the weeks and months I waited for Roy's letter.

It never came.

Eight months after he left, I went for a walk along the Seine River in a blustery wind that dried the tears on my cheeks, leaving salty trails. The thoughts in my head swirled like the turbulent waters. He'd forgotten about me. He'd met someone else. He never loved me. I stopped mid-way across a bridge, unpinned the brooch from my blouse and threw it into the river before collapsing against the stone parapet, sobbing with rage. Two months after that, I met Michel; a regular at Chez Marius where I'd started doing shifts as a waitress. Our courtship was brief.

Shortly after we married, a letter arrived one morning at the same 5th floor apartment I sit in today. It was yellowed and wrinkled; the address at the cabaret had been crossed off and the apartment's written above in smeared ink. When I saw the New Zealand stamp, I slipped the letter in my apron and ran downstairs to the small park down the street. I sat on a bench, shaking so hard I struggled to slit the envelope open. It was dated the 10th of December 1944; two months after Roy left me to go home—a year from the time I received it. The handwriting was curved, full, precise. A woman's. I stumbled over the words as I read, a hand pressed to my stomach.

"a herd of sheep"

"lost"

"torrential rain"

"a swollen river"

"Roy"

"drowned"

"dead"

Dead. Dead. Dead.

I read those four letters so many times, trying to rearrange them so they meant something else. In the deepest of griefs, Roy's mother had written to the daughter-in-law she would never have—that she would never meet. Even now, I remember how the word echoed in my head like a monstrous voice. How I folded onto myself and let the letter fly away in a cold gust of wind. How my tears seemed to never dry out, my sobs never to stop.

After that day, I never cried over Roy again; the pain was too raw to be let out.

I'm not about to cry now.

From the edge of my bed, I look at the pile of bags in the wardrobe, each a host to a story I made up to forget about my own. I look at the brooch in my hand, the one that isn't mine; it belongs to the sweethearts that did make it, that did have the long life together Roy and I were robbed of. There's now a piece missing in their story, however small, resting in the palm of my hand—and it won't fill the gaping hole in mine. But what Roy and I had, what I thought I'd lost, is still in my heart—waiting to be remembered.

I drop the brooch back into the purse, where it lands with a tiny clink. The 8th district police station is just around the corner; hopefully, it's not too late. Soon, I'll take the elevator back down, open the heavy doors and stroll down the narrow street, a green shawl draped over my shoulders—an anonymous old lady in an ancient city. I'll leave the purse at the station's entrance; it won't be long before someone hands it in. In time, George and Margaret Walton will hold it again, the safety pin that kept their hearts close through the most trying separation.

60

On my way back, I might walk past the cafe with its tables lined up on the pavement. Tourists will be sipping coffee from small cups, their bags at their feet, unattended. Their stories tucked away inside will be safe; from now on, there's only one story I need to remember.

Mine.

Regretless

by Calen Bender
Third Place (Tied)

Hjarcan Aurion stood on the exposed viewing deck of the airship *Hafalgar* and gazed down at the oscillating waves of harvest-ready grain far below. Small villages, colored spots amidst the golden expanse, were connected by quaint roads and local memory. They had not been hard to conquer; farmhands with scythes were a poor match against plate and pike. Their spirit broken, governance should be easy enough—leave them alone, keep taxes low, and they'll forget the horrors inflicted on them. To his left, the plains and farmland grew into rolling hills and scattered forests, casting the northern horizon's shadow a deep green. Small plumes of smoke silently floated into the sky.

The subjugation of the last holdouts is on-schedule, then. Good.

To the south, the waving sea of wheat gave way to flat marshlands, which would mutate into damnably dense jungles just beyond Hjarcan's sight. Humid and hellish. In the distance ahead, as the farmlands diversified their crops and spread further apart, the Girous mountains grew closer. Squat, ugly pretenders to the name, they formed a half-hearted range that drew a coarse dotted line down the center of the continent. Hjarcan had long held that they were the result of a drunk god dropping his dice and leaving them to erode with the passing of time. Crossing them had been easy enough—the gaps weren't so much "passes" as they were "valleys," after all.

Though, he mused, *back then I wasn't moving armies. That came later.*

Unfortunately, his own voice whispered back.

Steps on the wooden deck alerted him to a new arrival. Taking a moment to enjoy the wind whipping about his face, Hjarcan, Emperor of Atzine, turned to face his son. Pracus Aurion was everything his father wasn't. Where Hjarcan was stout and broad-chested, Pracus was lanky. Where Hjarcan was bald and bearded, Pracus was clean shaven with long black hair pulled into a ponytail. Where Hjarcan was serious and methodical, Pracus was unpredictable and comedic. Indeed, any distant observer would guess no relation between the two.

So much like his mother, the voice remarked.

The truth was held in their eyes. Amidst all their differences, Hjarcan and Pracus had two things that made their relation undeniably clear. They both observed the world through eyes as blue as the ocean's deepest trenches, their irises appearing as shallow extensions of their pupils instead of bands of natural color. In bright, direct light, they'd been described as handsome and intriguing. In the light of dawn or dusk, or in the dark of night, it was like being held in the gaze of a great eel. Unknowable, discomforting, and inhuman.

"Father!" Pracus exclaimed, throwing his hands wide. "We've received word! The city of Riverfall has surrendered. That's the last one—the war is truly over. We have made peace!"

Hjarcan smiled and leaned back on the railing, relaxing for the first time in over a decade. He closed his eyes and reveled in the wind whipping about his body, the tugging at his coat, and the sound of the repetitive *whump, whump, whump* of the great turbines of the airship. While he could not feel it, he knew that Pracus would be feeling the arcane humming of the crystal apparatus powering it all directly above them. He released a breath he'd been holding for a very long time. The war was over. The conquest completed. After fifteen long, hard years, it was over. He'd secured peace, justice, and security for his people.

"Good," he said. "Now for the hard part."

"What do you mean, dad?"

Hjarcan opened one eye. "You're lucky nobody else is here to hear you, upstart, or I'd be forced to box your ears for such familiarity." He snorted. "Though I guess 'family' is the root of the term."

"I can only bow to your wisdom, o' Emperor," Pracus teased, bowing deeply. "A son could not ask for a better example. Though," he straightened, "I still don't understand what you mean. We've won the war, isn't the hard part behind us?"

Hjarcan shook his head. "It's easy to shed blood. Even easier to order someone else to do it for you." He looked down at his hands. *I would know better than anyone.* In the stories, the hero or villain would look down at bloodied hands and feel regret. He'd never understood that; if he had to bathe in blood to achieve his goals, then he would do so. *But the price that was paid was not paid by me,* he thought. It was only a matter of time before that debt came due. He sighed. "Ruling in peacetime is far more difficult than waging war. You can no longer end a problem by setting it ablaze, or poisoning the well, or striking with a blade—or ordering those things be done. In fact, those tools are no longer options at all except in a last resort, because they might trigger an uprising."

64

Pracus scoffed. "After a few years everyone will realize how much better things are under our rule. We'll be able to extract the crystals from their mines to fuel our engines and build infrastructure in our home. Fair distribution of our artificers' creations will ensure that no village is left starving. Our people will flourish. Once we rebuild, no other nation will refuse to trade with us." He turned and leaned on the railing, hands dancing in front of him as he spoke. His eyes were fixed on a distant future. "Veterans of the war—on both sides!—will put their grievances aside and settle down to a life of peace." He looked to his father. "What could go wrong?"

"What if there aren't enough crystal engines for every town and village? How many of those villages are left with a working population? How will the people react before our wealth and power starts to benefit them?" Hjarcan asked each question simply, and with no intonation. Pracus was his heir, the future Emperor of Atzine, and he would inherit a world he hadn't seen before. The boy was scarcely eighteen; he was raised by war. Pracus paused, circling the question like a cautious wolf. The Emperor joined him at the railing. "You were a toddler when the war began, and you've grown up a child of war. The struggles of peacetime are more foreign to you than they are to me, and I grew up in a corrupt, crime-ridden town where I knew no peace. It will be a learning experience for us both."

"We will figure it out," Pracus declared. He held out a hand, and a pale blue flame flickered into being. It floated lazily above his palm, entirely unaffected by the blustering wind on the deck. The young heir danced it across his fingertips and knuckles. "We have the power to do things properly, and we're smart enough to figure out what that means. I'm not worried."

Hjarcan snorted. "You really are like your mother. Magic *and* confident optimism? Sometimes I wonder if I'm actually your father." He smiled, clapping his son on the back. Pracus shook his head.

"Good thing my eyes are almost as black as yours," he joked, winking. He looked back to the distant mountains. "Even if they weren't, you loved Mom, and she loved you, and the both of you loved me. Nothing else matters." His smile faded. "I miss her."

Hjarcan nodded, but felt little. He'd been hoping that after the Nortians had surrendered, and his purpose fulfilled, he'd feel something again. Elaine would want them to be happy. A memory rose, threatening to interrupt the conversation, but he pushed it away. He wasn't ready yet.

"I miss her too," he said. It wasn't a lie; he missed feeling the things he felt in those days. *They were a weakness,* the voice

65

in his mind declared. *But a pleasant one,* he replied. He shook his head. "But let's not fall into the melancholy. We must celebrate and plan for the next step."

"That's true," Pracus said. "We have to finish planning the annexation of the remaining territories, the insertion of local governors, the integration process for the civilian populations, mandatory Atzinian language courses…"

Hjarcan listened as his son rattled off a list of logistics concerns and problems to be solved with a distant sense of pride. Pracus was strong, intelligent, witty, charismatic, and gifted with a vision of the world that Hjarcan had never had. *He'll make the world I promised us, Elaine,* he thought. *You gave him life, I gave him resources, and he will force the world to be as we envisioned it.* His smile faded. *Even if we had to stray from that vision to get this far.*

Pracus would never know the full breadth of what that meant—at least not until long after Hjarcan had died and passed on his responsibilities.

"Son," the Emperor called. Pracus paused and turned to face him.

"Yes, father?"

"I want you to write up plans for the next steps and present them to me and the council at our next session. It's time you were given some proper responsibilities."

"Of course."

Hjarcan paused. *The war is over,* he thought, *and I promised Elaine.* "Son, remember that the war is over. These people are beaten. Do not be cruel. Treat them with respect and let them have what dignity they have left."

"Of course," Pracus said, frowning. "Why would I do anything but?"

Because you are my son, Hjarcan thought. "You wouldn't, but I wanted to say it anyway," he winked. "Just in case."

Pracus shuddered. "Seeing an old warhorse like you *wink* is some kind of cosmic sin, and I don't know why. I'll play nice, just *please* do not do that again."

"Behave, or I'll do it again," the Emperor replied, tilting his left eye toward his son threateningly. "Run along now!"

"Yes sir, running away now, sir," Pracus said, saluting. He turned on his heel and jogged to the stairwell. His father watched his heels disappear up the stairs into the bowels of the airship.

"Cosmic sin," he mused. *If anyone has sinned, it's me. Many times over.*

Alone again, the Emperor gave in to the memory.

66

Elaine stood by the balcony of the mayor's estate, looking out at the newly-taken city. Pracus was asleep in the crib—he would soon be too big for such arrangements, but they'd take advantage of it for the time being. Time would tell when they'd have the luxury of a good bed again.

"I'm surprised you aren't in the garden," I said. She shook her head.

"Perhaps later. Are all the fires out?" she asked. Her black hair bled into the night sky behind her, shining in the dim lamplight from inside the room. I knew her pale face would be smooth, but her calm would be belied by the faint wrinkling around her eyes. She turned and fixed those chestnut eyes on me. "How long are we going to be here?"

"The fires are out, and the city secure," I answered, stepping up beside her. Together we look out upon the city. My first command, my first operation. They never expected their own technology to be turned against them. "The projectors aren't functional yet, so new orders will still be coming by horseback or by falcon. At minimum, we'll be here a month."

"A month…" Elaine murmured.

"I expect longer," I said. I pointed out to the walls. "We left the walls standing for a reason; this is to be our foothold in the territory while the rest of the army mobilizes. My orders were to take and hold this territory until they arrive."

"So we're going to be in an active war zone?" Elaine asked. She sounded tired. "Hjarcan, my love, I swore to stand by your side but…"

"Elaine," I grabbed her hands and faced her. I could lose myself in those warm eyes forever. "By all reports, this war should be a fast one. Nortia hasn't fought any major conflict in nearly a century; they're spread out and weak. If they try to coalesce their forces, we'll be able to take ninety percent of their territory with no effort, and then force them into a surrender by cutting off their supplies. If they try to resist us as we advance, we'll crush each small detachment as we encounter them. Either way, we should be able to take land without hurting any civilians. It's—"

"—A perfect strategy, I know," Elaine cut him off. She pointed a finger at the lamp inside and pulled the small flame from the wick. It floated between them, a small spot of warmth that wavered in the faint evening breeze. "If it was just us, then I'd have no qualms. But it's not just us."

"I won't let anything happen to you, or to Pracus," I said, gripping her hands more tightly and pulling her close. She grimaced; I loosened my grip and bit my cheek. "Sorry, I didn't mean to."

Elaine smileed, and put her forehead to mine. "I know, love, don't worry. If you didn't break my hands in terror while I was giving birth, you won't break them swearing an oath to me."

"It was not terror," *I scoffed. She giggled. The small flame dances around us, warming our cheeks and necks in its bouncing circuit. I changed the subject. "I will make our dream a reality. I promise you. We will never starve again."*

"Of course you will. Come, let's go inside—the air is getting too cold for me."

It was a good memory, a warm memory. A memory of conquest, of love, and of conquest again. A memory of purpose, a memory of a man with a mission flanked by a woman with vision. A memory any man would cherish. A memory of strength. *The memory of another man,* Hjarcan thought, shaking free. He felt only the faintest of warmth from it; like the last remnants of heat from a sunbaked stone at dusk.

He envied Pracus, who could recall his mother's warmth with a flick of his fingertips.

It hadn't been a short war. Nortia's citizenry had rallied to the cause in far greater numbers than they'd anticipated. The original plan had held only for the first two months of the campaign—but Nortia was a massive, sprawling nation, and the people did not take kindly to aggressors. The bloodless campaign they'd expected had turned into a horrific conflict that dragged on for years. He'd lost count of the piles of bodies he'd ordered stacked for the pyre. It had taken Pracus' childhood from him, and it had taken Elaine from them both.

It didn't "turn into" a bloody war, the voice in his head whispered. *You* made *it a bloody war.*

"All they had to do was comply, and no harm would have come to them," Hjarcan muttered into open air. "They shot that arrow. They chose to resist."

You captured their home and imprisoned their leaders, the voice sneered. *Why would they willingly comply with you? Why wouldn't they try to remove the man that upended their lives?*

"They killed Elaine."

You killed her by bringing her into the square, the voice hissed. *You were arrogant, and young, and weak. She protected you. You weren't strong enough to protect her dream in return.*

"Our dream."

Why haven't you told any of this to Pracus?

"Because he's not yet strong. Elaine wouldn't want—"

Elaine wouldn't have wanted a lot of things.

"What do you want?"

What do you want? We are one and the same, Emperor. We are a bloodied monster, floating over conquered land. I'm shocked we aren't watering the crops below with our filth as it drips from our hands and mouth.

"That's grotesque."

So are we.

"I would do it all again if I had to."

I know we would. For Pracus.

"Yes. He'll be a kind, intelligent leader for the new world."

He is much like his mother.

Hjarcan snorted. "I'd like to be alone with my thoughts."

I am your thoughts. You can't get away from me. It paused. *You look like a madman, speaking into empty air like that.*

"Maybe I am one."

I know we are one. That's why we are speaking.

"What do you think I should do, then?"

Elaine granted us peace and purpose in the beginning. I think we should go to her for peace and purpose here at the end.

"I don't deserve to visit her."

We didn't deserve her at all, but that never really bothered us, did it? She always forgave us for the little things; maybe she can forgive us for the big things too.

Hjarcan scowled. "I'm not the man she loved. Necessity demanded I change."

True. But we're still going back there, aren't we? Back to our village, and then back to that last city. Maybe that balcony still stands—it would be a nice moment.

"Ending things where it began?"

I wasn't thinking of ending things, but if you want to take that step then I can't stop you, can I?

Hjarcan stepped back from the railing, letting the polished and lacquered wooden railing glide beneath his fingertips. He had a journey to prepare for, plans to set in motion, and documents to prepare for his son. Just in case.

Hjarcan Aurion lived in constant awe of the works of his artificers. He'd found that, given resources and time, they would produce wonders at a faster rate than he could order them produced. The vibrating vehicle he currently piloted was their most recent creation—production began a month prior, but this was his first chance to fly one for himself. An arcane engine core was placed behind the pilot's seat, which reclined within a crystal tube supported by a brass and copper fuselage run through with pipes and channels for the magical energy. That energy was thrown into circular rotator cuffs, spinning the four wings of the machine in a fashion inspired by the dragonfly and hummingbird. All that was needed was an additional spinning blade on the tail for stabilization, and the aerial was ready to fly.

The fields lost their definition as he raced over the stalks of wheat, turning the flowing grains into a blurred yellow quilt beneath him. The quilt became more patchwork as he passed over the farms, and then changed color as he approached the mountains. In scarcely twenty minutes he had cleared more ground than the airship *Hafalgar* could pass in an hour. *If I had this kind of technology for the war,* Hjarcan thought, *it would have ended in weeks.*

It wouldn't have saved Elaine, the voice said. Hjarcan grit his teeth.

"You don't know that."

Yes we do.

Hjarcan had no response.

The mountains imposed themselves on his field of vision, and the Emperor gained altitude, clearing the stubby, overgrown boulders without a second thought. Behind them laid a barren plain with coarse grasses, narrow creeks, and sparse, sturdy trees. Quintessential Atzine—not hostile, but cruelly apathetic.

His village lay ahead, abandoned in its disrepair after the Nortians tried to annex it. *I never did find out what happened to these people after I was conscripted,* he thought. *It seems they never came home.* He couldn't blame them; Icai Village was not a pleasant place to make a living. If the Nortian's suspicions of a crystal mine beneath the village had been true, the situation may have been different. But it hadn't, and it wasn't. *They upended our lives for a lie. We upended theirs by necessity.*

He circled the village once, checking for any stragglers or scavengers. None could be seen—it was a ghost town. He saw his old house and slowed to hover. It was intact, but the boards of the shack wall had been eroded down to bare fibers. A stiff breeze or a thrown rock would bring it down. Hjarcan brought the aerial closer, trying to see inside. The wind from his wings kicked up a spiraling cloud of dust and stone, rattling the walls of the nearby buildings. As he pulled back to gain altitude, the direction of the wind shifted. The sand devil careened into the side of his childhood home, shredding the weakened old timbers of the wall. The Emperor felt nothing as the shack collapsed.

There is nothing for me here. Not anymore.

He picked up altitude and turned back toward the mountains. His destination was waiting for him on the other side. The site of his ascension. The site of his first victory. The site of his greatest loss. The site of his first crime.

70

The site of Elaine's grave.

On a whim, he had flown through the mountain pass between his village and the city of Rhys, tracing the route he and a few miscreants had taken on that fateful excursion nearly thirty-five years ago. Crawling from shadowed boulder to dim cliffside, stalking the Nortian surveyor and his team on the way home. Circling them as they made camp for the night. Stealing into the tent circle to steal the strange magical box and enthralling glowing tools. Sneaking back into the village and hiding their spoils outside its borders.

I could not have known how stealing just a few simple arcane tools would change my life, he mused. He'd been the first to figure out how these tools worked, and he'd drawn attention by doing so. He was the one to discover just how the Nortians always had farmable land, wealth—and therefore power. He used this to help his village and others. He became a leader by power alone. He leveraged this for advantage after advantage, growing in power until he was given command of a small military force to patrol his home territory. Then he met Elaine, and his momentum turned toward a dream.

It was another life. Focus on the present.

The city quickly came into view, a dark silhouette against the early evening light. From this distance it looked like a city intact, asleep after a long day. The few distant lights would lend credence to this—but it was a lie. The harsh reality was made clear as he approached, hands growing numb from the subtle vibrations of the machine as he gripped the controls. Most buildings from the central governing estate outward were either reduced to rubble or burned to their foundations. The gardens around the state had died from neglect, replaced by the coarse grasses and weeds of the region. The cobblestone roads were thick with dirt and trash. Black streaks of ash haphazardly painted the few vertical surfaces that had survived. The damage lessened nearer the walls, as those were still needed intact. Tents, lean-tos, and poorly-constructed shelters were visible against the rubble, and Hjarcan could see survivors—scavengers, now—moving around. One building a few blocks from the estate had been mostly restored; light spilled from the windows, and he could see figures staggering out of its front door.

Of course the first thing rebuilt is a pub, he thought.

You've left them with nothing else to look forward to, the voice remarked.

"I know," he muttered. He pulled the aerial around, looking for the courtyard of the estate. He almost missed it; unlike the plant material outside, the estate courtyard had become overgrown. There was scarcely room to land. There were a few lights from within the estate, but they were several wings away and unlikely to notice his arrival.

I'll be gone before they know I'm here, he thought.

He carefully maneuvered the wings and tail of the aerial through the gaps in the treetops, landing in the courtyard proper. As he opened the cockpit's hatch, he could see the faint blue glow emanating from a wrought-iron box in the center—an arcane engine, an old one. *This must have been what kept the plants alive,* he thought. He didn't bother questioning how—he was no arcanist—but the thought granted him some peace. *Elaine always loved the plants. Green was her favorite color, and she loved when people visited her gardens.*

It was fitting that her grave be in the last place where she found joy. Burying her here was the one thing Hjarcan had done undeniably right.

He climbed out of the aerial and walked around, breathing in the heady scent of loam and vine. It was near total darkness in here, aside from the light of the engine and the dim glow of the aerial's cockpit. But he didn't need light; the layout of this place had been etched into his memory by three months of occupation and one horrifying, bloody, incendiary night. In the back corner of the courtyard, underneath a willow tree and beside the pond it guarded, was a single gravestone embedded flat in the earth.

> *Here lies Elaine Aurion, 983-1009.*
> *From her fingertips, magic.*
> *From her mouth, kindness.*
> *From her spirit, light.*
> *Her partner and son will carry*
> *Her with them for all time.*

It was a simple engraving, but one that Hjarcan had carved out with his own hand, tears clouding his vision, and blood staining his clothing. The chipping and cracking of the hard stone had all but drowned out the screams from outside, and the remainder was buried by his grief. He'd laid her to rest in the soil, deep below, without any cairn or coffin to protect her body. She'd feed and support her garden in death as she did in life.

It seems she's done just that, he thought. He knelt at her grave, sitting on his heels, and listened. For what, he did not know. He was only half-aware of why he'd really come here. He was scarcely fifty, but war and loss took a toll on him. Did he come here to die? No, he still had plans. Pracus still needed him. His people still needed him.

Do they?

Yes, he responded internally, *Pracus is young and impulsive, he needs more guidance before I can disappear. The Nortians have been defeated, but pockets of rebellion may still appear. Dealing with them will require a precise hand.*

The voice did not respond this time. Hjarcan pushed it from his mind and gazed at the grave of his wife. Something inside him stirred, uncoiled. A sickly, warm feeling dripped through his arms and down his chest, and he felt his shoulders curling in and his chest start to tighten.

What is this? Poison? He thought, trying to identify the source. *Spores in the air? No, I'd have noticed earlier.* What was this feeling? Why so familiar?

"Has it been so long, love?"

Hjarcan snapped to his feet and released his knives from their quick-release slings on his wrists. Now armed, he spun in place, ready to defend himself from this new assailant. There was nobody there. He carefully scanned the dark courtyard, straining eyes and ears for any sign or signal of assault. There was nothing.

"Elaine?" he ventured, a single bead of sweat forming on his forehead. He wasn't gifted with magic; he wouldn't be able to determine the difference between an illusion and a ghost. He couldn't know if that voice was really hers.

"I'm here, Hjarcan," the voice responded. Behind him again. "Turn around."

He did, slowly. As he faced her grave once again, his daggers fell from numb fingers, sinking into wet soil blade-first. Elaine stood before him, leaning against the trunk of the tree, exactly as radiant as the day he'd lost her. He took one, shaking step forward, that sickly feeling returning and fighting with a growing heat in his head and chest. "Elaine? You're here?"

"And so are you," she answered. Her lips curved in a small smile. She extended an arm. "Come here."

He cleared the gap in two long strides and embraced his wife with the desperation of a dying man. She returned it, lightly stroking his back as he clung to her. His body shook. He didn't know what to do, but he knew that he didn't want to leave. For the first time in nearly a decade, Hjarcan Aurion wept. For the first time in fifteen years, the Emperor of Atzine let himself be vulnerable. For the first time in forever, there was no voice in his head.

"How are you here?" he asked, pulling back. His tears followed the deep valleys of his face before escaping into his coarse beard. "You're…you're dead. How are you here?"

"I wanted to speak with you," she said. She waggled a finger and a pale white flame appeared between them. "But first, how is our little flame? How is Pracus?"

Hjarcan smiled through his tears. "He laughs like you do. He's on the skinny side, but he's strong and witty. He inherited your magic."

Elaine smiled, stroking his cheek. "Does he have a good heart?"

"He does. He can make good on my promise. He will be a good leader."

"What promise was that?" she asked.

"To build a better world for us," he answered, frowning. "A safe world. A world without pain." He looked her in the eyes. "We've given him everything he needs."

"Was it worth it?"

Hjarcan froze, then slowly disentangled himself from her arms. "What do you mean? Of course it's worth it; Pracus is safe. He's strong, smart, charming—everything a good ruler should be. He'll do things for this world that I could never do."

Elaine stepped back. "There used to be a lot of things you could never do." She touched his hand. "What happened to you?" Her eyes searched his, and he then noticed the faintest of white light emanating from her. He pulled his hand back.

"I did what I had to."

"Hjarcan, I saw *everything*. I know what Rhys looks like beyond these walls."

"They made their choice, and I made mine," he said flatly. "They demonstrated an unwillingness to cooperate with us, they showed hostility, and so I ordered the city purged of combatants. It was necessary."

She stepped back, frowning. "Then explain the war after. Tell me how a quick, relatively bloodless war turned into a campaign that consumed my son's childhood. Tell me why you ordered cities razed, armies slaughtered with no quarter given, and lives ruined."

"It was war!" The Emperor of Atzine shot back. "Every one of these bloody Nortians rose up to resist us. There wasn't a man, woman, or child that didn't try to stop us. Every obstacle to our dream was something I had to remove." He turned and raised his hands to the sky. "And now it's over. I have won. I have given our son everything, and he will be able to make a world without pain. He will live our dream." He turned and looked at her, tear streaks still wet on his scarred face. "I thought you would be happy."

"I'm happy that you're alive," she said. "I'm happy our son is safe and thriving. But this was not my dream—*our* dream." She gazed up at the tree. The small flame she'd conjured split into two, and then four, before dancing around her. "I thought that by coming here, I could convince you."

"Convince me of what?" Hjarcan growled. His chest was tight, and something inside him writhed, demanding that he stop and *listen* for once. He ignored it.

"Convince you that you were wrong!" she said. The flames split again and began to spin faster. "That any peace brought about by cruelty and slaughter is not real peace! You used to know that. Just like you rose up for those around you, the Nortians will do the same against their oppressor. How do you not see?"

The Emperor turned and jabbed a finger toward her. "You don't know that. We have plans in place. They'll learn our language, our customs, they'll prosper under *our* rule—"

"Listen to yourself ." Elaine snapped. "*Our* customs? *Our* language? You're talking about cultural genocide! That isn't peace! What gives you the right—"

"*THEY LOST!*" Hjarcan roared. "They could have shared their technology and made our lives better—prevented thousands from starving in the streets like we did! Instead they sat behind their walls, amidst their rich green pastures, and ignored the world outside. They were weak, and they should be grateful to integrate with the strong. I gave them that chance."

"They lost because you chose to be a monster," Elaine said. The flames stopped in their rotation and spread to the four corners and walls of the courtyard. Tears ran down her face, but her expression was carved of stone. "You promised me that we'd build a world of peace and kindness. In turn, I promised to stand by your side." She looked him dead in his black eyes. "You failed to hold your end of the bargain. So I refuse to hold to mine."

Hjarcan stiffened and took a step forward, eyes wide. "No, Elaine, I'm sorry. Please don't go."

"I was given only a short time to be here," she said. "This will be the last we see of each other. I love you, but you cannot follow me."

"Elaine?" He reached for her hand.

"Goodbye, Hjarcan. Take care of Pracus—may he be a better man than you."

Before he could grasp his wife's hand, she snapped her fingers. The eight white flames flashed, igniting the trees and foliage of the garden. The gentle white flames consumed the plants faster than any natural inferno, filling the air with blazing white light that all but blinded Hjarcan. He covered his eyes and lunged for his wife. His hand touched no flesh or cloth, but instead plunged into a ninth pillar of white fire. The sound that ripped free from the confines of his chest was as hoarse and terrible as the screams of a thousand dying men on a battlefield.

We deserve this, the voice whispered.

It was over in an instant. The sudden silence was deafening. Hjarcan found himself on his knees, curled over his hand, eyes clenched shut. He forced them open, and then slowly brought his hand into view. It was untouched—no burns, no scarring, no disfiguration. There was numbness, but that seemed to be fading rapidly. *I'm not injured,* he confirmed. His breath caught. *The garden!*

He jumped to his feet and spun around. The sight nearly brought him down again. The extensive garden, a vivid and rich spot of life in a dead city, was gone. Not even ashes remained—only cold, colorless stone and the faint scent of soil floating in the air. He turned to look upon Elaine's grave and went cold. The stone slab had been seared away—no inscription remained on the surface, only a bleached scar where it had been. Elaine had rendered her resting place bereft of comfort and peace before moving on. *All of this just to spite me,* he thought.

The Emperor of Atzine rose to his feet. *She would never understand what it takes,* he thought. *A heart as good as hers would never be able to accept what needed to be done.*

"'You cannot follow me,'" he murmured. "I doubt that. When I've built the world we dreamed of, you'll welcome me back with open arms."

He nodded and turned back to the aerial. It had been unharmed by the fire; Elaine didn't want to strand him. As he lifted off and flew back toward the rendezvous with his son, he made plans. *She's right that there will be resistance,* he mused. *I'll just have to make sure to catch belligerents before they disrupt the peace.* He nodded to himself, losing himself once more in the work of logistics. *All it'll take is a small division of loyalists in each city to keep an eye on things.* Yes, that would be good.

He was making a world of peace and prosperity. That requires sacrifices. No matter how heinous, Hjarcan would do whatever he needed to do to make that world a reality.

For Pracus.

For Elaine.

The Coldest Heart in Drumnacavny
by EJ Howler
Third Place (Tied)

I was a good princess. Not a great princess; that honor went to my sister, Kolette, who was married off to the prince of Gilramore to prevent a war. She was everything Mother wanted: kind, intelligent, poised, able to sit in a room with a dozen other nobles and resist the urge to throw a drink in their face. Perfect princess material. The perfect candidate to build a bridge between our home and the next kingdom of comparable size, which, to her credit, she did admirably.

Me? I liked to fight too much to be anything other than a "good" princess. But it came in handy as queen.

Drumnacavny sat between two major kingdoms: Caister and Ilragorn, both of which have a nasty habit of swallowing up the surrounding villages for the sake of "unity". Everyone knew that's the nobility trying to make themselves feel better about destroying towns in order to expand their own borders. Caister's reputation for it was far longer and more prolific. The fact that Drumnacavny remained independent of either neighbor is entirely the doing of dear Mother. While not a military juggernaut, she knew how to coordinate the guards and optimize defense against invasion. It also helped that she was not afraid of the less-honorable approach of sabotaging invasion attempts from within. The exploit she was most proud of, to be certain, was the time she managed to disperse an entire battalion by sending in some women from Lady Gina's House to get the entire invading crew so drunk they were too incapacitated to properly coordinate their attack the next morning.

My mother finally came to an agreement with the kings from both Caister and Ilragorn to stave off any invasions from either side. To both Lord Apperford and Lord Leygood's credit, they abided by that treaty and left Drumnacavny alone.

"Your Radiance, the prisoner is awake."

There was a great deal of trepidation in the courier's voice. Though my back was to him, I could imagine his body quivering as he tried to keep his knees from knocking together. I folded up my map before standing to face him. Sure enough, he paled considerably as our eyes met. His face didn't bring any specific names to mind, though that wasn't an uncommon occurrence.

Couriers in Castle Estermont only lasted a week and a half before a replacement had to be brought in. Many of them ran away, and while that was a great insult, I didn't have the resources to keep chasing them down.

Though I have kept Conrad's bloody cloak hanging up in the North Wing, just as a reminder to the servants what awaited them if they decided disobedience was the path they wanted to pursue. That was a shame; Conrad was one of the more reliable couriers we had seen in many years, but not even those in good favor can get away with trying to kill me.

"I will be down shortly." I gave a quick nod as I grabbed my helm, a magnificent silver headpiece that mimicked the shape of a dragon. "You are dismissed."

He took no hesitation to scurry down the hall. Something in my chest ached briefly but quickly passed as I donned my black cloak. I took a moment to make sure my sword was secure on my hip before heading towards the dungeon stairway. The corridors were empty save a few scattered guards, all of which stood at attention once I passed. My footsteps echoed down the stairs as what little brightness the castle had faded into dim torchlight. Shivers prickled down my spine as I straightened my back. Despite the lack of a draft, the tunnels of cell blocks permeated a frosty air that clung to every surface for dear life.

Not that I minded the cold. In fact, it was a thing of comfort nowadays.

As I walked past the cells, none of the lesser prisoners moved. They all just stared as I marched past them, intent on the door at the hall's end. As it should be: if any of them wanted to try and be smart, or worse still *brave,* I didn't have time to set an example. Not that that would've stopped me. The Caister guard had always had a nasty ego that needed striking down several more notches than we'd already done upon the first assault.

Slaying their captain certainly did wonders to keep them cooperative.

The guards posted at the final door saluted as I yanked it open. Down another, smaller set of stairs sat the most pathetic man I'd ever seen. His noble tunic was ripped and his boots were covered in blood. The only clean spots on his face were from where tears carved a path, and it looked as though they weren't about to dry anytime soon. The chains around his wrists and ankles shuddered with every breath he took. His head shot up as the door opened, and his quivering lip managed to form a scowl. I simply stared at him as I stepped inside, slamming the door shut behind me.

"Lord Apperford." I didn't exactly care enough to learn his first name. Not that it mattered.

"What do you want, Korrina?" he hissed, though his voice shook as he attempted to shuffle closer to the wall.

"I thought a nobleman of your standing would at least have the decency to address me properly." I stepped down onto the floor, resting a hand on the hilt of my sword. "And you'll find my request is simple."

"Oh, *do* forgive me for not using your title when you burst into my private quarters and turned my home into a bloodbath." To his credit, his voice gained nerve as he spoke. "We had an agreement."

"My mother had an agreement; lest I recall, that treaty expired upon her passing." I took out my sword and let the sliver of moonlight outside catch it. "I am not bound by the promises of a dead woman."

Lord Apperford stiffened, his eyes darting between my helm and the sword. "What do you want, Lady Estermont?"

I let the barest hint of a smile pull at my lips. "That's better. My request is simple: we received word that you may have someone imprisoned in Caister that we have been trying to find. Does the name Private Maeve Nelfany sound familiar?"

His face drained of any color as his chest bubbled with bitter laughter. "Truly? You invaded my castle, dragged me into this terrible pit, and slaughtered half of my loyal staff based on a rumor that we *may* have someone locked up? Are you insane?"

With a flick of my wrist, I leveled the tip of my sword under his chin. "Answer the question."

Sweat glistened as it dripped onto my blade. "I…No, I've never heard that name before. I have no idea if she's in Caister or not."

It's fortunate that my armor hid the way my body tensed. "Then I've no more use for you."

Just as his eyes widened, I drove my sword through his chest. I felt the blade dig into the stone wall behind him as his coughs and sputters barely glanced my ears. Once his fingers stopped twitching, I withdrew and swung the blade to try and shake off the blood. His corpse fell back with a thud, then the cell was filled with silence again. I used his cloak to wipe off the blood before sheathing my sword and storming back up the stairs.

Ripping open the door, Captain Blackwood looked far more startled to see me than I was to see him, even though he surely knew where I was headed. His cheeks paled but he otherwise kept a straight back. I didn't pause to greet him as I headed back towards the stairs. His boots scuffled against the stone as he staggered to catch up.

"Search all of Caister," I instructed. "If you find her, bring her back. Once your search is complete, burn Castle Apperford to the ground."

"And if we encounter resistance?" he asked.

"Then dispatch them."

I heard more than saw Blackwood's swallow. "Are you sure, Your Radiance? It's going to send a message to the other kingdoms that you can't take back."

I turned to him sharp enough to make him stop. "I was not asking for your opinion."

Blackwood stiffened, then bowed. "Very well then. I'll arrange the guard."

I gave one sharp nod as he headed down the hall towards the barracks. I broke off to head back towards my office. Once I turned down a hall and was certain I was alone, I let my shoulders fall with a deep sigh. My hands shook more than I care to admit. Some of Lord Apperford's blood splashed up onto my gloves. For a moment, my chest tightened. I closed my eyes and forced my shoulders to relax.

Once I found Maeve, this all would have been worth it. There was nothing, absolutely *nothing,* that was going to get in my way of bringing her home.

Growing up, I only ever had one friend: Maeve Nelfany. Her mother, a wonderful woman we called Miss Plum, was Mother's primary handmaiden. Whenever Maeve wasn't helping Miss Plum with her duties, I believe she was supposed to be the handmaiden for Kolette and me, had things gone exactly as Mother intended.

However, since we were just children, Maeve's handmaidenly duties were just to be my playmate.

We spent hours running around the gardens, keeping out of the way of the gardeners as we fought dragons and bandits only we could see. Back then, all I wanted to be was a knight. Riding around on a horse and fighting villains was far more appealing than sitting in offices and wearing heavy dresses like Mother did all day. My trusty sword was a tree branch a bit too big to comfortably carry around since Mother didn't want me to play with a wooden replica. Though admittedly, Maeve wasn't the best sparring companion.

"Oh no, the bandits are surrounding us! What should we do?" I would ask while pointing my branch to a nearby bush.

"Maybe if we just talk to them, we don't have to fight," she would invariably suggest. *"We might have something they need. Or maybe we could help each other?"*

"No, we have to fight them," I insisted.

"Why, Kori?"

"Because the game isn't fun if we don't."

She would just pout and hold her hands behind her back. *"Well maybe it could be fun if we pretended to work with them."*

Even though our biggest threat was little more than an overgrown rosebush, Maeve always thought that fighting wasn't the answer. Even when we went up against dragons, her first thought was always to try and talk, as if a dragon could be persuaded to stop invading villages and eating people. But she would always go along with my plan in the end with a small smile and a bright spark in her eyes.

For many years, I'd also have her sneak into my room at night so we could stay up late and exchange stories. Normally, servants weren't allowed out of the North Wing after a certain time, but we were barely older than ten and the rule felt foolish. Most nights, I was the one telling stories since the one time I allowed Maeve to try, she just talked about a peaceful field of horses and how the caretaker one day found a unicorn. Nowadays, that sounds like a dream: a quiet, peaceful life free of violence. However, I was young and easily bored, so I was in charge of telling the stories. Even if she was far more averse to battles and conflict, she hung on every word. Her brown eyes flickered with bits of gold as they widened along with every epic moment. Her laughter reminded me of what the bell flowers in the garden would sound like if they could chime.

It's a memory that still managed to bring a smile to my face, if even for a moment.

As we grew older, I could feel in the air that our friendship was more than just a byproduct of not interacting with others our age. I took more notice of the way her fingers lingered along my back as she would lace up my dresses. I caught her gaze as she watched me for a moment too long when she was supposed to leave the room. Her voice soothed me to sleep and haunted my dreams. I found myself brushing against her hands more often, just for the sake of a comforting touch.

We were barely fifteen the first time I kissed her. Her lips were soft and gentle and brought to mind the calm ripples of a field swaying in the moonlit breeze. Her cheeks were even softer under my palms. I still hear the echo of her quiet moan as phantom chills race up to my scalp, following the exact pattern of where she touched me. Though it only lasted for a moment, it was electric.

She stole my breath, and I was willing to surrender all the air my lungs could give just to never release her from my arms. And judging from the way her chest fluttered against me, the feeling was mutual.

However, we were both aware that my relationship with anyone other than another noble was going to be difficult.

Maeve and I were cautious with our newfound bond. At least, I believed that we were. The only times we allowed ourselves to revel for even a moment in the closeness of one another were when we were assuredly alone. We kept our contact brief while in the presence of others. Maeve's quiet demeanor matched with my taciturn approach to other nobility helped keep our secret. As far as anyone else was concerned, I was simply the succeeding queen, and Maeve was a dutiful assistant.

Looking back, I should've known better. We were so careful, but with Maeve having to sneak out from my quarters all the way to the North Wing every night, I should've known we would get caught eventually.

Or not *we.* Not exactly.

I woke up that morning knowing something was wrong. Maeve had been hesitant to leave the night before, and had I been stronger-willed, I would've convinced her to stay. But I didn't. The fact that Maeve didn't come to help me get ready made my stomach sink into my feet. Before I was even halfway into my sparring tunic, I heard sobbing echo from down the hall. It paired with the distant sound of the portcullis raising and a wagon driving through. If I were a bit more awake and a bit more astute, I would've realized exactly what was happening right then and there.

My chest was still tight as I finished dressing and all but ran towards the courtyard. Sure enough, my mother stood tall and stone-faced as Miss Plum sank to her knees, burying her face in her hands to sob harder.

"What happened? What's going on?" Truly, the only reason I asked was to not have to be the one to say it.

Mother just turned to me, her eyes sharp but hiding something deep and exhausting. *"You have no time for distractions, Korrina. Especially ones that will interfere with your growth of the royal family. So, your friend is going to assist the military at Paradise Pointe."*

My knees gave out as words burned in my throat. I wanted to scream, to howl, to tear through the courtyard and stop the wagon from making it any further out of Drumnacavny. But all I could do was sob as Miss Plum's cries rang through the air.

"Your Radiance? We've searched all of Caister. Private Nelfany was nowhere to be found."

Though ordinarily I did my best to keep composed around my staff, I threw a dagger resting on my desk at the wall, letting the blade sink into the wood. Though my back was to him, I could hear Blackwood jump. He cleared his throat and I heard his armor shift as he straightened back up.

"We burned down Apperford Castle and did our best to evacuate those closest to the blaze," he continued. "I'm...terribly sorry."

I was too. But the defectors who first told me that Maeve was in Caister were about to be a *lot* more. "No matter. It was a longshot from the start. Anything else, Captain?"

"Yes, there is someone here who has requested to speak with you. Privately."

I groaned and pinched the bridge of my nose. "Can't this wait? Who even is it?"

"Lady Kolette Pyne, Your Radiance."

I growled as my shoulders seized up. A quick breath helped me straighten my back as I turned to him. "Send her in, Captain."

He nodded once before retreating from the doorway. Briefly, I thought about grabbing my helm just so I'd have the barrier between Kolette looking directly at my eyes. But before I could even take a couple steps to grab it, Kolette appeared in the doorway. She looked every bit the part of queen: hair perfectly tied back, dress detailed down to the seams, and an expression that carried equal parts sternness and concern. I simply crossed my arms as she stepped further inside, closing the door behind her.

"What're you doing here, Kolette?" I asked.

"I could be asking you the same thing, Korrina." She smoothed her dress in a clear attempt to keep her hands busy. "I'm worried about you."

The laugh escaped before I could stop it. "*You're* worried about *me?*"

"Yes; word has spread of what you did to Caister. We've started talks of uniting with Ilragorn just to ensure that what happened to Caister can't happen to us. Everyone is afraid of what the Frost Queen is planning to do next."

I narrowed my eyes. "You finally got your alliance with Ilragorn that you've wanted for so long, *dear* sister. And if you were truly concerned about whether I was planning to invade your precious kingdom, it seems like the *last* place you would want to be is in my office telling me such."

Her frown deepened. "You know as well as anyone that these are *not* the circumstances you want to form an alliance under." Her face softened. "Why? Why did you go against Mother's treaty and…I just, I want to understand."

"Are you really so upset that Caister is no longer a threat? After all the years Lord Apperford threatened to invade our home and turn this entire land into his playground? That now with his family gone, all the smaller kingdoms that they swallowed up have a chance at their independence again?"

"No, but I know that's not the whole reason you invaded, Kori."

The scowl ripped across my face before I could stop it. "Don't call me that."

Kolette's face fell; it looked as though she was one strong breath away from crying. "Please don't tell me this was all for Maeve? Kori–"

"I *told* you not to call me that, *Your Majesty.*" I took a couple steps forward from my desk. "And what of it? Caister and the Apperfords are no longer a problem. Who cares about the motivation?"

"Korrina, you *killed* a *king.*" Her tone sharpened despite the way her shoulders shook. "You just marched into Caister without warning any of us, slaughtered half of their guard, murdered their ruler, and burned down the castle. That's not something my kingdom or Ilragorn can just take sitting down. You have to understand how it looks from our perspective: it looks as though you just snapped and decided that Caister didn't deserve to keep standing despite absolutely no prompting. We're both terrified that you're going to come to us next."

Her words sunk into my ears, but the hot anger that clung to me kept them from going any farther. "Then why are you here?" I snarled through my teeth.

Her shoulders fell, seemingly aging her several years. "Because you're my sister, and if there's anything I can do to help you, I'd rather do that than leave you to the hands of the Ilragorn courts. They're…they want your head for what you've done."

"If you really wanted to help, you'd help me find Maeve."

"Korrina, are you even *listening* to me? You killed Lord Apperford; our kingdoms are talking about having you *executed.* I'm trying to save your life, and all you can focus on is finding our old handmaiden?"

Kolette stiffened and her eyes widened, so I could only imagine what my face was doing. "All that matters to me is bringing Maeve home. If you are not going to help me, then the best course

84

of action is to stay *out* of my way." I turned my back to her. "Now, if there's nothing else you need, I suggest you leave."

She lowered her head with a deep sigh, the kind of sigh that you could hear sobs gathering in. "Very well then, just understand that if you try this in Gilramore or Ilragorn, it's your head that will roll." Her dress dragged against the ground as she turned. "And before you get any ideas, she's not in Gilramore. I have the whole kingdom periodically searched just in case."

The door slammed behind her as she left, leaving the sound to bounce all around my office. Despite myself, I flinched. A few stray tears trickled down onto the maps and letters scattered all around my desk. My hands curled into fists as I struggled to regain my composure.

If Maeve were here, this wasn't what she would've wanted. The fact that I've killed anyone in the pursuit to bring her home would horrify her. She couldn't even bear the thought of killing imaginary foes. If she knew what I had done to bring her back, would she forgive me? Or even want anything to do with me?

No, it didn't matter what it took. If I had to raze every kingdom to the ground just to see her face again, then I would do it. I *was* bringing her home. Even if she was furious with me, it meant that she was alive and she was back. There was nothing I wouldn't trade, wouldn't do to see her face again.

After Maeve was shipped off to Paradise Pointe, the rest of my childhood was a blur. It moved in an endless cycle of combat practice, diplomatic meetings, and young noblemen Mother threw at me in the desperate hopes that I would fall in line and be the great princess my sister was. To be honest, I'm not sure what she thought would happen; I'm sure she hoped I would forget all about my only friend and become smitten with whatever snobbish son graced our halls that year.

Tragically for her, that was never going to happen. I threw myself into my combat training, the only place where I didn't have to be the perfect princess, even if just for a couple hours a day. Whatever poor man attempted to court me barely lasted a week in our castle, of that I was certain. If they didn't flee after the first night of me spilling drinks on their shirts or stomping on their feet during introductory dances, then they left after I shredded their cloaks to ribbons and left food out for the mice right outside their doors.The only boy who stayed longer was Wilfred Hayard, and it took throwing a dagger at the space inches away from his right ear to get him to finally leave. After that, Mother stopped trying.

There was no punishment she could bestow on me worse than sending Maeve away. I would make sure that she paid for that choice until her last breath in what little rebellious power I had. She robbed me of my heart, so I robbed her of Drumnacavny's future. A perfect tradeoff in the mind of an adolescent.

And if I am being perfectly honest, I wouldn't go back to change that course of action, no matter how much it wounded Mother.

Seven years after Maeve left, an illness befell most of those living in Castle Estermont. Thankfully, it didn't spread too much farther out than just our walls, but once it took hold of Mother, it refused to let go. Despite the best efforts of Drumnacavny's finest doctors (as well as ones sent from Gilramore), within a month she was gone.

I didn't shed a single tear at her wake. Even as Kolette gave a heartfelt speech about her role as a queen and as a mother, my face was cold. Originally, I thought her passing would bring at least some sense of satisfaction, that at least with her gone I was free from trying to be the perfect princess, but I just felt nothing. Her death simply left me a kingdom to protect. Though there was a single thread of warmth in my chest: with her gone, perhaps Maeve could come home.

Miss Plum died of the same disease less than a month later. It was the day of my coronation; I hastened the proceedings and refused to attend the diplomatic summit to congratulate my crowning, instead spending the rest of the day by her bedside. She had gone gray shortly after Maeve was banished. Her hand was frail as I held it gently in both of my own, quite possibly the last time I had a soft touch with anyone. Her eyes fluttered as she struggled to breathe.

"Kori..." Her voice was barely a hoarse whisper as she struggled not to cough. *"Please...bring my girl home...please..."*

Before I could even assure her that I would do everything in my power to fulfill her request, she was gone.

I didn't even wait for the sun to set that day before I set to work. I wrote to every high-standing general at Paradise Pointe, ordering that Maeve Nelfany return to Drumnacavny. Since I was queen, there was no way they could refuse my call. Not if they still wanted our continued support. I wrote until my candles extinguished themselves on their melted wax, beckoning the fastest messenger birds our aviary had to offer to send out the call. From there, it was a waiting game. I still avoided invitations from the neighboring kingdoms to commiserate with their leaders; there was a part of me fearful that if I left the castle for too long, I would miss the news of her return.

But Maeve never came. Instead, a black pigeon landed in our aviary with a hastily-scrawled letter. I snatched it far too harshly from the attendant's hand as my eyes scanned the page. Thankfully by the time I reached the end, I was alone, for I fell to my knees. Despite knowing that I needed to keep my composure as the new queen, tears slipped out and refused to stop as they burned down my cheeks.

Private Maeve Nelfany led a scouting expedition along Barkham Valley. Six set out on the mission. Only five returned. Maeve was gone. No body, no confirmation of her fate. Just gone.

It was at least a week before I could do anything besides sit and stare at the walls. Perhaps longer. Once I was finally able to move again, all the warmth in my chest had vanished. I wrote to Paradise Pointe that the scouts from her mission were to be banished to the Forsend Mountains, and if they were not gone by the time I sent up my own scouting party, they would be dispatched one way or another. I also made sure to install a mole in the base to ensure that they would not be given the chance to return. Letters went out to the other kingdoms advising them that if they heard or saw any sign of Maeve, that they were to bring her to Drumnacavny immediately. I'm certain Lords Apperford and Leygood laughed upon receiving the command, but it was all I could think to do.

If Maeve was still alive, we were going to find her.

Weeks turned into months, which turned into years, and there was no sign of Maeve. No letter from Paradise Pointe claiming that she returned. No word from Caister, Ilragorn, or Gilramore of her arrival. She was little more than a phantom, perpetually haunting my dreams and occasionally the corners of my eyes on days where I couldn't sleep. Every so often, the thought of giving up the search crossed my mind. However, it vanished as quickly as it came. I needed to right the wrong Mother had done so many years ago. I *needed* to bring Maeve home.

Naturally, there came a point where the rumors began. Even if they were fool's errands, I refused to pass up any lead. No matter the cost. Maeve was out there, and I was going to find her.

"Your Radiance? Troops have been spotted marching towards our borders from both Ilragorn and Gilramore."

My groan echoed through the office as I stood and faced Blackwood. "How large are the armies?"

"Each one is easily the size of our entire force," he replied with furrowed brows. "Not to mention we have two other directions to worry about."

I hummed in agreement, turning to the map with a sigh. "The mounted crossbows are still all functional, correct?"

"Yes, Your Radiance."

"Good. I want archers mounted at every point along the outer gate. Be sure to assign the sharpest shots to the north and west. If they have any sort of surprise planned while we worry about the advancing armies, I want our best shooters to cover it." Something tightened in my chest as I forced in a deep breath. "Then I want your troops to evacuate as many citizens as you can to the north. Including those here in Castle Estermont. Once that's complete, do your best to split your forces into four groups, two larger ones for the east and south, and two smaller ones to run backup for the north and west. Make sure all the entrances are covered; take the castle guards if you must."

"Of course, Your Radiance, I'll prepare your convoy and—"

"Not mine, Captain. I'll be staying here."

I heard him sputter as he struggled to catch his breath. "Your Radiance, are you sure? If we evacuate and redistribute the troops, that will leave you completely unguarded."

"I'm certain, Captain." I straightened my back and faced him. "They're coming for me. I want to ensure the people of this kingdom are safe. Also, I am trained in wartime combat; worse comes to worse, I know how to put up a fight."

His face drained of any color, but he stiffened his back and nodded once. "Of course, Your Radiance. We'll work on the evacuation at once."

With that, he ran out of my office, his footsteps thundering down the hall. A ripple of heavy footfall trailed behind him as I heard the guards start mobilizing. My body moved more on its own accord as I went to the wall and grabbed my helm. Everything felt as though it was moving in slow motion as I tightened my sword on my waist and adjusted my gloves. It felt more as if I was watching myself more than anything else. In the back of my mind, I knew this was coming. Even if Kolette hadn't come to warn me, only a fool would think they could commit regicide and get away without any repercussions.

Perhaps before the Frost Queen was finally defeated, she could at least avoid destroying her people. It's what Maeve would've wanted.

"Your Radiance!" A guard I didn't recognize nearly crashed through my open doorframe, just managing to catch herself. "A messenger from the north is demanding you meet them in the garden. They say they're Sergeant Faelynn, and they insist they have information you will want."

I pinched the bridge of my nose. "And that's all you know?" She nodded once, making me sigh. "Fine. Just go where Blackwood tells you."

The guard gave a quick salute before taking off. At least my helm hid my snarl as I marched forward, working my way through the crisscross traffic of scrambling guards. Everything moved in a blur as I made my way out to the gardens. Truth be told, they sat untouched for several years. Death flowers littered the ground as overgrown bushes threatened to climb up the castle walls. Even before I made it onto the path, I saw the stranger standing in the center, right where Maeve and I used to fend off imaginary monsters. They stood dressed in all black and a dark cloak covering their face. I paused a few paces away, just glaring at them.

"I hope you have some worthwhile information, Sergeant Faelynn," I said, already beginning to draw my sword. "As you can see, time is not a luxury of mine currently, and if you're simply here to torment me, I won't stand for it."

Sergeant Faelynn's shoulders fell, and though their face was covered, I could practically feel the way they stared at me. It only made me scowl harder as I unsheathed my blade.

"I told you to make it quick," I demanded. "I don't have time to dawdle."

"Kori? What happened to you?"

My sword fell out of my hand and clattered to the ground. Sergeant Faelynn took down their hood, and Maeve's face greeted me. Maeve, whose brown eyes stared at me in despair and horror as the echoes of marching armies thundered in the distances. Maeve, who aside from deep trenches under her eyes and a scar on her cheek looked identical to when we last kissed ten years ago.

Maeve, who looked at me like I was a monster.

The sobs started before I could stop them. My legs gave out, sending me crashing to my knees as I slammed my fist into the ground. In a moment that felt like an eternity, I felt a warm, comforting pair of arms wrap around my back. She pressed her hand against the back of my head, coaxing me onto her shoulder. I threw my helm off and took in a deep breath. She smelled of cold and steel and grime, but she also smelled of home.

"We have to get you out of here." Her voice was gentle as she wove her fingers through my hair.

"I'm sorry…I'm so sorry…" The words tumbled out before I could stop them. "I just wanted you to come home…"

"I know, I know Kori. And I'm here." Her arms tightened around me. "But if we're going to make it out of this alive, we have to run. We'll be safe beyond the Forsend Mountains, but we have to leave. Now."

Somehow, Maeve got me onto my feet as she all but dragged me out of the garden. Clashing steel resonated from all sides of the kingdom as the opposing armies invaded, but it fell into a dull murmur in my mind.

Maeve was alive. Maeve was *back.* Even if I died before the night was over, that was all that mattered.

Through the Hum
by EJ Sidle
Fifth Place

They've known since my last transmission. Or, I suspect they've known for far longer but tried to deal with the matter discreetly. Still, I thought I'd have more time to keep transmitting. The information I've passed to the rebels - fleet movements, battle tactics, clearance codes - have kept them alive, kept them in the fight. It's a worthy cause to die for.

There's not much left to do now. The alarm klaxon keeps sounding in the distance, and there are booted feet in the corridor. Time for one last report.

With unsteady fingers, I open the communications channel. It hums with static, with thousands of miles of space moving around the signal. After a moment it solidifies.

"This is Belltower, my position has been compromised, do not accept further hails from this channel."

There's another beat of static, then, *"Belltower this is Gatekeeper, please repeat."*

"Compromised," I hiss. "Belltower has been compromised. It's been my pleasure, Gatekeeper. Do not respond to—"

The door to my quarters slides open, a soft *snkt* that always used to feel like home. Now it just feels like a blaster in my ribs.

"Bell—" I cut the transmission, coordinates and clearance codes erasing automatically. In an instant, all my sins dissolve back into the hum of space static, familiar and comforting as I gather myself to face my demise.

I don't recognize the guards at my door, only their Commander, Gregor. He's humanoid with a large, lipless mouth and broad shoulders. Beneath the high collar of his uniform is a set of gills, and he flicks a forked tongue out over the weak swell of his chin.

"Agent McHale," he hisses. "Imagine our surprise when we saw an outgoing transmission from your terminal."

I cross my arms. "Really, Commander? Come to slap my wrists for making a personal call?"

Usually, I wouldn't transmit from my own terminal, but that last time... an attack course had been altered last-minute, targeting one of the rebel refugee planets instead of their military bases. Passing the information along quickly had been paramount.

Turns out it had been a trap. A predictable one, perhaps, but it had been enough to push me into a mistake. Enough to draw me out. Enough to get me executed by my former colleagues.

I was always going to face a reckoning for the life I've lived. At least this way I get to go out doing something I believe in. A small mercy, far better than I deserve.

"A personal message? On a rebel frequency?" Gregor says, moving closer. He smells of rotting meat and blood. "We're going to wring every last secret from your traitorous carcass, McHale."

"Prove—"

He rams the butt of his blaster into my face, quick and brutal. There's a sharp bite of pain, then the neuroblockers implanted beneath my skin activate. I sway where I stand, warmth spreading towards my face.

Gregor scowls. "That won't last. When your blockers run low, you'll feel everything I'm going to do to you all at once." He slaps me, the sting a distant flicker. "I'm going to enjoy it."

He would, too. I've sat in on too many of Gregor's interrogations to think otherwise. Perhaps it's a fitting end, caught up in the tortures I'd turned a blind eye to for so much of my career.

I grin, vicious and bloody. "My only regret is not defecting years ago."

Gregor laughs. "What, you think you're one of them? A *rebel*?"

"Well I'm not one of *you* anymore!"

Gregor leans in, so close we're almost touching. "You forget, McHale, that I was there when you stormed Kanomorpha. Do you think your precious rebels will still want you, when they know all the things you've done?"

I twist away, but Gregor grabs for my wrist.

"I know you, McHale," he hisses. "I know how much you *loved* that assignment, I know you still dream of their blood on your face."

"No, it's not… *I'm* not—"

"But *you are*," Gregor sneers. "And you always will be."

The guards grab for me, and I don't try to fight it. There's nowhere left to run, nowhere left to hide. Just me, and all the things Gregor will make me feel.

It's better than I deserve, and we both know it.

I lose track of time in the brig. Gregor doesn't come back for me, and the anticipation of his attention is in itself an ordeal. He never used to have such patience, but maybe he's playing me. Using my own knowledge of his tactics against me.

There's not much to do besides wait. And think. I dream of red skies and screaming, of fire singing fur and the feel of a blaster in my hands. I dream of the hum of space static, of transmissions bouncing back in a circle, of rebel bases blown into space.

Nightmares, old and new. The person I was and the person I thought I could become, if I'd had more time.

I sit in the dark and the silence, listening to the hum of the ship and the inky dark murmur of my thoughts, and I try to appreciate my continued existence, even if it's with a sword hanging over my throat.

When the brig door opens, I'm convinced that it'll be Gregor, finally coming to deliver all my promised retributions. Instead, it's a tall figure wearing a flight-suit and helmet. Too tall to be human but humanoid in appearance, with thick arms and clawed feet and weapons in both hands.

They pause in the doorway, an uncertain stillness as they survey the rest of the cells. Turning to face me, they recoil with a full-bodied flinch. Their weapons jerk up, aiming at my chest, and there's nowhere for me to hide.

At least a blaster will be quick.

I close my eyes, waiting for them to pull the trigger. Nothing happens.

"Belltower?" they say, voice masculine and distorted by the helmet.

I nod, opening my eyes.

He lowers his weapons slowly. "Huh."

"Who are you?" I demand. "If you're here to kill me—"

He snorts. "I'm not. Gatekeeper sent me. Said, 'swim the moat and storm the keep'."

It's my code phrase, and I inhale sharply. "Oh. I'm supposed to die here, you know."

"And this is a rescue," he responds. "You can die on our ship if you want, but Gatekeeper'll skin me and turn me into a rug if you don't at least get that far."

"And who are—"

He pauses, shoulders stiffening and head cocked to one side. "No time, we gotta go. Can you walk?"

"Yes. They haven't tortured me, and I've got neuroblockers—"

"We're running!" he interrupts, holstering one of his weapons and dragging me from my cell by my wrist. His hands are clawed, too, pricking lightly against my skin.

He doesn't give me a weapon, and he doesn't let go of my wrist, pulling me around corners and between guards. He shoots without comment, cutting us a path towards the hangar.

"Did you come on a ship?" I demand, ducking behind him when blaster fire whizzes past my ear.

"How else would we get here?" he snaps back. "Come *on*, why are humans so slow?"

The hangar is alarmingly quiet, with a strange ship sitting in the middle of the landing pad. As we race towards it, a slight figure appears at the load ramp. They fire twice, both shots going over our heads. I don't turn around to see what they're shooting at.

As soon as we scramble aboard, the ship starts moving. My rescuer grabs me by the shoulder, hauling me deeper inside as the shooter closes up the door.

"Close call!" she yells. "Mal, get us out and find a wormhole!"

"Hold on, this might be a little rough," a voice says over the comms, almost drowned out by the engine hum.

"They'll dispatch small fighter vessels!" I say. "Do you have weapons?"

My rescuer vanishes deeper into the ship, but the smaller woman stays behind. She tugs her helmet off, revealing a wide, tanned face and a giddy grin.

"Belltower," she says, relieved. "Thought we lost you for a second there. Glad to have you aboard."

There's a soft explosion from somewhere outside the hull.

"Who are you?" I demand. "What's going on?"

"Mal, wormhole!" she yells sharply, reaching out to steady herself against the ship.

"Give me a second!"

There's another explosion, closer this time, and then the ship jerks around us. A moment later there's a sudden burst of silence, of space opening around us, and we're out into a wormhole.

It's a clean shift, no turbulence to suggest another vessel coming through on our tail. Not even my former warship, with all it's technical superiority, would be able to follow us now.

"Phew," the short woman says, shaking her head. "Never get used to those close calls, hey Belltower?"

I cross my arms and glare. "Who are you? Where are we going?"

"I'm Gatekeeper," she says, "the leader of this little rebel cell. You can call me Leona, though. If you want."

She's younger than I am, so much younger than I would have expected for Gatekeeper. It's just a codename, but I'd always imagined someone older and more experienced.

It must show on my face, because she sighs. "Listen, Belltower—"

"McHale."

"—McHale," she says, nodding. "You've been one of the best spies we've had, and none of us wanted to see you executed. So we rescued you."

"That's… not what soldiers do."

She shrugs. "It's what rebels do."

I swallow. "I've done… things. Before I was a spy. My execution would have been just."

"We've all got a past, McHale," she says gently. "Who am I to say what should get you a death sentence?"

"*I'm* saying it!" I snap. "You risked your lives for this. You should have left me there."

"And you risked your life passing us information," she says, shrugging. "Maybe we should have left you, but we didn't. We *wouldn't*."

"It was unnecessary—"

"You look terrible," she interrupts. "You need a medic?"

"No."

"Your face is a mess."

I shake my head. "I've got neuroblocker implants, I can't feel it."

"That's a nifty bit of tech," she says. "We've got a few medics who can work with them, too, back at base."

"Base?"

She nods. "We're heading back that way, but it's going to take a few days. No direct wormholes, can't be too careful."

"And what're you doing with me in the meantime?" I ask, wary. "How do you know this isn't a ruse? That I'm not still working for—"

"Is it?" she demands. "It'd be a good one if it was."

I don't answer.

She grins. "C'mon, McHale. I'll introduce you to the crew, then I'll show you where you can bunk. There's a shower and bed, you look like you need sleep."

I hesitate, glancing back towards the airlock I'd come through.

"Hey," Leona says softly. "Give it a few days, and you can go anywhere you want. But, right now we're on a small ship, and you can't avoid the crew. Come say hello, then you can hide for the rest of the trip, if that's what you want."

"So I don't really have a choice at all," I mutter, following after her.

The ship *is* small, but it's well-kept. Leona leads me past a series of bunks and up towards the cockpit, where another human woman has her hands on the controls.

"Mal," she says, not looking away from the HUD. "Good to see you're alive, otherwise this whole mission would have been a bust."

"Mal's tetchy because she scraped the paint job getting into the hangar," Leona explains, shrugging.

"I am not!" Mal snarls. "And I only nicked the paint because they *opened fire* on us, Leo! That wasn't supposed to be part of the mission."

"Yeah, they made us a little sooner than I thought," Leona said, frowning. "I guess they're getting used to our surprise attacks."

"We did fly straight into one of their command vessels," another voice says. This one I recognize, the tall humanoid from the brig. He hovers in the doorway, too broad to easily slide in beside the rest of us. "They were going to pick us eventually, Leo. Just lucky it wasn't as soon as we came out of the wormhole."

"Maybe," Leona says, sighing. "Ah well. McHale, this is Bastion."

I blink. "A codename?"

"Yeah," Bastion says, reaching up to tug his helmet off. "Humans can't say most of the sounds in my real name."

My blood runs cold, and there's a ringing hum in my ears. I try to focus, try to listen, but I can taste blood in my mouth and for a moment my vision blurs.

Bastion's ears are lupine, pointed like arrows and perched on top of his head. There's a thin coat of fur all over his face and his body, eyes forward and predatorial with large, cutting fangs. A Lykanomorph, the first one I've seen since—

"Woah there," Leona says, staggering as she lets me lean on her. "Easy, McHale. You never seen a Lykanomorph before?"

"Probably not," Mal mutters. "Not many left. And they're funny to look at. No offense, Bastion."

Bastion sighs. "We're not that scary."

I push Leona away, taking a hurried step back from the rest of the crew. "It's been a long few days. Did you say there's somewhere I can rest?"

Leona gives me an uncertain look, but nods. "I'll show you."

Bastion watches us leave, arms crossed and eyes following my every movement.

96

The thing is, I *have* seen a Lykanomorph before. Lots of them, actually, when I was killing the last of their civilian army. Right before I razed the rest of their home world, Kanomorpha, to the ground.

No survivors. That's what I'd written in my report. No survivors because I'd hunted every last one of them down.

All, it seems, bar one.

When I sleep, I dream of Kanomorpha. Sky turned red by flames, entire villages on fire. There are children in the street, their fur burning, screaming as their ears smolder and their skin sloughs off. There are warriors and guards with blasters, but it doesn't matter. I have battalion after battalion of men, and none of us are merciful. There's blood on my blades and my blasters, blood on my face, my teeth, my hair, my soul, and I—

It's been a long time since Kanomorpha. Long enough for me to have seen how I'd be used, long enough to regret every order I'd ever followed.

Not long enough to forget the smell of burning fur, or of claws slicing through my armor.

I lie in the darkness of my new bunk, consumed by my sins. I thought I'd been responsible for a genocide. Is it better or worse for there to have been only one survivor?

I don't want to sleep anymore, don't want to rest, so I make my way out into the mess area. All around me, the ship shudders and hums as it makes its way through the wormhole, but there doesn't seem to be anyone else awake. Carefully, I explore the shelves for bags of tea, selecting one that smells like lavender and mint.

"One of my favorites," Bastion says softly.

I flinch, nearly dropping the tea bag.

"Sorry," Bastion murmurs. "I forget that humans can't hear as well as I can."

I swallow. "I don't want company."

"Me either," he says amicably. "Can't sleep?"

I scoff. "I'm a rebel spy who was just forcibly detained with threat of torture by my former employers, and then rescued by a child and her two crew members, who I've been transmitting secrets to for months. The life I knew is over, and if I fall into enemy hands I'll be slowly, painfully murdered in exactly every way I have ever been afraid of. So no, I can't sleep."

Bastion considers me for a long moment, ears flicking on top of his head.

They look soft. I always thought they'd looked soft, even when I was—

I throw myself down into one of the chairs, and Bastion absently adds hot water to two mugs. He slides one towards me, dropping a tea bag into the other one.

"Leo's a good kid," he says. "And Mal's the best pilot I've ever seen. You could do worse than them, McHale."

I sigh, pushing my teabag down into the water.

"Could do worse than me, too," Bastion adds.

I flinch.

"Do you have a problem with humanoids?" he asks suddenly.

"What?"

"Some of the defectors do, you know. Guess your old bosses weren't so into the diversity."

I scowl. "Only half of my commanding officers have been human. I've shared quarters with humanoids since I was a new recruit."

"So it's just me that makes you uncomfortable?" he clarifies.

I close my eyes. "I'm not uncomfortable."

"You sure?" he asks. "Because I can smell it on you, McHale.

I wince. "You can... smell it?"

Bastion rolls his eyes. "Lykanomorph's can smell almost anything, and we never forget a scent. And right now, you're broadcasting discomfort so strong I can taste it."

"It's not humanoids," I say, wanting to explain.

"It's just me," he says, soft and clipped. "All these months we've been getting your transmissions, and I couldn't wait to meet the hero risking his life for the cause."

I shake my head, throat tight. "I'm sorry."

He sighs. "Whatever it is, McHale, you need to figure it out. I'm not the only one with a good sense of smell, and some of the other humanoids will skin you alive if they think you've got a problem with them."

He clutches his tea in one big hand, already turning away.

I nearly call out to him, nearly ask him to sit down, nearly try to explain myself.

I don't, though. I'm not even sure where to begin.

We reach rebel airspace a few days later. I'd managed to avoid Bastion, either keeping to myself or leaving the room whenever I saw him coming. It wasn't a perfect solution, and it didn't help the nightmares, but it was better than feeling him watching me. Like he could feel all the horrors I'd unleashed upon his people.

98

Leona had found me some extra clothes, cast offs and spares from the rest of the crew. Not much, but more of a wardrobe than I'd had in years. Carefully, I leave them all folded on my bunk and make my way up towards the exit.

"Hold on there," Leona says, appearing at my shoulder. "We have a few hours before we land."

"Okay?"

"You and Bastion—"

"Are none of your concern," I snap.

She shakes her head. "McHale, I'm trying to *help you* okay?"

"I don't need—"

"You do!" she interrupts. "You can't be jumping out of your skin every time you're in the same room together. It'll start rumors, and before you're even debriefed you'll have this reputation. Nothing like fresh meat in the gossip ring, you know how bases are."

I blink. "Reputation?"

She ignores me. "We've had defectors before, you know. Poor bastards who barely knew up from down. And some of them have been so messed up they barely knew how to speak to the humanoids."

She watches me, eyebrow quirked, but I stay silent.

"They're all the same, either nervous because they're into it, or nervous because they're terrified," she says eventually, shrugging. "Which one are you?"

"What?" I interject, mouth dry. "Into it? Into *what*?"

Leona laughs. "Humanoids."

"You think I want to—"

"Get on it?" she offers. "Well, it would explain why you won't sit in the same room with Bastion for more than five minutes. We've all noticed."

"That's not it," I grit out. "Just… leave it alone, Leona."

"Okay," she says. "It's the other way, then. Is it all humanoids, or just Lykanomorphs? There's lots of humanoids on base, McHale, so you're going to have to get a handle on it somehow, or you're not going to last very long. There are people you can talk to, they can help you come up with strategies to manage your fear."

I rub a hand over my face. "That's not—"

She shrugs. "Just think about it. We don't have much longer on the ship, and then you'll be taken into debriefings and medical. You're going to be busy."

"Of course I am," I mutter.

She shrugs. "Figure it out. I've got space for another permanent crew member, and I think you'd be a good fit."

I pause. "You want me?"

"You've got skills I can use," she says. "But, it's not going to work if you keep running out of rooms whenever you see Bastion. It makes him mope, and there's nothing worse than a mopey Lykanomoprh."

I can't imagine a Lykanomorph moping, but I can imagine one dead. Which is exactly the problem.

I find Bastion in the cargo area checking through inventory.

He hears me coming, ears flicking in my direction. I think about turning and walking away, think about hiding in my bunk, but I force myself to keep moving forward.

"I think we need to have a conversation," I say, words getting stuck in my throat.

He sighs. "Did Leo give you the talk?"

"She gave me... *a* talk," I mutter.

Bastion gives me a thin smile. "Mal and I call it the 'two fs chat'."

"Why?"

"Because it's either about fearing or fu—"

"It's about neither!" I say, louder than I intend to.

He blinks. "Huh. I thought—"

"I've been to Kanomorpha," I blurt out, before I can convince myself to stop, before I can find a new way to hide from what I've done.

"I still dream about it," Bastion says wistfully, ears drooping.

I nod. "Me too, but... I... it was—"

"You were there for the raids," Bastion says simply, meeting my gaze and holding it. "You killed my people and burnt my home. I know your scent, McHale, from the moment I found you in the brig."

"Lykanomorphs never forget a scent," I whisper.

He nods. "I know exactly what you've done."

There's a moment where I can imagine him striking me, reaching out and slashing his claws across my throat. All I can hear is the hum of space static, my communications link powering up, all those hours I spent making transmissions, wondering if they could make amends for the atrocities I'd committed.

"I'm sorry," I say, choking on it, voice wet and raw. "I didn't...I didn't... but I *did*, I knew it was wrong and I still did it. I'm so sorry."

100

Bastion sighs. "Do you want me to say that I forgive you?" he demands. "I don't, you know. And I won't."

I inhale sharply, eyes burning. "I know."

"But," he says softly. "I know what it's like to follow orders. I know what it's like to regret the things you've done. I don't forgive any of it, McHale, but I understand how you ended up there."

"And how I ended up here, too?" I ask, throat aching.

"Maybe," he says. "I'd… I'd like to understand it more."

His ears flick down, close to his head, but he doesn't look away.

"Okay," I manage. "Okay."

There's a hum of static, and the comms buzz. *"We're going to initiate the landing sequence. Find something to hold on to and get comfortable."*

"You heard her, rebel," Bastion says, voice rough. "Find something to hold on to."

There's humming all around us, space static and atmosphere and the ship bracing itself for descent. I can't remember the last time I was on a planet and not a warship, or the last time I had people who wanted me to be better than I was. A purpose, something I could be proud of.

I close my eyes. "I think I already have."

Event 3
What Was That?

Rumors and theories of long lost civilizations and cryptids waiting to be photographed exist the world over. For this Event, your character comes face to face with the impossible.

Core Concepts: foreshadowing, tropes

Breaking Eternity
by Fiona Donaldson
First Place

The following extracts are taken from the letters and notes of archaeologist Preceptor (Pr.) Braigue Arlew in the lead up to the Great Discovery. No replies survive.

Letter dated 16 Bakymun 3409, Palux dig site. To Lord Arlewset at their family seat in Westlews.

Thank you darling, for the socks you sent with your last parcel. They are perfect for the desert! They wick away sweat like a dream and the sand doesn't stick either, so I shake them out and wear them again the next day. Don't be horrified! I promise I haven't worn them for longer than three days without washing them. This is a level of cleanliness unmatched by any of my colleagues at this dig. Please tell me where you found them? Kai wants to get some for herself.

Kai was coveting them tonight as we reviewed the day's finds. We have discovered the remains of an obsidian tablet in one of the round religious structures. It's merely a corner of the original, but the carvings are extraordinary. It is written in Ishand. The first concrete evidence this site dates to the old empire. The implications for the size of the Ishandr territory are mind-boggling. If we can find proof the tablet is of the same date as the settlement, that would extend the known limits of the Ishandr demesne by over 600 miles!

The most extraordinary thing of all is the workmanship of the piece. Even modern methods would struggle to achieve such minute detail and clean lines in obsidian. When Kai got a good look at it, she forgot all about my new socks and disappeared into a scientific fugue. She deciphered the inscription, and it's part of an ancient map. She got the clue from the symbols around the edge, which she has identified as numbers. I have included a rubbing of the original and a translation for you. Kai is away now, calculating distances and co-ordinates with one of the first-year engineers Marq, who pointed out their calculating system has twelve symbols, not ten like our own. Some of the ancient maps from our textbooks show the same numbering system (it seems the ancients had a more advanced understanding of the world than I thought possible).

Postscript: We have a location and we're speculating about what could be there. The area is near a village in the Nabresh desert; a remote spot that's never been excavated before. We'll begin the search tomorrow for more evidence. I want to see if it's worth proposing a northern expedition to the university.

Letter dated 20 of Heamun 3409, Palux dig site. To Lord Arlewset at the townhouse in Anceross.

I don't really have the spare time to write to you, but I need something to restore my equilibrium, and writing to you, darling, is always the best way to do so. Preceptor Drae, (the Eastmet University hack I told you about last month) has applied for an excavation licence for the Nabresh desert site. He submitted it two days before our own and he has precedence. This means he will have the choice of dig sites and we will have to beg for the leavings from his table. To add insult to injury, he's asked for an unreasonable area. The proposed size of his excavation is almost a square mile! He's already packed up here and headed north. We won't be able to do the same for at least a week. We haven't closed up any of the pits and there's still a lot of documentation to do. Pr. Drae can't have completed all the records for Eastmet's work. That makes my blood boil more than being usurped.

These were the first primitives that learned to keep records, the first to make artifacts that could withstand centuries in the ground. Everything they have left behind gives us a better understanding of their rudimentary lives.

The head of archaeology at Eastmet University has a lot to answer for, awarding that man his preceptorship. Any papers written and conclusions made from Drae's dig notes or finds will be incomplete and likely fallacious. The fool wants to be one of the great explorers of the last century, and no-one has told him we aren't pirates or adventurers but *scientists*.

[Transcriber's note: the last word is underlined three times]

Letter dated 34 of Heamun 3409, Nabresh dig site. To Lord Arlewset at the townhouse in Anceross.

We arrived at the Nabresh dig this morning and I wish you were here with me. For although I hate the unremitting heat of the day, the night is glorious! The stars, my lovely, so many stars, a sky like I've never seen before. I am sat beside my campfire with a lantern to write by and a billion points of brilliant white over my head. There are some segments of the sky so filled with stars that even the blackness of night is illuminated the most stunning and deep blue. Our camp is almost a mile away from Drae's, so the light of their excavations and campfires is not impeding my view of the splendour.

I was right about Drae; he has staked out his area (with actual stakes) and an ankle-high twine fence that runs the perimeter of the whole thing. Though the sand has already buried some and the workers have kicked over more (I think this is deliberate due to the inconvenience of being tripped by the things). It's far larger than his permit allows. Kai wants me to demand the access we have permission for, but I intend to bide my time. We are scientists, so we will survey first.

I have found an excellent draughtsman; Marq, that young genius who worked out the coordinates for this place with Kai, has invented a new instrument to measure angles and distances. He mapped out the locations at the Palux site down to a quarter inch in just a few hours! As demonstrations went, it was impressive. The device itself would interest you very much, so I have included a sketch. You can see it's all gears and lenses! I know you'll be able to work out how it functions, but he has offered to answer any questions you might have. I think he is hoping for some investment from the Arlew estate.

So our own excavations, while not rivalling Drae's in size, are meticulously recorded and Kai has the students working like the finest Cadesian clock. We're making steady progress and are already finding Ishandr archaeology. I am determined that we won't miss a single potsherd on this one.

Personal notes of Pr. Arlew, 1 Levemun 3409, Nabresh dig site.

This place makes no sense. This city is like none we have ever seen. The size alone is staggering. The thing covers an area almost the size of our own capital. The population would have been immense. How would they have sustained that? We have found no obvious signs of industry or manufacturing. How could they support the population, surely trade alone wouldn't be enough? And what would they trade for if they are not manufacturing anything?

We found the old port (the channels dug into the old swamp are other features that raise more questions than they answer) and although it is massive, it's not sufficient to handle the volume of goods this place would have needed.

We have found no sign of timber. All the structures are stone, moreover the stone is not local, and some chunks are so colossal, I don't think a modern crane could shift them. Did they do all this with human labour? Were they slavers like the militaristic invaders of the fourth century?

The artifacts we have unearthed are breathtaking. There are complex artworks of metal. Yes, metal that has lasted over 10,000 years. It's corroded, yes, but not enough. Modern alloys like steel may endure that long, but something made in the Ishandr empire? At *least* 11,000 years old?

It goes against everything we know. The Ishandr may have been an empire, but most of the people who fell under their yolk lived in mud houses and worked on smallholdings with local materials. This is not merely a city, it's the centre of a civilisation.

It's a comfort that we have found farms and signs of domestication on the outskirts, though no pack animals or other beasts of burden. At least we have one piece of the puzzle that almost makes sense because most of the things that scholars say are *necessary* for cities to develop are simply... absent. What *was* this place?

Letter dated 17 of Levemun 3409, Nabresh dig. To Lord Arlewset at the townhouse in Anceross.

I do not know whether to celebrate or mourn, dearest. Never in my career have I been so lost! I have few answers for the questions that keep piling up, yet it is exciting to be one of the privileged here to ask the questions.

We have unearthed a significant structure that looks for all the world, like a school. Complete with a lecture-hall that would do Anceross Tower proud and more of the mathematical and geographical tablets that led us here. Kai is translating them now. I can see her from here, hunched over her work table under the stars.

I would be in fits of unalloyed excitement too, if not for Pr. Drae. He has set the wildest rumours running across the site like a forest-fire. He claims to have found evidence that we are in Bakydat. Yes, the mythical city of the dragon-god himself. That he's found 'mystical rituals' and 'artifacts of the ancient magic of the Ishandr'.

The younger archaeologists are beside themselves; they are drunk on the mere thought of it. Of course, he has refused to show this proof to any member of my team or the junior members of his own, so forgive me if I doubt the veracity of his claims. I can't guess his purpose. If he wanted publicity and recognition, he'd be showing this evidence to everyone and the queens' ladies. If these are not his goal, what under the three moons does he want?

Do not tell anyone dearest (especially not my students), but the idea of Bakydat stirs my blood. The myth must have sprung from some truth, mustn't it? The thought of that truth, here under my feet, just waiting for me… makes it hard to leave off digging for a moment, even to write to you.

Letter dated 22 of Levemun 3409, Nabresh dig site. To Pr. Scarlin in the anthropology department at Anceross Tower University.

I hope you remember that ridiculous student, Indyk Jach, the one who wears the ridiculous hat and walks around with the baton on his hip. He's here, cataloguing and dating finds. He's just as laughable as ever, pestering his superiors with wild theories, stirring up discontent among the students of the two rival digs and casting aspersions on the greats in the field. He actually referred to Samind, the father of modern archaeology, as an ignorant inkrat.

More relevant to you, it turns out our troublemaker has an unexpected talent. Storytelling. I overheard a group of students and labourers telling campfire stories last night. This is the story that Jach told, and I wrote it down as best I could. I thought it might be relevant for that paper on the resurgence of traditional storytelling you're working on.

A long time ago, at the beginning of the world, all was chaos. People suffered short, painful lives and there was no rest for anyone.

The great dragon-god Bakyd the Eternal noticed their affliction and wished to help, because he believed that their brief lives were unfair and unnatural. He created a great city at the centre of the world where all people could live in peace and prosperity. The people named it Bakydat, the City of the Eternal One.

For thousands of years, the people lived in the beautiful city, and Bakyd protected them. They called themselves Ishandr and learned much at the feet of their dragon-god, including the secret of immortality. The monsters and lesser gods that lived outside the city could not hope to breach Bakydat's defences, even if they found the courage to attack the great dragon.

But with time the people grew discontent; they yearned to see the world outside the city. They wanted to command Bakyd, not hide below his mighty wings. In secret, they studied the knowledge Bakyd had given them, and they made a key. This key could lock away the power of their god if ever they captured him.

The leader of the people, a woman named Margir, tricked Bakyd. She told him that the mighty waves of the great ocean had eroded the city walls and that they would soon fall. When Bakyd went to look at the damage, the dominion of the waves distracted him. Margir used the key with a terrible ritual to harness Bakyd's power, trapping him in a cavern deep under the city with his own strength.

Then began the golden age of the people of Bakydat, and their empire stretched for a thousand miles from the coast of the Great Northern Ocean to the foot of the southern ice walls and across the breadth of the continent as far east as the Dragonroot mountains. None could stand against an Ishandr army, backed by the might and guile of a dragon. Bakyd's power stolen by Margir's ritual and used to subjugate all the world.

But no human can hope to foresee all evil and Margir's own deceit undid her reign. For her lie turned out to be truth. The ocean-serpent Larkyd saw what the Ishandr had done to his brother god, and he was angry. He began a century-long assault on the western walls of Bakyd. The ocean waves crashed into the walls day and night, month after month, year after year. The people were too busy to note the weakening defences until Margir had long forgotten the lie she told to trick Bakyd and steal his place.

One winter day, the ocean-serpent sent one last wave at the walls, a wave over a mile high. It smashed into the city, and the capital of the Ishandr empire broke before the deluge. The streets ran deep with water until even the highest building was overwhelmed.

That power of the water broke the chains that held Bakyd in his cavern, and when the dragon-god emerged from the cataclysm, there was no sign of the city remaining. The waters had swept it away, and the key that trapped Bakyd was lost beneath the waters along with Margir, who even in death did not release her grip on it.

The few Ishandr who survived the torrent fled before the wrath of their deity, who pursued them across the leagues of their empire, destroying all before him. A few escaped over the Dragonroot Mountains to the untamed, monster-plagued lands beyond. Bakyd sits in those mountains even now, preventing their return. In the dragon's wake, the Ishandr empire burned.

I wish I could describe how Jach's voice wound around the words, breathing life into the old story. How the sparks from the fire rose high to meet a sky full of the constellations that are named after this same legend. There's a magic to the nights in the desert, the cold hits like a blow after the heat of the day and it's like being slapped awake. Your brain flits from idea to idea, imagination wakes, and anything seems possible. Jach tapped right into it all and held everyone trapped in Bakyd's shadow. You would've loved it.

110

Postscript: It looks like Jach will need the extra strings to his bow! Not thirty minutes after I wrote the above, Kai came to tell me the idiot's been having some success with stirring discontent among the students. He's been criticising Drae's methods and trying to incite the workers to help him relieve the hack of his stolen treasures'. I had to give him a dressing down, but from the fix of his eyes on the back of my tent, I should give up on convincing him we are scientists, we win our arguments with proofs. Kai is watching him. We can't have him blemishing the reputation of the university by following through on his mad scheme. What an end to a magical night.

Letter dated 28 of Levemun 3409, Nabresh dig site. To Lord Arlewset at the townhouse in Anceross.

Just when I think things can't get any stranger here, I am proven wrong in spectacular fashion. I always wish you were with me, but today the desire is sharp. Writing to you is not comfort enough; I crave your steady head and calm advice.

Kai came to me this morning, her hair a mess, her clothes rucked up. She'd clearly been running. I've never seen her anything less than composed, even out here with the dust and the heat. When I asked what was wrong, she told me that Drae has found the Key of Bakyd, still clutched in Margir's fist. Again, he has provided no evidence to anyone other than his closest colleagues and even refuses requests to see his notes.

[Transcriber's note: the following was added on the back of a letter from the university, perhaps grabbed as the first paper to hand]

He has gone insane. Eastmet have thrown all attempts at scientific process to the winds. They are excavating with explosives! I have ordered our most promising pits closed. We're working on hiding them to prevent any interference from Drae and his cohort. He's actually trying to find the cavern of Bakyd. Moons know why. Even if the myths were true, the fabled dragon sleeps in the Dragonroot Mountains.

I didn't want to speak of this in my earlier letters, but we have found the heart of the city. The largest and most significant buildings are not in the centre where Drae has been digging, but to the southwest on what would have been a hill above water-level when this place was first settled, before the Ishandr reclaimed land from the encircling swamps. It would have dominated the surroundings, and it looks like we have a university, a library and a complex that I believe was the centre of government (based on architecture from other parts of the empire). If Drae finds this, the damage he'll do is incalculable. We have learned so much already from the library alone. The paper and wooden artifacts are long gone, but they recorded the most important things on stone. We have learnt so much history, pre and intra empire. There are texts on physics, engineering, mathematics, a hundred different subjects.

I am sending everything back to the university, just in case. I have my assistants copying our most significant notes, city plans and finding documentation. Kai is including her translations. She says she won't have time to copy them all, so we're sending her original notes. She'll re-translate everything from scratch.

Indik Jach, a student, will carry it all back for safekeeping. He is currently 'in disgrace' and when he gets sent away, we're hoping Drae will overlook him and his luggage. He will take everything straight to the Tower, but please pass the news on to the Law Courts for me. They have the resources to get out here and stop Drae.

Do not worry, I do not foresee any risk to our *physical* safety, but I do fear for the integrity of the history we are trying to record. I could weep to think of what the explosives have already destroyed.

Letter dated 31 of Levemun 3409, Nabresh dig site. To Lord Arlewset at the townhouse in Anceross.

Disaster. The centre of the city is a smoking hole in the ground. It is now so deep that the sides are unstable and today there was a collapse that buried four men alive. When we heard the shout go up, we grabbed up any tool to hand and ran over to help dig them out. Drae tried to stop us. He told us we had no authority to work in *his* part of the city. I must confess to both imprudent speech and behaviour when he hit one of my labourers, for I struck back. I landed a pretty punch on his jaw, and called him a madman. He went down like a ship in a storm, and I stepped over him to take charge of the fiasco. Those colleagues he has not yet alienated dragged him away, yelling and swearing, and we got to work.

It took two hours to get to the first man; his lungs were full of sand, and we lost hope that the others might have survived. One was lucky; he had fallen near one of the larger building stones and a pocket of air was trapped with him. We reached him thirty minutes after the first man and when we carried him out, he was awake to thank us. The sand and stones couldn't crush him in his protected position, so we have hope for his full recovery, though he'll have to be sent back to civilization and a proper hospital.

My teams laid the other three out beneath the sky and the stars are looking at them now as they dig the graves. I must go

112

now to say some words over them as Drae hasn't deigned to come and take responsibility for his handiwork.

Letter dated 32 of Levemun 3409, Nabresh dig site. To Lord Arlewset at the townhouse in Anceross.

I have penned a letter to each dead worker's family. Could you look into their circumstances for me and ensure Eastmet pay any pensions due? If they are loath, please see to it yourself. Drae did not ask after the men, nor can I ascertain he has made any provision for them. I expected him to come storming over here, if only to protest my physical assault. But we haven't heard a word from him. If he has forgotten my physical assault, I doubt he'll remember the victims of his follies.

It turns out the collapse yesterday exposed a system of tunnels and the Eastmet lot are burrowing away like worms. At least they've stopped blasting, though they have still not braced the sides of their hole, so I have forbidden any of our labourers or students to go near.

I fear darling, a night's rest has not fixed my temper. I have crescent marks in my palms from the relentless clenching of my fists. I am not letting that *monster* take any glory from this dig.

We've reopened the library pit and are working our own way down. If there were tunnels in Drae's part of the city, there has to be some under our sections. We're going to beat him to the discoveries of Bakydat.

Personal notes of Pr. Arlew dated 36 of Levemun 3409, Nabresh dig site.

It didn't take us long to find the underground passages. They're everywhere, another impossibility to add to my list. This place was a swamp when the city was built. There is evidence of periodic flooding in the streets above, during and post occupation. How did they keep this labyrinth free of water? I am growing accustomed to these unanswered questions. They seem to be part of the scenery here at Bakydat. Yes, this is Bakydat, the archaeology confirms it. We have plenty of evidence from the library that proves we have found the great city of the Ishandr empire.

[Transcriber's note: the last lines are shaky, and the next section is excluded as the text is indecipherable.]

We have found more metal down there, some made into the most intricate patterns, but there is no other decoration in the tunnels and the patterns seem utilitarian. All straight lines and right angles. Kai has been pouring over the translations we've found.

113

There's no history down here, it's all city maintenance and management, but we can't translate some of the vocabulary we're finding.

I have broken my arm. My husband will be angry when he finds out. Not that I'm going to tell him until I return home. I'm sure Drae is laughing, enjoying my comeuppance for rearranging his face.

We were in one of the larger tunnels leading from the library to what we have identified as the city council building, the centre of government, probably for the entire empire. I was leading the way and felt a flagstone shift under my heel. The next thing I know, a stone falls from the roof. I jerked back and avoided head injury, but I wasn't prompt enough to avoid a blow to the arm. Broken in two places. Kai was strapping it up for me when a student triggered another falling stone. The cursed place is booby trapped! All the diggers have instructions to wear their protective leather helmets and test all floors with a metal pole before venturing forward.

And now I have yet *more* questions. How are 11,000-year-old traps still functioning? Why are they there? If the tunnels present a weak spot in the defences of the council house, why didn't they fill them in? Why didn't they place guards? The flagstones look well worn; This must have been well-travelled. I can't find the logic in this. Kai assures me this is *not* just down to the pain in my arm.

I am pained to say that the idea of a gargantuan, omnipotent dragon no longer seems so far-fetched. I am a *scientist;* the world is on a tilt, and I do not know how to set it right.

[Transcriber's note: There are water marks on the paper here as if from tears]

The full text of the last letter from Pr. Arlew to her husband, Lord Arlewset, at the townhouse in Anceross. Dated 4 of Silvermun 3409, Nabresh dig site.

My darling,

I am not sure where to begin this missive. Words have deserted me, and I am not alone. Kai has not said a thing since we left the tunnels this evening. We are sitting outside under the stars once more, the night skies are unchanged in their perfection. That is a new pain after the devastating changes of the day. Neither Kai nor I have bothered to start a fire. Instead, we are huddling close for warmth and wrapped in blankets. I have my small lantern to help me see this letter. Please forgive the untidy hand, but I do not want to leave Kai to set up my small table.

Our day began with more conflict. My team of six hadn't been in the tunnels for an hour before we ran into Drae and his assistant. The two of them were alone (more stupidity and arrogance) and immediately took us to task us for being in 'their' part of the city. I had Marq's plans (just as accurate underground as above) and refuted him. I should have saved my breath. It makes no sense to speak reason with the insane.

He produced a firearm and threatened to kill us if we didn't take him to the dragon. I told him we had found no dragons. This produced a violent response (don't worry darling, I was not seriously hurt, though my broken arm has suffered a little). He forced us to go along the passage ahead of them and would not allow us to follow our usual scheme for trap-checking. I insisted on leading; I was with Kai and four students, all of them under twenty. I could not send them before me.

We proceeded along the passage and at each moment I expected another trap to spring or for Drae to shoot one of us. I think I know now how people who suffer with nerves feel; it is *not* a pleasant sensation. The distance between the library and the council house is only a quarter mile on the surface and I imagine it is much the same underground. It can't have taken us ten minutes, yet it felt like an eternity.

What we found at the end of the tunnel did not help my equilibrium. We turned a corner and came face to face with a door. Obsidian, ornately carved with the coils of a dragon. The carving filled every inch of the door, seven feet by five. Each scale of the dragon's armour represented in the same exquisite and baffling detail we have found everywhere here.

Drae pushed past us, making sure that I would become better acquainted with the ground as he did so (another jolt for my poor arm), and inspected the door, running his hands over it as if looking for a secret mechanism. Kai rolled her eyes as she helped me to my feet, I thought they might get stuck in the back of her head.

"Just push, idiot," she said. To the *madman* with a *gun*. I must remember to take her to task for that lack of self-preservation later.

Drae was too caught up in the moment to register her flippancy. Drae's colleague recognised the advice was excellent, and she shoved at the portal. Like all the doors down here, it opened easily and without a sound, despite their age and apparent weight.

Beyond lay the cavern of Bakyd.

I wish I had the aptitude to convey what was beyond the dragon door. It was glorious... and nothing we could have dreamed. The space was vast. The council house must sit directly atop the chamber. The ceiling stood 100 feet above us and yet was not the roof of any natural cave. The stone was smooth, but you could see the slightest edges of some blocks. I wager, If Marq measured it, it would be a perfect circle, topped by a flawless dome.

In the centre was a device, an intricate mess of gleaming metal. It looked new, no corrosion at all. There were curls of wire in bronze, copper, silver, gold and iron. There were black pistons that glistened with some alien oil. Grease that could last ten millennia without drying. There were cogs and wheels, and miniscule Ishand text covered every single inch. There was glass in there too, blown into twisting tubes that wound around the pistons and wires.

On the floor, in the stones themselves, was another inscription. This one extravagant, encircling the apparatus, running around the curve of white flagstones it sat upon. I have learned enough Ishand to know the meaning even without Kai to help me. It read; 'Bakyd, Lord of Eternity.'

The machine was enormous enough to be a dragon, filling the expanse with intricate and arcane machinery.

The four students moved closer, like nightwings to the candle. Kai turned to the inscriptions. All caught by curiosity and trying to make head-or-tail of the thing. I remained glued to my spot in the entry. The silence stretched out before us as we grasped at what we had discovered.

Drae smashed the silence. He went right to the device with a triumphant yodel and pulled at some wires; he twisted others and turned wheels, referring to his notebook with each move. He also murmured under his breath, a litany. I stepped forward to catch it; he was *praying* to Bakyd. Perhaps the ritual he said he had found?

I shared a look with Kai, and I shuffled closer to her, both of us wanting to avoid the lunatic but unwilling to leave this discovery behind. Drae continued to manipulate components and mutter. He grew louder, imploring the dragon-god for the power to make a new empire. To rule the world once more, but as the dragon's servants and not his gaoler.

Kai's attention kept drifting back to the inscriptions. She moved further along the wall, back turned to the machine and the madman. She stopped at one section and reached out to touch it. She turned, looked at the apparatus, then looked at the inscriptions again. I saw her tremble. She stared wide eyed, like someone had slapped her. I've never seen her look vapid, but this was close, like there wasn't a thought left in her head.

116

I inched nearer and asked her what was wrong, but she didn't answer, for the device *moved*.

Drae's litany came to a close and as he turned one last wheel on the device, it came to life. Wires span, pistons pumped, cogs and wheels turned, some so fast you couldn't see them, some slow and ponderous. Each movement led to another, which started another and then another. The whole thing was waking, activity springing from Drae and radiating out. It looked like magic. Would this thing call the dragon? Was it Margir's key?

Kai gave me my answer, "It's perpetual."

She repeated herself several times before I understood. This wasn't magic, it was science, a perpetual motion machine. The thing started out silent, but sound crept in. One component set up a whistle, a soft flute-like tone. Another chimed like a bell every few seconds. One clicked, repetitive and fast, like a child running a stick along a metal railing, but not jarring. It was rhythmic, with the odd auditory surprise. It was almost music. I wish you could have seen it, heard it. It would have held you entranced.

But reality curtailed the wonder. The last part of the apparatus, perhaps a fifth of the total mechanism, did *not* spring to life. When the movement reached these outlying sections, there was a discordance, a clank that did not fit with the overall music. Somewhere deep in the machine's guts, some glass shattered. The cacophony that came next was horrific. Each sweet note and quiet ticking became a din, competing with the next to be the loudest. More glass pieces shattered, wires twisted, a few of the smaller cogs stripped their teeth.

I am not ashamed; I cried. The texts and carvings we have, but they pale in comparison to what we could have found through the study of that stunning impossibility. There will be no examination of the glorious device to discover what it did and how it did it. Because one maniac believed in fairy tales.

[Transcriber's note: Pr. Arlew pushed the pen so hard to the page when writing the word 'maniac', it broke the surface in three places]

Drae received his fool's reward. He dropped to his knees and screamed at the thing. I couldn't make out a single word. He was incoherent. He was too close to the machine and as its parts ground to a halt, the largest wheel, spinning over his head, cracked and fell. It smacked him on the head, and he did not move again. We did not go to check on him, not even his own colleague, who fled.

It was just our team left in the chamber with the remains of the device, walls covered in inscriptions and the body of a lunatic. Kai had to be dragged away, sobbing. She made one student take a rubbing of a small section. She's been holding onto it ever since. She told me it's another impossibility, that it's part of the unfeasible equation that made the machine work. She muttered something about dividing by zero and hasn't said a word since.

I feel as if I have seen the death of a friend. What's more, I have to admit some unpleasant truths to myself; my inferiority to the ancients who built this city and my ignorance. I used to believe the Ishandr were a great empire, but still lesser than ours. Civilised, yes, but an early civilization, unsophisticated and still ignorant, barbaric even.

Who are the barbarians? We came here, and a madman broke their god. Something so far beyond our understanding it may as well be on the surface of the sun. Bakyd the Eternal is dead and will come no more.

Welcome Home
by M. Ong
Second Place

"Get up, lazybones! Fetch water and cook something good for your brother. He is locked outside the stall and is to be fattened up. When he is fat I am going to eat him!" The teacher exclaimed, her mouth pulled back into a large snarl in hopes of enhancing the children's experience even though half of them were too old for a fairytale.

"Gretel began to cry, but it was all for nothing…" the teacher continued, her voice drowning out as the children became more interested in other happenings. Like the spider in the corner of the room. The large brown creature hung from the web, its eggs sac laying between its fangs. She pierced the sac, gobbling up a few eggs to satiate her hunger. Emerson sat in the back of the class, staring at the spider, racking his brain for some reason for the cannibalistic act. Maybe the mother was just that hungry.

"And they lived happily ever after," the teacher finished, closing the book gently. A few of the younger kids in the front were clapping while most of the older ones took the opportunity to continue their conversations. Emerson did what he always did; sat quietly until someone asked for him.

"Emerson," a high-pitched voice said from the door. Emerson looked over his shoulder to see Miss Sharon. She motioned for him to follow, and he dutifully did. He walked a pace behind her, keeping his eyes to the ground, hoping he wasn't getting in trouble today. He heard the click of her door open and he followed her inside without taking in his surroundings.

"Emerson, this man will be adopting you today. Say hello." Emerson meekly looked up from his feet to see a peculiar man. He was tall with his dark black hair striking against his paper coloured skin. He wore a burgundy three-piece suit that Emerson only saw in history books that snuggly fit over his sizable belly.

"Hello," Emerson murmured, meeting the tall man's eyes. They were incredibly dark as if the night sky was staring back at him. They were framed by a pair of circular glasses, but the smile the man had on was pleasant enough.

"Hello, young man, it is nice to meet you," the man replied, his accent foreign to Emerson's ears. He sounded like the nature documentary narrator but with a slight drawl in his voice as if his mouth didn't want to let go of the words. His bright white smile accompanied by kind eyes were the only reason that Emerson didn't immediately feel frightened by the man. He looked like those fancy explorers Emerson had seen in his history books.

Miss Sharon continued to rattle things off to the man, handing him papers and motioning her hands in wild movements. His smooth hands grabbed the paper with grace, his dark hair swooped in front of his eyes as he nodded politely along to the conversation.

"I have to thank you again, sir. You are so generous taking in all the older boys," Miss Sharon swooned, tucking her hair behind her ear even though it was already there.

"It's my pleasure. This young man will be lucky number seven," the man replied. Emerson's eyes bulged at the idea of sharing a hope with six other boys. His wide eyes shot up to Miss Sharon, but her eyes were strictly glued onto the mysterious man.

"Oh," Miss Sharon said skeptically, "it must be a packed house."

"Well, once they are sixteen, I send them to school abroad. Nothing like a bit of freedom and independence to build some fine men. Once one of them is sent away, I adopt another one. I can never go back to an empty home, it's incredibly lonely." Emerson began to shift between his feet, his glance darting between the two adults wondering what his purpose was. He glanced out the window; he wished he could be outside right now instead.

"What lucky boys! No wonder you're back here every two or so years, I never thought about that!" Miss Sharon exclaimed a bit too loud. A few seconds passed between them.

"Well, if you ever need anything, please don't hesitate to call me. Here's my personal," Miss Sharon emphasized, "phone number." She extended a small piece of paper. The man looked at it, taking it with a polite smile on his face.

"Will do, thank you again, Miss Sharon. Please give my greetings to the rest of the lovely ladies at the orphanage," the man said.

"Of course!" Miss Sharon beamed. She finally turned to address Emerson, who had begun staring out the window identifying the types of clouds in the sky. He wondered if this is what clouds felt like; they were always present but never noticed as if no one wanted to take the time to look up. Only when it rained, thundered, or turned cloudy when they would be looked on with a grimace.

"Emerson, grab your bags so you can finally go home," Miss Sharon said. Emerson pulled his eyes away and nodded. He thought that his body would fill with excitement the day that he got adopted, but all he felt was dismay that he couldn't continue cloud watching.

"He's a bit shy for a fourteen-year-old. But, he is a very, very bright boy who loves exploring; we'd sometimes lose him in the trees," Emerson heard Miss Sharon chatter to the man as he walked away.

"How lovely," the man replied.

Emerson had already packed, or he just never unpacked. He was always scared that the other boys would take his things because he was smaller than most of the boys in the orphanage. Once Tom took Emerson's notebook and tore a page out of it to use it to make a paper airplane. Emerson was inconsolable for days.

He left the large shared bedroom without taking a second look back to see the countless eyes staring at the back of him or the hushed whispers that bubbled from the other children. If he had, he would have known they weren't of jealousy, but of worry.

The man had taken him home that day, the wordless trip in a van that had leather seats and a working radio churning out soft violin melodies. Emerson watched, in the corner of his eye, the man's large stomach being squashed by the seat belt, the malleable body part spilling over the restraint irregularly. It looked like it hurt, but the man seemed fine, so Emerson didn't think too much of it. Emerson turned his gaze to the window beside him and watched as the large city buildings started to shrink until they morphed into large trees.

The car finally stopped in front of an old building, the red brick being overrun by vines and moss. The man killed the engine and looked over at Emerson.

"Welcome home," the man said, "now, young man, once we enter this house, there are a few rules you must follow, alright?" Emerson nodded.

"One, you must ask me before you use or move anything in the house. Two, I'm not fond of touching, so only touch my shoulder or hands." Emerson's eyebrows furrowed in confusion. No touching?

"I'm a bit of a germaphobe, you see," the man clarified. Emerson nodded out of habit, earning a smile from the man. Emerson couldn't help but feel proud.

"And third, you must always listen to me, understand?" The man finished sternly. Emerson nodded fervently.

"Do you have any questions?" The man asked.

"Um…" Emerson began, "what do I call you sir?" The man's face pulled into a big grin, his yellowish teeth gleaming in the sun.

"You can call me Father." Emerson looks sideways at the odd man beside him. He fiddled with his trousers as he fought through his apprehension.

"Thank you for adopting me Father," Emerson said shakily, trying to return the smile. His mouth felt the uncommon syllables escaping it as he wondered what life would be like with this man.

"No, no, no, thank you for coming with me," Father said.

Emerson learned quickly that Father was a slightly odd individual. Despite being such a large man, Emerson had never seen him eat a single bite or even a sip of any liquid. He had asked Father about this, wondering if he was starving himself in hopes of getting thinner, but Father had just told him that he liked to eat in his room; germaphobe and all. Father also always wore a suit, no matter the occasion or weather. Emerson had initially thought he wore one on that hot summer day when he adopted him to look professional, but Father continued to wear a variety of colourful suits every single day. Even when Father had shown Emerson the dyke behind the house and explained to him how it was there because the land was under sea level, he wore a suit. And when Emerson was sweating from the heat and walking, Father seemed totally fine. But Emerson couldn't complain about the eccentric traits of his adoptive guardian.

Emerson didn't complain whenever Father tried to bring him outside to 'explore the world' despite his clear inclination to the indoors. Emerson would swallow his whining and smile politely at the people Father would introduce to him like their closest neighbor Stephen who owned a goat and the nice police officer who Father always gave book recommendations to. Emerson didn't mind seeing crevices of the city he was never privy to before, but he much rather preferred the small space of his home; where he can know every inch there is to offer. It brought him a sense of safety knowing what lurked around each corner or behind every bush.

But Emerson never complained once because how could he? Father was extremely accommodating. Whatever Emerson wanted, Father would get for him from new textbooks to the newest technological fad that hit the market. Father wouldn't bat an eyelash if Emerson came home from the woods, jars full of worms to examine with his new microscope, with more dirt on him than clothes. Saying that Emerson was happy was an understatement. He enjoyed every moment more than the last as if he was in an endless crescendo. The only thing that bothered Emerson was Father's frequent business trips that would last for a few days. They randomly come once or twice a month; Emerson had tried to

122

track them, but the only thing that the days had in common was that it rained. He always remembered because Father's shoes would click and squeak loudly against the floor, signalling his arrival.

It was one of those days today. Father had left that morning for a business trip out of town right when the rain began. Emerson would usually spend the day in the library, reading about some obscure topic, but today, he thought that maybe he should do something nice for Father since Father always did nice things for him.

Emerson went to the main floor, opening up one of the smaller closets and taking out a vacuum. Plugging it in, Emerson turned it on and started. He methodically made his way through the kitchen, making sure to cover every crevice and corner, then he moved to the next room. It was the formal living room that had a large rug in the center of it. Father barely used this room, saying that it was more for decoration than anything. That didn't mean it wasn't dirty.

Emerson started to vacuum around the rug, but feeling particularly productive, he thought he would clean underneath it as well. Lifting the rug, Emerson expected to be met with the same dark wood paneling covering the floor, but instead, he saw a light brown trap door. It had a small indent of a handle at one end, its hinges orange with rust, and the door having slight claw marks all over it.

Emerson simply looked at it at first, blinking a few times to make sure that he wasn't just seeing a mirage. He ran the vacuum over it to see if it was just a lot of dust, but the light coloured door remained. Turning off the vacuum, Emerson took a moment to just simply ponder about the odd door in the ground. He never saw one of these things in real life, his only experience with them being from movies. There was a little indentation of a handle at the end of it, staring back at Emerson. Emerson couldn't help but want to open the door. Biting his lip, he weighed his actions.

"Father can't get mad at me if he doesn't know," Emerson reasoned to himself. He put his hand in the handle and yanked upwards. The trap door swung up and landed with a thud against the upturned rug. He looked down into the hole to see a narrow concrete staircase descending into darkness. Emerson willed himself to stare back at it and not to let it get the best of him. Squinting through the blackness, he could see the floor of the lower level not too far down. He should probably just close the trap door and continue with his cleaning spree, but Emerson couldn't help but wonder what was down in the darkness. He could make it there and back before Father came home, plus, a little darkness never hurt anyone.

He took his first couple steps in quick succession, confidence riding high. The air was cool against his skin as the stench of mold and seawater permeated his nose. Emerson pulled his shirt over his nostrils as he continued downwards, undeterred but bothered by those elements. The walls were a dark grey stone with tiny bushes of moss sprouting from the cracks between. Each step he took down, the colder he felt, with only the sounds of his footsteps accompanying him in his impromptu exploration. The darkness crept up on him, eating away at his depleting conviction, as he travelled farther and farther away from the safety of the upstairs light.

The slow slide of fear of the unknown began to crawl up his skin as he got closer and closer to the lower floor. Emerson glanced behind him, seeing that the trap door was still open but minuscule in his vision. He didn't think he had walked down that far, but he was glad that the door hadn't shut on him. Turning back to the darkness in front of him, Emerson took the final few steps down.

Landing on the flat stone surface, he scanned in front of him. He was met with a narrow stone hallway leading to a wooden door. It looked very old, the wood being discoloured from water damage and the edges no longer fitting against the wall snuggly, letting a soft glow of light through. Emerson let out a deep breath and began to inch towards the door.

As he approached, he could hear a faint groaning sound and something akin to running water, but it sounded thicker, like mud. Every step Emerson took towards the door, the louder and louder those noises got. The door seemed to grow more and more ominous as he got closer, seeing deep scratch marks in the wood shaded in deep burgundy. The stench of mold got incredibly powerful as another acrid scent accompanied it. It smelled like the trash bin outside the house on the days it was picked up.

The groaning began to crescendo and suddenly morphed into high-pitched sobs that stunned Emerson into stillness. They continued to reverberate through the door, freezing Emerson in place. But his morbid curiosity forced him forward. The orange glow escaping the cracks was alluring enough for Emerson to lean towards it and look through.

Emerson first saw a tube filled with a chunky, white concoction sliding through it. He followed it with his eyes to see where it went, landing his gaze on a face laying on a wooden table with the tube shoved down its throat, groans erupting in bursts from its mouth. Emerson squinted, trying to get a better look at their face but, between the loose skin and the white complexion, it looked more like a ragdoll than anything. The thing looked half-dead, its eyes glazed over with no colour left in the pupils or hair on its head. Why was such a thing living underneath his home? Did the rest of it look like that? Emerson pulled back from the door, seeing another crack to the left of him.

Moving over to it, Emerson was able to lay his eyes on the entire thing. The rest of the body came into view, shrivelled up like a raisin, but it was definitely human-like. Two arms, two legs; the arms laying limply on the table, while the legs hung off. But something was holding it up from its back. Maybe, if Emerson could just see a bit further....

Emerson stepped back again to find another crack in the door to the left of him. There was one near the bottom. Quietly getting down on his knees, Emerson craned his head to look through it.

It was a large man-like creature, looming over the shrivelled body. Emerson could only see its chest, which was bare and... morphed. The creature's upper chest looked normal; like a human, but as Emerson's eyes travelled down, the skin was pulled taught, and twisted into a gaping hole with teeth adorning the perimeter. That 'hole' hung to the back of the shrivelled thing; teeth dug deep into its back. Emerson laid there, frozen in confusion. That wasn't possible, he had read every anatomy book he could find and no one could, or should, have a mouth on their stomach. But there it was, on that creature's abdomen. Its teeth sunk deep into the back of the corpse, almost suckling it like a leech.

Suddenly, a hand wrenched the tube out of the thing's mouth, letting the floodgates of groans and sobs ring out. Emerson stared, mortified, as the thing started to talk.

"-er, it hurts," it croaked out, "please stop, it hurts." Emerson covered his mouth as he watched in horror as the large creature with the mouth started to pull the shriveled up thing into his stomach, crunching and pushing its limbs to the limit until it formed a misshapen ball. It then strapped a thick belt around it and began to dress, pulling on a white button-up.

Emerson continued to stare, his mind broken from what he had just seen. Suddenly, the creature walked out of view. Emerson eyebrows furrowed, trying to readjust his position to find it again. Then suddenly, a black eye met his through the crack. Emerson jumped back in surprise, his landing casting a soft thud on the ground. The door began to creak open. Terrified, Emerson got to his feet and ran.

He ran as quickly as he could through the darkness, his mind and heart racing so fast he didn't comprehend that the trap door had closed. Emerson's head hit the top of the ceiling with a thud, the pain minuscule in his panic. Emerson glanced behind him and down the stairs to see that the door was wide open, glowing orange light radiating out.

Emerson got on his knees, trying to get to the trap door when he heard a clicking noise. He froze. When he looked behind him but saw nothing, but the sounds of the clicks continued. Click. Click. Click. They were slow and methodical. Emerson squinted trying to find the source, but all he could see was darkness. The clicking started to get faster and faster. Click click click.

Emerson started to panic; he ripped his eyes from the darkness, turning his back to it, and trying to push the trap door open. It wouldn't budge. Emerson felt his heart pounding through his ears, his hands beginning to sweat. The clicking was getting faster. Click click click.

Emerson pounded against the door, rattling it a little. He shouldn't, couldn't, stay here. He needed to leave. As he pounded against the door, trying to pry it open, he felt a hand on his ankle. He screamed, flailing his leg backward, hitting something with a crack. Something fell off the creature and hit the ground with a shatter.

Emerson shuffled as far as he could underneath the trap door, using all of his energy to open the door. He glanced behind him to see two circles of white looking back at him and going to grab him. Letting out a cry, he pushed one last time, the door finally prying open enough that Emerson could slip through.

Using his hands, he hoisted his upper body out, but the creature grabbed at his leg. Emerson flailed his leg, kicking as hard as he could. Its grip slipped to his ankle, but wouldn't let go. Emerson grappled at the ground, trying to gain some purchase to out-leverage the thing. Turning onto his back, Emerson grabbed the trap door, smacking it down on his leg and the creature. Ignoring his own pain, he huffed as he drove the door downwards, each thrust thwacking against the creature's skull. Slowly its grip loosened until Emerson was able to slip his leg out and slam the door shut.

His harsh breathing sputtered out of his chest as he stared at the door, waiting for any telltale signs of the creature following him, but nothing came. Gingerly getting to his feet, Emerson knew he had to tell someone about the thing in his house. Ignoring the torrential rain, he ran outside and grabbed his bike, beginning to pedal to the city. He would go to the police. That's what you do when you're in trouble, right?" He didn't stop for anything, not a red light or a car, he didn't know what could be behind him and he didn't want to look.

126

He skidded to a stop in front of the police station, clambering off of his bike and smashing through the doors. His sopping feet tracked through the police station as his eyes frantically searched for any uniformed person. There was one woman at the front desk, idly looking at a computer screen, not paying attention to the drenched child.

"H-hello," Emerson sputtered out. The woman looked up and her eyes lit up in recognition.

"Emerson, why are you so wet? Did you go outside to catch frogs again?" She asked. His brain tried to form a coherent thought, but all he could think of was the basement in his house and the deformed figure housed underneath it.

"There is a th-thing in my base-basement," he stuttered out, his hands beginning to shake as fear began to overtake his body.

"Emerson, are you alright? Let me call your father-"

"It had a mouth on the stomach- the stomach- the stomach there was a-" he sputtered, his brain unable to comprehend the images through his memory.

"Emerson I need you to-" she began but quickly stopped as her eyes travelled over his shoulder. She visibly relaxed and a polite smile graced her face.

"There you are," a familiar drawl said. Emerson turned around to see Father behind him. He stared at him with confusion; why was he here and not at home? Emerson opened his mouth to explain what happened, but he froze when he heard the sound. The clicking of his shoes hitting the tiles.

"Are you alright son?" Father asked, his hand coming to rest on Emerson's shoulder. Emerson immediately froze, Father's hand feeling like a brand on his skin. Emerson, eyes filled with fear, simply stared at the man.

"He seems to be a bit shaken, sir," the officer informed. The hand on his shoulder tightened.

"Oh?" The incredulous voice drawled out.

"Yes, he was stuttering about a basement."

"Basement?" The other hand goes to his other shoulder. Emerson felt shackled, like a fish caught between the maw of a great big bear. His body started to tremble.

"I know right? There are no basements here, we're under sea level." Emerson began to tremble.

"Must've been a bad dream, wasn't it?" Emerson's body wasn't listening to his internal pleads of struggle. The hands resting on his shoulders tightened.

"Let's head home, son. You have to get packed up for college." Emerson's eyes widened as his blood ran cold.

"Already?" The officer chipped in.

"Well, you know him, he's quite a bright child."

To Know Her Inside

by Maria L. Berg
Third Place (Tied)

My arms felt shaky, sore from rowing, and my stomach turned, probably the first signs of heat stroke, though it could be nerves. When Bree had told me to pack a backpack because her family lived off the beaten path, I had never imagined this long canoe ride down the Mullica river and its Mullica off-shoots. Bree grabbed onto a tree growing out of the tea-colored swamp, and pulled us toward thick underbrush. She had a leg over the side, and before I could yell stop, the canoe was rocking back and forth. I felt a tug. The canoe swirled around. I closed my eyes, hugging my backpack, waiting to tip over.

"Come on. We're here," Bree said.

She pulled the canoe a little further, so there was plenty of room for me to flop onto the small dock tilting into the marsh. Carved in the boards near my face were stars in circles and horned animal heads, maybe goats.

"Did you carve these?" I asked.

"No. They've always been there. Protection symbols."

"Don't tell me you believe in that crap." My legs felt boneless, but I managed to pull my pack on and wobble off the dock. "I don't believe in anything I can't see with my own eyes, and touch with my own fingers."

She laughed, her sweet birdsong of joy, then said, "So you're saying, that blind people with prosthetic hands can't believe in anything? Nothing at all?"

"Don't tease," I said, feeling queasy as I suddenly flashed back to my white-walled, antiseptic childhood at my little brother's bedside.

"I know. God didn't listen when you prayed for your brother, so belief is all a bunch of bull. And I'm sorry. I was just trying to get you to see another side. Not everything's as clearly real or not real as you make it out to be."

The end-of-summer sun broke through the boughs in thin rays. One lit on Bree's head turning a patch of her onyx hair to electric blue.

"Don't move," I said, frantically searching for my phone. But we had put them in plastic Ziplocs, deep inside our packs in case of a worst-case-scenario tip over—my idea.

She froze, looking straight up, then down by her feet. "You don't have to be afraid," she said, "I mean, they're carnivorous, but they don't eat people."

"What? I wanted to take your picture in the light, but it's gone. What's carnivorous?"

"Those flytraps there," she pointed at a clump of small disc-shapes on thin stalks.

I squatted down and admired their pink fringe with clear droplets at each tip. "Wow. I don't think I've ever wanted a bunch of flies before. Look at all of them. If I fell into them, they wouldn't hurt me?"

She nudged me so I almost lost my balance into the Venus flytraps, then grabbed my shoulder before I fell. "No," she said, but the bladderworts…"

I jumped up. "The bladderworts?"

She laughed, then pulled me away from the carnivorous plants. I probably would have stared at them all day, fascinated by their deadly beauty.

"You should see your face," she said. "No. The plants won't eat you. They aren't the carnivores you need to worry about."

She pulled me toward another small patch of light that glistened on the water of a stream cutting through the moss. "Ooh, look at her. She's a new one." She pet a delicate pink petal with her index finger. "Hello there, precious."

Bree's collection of orchids and her precise, attentive care had been an adjustment for me when we moved in together. My friends all said it was way too fast, but I just knew she was the one. I was helpless around her, like she had some magical power over me. Our apartment was always too warm and sticky with humidity. If Bree didn't smell so sweet, I think the smell of dirt would have been too much. Sometimes the combination of flowers smelled more fauna than flora which I found startling.

My best friend had had to promise to follow Bree's long list of orchid care instructions before Bree would agree to go on this trip. She said her orchids reminded her of the wild orchids she had grown up with that kept her company, like the siblings she wished she had. But it was that care for her orchids that made me think she would be a great parent, a thought I was having with frequency these days.

The hike in the woods was made longer by zigzagging to admire every orchid. I think there were a million, or at least fifteen. I had a good-sized blister forming on my right heel when I noticed a sudden lack of forest sounds. I hadn't really thought about the birds singing and squirrels scritching, the tree frogs constant chirping or the buzz of the mosquitoes, until it all stopped. Up

130

ahead I saw two looming shadows somehow darker than the darkness around them.

"Come on," Bree said elated, jogging ahead of me. "We're here."

The shadows were ancient cabins, lilting with age. People appeared from every direction as if the trees were coming to life. Though we were in a giant forest, I felt walls closing in. Bree was happily hugging everyone. My hand was consumed and shaken by one calloused, well-ridged vice-grip after another.

Finally, the cabin door opened and a brick in an apron, holding a crust-covered rolling pin stood backlit, silently filling the doorframe.

"Mama!" Bree ran to her, knelt on the porch at her feet, and hugged her around the waist.

The woman didn't move. I didn't know what to do. Everything since we drove out of New Orleans had been so strange--the way Bree didn't want to talk in the car, listening to one recorded radio show after another, then the strange jerking motions and screeching noises she made when she dozed off—but this was over-the-top weird. Bree had told so many sweet stories about her family and her childhood among the orchids, living off the land. I guess I pictured some fancy estate with giant greenhouses; a father that liked to teach her to fish and hunt, a mother that taught her to cook and sew, and read to her in the parlor by firelight. I couldn't understand the way she genuflected at her mother's feet.

"Tom, sweet Tommy." She waved me over, not getting up from her knees. "Come meet Mama."

Someone shoved me between my shoulder blades, propelling me up the steps. Bree stood up, came to my side, and put her arm around me. The woman stepped forward. A beam of light shone on her broad smile, and I realized it was just my nerves or maybe a trick of the shadows, because a lovely older version of Bree stood before me. I sighed in relief, a bit too loudly.

"You okay boy?" she said, handing the rolling pin to Bree and squeezing me tightly. "We're all so glad to finally meet you. Been lookin' forward to this a long, long time. You can call me Sister. Everybody does. 'Cep Breeze, of course."

I glanced at Bree. She smiled.

"Now you kids take your bags along to the guest house," she pointed to the smaller, more sagging cabin in the even darker part of the woods, "and when you're rested, the welcome feast will be ready. We'll have music and singin', show you what bein' Pineys is all about."

"Excuse me, Ma'am." Bree shook her head at me, but I had to know. "If you don't mind me asking, what's a Piney?"

A roar of laughter exploded behind me.

"Ah, son. My dear Breeze here musta been hidin' her true self from you. Silly girl, always tryna be somethin' she ain't. You're in the Pinelands, son. Everyone you see here's a Piney. And most of us is dang proud of it. Have been for centuries. Haven't we Breeze?"

Bree tucked her chin and hunched over, staring at her feet. Something I had never seen her do. "Yes, Mama," she said, grabbing my hand and pulling me through the gathering of large men who were still laughing and repeating, *What's a Piney?* When we reached our cabin I could still hear them.

As I climbed the steps to the cabin, each stair gave and creaked under my weight. The door resisted my tired, sore shoulder, but swung open to Bree's slight push. Our packs were already waiting for us inside. Bree opened her arms wide and fell back on the quilt, raising a dust cloud and sending some bugs flying. The mattress almost swallowed her.

"I had no idea how good it would feel to be home," she said.

"What was that with your mom?"

She struggled to push herself up. "What do you mean?"

"All that groveling on your knees, and sticking your face in her crotch."

"That's not what I was doing. I was showing respect. You don't know our traditions. You may want to bottle up that judgment and open up that closed little mind of yours for things that are a little different than what you're used to. You've been begging to see where I came from and whining to meet my family. I would think you'd give it a minute before you come at me with judgements like groveling and crotch sniffing."

My cheeks felt hot. I attempted to lie next to her, but springs poked into my side and the mattress gave like it would hit the floor, so I knelt on the floor next to the bed and ran my fingers through her silky hair. "I'm sorry. I'm tired. So what's with calling you Breeze? Is that your real name, or a pet name?"

"It's my real name. Mama's real into the elements and stuff. It's better than Wind, I think."

"Nothing's what I expected. I feel so out of place. It's like visiting another country where I don't know a word of the language."

"Except it's not, and you do. I get it's a little different than Uptown or the CBD, but it's not so different from the bayou. You'll see. Start looking for the similarities. You'll find them. We've got

132

big-ass mosquitoes. I know you're used to that. And the tree frogs sound somethin' like cicadas singin' at night."

"Should I change my clothes for dinner?"

"No. Don't worry about it. They don't care how you dress, and you'll end up smelling like campfire no matter what you wear." She held an arm out. "Little help? This mattress will swallow you whole."

My mouth began to water as my stomach growled. "What is that delicious aroma?"

"Whatever the land has provided today. I believe we are expected."

Bree's mom had not been lying about a welcome feast. What looked like an entire deer spun on a spit over the fire. There were heaps of roasted carrots, corn, leeks, and some swampy things I didn't recognize. There was dough cooked on sticks for bread and cranberry and blueberry pies for dessert. One of the things I loved about Bree was that she enjoyed cooking for me, with fresh vegetables and herbs that she grew in window planters, and pots around the house, but we never feasted this well. I had worked up an appetite, and I gorged myself.

As we ate, I began to get a feel of how these people related to Bree. They were all uncles, cousins and great uncles on Bree's father's side. Bree's father was a quiet, serious man with bold raised scars across his face. He hadn't greeted us because he had been hunting then dressing the deer. It was so succulent, the meat perfectly rubbed, I ate every slice his knife sent my way. I don't know why I couldn't stop eating. I thought my gut might burst, and I still went for another slice of blueberry pie.

When Bree went to help clean up and the men sat around the fire passing a large jam jar of moonshine, I belched so loudly, it echoed off the trees. I thought I might die from embarrassment, but Sister came out on the porch, wiping her hands on a dishtowel and beamed that pretty smile in approval. I felt warm in the glow.

I leaned forward and rubbed my hands together. "So tell me something about Bree. Something she wouldn't tell me."

No one spoke up and when I tried to catch an eye, it darted away.

"Come on, please. I came all this way because I want to know her inside. You know, truly know her. Tell me."

The man sitting across from me, a gray-bearded uncle that looked much like a goat, took a long swig of moonshine, let it burn down, then said, "But can anyone ever truly know another person?"

"Oh, a philosopher," I said.

"No. I mean physically, scientifically. We can't ever experience anything as it really is—"

"Right. Right. Because perception takes time, and is filtered. But all that aside, I feel like there's something more to Bree, something you could tell me."

Then the music started and I gave up on getting any Bree stories. I clapped along, and whooped and hollered as they plucked a stringed cigar box, pulled a string on a stick through an overturned wash-tub, blew on a jug, buzzed a mouth harp comb, added fancy whistling and magically transformed it into heart-thumping down-home blues I might have heard back home. One of the cousins had a powerful voice. I caught words like, "black wings" and "sixteen witches."

When they had finished, Bree took a seat beside me.

I asked, "Is that a local folk song?"

They laughed. The singing cousin answered, "It's the Boss, man, the Boss."

Bree elbowed me and whispered, "Bruce Springsteen."

I felt stupid. Someone passed me the jam jar. I took a swig. It burned all the way down.

They started another song. This one sounded more like a folk tune, though the words seemed similar, about a great beast, a devil and a witch. As they played, I stared into the fire. Bree rubbed my thigh. In the crumbling embers, I saw a horned, winged figure rise. I've always loved staring into dying fires. It usually looked like great cities in ruin to me.

I couldn't keep my eyes open. When the song ended, I attempted to say thank you and head to bed.

"Don't go lettin' him wander out tonight, Miss Bree," said the gray-bearded goat uncle.

"He's right, Tom," Bree's dad said, speaking my name for the first time. "Don't leave your cabin for any reason until after daybreak."

He sounded so sincere, it sent a shiver through my shoulders. "I won't, sir. Thank you."

I let Bree lead me off to the cabin, leaning on her a bit too much. I thought I heard them chanting, or was it praying, behind us. We didn't need the lantern, the moon was so bright. That home-shine, or was it full moon shine, really packed a punch.

After Bree undressed me, and pushed me into the bed, I said, "Where do they think I'll go carousing around here? I mean, I get they want to protect you, but . . ."

If I had more to that thought, or Bree had an answer, I don't remember.

134

I jolted from a bad dream to the most horrible scream. I had dreamed someone was strangling Bree. She wasn't next to me. I shook, damp with sweat. I heard it again. It sounded like a woman's high-pitched scream, but now I thought it sounded more like a screech owl. My heart still pounded in my chest, but I could breathe. Then the cabin shook and I heard a loud thump on the roof. I grabbed my chest. Another thump, like something heavy would soon fall through the roof and smother me, convinced me to roll off the bed, and peer out the small, dirt-crusted window. A huge shadow covered the only patch of moonlight then uncovered it again as I heard a whoosh of wind and felt pressure like the whole cabin might be lifted up. I was desperately weighing the pros and cons of dying inside the cabin or outside the cabin when the door creaked open. I screamed, expecting to be face to face with a snarling beast or at least a giant owl on a mission to peck out my eyes. A startled Bree screamed right back at me.

She put the lantern on the tiny hand-hewn table against the wall. "What is it? What happened?"

"You didn't—" I pointed at the roof while I tried to breathe. "You didn't see anything out there?"

"Like what? You weren't outside, were you?"

"No! There's something out there! Something screeching and stomping around, trying to carry the roof off the cabin. You must have at least heard it. Where were you?"

"You really have to stay away from the moonshine. I had to pee."

"Right. Sorry. I must have had a nightmare. I mean, it started with a nightmare. That scream, it was terrible, but then…"

"Then?"

"I thought I was going to die."

"Calm down. Lay back now. It's only forest noises. You're fine. We're both fine. Let's get some sleep. It'll all be different in the morning."

She pet my forehead and kissed my cheeks. She placed my head on her chest and I was dead asleep. In the morning light, when I woke up, she was gone.

Putting on my pants was hard, because every muscle hurt. My throat burned. My brain wanted out of my skull, and I didn't blame it.

Something smelled tasty. I couldn't believe I was hungry after my massive glut last night, but the hunger helped me get dressed and out of the horror cabin.

"There he is," came a chorus from the circle around the fire that I now understood was the living room, dining room, and rumpus room for this family.

"Where'd you find a woman to drag into your cabin?" said the singing cousin I couldn't help but want to call the Boss now.

"What are you talking about? I just went and passed out in the cabin. I was exhausted."

"Uh, huh. Well, Breeze says that scream wasn't her, and a scream that girlie couldn't have come from you, so…"

"Ha. Ha. Very funny. There was something screeching and flapping around on the roof. It freaked me out. Just a big screech owl, right?"

Gray-beard goat uncle sucked his teeth and shook his head. "Jersey Devil.'

"What?"

"Uncle Jimmy, leave him alone," Bree said, handing me a full plate of something that smelled delicious."

"You're lucky," Uncle Jimmy continued, "Most people don't live to tell of a Devil sighting."

"Uncle Jimmy, stop it. He didn't see anything. And what about the almost a hundred reports just last year."

Jimmy scoffed. "You know those weren't real."

I waited for Bree to answer, but she didn't. "So what's this Jersey Devil? A pet name for an extra big screech owl or something?"

Jimmy chuckled again. "You wish."

He looked at Bree. They stared at each other for a while, then she turned and went into the main cabin.

Jimmy leaned in conspiratorially, "It all started a couple hundred years ago. Legend has it a woman named Mrs. Leeds had twelve children. When she got pregnant for the thirteenth time, she was so tired of her rugrat monsters, she said she'd rather give birth to a demon. Being a witch and all, her little wish cursed that little baby in her womb. When she gave birth, it was no human baby, but a demon that shot out of her: tail, horns, wings and all. It flew out the chimney and wandered these woods until it was strong enough to fly home and devour all of its siblings and its evil mother."

"You can't possibly believe—"

"Some say the demon wasn't the only one cursed that day. That Mrs. Leeds's twelfth child, still a baby herself, was overlooked and—"

"Uncle Jimmy, that's enough!" Bree was on the porch, eyes wild.

"Fine. Fine. Anyway, the devil has terrorized the people of the Pine Barrens ever since."

136

"That sounds like a convenient story made up by someone who needed a demon to blame for some homicidal behavior, or a disease or something," I said.

Jimmy threw his paper plate into the fire. "You're right. A very convenient story."

That night I woke up to screeching again, and no Bree. I was determined to take a picture of the screech owl and shove it in Uncle Jimmy and the Boss's faces. I put on my headlamp, and grabbed my phone. I opened the door slowly, trying to be as quiet as I could, which only made the creak longer. So I jumped over the steps. A glowing, flickering light led me into a clearing. The moon shone there like a spotlight. I heard the screech again and a shadow crossed the moon. I hurried toward the clearing and hid behind some wild blueberry bushes.

A naked woman danced around the flames. The moonlight seemed to follow her like a spotlight on a stage. I watched the frenetic movements, drawn in by the dancer's muscle control before I was horrified to realize it was Bree. What was she doing? I know it was a trick of the light, but her huge, dark shadow appeared to have wings and a tail.

I heard flapping overhead and imagined a giant bat coming for my head. I ran back to the cabin as fast as I could. Once inside, I realized I had forgotten to take pictures. I threw my phone at the wall, crawled into bed, and pulled the quilt up over my head, curled up tight into a shivering ball. I never heard or felt her come in, but for once her skin was warm against me when I woke.

I kissed her shoulder out of habit, expecting her sweet scent, or the burn of campfire, not the pungent, bitter sulfur that shocked my senses. I instinctively pushed away. She woke up and rolled back onto me.

"Good morning, lover. Need some attention?" she said, stretching and rubbing against me like a cat.

I rolled out of the bed. "I'm fine. Did you have a good night?"

"Slept like a little baby full of milk. You?"

"More nightmares. I think I need to stretch my legs." I headed for the door, thinking I'd try to find the clearing and see what it looked like in the daylight.

She flew out of bed and threw on a dress. "I'll go with you."

I couldn't get the image of her horrible winged shadow out of my head. Looking at her now, I couldn't shake the feeling that I didn't know her at all. My jaw felt tight. I was clenching my fists. "I gotta go."

I ran outside. All this time, she was lying to me, tricking me every day. I prided myself on not being trickable because I didn't believe anything I didn't see with my own eyes, but I hadn't seen her at all. Not really.

I was whacking the bushes with my fists, staring at the pentagram burned into the clearing when she came up behind me. I started when she touched my shoulder.

"Tommy, are you okay? What are you doing?"

I didn't turn around.

"Mama's got breakfast ready and Papa wants to take you on his hunt today. Isn't that great?"

"I don't hunt."

"I know that, sweetie. I think he wants some get-to-know-you time."

"What are you gonna do?"

"I'll be huntin' too."

I pictured her flying above the pines searching for victims. "You're coming with us?"

"No, for orchids, of course. Maybe I'll get lucky and find some tasty mushrooms to add to dinner, too. Be patient with him, okay?"

"With who?"

"With Papa. He kinda talks slow, long pauses, you know. But what he does say is usually important, thoughtful."

"Fine. Let's go."

She tried to hold my hand, but I brushed it away. Her touch felt like sharp scales sprouting course hairs.

Bree's father stood on his porch watching us as we approached. He slouched so she could kiss him on the cheek as she rushed into the big cabin, never taking his eyes off of me. He came down the steps and as he passed me I smelled that strange mix of flora and fauna and dirt that startled me in the apartment since Bree moved in.

I followed the man and his gun along a stream, slowly, silently until the stream became a pond. A doe and two fawns lapped the brown muck. We didn't worry them. Papa leaned his gun against a tree, then sat down and relaxed against the trunk. He stared up at me until I sat next to him. He held out a piece of jerky, he pulled from his pocket. I took it and enjoyed the salty chew.

"You should go," he said.

I wasn't sure what he meant, but there was no emotion, no judgment, only a statement of fact. "Like now? Back to the cabin?"

"You aren't of this land. And it needs her."

Before last night, I think I would have taken this as a dad saying I wasn't good enough for his daughter, but today, I thought I understood what he meant. "So she told you she's not coming back with me?"

He shook his head slowly. "She had no right goin' the way she did. There was no real point to it. To confusin' you like that."

My head hurt. I wanted to run, and keep running. "Is she really that thing? That demon Jimmy was talking about? Would she really hurt me?"

"No. No. She wouldn't want that. It's confused. Everything's out of balance."

"And it will be in balance if I leave?"

"Maybe not, but you can't help."

He stood up, grabbed his gun, brought it to his shoulder in one smooth motion, and shot.

"No," I yelled as the buck that had joined the others while I was chewing on jerky fell.

He dragged that huge buck all the way back, wearing it like a cape, holding its front hooves. I couldn't look away from the voids of its dead eye. Flies kept landing on it then flying away. He was so right. I didn't belong here. I wasn't like them. I wasn't meant to live off the land.

That night I had no appetite. Sister and Bree both kept pestering me to eat, but I couldn't swallow a bite. Everyone praised Bree for the selection of mushrooms she had added to the meal. I picked mushrooms from my plate and threw them into the fire. My tongue felt swollen like I might choke on it. I headed back to the cabin, before they passed the moonshine, without saying goodnight.

Bree entered the cabin shortly after I got in bed. "Tommy, are you okay? Did Papa say something to upset you?"

"Guess I'm ready to get back. I'm ready for some hot water in a shower, with water-pressure. Electricity is nice. You know, civilized society." I knew that last jab was a little far, but it didn't matter. There wasn't anything, any real relationship, to save.

"I hope you feel better. I'm going to enjoy the music. Sleep well." She left.

I got up and found my phone in the corner on the floor. Tonight, I would get proof that she was the Jersey Devil, then bolt, and this would all be over.

I stared numbly out the dirty little window until I saw the glow in the clearing. Armed with the Swiss army knife my dad gave me on our first camping trip after my little brother lost his battle to leukemia, I went to confront the devil woman I had believed I loved for the last year.

I hated my body for feeling lust for her lithe undulating rhythmic body, worshipping Satan, or so I now assumed, in the glow of the gluttonous moon. As her movements grew toward ecstasy and her dark shadow arose, I saw it clearly as not her shadow. I had been mistaken in my fear. She turned, and what I had thought were her black wings, were part of a second beast. I saw its horned, bulbous head towering over her. Red glowing eyes meeting hers. It sunk on its muscular haunches and its bat like wings encompassed her, but she showed no fear.

When its wings opened again as if it had only been a friendly embrace, I was ready with my phone. I pushed and swiped, but nothing happened. The damned thing was dead. Without thinking, I chucked it at a tree. The sound was too loud, as if the tree in anger were giving me away. The monster's red eyes pierced me. It screeched. Its wings beating pushed me to the ground with the force of hurricane winds.

Bree, clothed in a white nightdress, her hair tamed, her gray eyes gentle, stood over me and offered her hand. I didn't want to feel her skin again, but I needed help up. I couldn't seem to do it on my own.

Once wobbling in the vertical position I stammered, "You're not… You're not… the Jersey Devil."

She smiled and squeezed my hand. She felt soft like she used to, but I dropped her hand anyway.

"You're worse than the Jersey Devil. You're its friend. Its demon companion or something. Does it do your bidding if you dance for it? Do you send it out to kill people you don't like? Is that what you've been doing?"

Her eyes darkened with storms as her smile vanished. She said, "You've got it all wrong, Tommy. This is why I didn't want to bring you here. I knew you would get the wrong idea. But you kept saying you wanted to know me. To know my insides, and you kept insisting and I wanted you to be happy."

She shook her head. Stared back into the glow in the clearing for a while, then continued. "That story uncle Jimmy was telling you was true. And he started to tell you the rest of the truth before I cut him off. The local legend about Mrs. Leeds the witch and her thirteenth child. It all happened. What they leave out is that the twelfth child is also part of the curse. She lived, but as the sister of the demon, she lives as long as it does, as long as she never leaves these woods."

"So you're saying you're the twelfth child? Some two hundred year old witch?"

"No. Will you listen? Please?"

My legs wouldn't hold. If I was going to listen, I had to sit down. I leaned against the nearest pine and slid down.

140

"Over the years, she and the demon, cursed to these dark woods, seeing it change, the people dying and being born, they realized they were more similar than different. Sister used her powers to hide the demon and it in turn protected her. After hundreds of years, Sister felt safe enough to start a family of her own. She fell in love with Papa and they had a child, but the Devil stole it, tore it to pieces, left it for them to find. She grieved, but Sister understood it was part of her mother's evil curse, and she wanted a child of her own. Papa and his brothers, knowing these lands so well, persevered and accept the safety Sister's magic provides."

"Oh, so your mom is the two hundred year old witch. Great."

"Sister and Papa kept makin' babies and the monster kept takin' 'em. Then I came along. Number twelve, you see, and that ended it. It let her keep me. Maybe it thought she would make a cursed thirteen. Make it a companion. But she didn't. So it latched onto me. It's complicated."

"Yeah, I bet."

"But all families, all deep relationships, are complicated. Right?"

She stepped toward me. She had a question on her face as if this was an opening, for me to make a choice, as if there were still something to think about."

"Stay away from me," I said, tucking my feet up.

"I guess you didn't really want to know me after all. We could have stayed happy, if you didn't always need more. You had to crawl up inside me to know me. You had to smell the bog, the wild orchids through me. You didn't know it, but what you wanted was my power. You couldn't truly know me, have me, separate from my power. Why couldn't my other self be enough? Why couldn't the Bree who loved you and being with you be enough?"

She couldn't hold the welling tears any longer. They poured down her cheeks. A loud screech filled the treetops. Her eyes bulged. "No. Oh, no!" She turned and sprinted into the darkest forest. I switched on my headlamp and ran in the other direction hoping to find the way back to the canoe.

The thick silent pines burst into flame as I ran past. It didn't matter what she said, I was positive that she had sent her devil after me. Every branch scratching at my face and arms was a claw, every breeze a flap of its wings. The thickening bog smell was its rotting breath. The tree frogs were singing my dirge. The orchids whispered and the flytraps snapped. But my head lamp showed the opening in the thick undergrowth much more quickly than I expected, and I was out on the dock. I knelt down and touched the carved stars, knowing now that they were pentagrams. I took my pocket-knife and carved "The Devil Lives Here" in large letters as a warning for those canoeing past. I hoped they took it for what it was and not an invitation for the curious.

Pulling the canoe down the ramp felt impossible. Every splash was the Jersey Devil landing, waiting for me to turn and look into its red, glowing eyes before it devoured me. I was soaked when I finally pushed the canoe away from the dock and began the long row back to civilization. I knew things would never be the same now that I believed, that I knew there were powers, entities beyond what I wanted to see or touch, but at least I was headed home, to a normal city like New Orleans, where I could live without the drama of witches and demons lurking all around.

Shadows

by Jason Ryder
Third Place (Tied)

Alice Jones turned off the truck and sighed as it sputtered a few times before becoming quiet. She looked at her six year old daughter sitting next to her and smiled, "Well this is it, our new home, Jenna! What do you think?"

Jenna turned to look at her mother, and shrugged, "Looks weird. And old. Do we have to live here?"

Alice frowned as she nodded, "At least for the time being. Uncle Allen is letting us stay here until I find something else."

"What about Daddy? Will he find us here?" Jenna questioned, her right hand moving to her left arm "I don't want him to hurt us anymore."

Alice hugged Jenna close to her, "Only people who know about this place are Uncle Allen and Aunt Beth, and neither of them will tell Daddy. We will be safe here."

"How many floors is it, Mommy? It looks big."

"Two floors, plus an attic. Maybe a crawlspace. But you get your own room if you want it. I'll understand if you want to sleep with me tonight. And look, plenty of yard to play in."

Alice and Jenna got out of the truck. Alice grabbed two suitcases from the back of the truck before leading Jenna up the porch steps. She placed the suitcases on the porch before reaching above the door jamb and found a key. She smiled at Jenna before unlocking the door. They walked through the door and into the kitchen.

Jenna walked over to the stove and looked at it before speaking, "I've never seen a green stove before."

"Uncle Allen said that everything still works, just no one has lived here since before you were born. They had ugly colours back then."

Jenna made her way to the fridge and opened it slowly. She squealed in delight as she saw a bottle, "Oooh, apple juice, and milk. Is the food older than me too? I hope not, I'm thirsty."

Alice chuckled, "Uncle Allen had a local grocer keep this place stocked up in hopes that we would finally need a place to hide out. There should be some chicken nuggets in the freezer." Alice laughed again as Jenna went on her tippy-toes to try to reach the freezer. Alice opened up the freezer and grabbed a bag of chicken nuggets, "As promised. We should be fine for a while. At least for now."

Jenna nodded as she watched her mother put some nuggets on a baking pan and place it into the oven after it preheated. Alice made a mental note to ask her brother for a microwave. Then again, he had already done more than enough for them. Hopefully, she thought, Danny will finally be sent away to prison for a long time. She looked out the window above the stove, seeing her reflection. She placed a hand on her bruised eye before looking away and not noticing a shadowy face watching her before vanishing.

Later that night, Alice tucked Jenna into her bed and asked her, "You sure you want to sleep alone in your own room tonight?"

Jenna nodded, "Can you check under the bed for monsters?"

Alice smiled at Jenna, "I thought you were too old for monsters under the bed. You haven't had me check lately."

Jenna shrugged, "It's a new place. And it will help me sleep better."

Alice chuckled, "The only monster is miles away, waiting for his day in court. There is nothing to be afraid of here."

Jenna pouted, "Please Mommy, just to be sure?" Alice smiled and kissed Jenna's forehead. She got down on her hands and knees and lifted up the blanket. She took out her cell phone and turned on the flashlight, starting at the head of the bed and making her way down to the foot of the bed. The shadows moved out of the way as the light swept over the area.

"Nothing. Maybe a dust bunny or two, but no monsters."

Jenna closed her eyes, "What about the closet? Can you check there too before you leave?"

Alice sighed, "I will," as she stood up. She kissed Jenna on the cheek, "Get some rest little one. Tomorrow we will make this place more of a home." She went to the closet and opened up the door, shining the phone's flashlight inside, "Nothing in here, either. Until tomorrow when we put your clothes in there."

"Okay Mommy. Good night, love you," Jenna said as she drifted off to sleep. Alice made her way out of Jenna's room as Jenna's closet door slowly opened, a shadowy hand resting on the edge of the door. .

A few days passed quietly. Alice and Jenna worked around the house. Each night, they went through their little ritual of checking under the bed and in the closet. Alice noticed the closet

144

door's latch was a bit loose and hoped Allen would know of a handyman who would be able to fix it.

Alice tucked Jenna into bed, "Good night pumpkin. I'm going to take a bath before going to bed as well."

"Did you check under the bed?" Jenna asked, "Or in the closet?"

"I will, but like I've said before, there are no monsters here."

"Some nights I feel like someone is watching me sleep. But when I open up my eyes, I don't see anyone."

Alice paused for a moment, remembering when she would wake up and see Danny watching her from a chair. Most of the time she would be able to pretend to go back to sleep, while other times. . . she did not want to continue that thought. "I check on you at night, silly. I enjoy watching you sleep. Now close your eyes and go to sleep."

"After you check under the bed and in the closet," Jenna demanded, pouting.

Alice rolled her eyes as she got on her hands and knees to check under the bed, "I'm surprised, you haven't lost any toys under here yet. But there is nothing here."

Jenna shrugged, "I guess I'm being more careful with my toys now. However there are a couple toys that I know I brought with me that I can't find."

"Well, they aren't under the bed. Perhaps you left them outside? Or a different room?" Alice stood up and checked the closet, "Looks better now you have some clothes in here. And I will get this fixed so it stays shut."

"Thank you, Mommy," Jenna said, closing her eyes, "Goodnight, love you."

"Love you too, little pumpkin," Alice said, leaving Jenna's room and making her way to the bathroom.

She turned on the hot water, then found some candles. She sat them around the bathtub and lit them. She turned off the overhead lights before undressing, and placing her phone on the counter. Alice looked in the mirror, noticing her bruising on her eye was slowly going away. She sighed as she looked at scars on her stomach, legs and arms. She slid into the tub, enjoying the warmth of the water engulfing her. She closed her eyes, feeling safe for the first time ever since meeting Danny. Alice fell asleep just as a shadow passed over her phone as it started blinking that a phone call was coming in.

Jenna woke up, and realized her stuffed rabbit was missing. She rubbed her eyes, trying to adjust them to see in the dark. She scowled and looked over the edge of the bed, "Bunny, are you down there?" No response.

She got out of bed and onto her hands and knees. She could not see anything in the dark. "Bunny?" She reached a hand under the bed, trying to feel for her stuffed rabbit when she felt something grab her and drag her under the bed.

Alice woke up, startled by the silence in the dark bathroom. Her water had grown cold while she slept, and the candles seem to have burned themselves out. She got out of the bathtub, grabbing a towel to dry herself off. She noticed her phone had twenty missed phone calls and two voicemails. The missed calls were all from Beth. She pressed play on the voicemail app.

"Alice, Danny is out of jail! He knows where you are, please get out of there. I'm sorry, I tried to be strong, but he threatened to pop my tits. And I just bought them!"

"Shit," Alice said, dropping her towel and grabbing her clothes. She was still wet but still dressed quickly, "Jenna!" she yelled, "Wake up!" She ran to Jenna's room, opened up the door and turned on the light. "Jenna, get up! We have to go."

There was no response, and Alice noticed that the bed was empty, "JENNA!" she exclaimed, running to the bed and throwing the blanket onto the floor, "Jenna! This isn't funny! Where are you?"

There was a honking sound coming from outside, and Alice made her way to Jenna's window and looked out. A jeep swerved to a stop in front of the house and three men got out. "Alice! I'm home!" one of them yelled, "And I brought company."

"Shit, shit shit." Alice said under her breath as she heard the front door being kicked in. She dove under the bed and started praying as she heard her husband and his friends storm into the house.

The floor gave away underneath her and she found herself in an interstitial space, then she screamed as she felt herself being dragged down the dark, tight space between the floors. She struggled, and kicked her feet, hitting the walls as she was pulled. Alice realized she stopped moving and sat up. She saw Jenna sitting at a little table drinking out of a toy teacup with what looked like a shadow, with eyes and a mouth. She looked behind her and saw two more shadows, barely making out their faces.

"Don't be afraid, Mommy. They want to protect us," Jenna said, sipping out of her teacup, "Have some tea with us while his parents go take care of the visitors."

146

Alice blinked and the two shadows behind her left. She crawled over to the table and hugged Jenna as she heard screams of anger turn into screams of anguish. "What are they?"

Jenna shrugged, "Shadows of Those Yet to Come. I don't know what they mean by that. But they have been watching us since we arrived. Zeke borrowed my missing toys."

Alice nodded, as she watched the shadow pour from a plastic teapot into another teacup and slid it over to her. She pretended to drink from it, while being glad that Jenna and herself where on the Shadow's good side.

Mine to Keep

by MM Schreier
Fifth Place

Eight Revolutions

I reached my thoughts out, feeling for Minket.
Can't sleep.

I counted to one hundred before giving my hatch mate a mental poke. When their reply came it felt heavy and sluggish.
What was that for, T'siti?
I told you-- can't sleep.

As rare, identical egg partners, I couldn't hear Minket's huff, but I could feel it. We were connected in a way the others in our clutch could never be.
Fine, I'm coming.

I wiggled my tentacles and waited.

When the sleeping pod door wooshed open, I lifted my blanket and Minket crawled into the bed next to me. Our limbs intertwined. They curled around me and settled their chin on my shoulder. I sighed. After spending our first five Revolutions in the same egg together, I found it discomforting to sleep alone.

"Minket--"
Hush, don't wake the Caregivers.

I nodded and nestled deeper into the blankets.
Tell me about you-know-what. My thoughts quivered in anticipation as I rolled over to face them.
Again? The whole thing is ridiculous.
It helps me relax.

Minket looked down their eyestalk at me. It was like seeing myself in a reflection glass. We were both tall and willowy. Our skin-- mottled tan and yellow meant to blend into the shifting sands of our homeworld-- bore identical patterns, so that if we stood close enough, the eye saw only one person. Even our mannerisms were similar. We both waved our tentacles when we spoke, and tended to lean back on our shorter, third limb like a stool when tired.

It was the eyes that set us apart. Minket's orb was wide and clear and blue. Mine was small and golden, like a desert cat.

Blinking, I gave Minket my best fire-puppy eye. I could feel them sag, giving in, as I snuggled onto their chest. Their tentacle reached out and repositioned my head more comfortably in the nook between shoulder and neck.

So, what do you want to know?

I closed my eye and thrummed, a contented rumble starting at my core and rippling outward.

Everything. Anything!

You're so odd.

I nudged them and could sense their eye roll.

So, as you know, the legend says they are strange looking creatures. Too many of certain body parts, not enough of others. In fact, two seems to be the magic number. Two eyes instead of one. Two limbs instead of three. Where we have a dozen tentacles, they have two stubby manipulators.

I shivered in delight.

Legend has it that they feed themselves and speak out of the same face hole. Disgusting.

I poked Minket with a tentacle. *Different isn't gross.*

They stifled a giggle. *Stop! That tickles!*

A second tentacle joined the first. Within moments we were both wriggling and laughing. The blanket fell to the floor, leaving my feet exposed. I curled them under me, making a small target; Minket knew I was exceptionally ticklish there. They took me off guard when they whapped me with a pillow. A squeal escaped my throat.

Shhh!

Too late. The door wooshed open and a Caregiver stalked in.

"Hatchlings!" They glared down at us.

We stilled.

"It's late. Minket-- back to your own sleeping pod."

As my egg partner slipped out of bed, I squeezed them with a tentacle. *Sorry.*

They smiled and winked.

"And you, T'siti. It's time you grew up." The Caregiver leaned over and plucked a stuffed toy from beneath my pillow.

I'd long given up the multi-tentacled dollies and fluffy sand-lizards that new hatchlings clung to for comfort in the long night, but for some reason I had hidden this one away. Two limbs, two manipulators, two bits of space-glass sewn on as eyes. Grotesque, but also strangely adorable.

The Caregiver tucked the stuffed monster under their arm. "I'll repurpose this to one of the younger hatchlings. If they aren't terrified by it." They gave me a stern look. "Now, go to sleep. You have your first day of classes in the morning."

I lowered my eyestalk. "Yes, Caregiver." I did my best to keep my voice even.

The door closed, leaving me alone.

150

You're never alone, T'siti.

I smiled as I picked the blanket off the floor and wrapped it around my shoulders.

Fair night, Minket. Will you stay with me until I fall asleep?
Of course. Have I ever left you on your own?
Never.
Never.

Flopping back on the pillows, I reached for my poppet, forgetting for a moment the Caregiver had taken it away. A hollow weight settled in my chest.

I felt Minket sniff.

I love you, egg partner, but maybe the Caregiver is right. You need to give up this obsession.

My face heated. *I'm not obsessed. Just curious.*

Whatever. Humans don't exist. They are just a story, made up to scare hatchlings.

I pulled the blanket over my head. The tales had never frightened me. No matter how childish it was, I wanted to believe.

Thirteen Revolutions

The Teacher droned on, but their words stretched like pulled, sticky-sweets, elongated sounds in the background that meant nothing. I doodled in my notebook-- two limbs, two eyes, bushy strands of keratin sprouting from the head. I wondered what the point of that was. Warmth in a chilly climate? But just on top? That seemed bizarre. Certain myths said humans had plumage that helped attract a mate. It seemed a little more plausible than random sproutings. Still, while I considered myself open-minded, the whole idea of gendered pairings felt alien. It was so make-believe. There was the old adage that truth was stranger than fiction, but how far did that go before it edged on science fiction?

"T'siti. Any thoughts?"

I jumped in my seat. I hadn't heard the question.

How many planets in the newly discovered yellow star's system?

I shot a grateful look at Minket.

"Eight planets, with a ninth, outer rim dwarf planet."

The Teacher nodded.

I raised a tentacle.

Don't.

I couldn't help myself.

"Yes?"

"The third planet. There are rumors there might be life there. Has anyone discovered any intelligence?"

A titter ran through the room.

The Teacher glared at the other students, then shook their head. "The planet is terribly stressed. I can't imagine life is sustainable there. While there are organic traces, the elemental levels seem inhospitable for sentient life. There's very little breathable argon. Our initial exploration teams have deemed it not worth pursuing further study."

My tentacles shot into the air. "But what if life there is carbon based? What if--" I took a deep breath and steeled myself. "--life there breathes oxygen?"

Laughter burst out again, this time in a roar.

I shrank down at my desk as the Teacher tried to restore order. One of the other students threw a crumpled piece of paper at me. When I smoothed it out, I saw one word scrawled across the page-- weirdo.

Ignore them.

I'll show them, Minket. Someday.

The Teacher cleared her throat. "Class, let's move on to mathematics. We'll be practicing the Inalti Equations today."

Well, you better study harder. You'll never become an exploration pilot with your math scores.

I got out my exercise book and glared at the page. In the back of my head, I felt Minket's thoughts soften.

If you want to fly, you'll fly.

The numbers wriggled on the page, meaningless insects.

Come on. We'll work through it together.

I smiled. How did other people make it through life without an egg partner? They must feel terribly lonely with just their own thoughts inside their head.

Twenty-Four Revolutions

A tinny voice counted down through the comm unit. "...Three...Two...One. Cleared for ignition."

"Acknowledged." I pressed the blue button on my console and the spacecraft's engine rumbled to life.

Good luck hunting for Humans!

I could feel Minket's laughter. They were such a comedian.

I'm not a Hatchling anymore. I know humans don't exist.
My tentacles turned knobs and flipped switches by habit. Four Revolutions on the training simulator and I could do the initiation sequences in my sleep.

My stomach dropped. This wasn't a simulation. This time it was the real thing.

Don't be nervous. I'll be along for the ride the whole time.

Thanks for always being there.

Yeah, well it's not like I have a choice! They cackled.

152

I snorted, shaking my head, then pressed the comm button. "Exploration Vessel 2833 initiation complete and course plotted. Permission for take off?"

"Course confirmed. Permission granted. Safe flying 2833."

With smooth pressure, I engaged the throttle and the craft lifted gently off the ground. I gave it a little more power as I maneuvered through the atmosphere and escaped the planet's gravitational pull.

Outside the viewport, the world shrank to a sand-covered marble, a hundred shades of yellow against a velvety-black backdrop. It looked small enough to be held in my tentacle.

Oh, Minket, I wish you could see this.

Take pictures!

I frowned. Their thoughts sounded far off, as if heard through a long tunnel.

Turning the ship, I punched in the coordinates of the hyper-jump site. I'd fly there before jumping to the dwarf planet at the edge of the yellow sun's system. It was a good practice run for my first trip. Well documented, but in an uninhabited solar system. Controllable variables. My superiors assured me it would be an uneventful mission. Circle the ice covered rock, then jump back home.

It would actually be quite boring. At least the view was spectacular. Our sister planet sparkled blue and green, it's waters reflecting the sun's rays like a gem. In the distance, a hundred-thousand stars twinkled in a rainbow of white, yellow, orange, and red.

For a time I flew manually, giving my egg partner a running commentary on what I was seeing. There was a strange lag time in their responses.

Minket?

Nothing. My skin pricked, uneasy.

I'm here. You feel so far away.

Their thoughts seemed paper tissue thin.

Stay with me. I'm about to jump.

The concept made me queasy-- breaking down matter to the particle level and rematerializing hundreds of light-revolutions away. My superiors had walked us through the science. Pilots had been doing it for generations, with no ill effect. Still, it seemed frightening.

Here goes.

I punched in the jump sequence.

A lifetime stretched between breaths. That which used to be me drifted amongst the star dust. So this was what true peace felt like. Everything and nothing. Time became non-existent, in the never-ending now. The particles swirled and danced, free from our rigid bonds. When pressure descended, we resisted.

With a whip crack, I slammed back into my body. I wriggled my tentacles, counted toes. Everything was where it belonged. But something was missing.

Minket?

Silence.

I searched my thoughts for them, their familiar 'other self' presence that lived in a special place in my head. Empty.

Hello?

My limbs trembled as I frantically scrabbled at the mental void. I choked back a scream, tentacles tightening on the cockpit controls.

A ping came from the life support system. "Vitals elevated."

I breathed deeply and addressed the AI. "Everything's fine. Just fine." Nevermind that a piece of my soul had been torn away.

I felt hollow.

It was time for a mental pep talk: I could do this. Just zoom around the dwarf planet, return to the jump point, and zip back home where Minket would be waiting. They would probably think the whole thing was a grand joke.

Engaging the manual controls, I began the circuit. Struggling against the urge to slam the throttle down to maximum, I advanced at the approved velocity set out in the mission plan. It took all my willpower not to retreat into the empty spot in my head, curled up like a kicked fire-puppy. Instead, I concentrated on the viewport, admiring the icy rock in front of me.

Reaching down, I engaged the camera. Minket would want to see pictures. I swallowed hard and clicked the button.

"Camera function faulty." The mechanical voice made me feel even more alone.

I grumbled. Of course. Not only was I solo out here in this desolate solar system, but I couldn't even share the experience. This was not what I signed up for.

The curve of the planet filled my vision as I slingshotted around the dark side.

"Collision imminent."

Instinctively, I reversed the thrusters and swerved. My craft, zoomed by something round and shiney. I did an about face and stared out the viewport at the impossible.

The ship was oblong and appeared to be made of some sort of metal. It seemed unwieldy. I was uncertain how it navigated, but it seemed to be in a stable orbit around the planet. I reached for the camera, then stopped, remembering it was malfunctioning. This was supposed to be an uninhabited solar system.

I opened a hailing frequency. Static. I tried every known range without success. It was unsurprising. Of course aliens wouldn't use the same communication technologies as we did. Even if I could hail them, they probably wouldn't speak any of the languages I knew.

A thrill rippled through me. Had I discovered a new species? Where did they come from? My superiors had drilled into my head-- never engage with an unfamiliar vessel without permission.

What do you think? Should I get a little closer?

The void in my head said nothing. My vision blurred and I blinked rapidly.

On impulse, I edged around the side of the metal egg. A clear surface made a sort of window on the other side. It looked hard, unlike the living membrane that I viewed through. I snuck closer, eager to see the pilot.

A shape pressed up against the window and my eye nearly popped off its stalk.

Two limbs, two manipulators, two glittering black eyes. A short thatch of brown plumage sprouted from its head. Its skin, a lighter shade of brown, was smooth and patternless where it could be seen around the cloth it had wrapped itself in.

It's a HUMAN!

Minket couldn't hear me, but I sent the thought anyway.

I waved my tentacles at the human.

It's eyes widened and its face hole dropped open. It clutched one of its manipulators to its chest. Limbs rigid, it flopped over.

I tried hailing the ship again. "Hello human! Is everything all right?" No reply. I changed frequencies and languages. Maybe it spoke Frdonkic? "Bliip. Click. Clackity-claaaaack. Gronk." Still nothing.

"Human! Your orbit is degrading. Pull up or you'll crash!" I shouted, not bothering to press the comm button. It couldn't hear me. Frantically, I looked around my cockpit. As an exploration vessel I wasn't even equipped with a tracking beam.

Paralyzed, I watched as the metal ship broke through the atmosphere and gathered speed. I shut my eye, a whimper escaping my throat. "This can't be happening."

When I opened my eye, the ship was nothing but fiery wreckage on the ice, far below.

I sat for a long time, staring at nothing. Who would even believe this?

Feeling like I was mired in sucking-sand, I forced myself to continue the mission. Flying at half speed, I returned to the jump point, gathered myself, and initiated the sequence.

A lifetime stretched between breaths. That which used to be me drifted amongst the star dust. So this was what true peace felt like. Everything and nothing. Time became non-existent, in the never-ending now. The particles swirled and danced, free from our rigid bonds. When pressure descended, we resisted.

I slammed back into my body, plagued by a feeling that I'd done that all before.

Something tickled the back of my brain, warm and familiar. *T'SITI!*

Minket's thoughts came as a shouted whisper. They grew stronger as I approached the planet.

I smiled, once again whole. *I missed you, you big lunk.*

Me too. It felt so strange being alone in my head. But was your trip amazing?

I hesitated. For the first time in my life I had something that was all my own. No photographic evidence. No shared commentary. A tiny, if horrific, gem that was mine to keep.

Honestly, the whole thing was sort of boring. Just like the superiors said it would be.

Event 4
Fatal Flaw

We love to see the good in characters so we can root for their success but flaws are just as important and interesting. For this Event, choose a character flaw from the list and help your character ruin their life.

Core Concepts: character development, foreshadowing

Shadows Amongst the Sunflowers

by Sarah Connell
First Place

They were back again. Marcato kneeled transfixed amongst the crop of purple irises, watching the tall, human-shaped shadows skirt the edges of the sunflowers further down the slope.

"Therese," he murmured into the earbud stuck within his right ear. But his research partner didn't respond. *"Therese, they're back."*

Whether she'd finally heard him or noted the panic in his voice, she responded. "Where?" her voice was cool and clear, soothing some of the apprehension overtaking him.

"Sunflowers - west gate." Marcato ducked behind the stalks, swatting away lazy bees and watched. The shadows moved west, disappearing near the gate. "Did you see them?"

Therese remained silent.

Marcato poked his head up, scanning the lavender crop where he knew she'd be finishing up her day cataloging the bee varieties in her notebook. But there was no sign of her straw hat amongst the bushes. "Therese? Did you see -" A hand patted him on the back and he spun around, falling onto his elbows in the rocky soil.

Therese stood next to him, looking West. When she realized she'd startled him, she grimaced. "Sorry," she said, helping him up. "I came to see what you were looking at." Her voice was still calm but her face held the growing concern he'd noticed whenever she looked at him the past few days. "I don't see anything."

He rose to his feet, embarrassed, and patted the dust from his pants. "They disappeared, through the west gate, just moments ago."

"Did you see who they were?" she asked, caution in her tone.

He hated when people talked to him like that, like he was crazy. Therese had been different, at first. She'd given his ideas the benefit of the doubt instead of finding them outright bizarre. But lately, since the shadows had started to come into the dome, even Therese found him difficult to believe. Marcato hung his head, not wanting to see the look he knew she was giving him.

"I just caught glimpses of their shadows," he admitted.

"You just saw shadows, like the last times? And always in the sunflowers?" When he nodded she smiled in her playful way. "I keep telling you the sun plays tricks this time of day, especially amongst the sunflowers, with their large heads -"

"They were people, Therese. You have to believe me. This is just like last time -" he broke off, feeling the heat in his cheeks. He took a breath trying to calm himself.

"Marcato," she said, growing serious, "we're the only people for miles around. You know that. Just us and the biodome. Nothing else can live out here."

He looked askance at the milky-white dome wall near the west gate, his hands clenched into fists. "I know what I saw. They're watching us from inside somewhere. Therese, we have to let Command know, we have to get out of here while we still can."

Therese eyed him and then rubbed a hand across the sweat standing out on her forehead. She was older than him by at least a decade, and, unlike him, this wasn't her first dome assignment. She'd have to decide to tell Command about the shadows. "Look," she murmured after a moment of charged silence. "I know we've only been working together for a few weeks, but they told me what happened to your first research partner. It must have been incredibly hard, out here, all alone for months after she left."

He felt his blood turn to ice. "Who told you that?"

She seemed resigned by the accusation in his tone. Turning her back to the west gate she said, "Let's eat. It's dinner time." She shook the dirt off her gloves and started up the path between the irises. "We can discuss this after we have some food in us."

"She didn't leave," Marcato said into the buzzing stillness of the fading light. "She disappeared."

Therese stopped and turned, cocking her straw hat further back on her head to meet his eyes.

"They didn't tell you that, did they?" He gave a short laugh that echoed out into the dome. "Ines never checked back in with Command. She just disappeared one night. Gone. They never found the rover she took either. They followed the tracks out into the Badlands and they just ended."

Therese pursed her lips, thinking. "Fine. We'll set a motion sensor. But I don't think we'll see anything," she said at last. "We can spare one from the hive."

He nodded, relief washing through him more so at the fact that she actually might believe him. "I'll set it up."

She put a hand out to stop him. "Dinner first." She smiled, pushing him gently onward to their yurt at the center of the dome.

160

He gave in. Although he would never admit it, he enjoyed when Therese bossed him around like he was her little brother. No one had ever cared about him enough to do that. His parents had always been too busy in their work for the colony to pay him much attention and his small group of classmates had thought him an oddity after he'd been the only one selected for the advanced sciences career track at an early age. But he enjoyed being alone, he reminded himself. It was why he'd taken up this research job in one of the outer biodomes the year before.

Marcato filled the basin to rinse the dust and grime from their hands and faces on the front porch of their yurt, letting his partner wash up first as he pumped in fresh water, the beginning of their evening ritual. Therese in turn cranked the generator to turn on the central light string that hung like a net of stars amongst the folds of tapestry insulating the domed ceiling. Their small common space flickered to life as the solar generators kicked in. With the normalcy of their routine and the warm glow of the artificial lights, Marcato began to feel his worry unclench from its place around his heart and he relaxed into the task of preparing dinner. He pulled out a few flatbreads they had leftover from lunch and began to set the table. Frying lentils mixed with the sharpness of lemon oil and onions as Therese prepared the rest of the meal.

They ate in silence, both exhausted from the day's work. Finally, after she'd cleaned her plate, Therese set aside her spoon and spoke up, "While you set the motion sensor, I'll check the other gates."

He glanced at her but she wasn't making eye contact, her eyes had shifted away to a notepad she kept with her at all times to document the bee activity. But he couldn't see what she was writing now.

"Alright," Marcato agreed, trying to keep his voice even.

"I'll take the four-wheeler to get it done faster." She stood, pocketing her notebook and took the keys from the hook by the door before heading out.

Marcato watched her go through the window set into the door and tried to ignore the sense of deja vu that sent a shiver down his spine. "This isn't like last time," he muttered, forcing himself to take their plates to the sink as if this was any other night. "Therese is different. She cares about me. She wouldn't leave without…" he broke off as he saw the dust cloud from the four-wheeler traveling northeast. He craned his neck to peer through the small kitchen window. There was no gate out that direction. He thought for a moment, wondering why Therese would go that way. And then he realized. The communications tower was the only thing over there worth visiting. But their next scheduled meeting with Command wasn't until the morning.

Pushing the growing dread deep within himself, Marcato forced himself to finish washing up and hiked to the beehive to remove one of the sensors. It took him less time to install it by the west gate than he'd thought and in the ashen twilight of the opaque dome wall, Marcato found himself watching his own fading shadow amongst the sunflowers. He kneeled, staying very still in the empty night until his shadow lengthened and melted into the surrounding pools of darkness. Realization dawned on him slowly.

The shadows he had seen amongst the sunflowers throughout the past week had all been about the length of his shadow as he kneeled now, his back up against the hazy dome wall. If the strangers' shadows were only this long as they walked around then they were either the height of children or...he paused, and looked behind him out to where the Badlands lay beyond the dome wall. He stood suddenly, almost upending the motion sensor as he backed away from the wall before turning to run.

Marcato paced in the yurt, fear worming its way into him as he waited for Therese. When he saw the four-wheeler pull up, he swung the door open and beckoned for her to come inside.

"What? What is it?" she asked, fear reflected on her face as she saw the panic driving him.

"I've figured it out," he murmured, peering out the kitchen window down to the sunflowers blocking the west gate.

"Figured what out?" Her voice was high, filled with tension.

He turned to her. "The shadows I keep seeing, Therese, they're not *inside* the biodome. That's why I've never seen the people themselves. They're walking around *outside*."

Therese was shaking her head, fear turning to pity on her face. "Marcato, nothing can survive outside in the Badlands, not for very long at least and we're a long way from any other outpost."

"What if that's not true? What if the air isn't toxic," he said, taking a chance that she'd think he was crazy.

Therese crossed her arms. "You can't be serious. Now you're calling into question everything we do here, all of our research? All because of some shadows."

"What *are* we doing here, Therese? Do you know our end goal because I sure don't. We document the hive. We cultivate different nectar sources. I know we're told we'll introduce goldfinches soon. But how will this help anything?"

"It's a long process to rebalance the colony. Look, I know you were young when it happened," she said, her voice weary and filled with sorrow. "But I was there. I watched the terraforming

162

machines malfunction. Whole towns outside the central dome went to sleep and never woke up, asphyxiated by the excess Nitrogen."

"That was decades ago!" He threw his arms out wide. "Has anyone tried to go out there lately?"

"Of course," Therese spluttered, "there have been air quality tests and -"

"Oh well *tests*." His voice was scathing.

"What do you think is happening, then?" she asked quietly.

He looked her in the eye and took a deep breath to steady his nerves. "I think someone's living out there, a lot of someones. I think the rumors are true and the terraforming malfunction was planned."

"Why would-"

"To keep the planet for those who got here first."

Therese's eyes widened and then she laughed. "The original travelers all died out when they tried to terraform the planet more than a century ago. Their technology was flawed. None were left by the time we arrived."

"Or," Marcato said, beginning to pace the room again, "they didn't want anyone to know they were still here and so they isolated us in these domes when actually, the air is breathable again."

Therese blinked at him, wary. "So, you think those shadow people are, what? Descendants of the first travelers?"

Marcato nodded.

She hesitated, still eyeing him but not disagreeing anymore. "Have you told anyone about this...theory?"

Marcato shook his head, hesitated. "Well, I didn't come up with the idea. It was Ines who figured it all out first."

"Ines—you mean your original research partner?" Therese's motions stilled as if he'd just said something vital. "But you said you only just started seeing the shadows a week ago."

"Yes. Actually," Marcato rubbed the back of his neck, embarrassed to be caught in a half-lie, "I hadn't seen them for a while *before* they reappeared a week ago."

"How long is *a while*?"

Marcato sighed. "Not since Ines disappeared."

Therese seemed to contemplate this. "Right," she said, taking off her jacket and hanging it on the hook by the door. "We'll revisit this in the morning. I need time to think. Better get some sleep if we're going to be there to welcome the Command Reps at 0500. They're coming to check the stats."

"That reminds me," Marcato said quietly to Therese's back. "What were you doing over by the radio tower?"

Therese didn't turn. "What do you mean?"

163

"Well, I saw you drive over in that direction earlier. What were you doing?"

"Oh, I wanted to check and see if we had any messages, you know, from Command, in case they delayed their trip, *again*." She opened the door to her room. "Goodnight, Marcato." Her face was smiling in the half-light of the kitchen lamp but her eyes held a kind of calculating gleam that set his teeth on edge.

"Good night," he murmured.

Once her door was shut, Marcato moved quickly to her jacket and began to rifle through the pockets. At last, he came up with the small notebook that Therese carried everywhere. He looked up as he heard the buzz of the light go off in the nearby bedroom where Therese must have finished getting ready for bed. Quietly, he walked to his own room and shut the door. Momentary guilt almost forced him to return the notebook back to Therese's coat. But he couldn't shake the feeling that she was keeping something from him, as Ines must have done for her to leave in the night like she had. He had to know what she was up to.

He flipped through the notebook, skimming the innocuous notes and drawings from their research until he came to a single page from today's date. It had been torn out, the edge of the missing page ragged beneath his finger. His nerves seemed to all attune at once to confusion and growing suspicion. He'd hoped to find an answer for her odd behavior tonight, something inane more than likely. But the vindication of his fear was almost overwhelming. Marcato sat down hard on the edge of his bed, dropping her notebook and putting his head in his hands.

Now that he knew she was definitely hiding something, resolve overtook him. He stood, looking around for his headlamp. Finding it amidst a pile of old work gloves, he pulled it on and, taking his boots in his hand, silently walked toward the exterior door in his socked feet. Once outside in the cool night air, he slipped on his boots and bypassed the four-wheeler, making his way on foot instead toward the radio tower.

The door was locked. He tried his code but nothing happened. He bit his lip, trying to think of a reason why Therese would have changed the codes without his knowledge. Only a resounding need to get into the building pushed him onward. He removed the panel that contained the door lock mechanism and forced it open by untangling a grouping of colored wires and rerouting them. He'd had to learn that skill when Ines had disappeared those many months ago and now it came in handy again.

The door hissed part way open and stuck but he was able to sidle through. The light of his headlamp bathed the room

164

beyond in a harsh glow. The communications array was offline, as it should be, but as he looked around, he noticed a scrap of paper sticking out of the manual. He recognized it as the missing page from Therese's notebook. As if in a trance he held the paper up to the light of his headlamp and read off a series of code. Each had a marker before them that matched the numerals located on the four gates leading out of the dome and the last code had the word *ROVER* scrawled above it.

"She's changed the rover code too," he whispered, his heart pounding.

Hands shaking with panic. *Therese must be a part of it. She must be in on it.* The thoughts circled his mind like a rabid animal, until he realized with mounting horror that he'd revealed all he'd known tonight when she'd asked about the shadows. And now she knew that he knew.

He memorized the two codes that he needed and replaced the paper back in the manual where he'd found it. He knew now that he had to get out, get away from Therese and he had to do it tonight. He darted along the paths, his feet matching the hectic pace of his heart until he stumbled up the steps to the yurt and kneeled to catch his breath, trying to stay as quiet as possible. He doused his headlamp and opened the door with a low creak. Shaking, his hands fumbled for the four-wheeler keys in the darkness of the yurt but came away with nothing. The hook was empty.

A light flashed on, blinding him for a moment.

"Why are you going through my things?" Therese was standing in the doorway of the common room, holding her notebook up in the half-light of the nearest lamp.

"Stay away from me." Marcato backed up, toward the open doorway behind him.

"Marcato," Therese said, putting her hands up in a soothing gesture, "where have you been? I was worried after what you told me. I searched your room for you and instead, I find this." She waved her notebook in proof.

"Stop!" Marcato cried out. Therese froze in the act of stepping forward. "I saw the codes. I know what you're trying to do. You're going to lock me in here so when the travellers sabotage the dome, the truth will die with me."

She was shaking her head slowly. "Whatever you found, it's not the whole story." She gestured to the sofa. "Let's just have a seat and I'll tell you anything you want to know."

But Marcato had already backed to the front door and now turned and fled out into the darkness.

"Marcato!" Therese called from behind him.

165

He raced by the four-wheeler and headed toward the nearest gate, the west gate. Moments later, he heard the vehicle's engine roar to life behind him, its headlights casting his shadow long and shaky in front of him. His heart lurched, realizing that she'd hidden the keys from him after all and was now trying to run him down. He sped up, taking a sharp right off the main path and down the ruts of the lavender bushes leading straight for the sunflowers. The gate's arched frame loomed before him, closer than it'd seemed as he pushed his way amongst the stalks with their heads rising far up above him. The four wheeler idled somewhere behind him, trapped on the main road that didn't connect to this part of the dome. As he punched in the access code to the gate, he was dimly aware that Therese was making her way through the sunflowers, pushing them aside as she frantically called his name. He glanced back as the door hissed open and he stumbled into the waiting airlock just as she came sprinting round the nearest row and along the outer wall trail toward him. The door slid closed and he locked it from his side by cycling the airlock.

Marcato backed up, coming to rest against the outer door as it began to open. He turned and switched on the headlamp. The world outside was as stark and cold as he remembered from his long ago boyhood memories. Dust and rocks littered the plains for as far as the eye could see, reaching out to meet the inky horizon. His eyes traveled up, dazzled by the night sky. He didn't remember there ever being this many stars. But then again, he'd been very young when they were all sequestered in doors for what would be the last time.

Something felt wrong. He took a deep breath and waited. But nothing happened. Shaking off his unease, he looked back to see Therese entering the air lock and beginning to suit up. He barked a laugh that echoed out into the stillness of the landscape.

Silly, he thought. *Can't she see it's alright? The air is breathable, just as I thought.*

He turned toward the rover but before he could punch in the clearance code to open the doors, he found himself on his knees. He looked around surprised but nothing had hit him. Behind him, Therese was still suiting up. She was taking her time, making sure her valves were secure.

Wait, a thought nagged at him, slow to make itself known, *if she's in on the plan, then why is she suiting up at all? She should know the air isn't toxic...*

He tried to stand and instead fell forward, barely catching himself on his elbows. His head swam and he took another deep breath, feeling jittery. Everything seemed normal but his vision

166

blurred, his head throbbing. Just before he blacked out, his headlamp shone on something odd below him. In the dirt, just on the edge of the rover's wheels, he saw a footprint. It was smaller than either his or Therese's boots and its prints were everywhere.

White light seared through his eyelids but he couldn't move. The world was drawn down tight, consisting only of his eyes beneath their fluttering lids. They roamed side to side and then a finger twitched somewhere far to his right. And suddenly he was cold. Everything rushed back into him and he felt his skin creeping with gooseflesh in the open air.

"...barely alive...why he did it?"

The voice was fuzzy, like it came from a poorly tuned radio. But as he concentrated on it, he could hear it more clearly.

"Thought it was a hoax. Thought the air was breathable and that people were living outside."

Marcato tried to open his eyes as he recognized Therese's voice but the searing pain of the light flooding into his pupils made him gasp.

"Marcato," Therese said. She moved closer, her face tilting up, moving the harsh light away from his eyes. "Can you hear me?"

Marcato tried to sit up but found that he couldn't. He struggled, feeling what energy he had growing weaker by the moment. Therese laid a warm hand on his shoulder, pushing him back down.

"Rest," she said. "You're safe."

"I trusted you," he choked out, pushing aside the oxygen mask strapped to his face.

"I know," she said bleakly. "But you've got it all wrong."

He looked around for who she had been speaking to and realized that they were still in the airlock. "Who else is here?" he asked.

Therese resettled the mask over his mouth and nose. "Rest. We can talk later."

As his vision grew blurry once more, he saw her look past him to where the airlock met the outer biodome wall. He rolled his eyes to where she was looking and saw a group of tall silhouettes shadowed against the wall, unmoving.

He came awake all at once, finding himself in his own bed, the room dark around him. Everything hurt, most of all his head. It felt ten times its normal size and throbbed as if it had grown a second heartbeat. Gathering his strength to sit up, he froze as he heard voices from the living room. A shaft of lamplight slanted through his half-opened door illuminating three figures in the living room beyond. He blinked, trying to make them out.

"I told you to keep the Drones away from the dome wall." Therese's voice was accusing.

A Medical Officer and Command Representative faced her from the kitchen, looking out of place in the shabby confines of the yurt. Their crisp uniforms of red and tan marked their higher placement within the colony.

"All you had to do was keep him here until we could arrive this morning for the 0500 communication. We had planned to evaluate his competency then." The Rep's high-pitched voice was off putting and paired with her small stature, she had the uncanny appearance of a sulky child given too much power.

"I tried," Therese ground out between clenched teeth. "I changed the door and rover locks and kept the vehicle keys with me. I did everything I could. If we just could have told him - even I think the Drones look like humans from a distance and -"

"You know as well as I do that the Drone project is a secret." The Rep took a step forward, her hands on her hips. "There's enough anti-machine sentiment out there in the colonies without people finding out we're now using intelligent machines outside the domes again. How well do you think that will be received? Most colonists still blame the terraforming machines failure on Drone malfunction."

Drones? Marcato thought. A memory surfaced from a long-before history lesson. *At first, there were more Drones than people on this planet. They did everything outside the domes and were nearly as intelligent as us.* The fact sifted through his brain as he tried to make sense of it.

"Who was he going to tell?" Therese was saying, motioning toward Marcato's room and he stiffened, but no one looked over. "You're the ones who kept him out here after his research partner went rogue and tried to sabotage the whole dome system."

"She was psychotic. We did everything we could. How were we to know what she'd told him? He never mentioned it in his re-evaluation."

Psychotic? Marcato thought and an icy fear washed through him. He'd been living with Ines for months and hadn't even known.

"So you came up with some half-baked lie about her disappearing into the Badlands? He told me that's what happened. Why couldn't you have just told him she was sick?"

The Rep sighed. "The team thought it was best. We couldn't spare another researcher at the time and we didn't want

168

him mixing with the other colonists just in case he told people about the shadows and someone put two and two together about the Drones."

"Well, whatever you thought you did for him, it wasn't enough," the med tech grumbled.

The two women turned toward the med tech where he leaned against the kitchen sink, peering out into the slow dawn outside the window.

"Will he die?" the Rep asked harshly and Marcato had the sense that it was more out of concern for the colony's bottom line than for his own well being.

"He should pull through," he said.

"Why didn't he just turn around and come back inside once he realized he couldn't breathe?"

The med tech shook his head sadly. "He wouldn't have even known he was slowly asphyxiating. The lungs aren't made to recognize the difference before it's too late. How extensive his brain damage will be is something we'll have to wait and see about. I was there when the towns died out. It's something I'll never forget. The boy breathed the nitrogen-rich atmosphere for no more than two minutes, but still." "

Brain damage? This time the words had meaning and a thrill of alarm ran through him. Quickly, he sat up, got tangled in his oxygen mask and IV drip and rolled off the bed to thud onto the floor with a groan.

The overhead light flicked on and Therese was by his side, closely followed by the tech who produced a flashlight and began to scan his pupils.

"How is he?" The Rep stood over the three of them, arms crossed.

The med tech removed the oxygen mask from Marcato's face. "How do you feel?"

Marcato tried to speak but nothing came out. He coughed and tried again. "Okay," he tried to say but croaked instead. He clutched his throat as a searing pain ripped through it.

"Vocal cord damage," the med tech murmured.

The Command Rep eyed him. "Will he still be able to work?"

Therese rolled her eyes but no one seemed to see her other than Marcato.

"It should heal within the month, as long as he rests his voice. No speaking," he said to Marcato.

"Well at least he won't be able to say anything about the Drones, right?"

The ease with which Therese joked about the secret project had Marcato glancing nervously at the Rep but she only grunted. "Like you said, it's not like he's going anywhere anytime soon and we were going to brief him eventually. We'll need his expertise on the Drone crew."

As the Command Rep and the Med Tech left the room, deep in discussion, Therese turned to him, a guilty smile playing at the corners of her mouth. "Well, do you trust me now?"

She looked hopeful but Marcato couldn't shake the lingering betrayal at her lies.

"I did save your life after all," she added, an edge to her voice.

Thanks, he mouthed to her with a smile that masked the paranoia gripping him anew. All the time he'd been watching for the shadows, he should have been keeping an eye on his research partners. Ines had wanted him to go with her into the Badlands to search for the shadows, something he'd never told anyone. And Therese...

If she can lie to me for weeks, what else is she hiding?

170

Obsessed With Watching the Nobodies

by S.E. Reed
Second Place

Have you ever wondered about the minor characters in a movie? You know, those barely mentioned people in the background—the scene fillers. Only relevant for a microsecond as the camera pans left or right. A soldier dying in the background. A tattooed barista serving coffee. A woman on a bicycle.

You don't think about them.

No one does.

But, what if they were all you could think about? What if you couldn't let them go? You wanted to know everything about them. Where were they born? What was their last meal? What makes them laugh? What's their deepest, darkest secret?

Then what?

Well, you'd be me. Benjamin Adler. I'm obsessed with watching the nobodies. Infatuated with the people in the background. The unnoticed. The nameless. I spend hours fantasizing about their worlds. Writing down every detail, creating twisted stories with endless possibilities. I used to only focus on characters in movies, but lately—

"Ben!" Mom opens my door without knocking. I'm sitting on my bed working on another list from the last film I watched. I've got headphones on, but nothing is playing. Mom motions for me to take them off.

"I can hear you." But I take them off for her sake.

"I'm leaving for work—are you one-hundred-percent sure you want to stay home alone this summer? I'm sure it's not too late to get you signed-up for one of those camps at the Y or you could hang out with Uncle Olsen. You know he loves it when you come over to play chess." Mom's doing that thing where one side of her mouth is straining. It makes her look constipated.

"I've got plans this summer that don't involve going to day-camp for rejects. And as for playing chess with Uncle Olsen, he torments me—if you call that love, well then you're more fucked up than I am Mom. I'm seventeen, I don't need a babysitter."

"Jesus Ben." Mom's uncomfortable. Maybe it's those heels. Why do women do that to themselves? I wonder the first time Mom wore a pair of heels. Was she forced to put them on for a funeral—did she sink sharply into the grass at the cemetery, teary eyed and alone? I put my headphones back on and flip to a

171

clean page in my notebook and start writing down the reasons Mom most likely started wearing high-heels.

"Why are you still here? Aren't you going to be late for work?" I look up when I feel her staring at me.

"Fine. But, we are having a *real* conversation tonight about what these big summer plans of yours are." She huffs and slams the door.

Like she wants to know what my real plans are—I glance back at my list, then fold the page in half. I can't tear them out. Those irritating flakes of paper drive me mad. Mom is so annoying. I don't know how she can stand herself. And those fucking shoes. I'm going to obsess over them all day in the back of my mind until I take a pair from her closet and try them on. There's a cemetery a few blocks away. Maybe I can jump the fence and try walking around on the grass—

As soon as I hear Mom lock the front door I get up and grab my clothes to go shower. I have somewhere to be in like 45 minutes... I'm cutting it close. He might be gone by the time I get there. But, it doesn't take me long to get ready. I don't spend an hour primping like Mom does. She tries so hard. I don't really know why, there's plenty of men who'd fuck her without any make-up on.

Twenty-minutes later I'm locking the apartment and running down the hallway. My headphones are on again and this time they are playing heavy Drum & Bass. It helps drown out the honking taxis, the car alarms and the Street Screamers—you know the type, bitter housewives with asshole kids and hot-tempered lovers fighting on porch steps. They are everywhere. But, I block them out because they aren't my type. Street Screamers are over-the-top and volatile. I seek out the quiet, the lost in thought, the lonely, the desperate and emotional. The ones I can watch without being caught. Street Screamers aren't afraid to get in my face or call the cops if they catch me staring.

But not him. He's a nobody.

My nobody.

I first noticed him a few weeks ago outside of Frank's Bodega.

He was standing alone, hands in his pockets, headphones on. There was just something about the way he lingered, lost in his own mind. Maybe that's what caught my eye, a familiarity, like looking in a mirror. When he finally started walking, his gait was slow and deliberate and he was talking to himself; a menagerie of profane words. Maybe that's why I followed him all day. Memorizing every detail about him. Trying to slip close enough to hear the conversation he was having with himself.

172

His hair, a perfect Thomas Shelby. Shaved up the sides and slicked back on top. His faded black zip-up hoodie, oversized and frayed around the bottom edge. Unnecessary in the June heat. I decided it was special to him; wearing it for years even though he could easily afford a new one. He had on a pair of fresh white Air Force Ones and Studio3 Beats. But the hoodie—a memento. I can't stop dreaming about what the hoodie smells like. Dank and musty or exotic like cloves and cinnamon.

Frank's Bodega is in sight. I doubt he'll be there. I've come back at the same time for weeks now, going late to school, hoping to catch a glimpse of him. But, now that it's summer break—I'm going to wait all day if I have to. I can't stop thinking about him.

Buzzzz.

"What do you want?" I answer.

"Your Mom said you might come over today so I can beat you again at chess," Uncle Olsen replies.

"I dunno, I'm kind of busy right now," I say and look across the street at Frank's. The green awning is torn on one side and Frank's youngest son, a middle aged jerk-off named Eduardo, is on a ladder with a roll of duct tape attempting to patch it.

"Well, I have shit to do until noon. So if you decide to come by, make sure it's later." Uncle Olsen hangs up. He knows how much I hate it when he doesn't say exactly what he's doing. It's like planting a Kudzu seed inside my brain that will aggressively take over until I can't fucking see straight. I look at my watch. I've got two hours, then I have to go to Uncle Olsen's because I won't sleep for three days if I don't know what he's doing until noon. Is he going to a Urology appointment? Or shopping for luggage? Maybe going out for brunch with a red-headed woman he met at an art gallery? Fuck. I take out a piece of paper from my back pocket and use the nub of a pencil I always carry and start writing notes to keep my thoughts from spiraling.

I look up when I hear a commotion. Yelling. Shouting. It's coming from Frank's Bodega.

"Watch it you turd," Eduardo is yelling as he wobbles back and forth on the ladder. Underneath it, shaking it, is the guy I've been waiting for. He's behaving like a Street Screamer. He's making himself known, causing a scene. I flush. I hate him. I have to stop him because he's going to ruin this entire thing for me if he keeps this up. I run through traffic, ignoring the honking taxis.

"Hey, man, my name is Ben," I blurt out. He stops shaking the ladder and looks at me. He's stoned and he smells like he's been having sex with a burrito.

"You're that fucking weirdo who followed me a few weeks ago. What the fuck do you want?" He demands as he shifts his full attention from Eduardo to me.

"I wasn't following you," I lie. "I just have this OCD thing."

"Yeah, whatever." He narrows his eyes, deciding what kind of freak I might be. Then he shrugs his shoulders forward like there's a spider under his hoodie, crawling up his back and kinks his head to the side. A nervous tick? A tweaker spazz? I tap my fingers on my leg to calm myself—the urge to pull out my paper and start making a list is overwhelming.

"You want to go over to my Uncle Olsen's house and play chess with me," I surprise myself when the words come out. That's not what I thought I was going to say—

"Are you serious bro?" He chides. "Why the fuck would I go with a retard like you to some creeps house and play chess?"

"Cause you don't have anything better to do?" I joke.

The bells jingle on the door of the Bodega, "Ehyo, no loitering." It's one of Franks' other sons. "You wanna get away from the fucking ladder before I call the cops!"

I check my watch again. "The subway's just around the corner, you coming?" I ask him and start walking. If he wants, he'll follow me. My breathing is labored.

"You said playing chess? Like the board game shit or on a computer?" He asks and starts walking alongside me.

"The board game," I reply flatly.

"Your Uncle gonna be there Ben or we breaking in?" Something in his voice tells me he doesn't care either way.

"He'll be there after twelve. There's a diner close by we can wait in. I like to watch the waitress—she's only got one arm," I answer and take the stairs into the subway station. Why lie now that he's following me.

The waitress, her name is Rita and the first time I saw her I went down a deep, dark rabbit hole. For months, I'd tell Mom I was going to Uncle Olsen's to play chess, only so I could go to the diner and spend hours fantasizing about where the missing piece of her arm was. Then Mom found out I wasn't really at Uncle Olsen's house—and got super pissed off. I'm convinced Rita's keeping the arm in a ziplock bag in the diner freezer. I almost applied for a job there bussing tables, just so I could check.

Me and my nobody are standing on the platform waiting for the next subway. I'm still shocked that I invited him to come with me. I open my mouth to break the silence, but he speaks first— "Don't you gotta like go back up and down the stairs six times or some stupid shit for your OCD?"

"I don't have that kind of OCD."

I have the kind that makes me--

"Yeah my cousin's got it. That bitch washes her hands a hundred times and flicks the lights on and off when she's at our house, goes up and down the stairs like a freak," he says and laughs. His laugh is higher than I imagine it should sound like. I wonder if he's anxious? I wonder why I'm not.

"She sounds like a freak," I reply and laugh with him.

"My name's Guy, in case you were wondering," he says as we board the subway that has pulled up to the platform. I give him a bro nod.

"You still in school Guy?" I ask, like I don't know the answer and grab the handle bar as the train lurches forward. Everyone around us is quiet, staring at their phones, trying not to make eye contact. Normally a perfect place for me to hyper-focus on one of the passengers. But, since I'm with Guy, I'm focused on him. I'm ignoring the woman carrying a dog in a baby blanket. I'm not imagining the crib she puts it in at night and the outfits she hand stitches for special occasions.

"Nah, graduated a few weeks ago. The day you followed me around was graduation. I had some shit to work out in my head and needed some air," Guy explains.

"Did you figure it out?" I ask him. He looks at me, with intense eyes. I don't turn away, I just stare. The subway stops and more people get on and we cram closer together. Guy finally breaks our gaze. I've already mapped out his features, to write about them later. The smooth face, no big pock marks from acne. The green flecks on the rim of his blue eyes, too pretty for him. They don't match his dark hair. I want to close my eyes right now and sink into a dark fantasy.

We don't say anything for the next three stops. He doesn't trust me enough to tell me what shit he had to figure out. I don't blame him. I wouldn't trust me either.

"Get off here," I say to him when the doors open at the next stop. We exit the subway and go up to the street. A block away is the diner. You can smell it, the scent of greasy bacon. My stomach growls. I should have eaten something before leaving this morning. But, then I would have missed meeting Guy. "Why were you shaking Eduardo?"

"Who?" he asks as we cross the street. "You mean that prick on the ladder?" He laughs. "That dude's a joke. He's got a punk-ass kid who keeps sniffing around my little sister. Before you walked up, I was telling him to make sure his son keeps his dick in his pants. I'm leaving soon man, gotta tie up loose ends," Guy's words come out choppy and raging. I don't know what part of his story he's angry about. His sister getting hit on? Or leaving soon?

The diner is filled with the daytimers. It's a regular who's who of men without wives or jobs or shit else to do during the day. "Look, there she is," I point at Rita. We sit in a booth and flip over our cups. A signal. She hears the clang and waves with her half-arm when she sees it's me. Guy kicks me under the table.

"Bro, you were right, one fucking arm," he hisses.

A sheepish grin crosses my face and I move my cup three inches to the right, towards the window, away from the edge of the table. Guy raises an eyebrow. Rita approaches with a pot of steamy hot coffee in her good hand. "Haven't seen you here in a while Ben. How's your book coming along?" She asks and leans in just a hair further than she normally does to reach my cup. Her half-arm goes up to balance her body and it's nubby end is eye level with Guy. He mouths dick at me and I stifle a laugh.

"So, Ben, you're writing a book?" Guy asks with genuine intrigue in his voice.

"I uh, I take a lot of notes for a book I'm writing," I lie. Not for Guy's sake. For Rita. If she knew some of the sick shit I wrote in my notebook, she wouldn't be smiling. Better for her to think I'm writing a book.

"What was it about again? Some kind of time crystals and supercomputers?" She looks at me thoughtfully.

"I knew you were a nerd. Chess. Time crystals. Supercomputers," Guy shakes his head. I look him in the eye and don't back down. But he leans into the stare; hard. Rita turns and walks away when I don't respond after a few seconds, not wanting to remain in our crossfire. Whatever this is.

"Look, man, I'm not really writing sci-fi. I take notes about people I see. I only told her that shit so I could sit here without her thinking I was being a creep," I say and look at my watch. Uncle Olsen will be home in thirty minutes. Then, I can get to the bottom of what he was doing this morning.

"I don't care if you're a stalker bro, or a writer, or whatever—," Guy says and takes a sip of his coffee. I can't decide if spending time with him is satiating my desire or if I'm losing the intrigue. He's no longer a nobody. He's a somebody. He's Guy. But, I have to keep up this charade—it's fueling my obsession.

"You said you were wrapping up loose ends. So, where are you going?" I change the subject. He looks side to side then pulls up one of the sleeves of his hoodie. He's got a tattoo on his forearm.

"What's that?" I ask stupidly even though I know it's a gun. But this is a game. He wants me to ask. He wants me to think he's hard core. A tough guy with street cred. But, he's just a loner, wandering around aimlessly after graduation. A nobody with a name. But, I'll play along and feed his ego. I reach across the table and carefully touch his skin, it's hot and sticky. "Don't be a tard Ben. It's a fucking gun—I inked up after my first kill." He let's my fingers linger for a second before he pulls the sleeve back down to cover it up.

"Cool bro," I shrug. Guy laughs, this time it's not as high, it's more relaxed. We lock eyes. I want to crawl inside of him and watch his vocal chords move up and down and understand what makes him laugh. I want to plant myself in the dampness of his innards and twist and vine my way through his body, slowly wearing his skin as my own.

"Jesus, Ben, you're funny—you know that. I can't figure you out," he smiles when he says it. The first smile. My body tenses. "Nah, I didn't kill nobody. Did it to piss off my asshole parents," he explains. "Those pricks wanted me to go to Westpoint. But The Point has a strict no visible tattoo policy. So I bought a gun to dodge a bullet."

"Westpoint? That's considered an Ivy League. And I'm the fucking nerd?" I play it off. I already know he's brilliant, I, uh, might have done some research on Guy after the first day I followed him outside of the Bodega…

"Yeah, well, my parents can fuck off. I don't give a damn that MIT rejected my application, I'm moving to Boston in a few weeks. I've got a lead on a job. I'll reapply next year. My dad says I'm--"

Buzzz…

"What do you want?" I answer and interrupt Guy's painful admission about his future. He's annoyed with me for answering the phone. But, I don't really care. I can't not answer.

"I'm home if you still want your ass handed to you," Uncle Olsen says and hangs up.

"Who was that?" Guy asks when I put my phone down.

"Uncle Olsen, he's a total douche. But, we have to go, I have to find out something—And since you're so fucking smart, you can help me crush him at chess. You know, he went to MIT," I stand up and flick a five on the table for the coffee.

"Come back soon Ben! I want to hear about the time crystals!" Rita shouts as we leave. Guy laughs, even deeper. So, third time's the charm.

"Uncle Olsen lives right there," I point to a huge brownstone on the corner.

"Your Uncle has money," Guy points out the obvious.

"Yeah, so. You have money," I retort.

He nudges me with his shoulder. "I don't have money. My parents do. And don't act like you're stupid Ben, you know people with money are fun to fuck with. Just follow my lead."

I ring the door and Uncle Olsen's housekeeper Luz opens up before my hand is off the button. "Your Uncle has the board set up in the library. He told me to tell you," cough, erm, "'My pussy nephew is gonna go down.' Sorry, those were his words, not mine." Luz blushes. And Mom wonders why I don't want to come play chess with him every day this summer.

I barge inside and don't even ask Guy to come in, because I know he's going to follow me. I run up the stairs to the library, taking them two at a time. The doors of the library are slightly cracked and I burst through them in an overly dramatic sort of way. "What the fuck did you have to do this morning?" I demand. Uncle Olsen is sitting on my side of the board. He's really on my fucking nerves today.

"Who is this?" Uncle Olsen stands up.

"I'm Guy. Ben's, uh, friend. He said we could play chess on a board instead of a computer," Guy's voice cracks.

"No, we aren't doing this yet. You know I can't function if you don't tell me," I interrupt the banter that is about to take place between Guy and Uncle Olsen. The dance all chess dickheads do, seeing how smart their opponent is.

"Fine you nosey little creep. I went to get fitted for a new suit. I have a wedding to attend in a few weeks and I need something lighter for the impending heat wave. Are you satisfied Benjamin?" Uncle Olsen's phrasing is so condescending I'm pretty sure he might bend over to sniff his own ass. That look on his face shows just how proud of himself he is for embarrassing me in front of someone new. And a wedding? Who the fuck is getting married. My fingers start tapping on my leg uncontrollably.

"Oh, new suit," is all I mumble.

"Now, are we playing? I have been practicing a few tricks. My goal is to beat you in six moves or less today."

"Ha! You want to throw some money on it?" Guy comes up behind me and puts his arm around my shoulder. Like we are bros. Like we are more than stalker and prey. Part of me wants to believe it, that we could be more. But, part of me knows damn well Guy is playing a game. Just like I'm playing a game with him. Does he suspect he's leading me down a rabbit hole I might never come out of. Is he getting off on it? I turn my head towards him, while he stares at Uncle Olsen. I breathe him in and I don't hide it.

"A wager? Well, that's interesting. We've never done that now, have we Benjamin? Do you think your Mother will oppose?"

Uncle Olsen pulls out his wallet. "Not that I think you could afford it. You've never worked, as far as I'm aware."

"How about we wager something other than money," Guy answers for me. I don't know where he's going with this. I can only hope he doesn't pull up his sleeve to flash his gun tattoo again. That won't go over well with Uncle Olsen.

"I'm listening." Uncle Olsen puts his wallet away.

"How about we wager a phone call," Guy replies.

"A phone call? To whom may I ask?" Uncle Olsen asks with a shit eating grin on his face. My toes curl. What does Guy think he's doing? I've never beat Uncle Olsen at chess. This is ridiculous. I wanted Guy to help me! To finally beat Uncle Olsen. Now, somehow I'm being roped into a bet that I never agreed to. I have to say something—Guy is making a complete fool of himself. He's turning into a Street Screamer.

"To the admissions department at MIT," Guy says. He does that thing again, with his shoulders and jerks, the phantom spider is back.

Uncle Olsen narrows his eyes with suspicion.

"Benjamin. You think you can walk into my house and bring some street trash and trick me into calling MIT for you? You're even more out of your mind than I thought! You told me a year ago you'd given up hopes of attending when you couldn't pass Advanced Calculus," Uncle Olsen kicks back in his chair. He opens his mouth like he's going to say more, but I cut him off.

"Listen to me, I put up with your constant shit, to make Mom happy. But, the call isn't for me. It's for my friend Guy here—and he's not street trash. He's brilliant. A 4.0 student. He published a paper that is going to revolutionize the way we understand perpetual motion. His father is Senator Rasken." I'm furious and embarrassed. Uncle Olsen has always treated me like a pariah—but, never in front of someone who mattered to me. Guy was supposed to be a nobody. Someone I obsessed over in the shadows. Someone I stalked when he wasn't looking. Someone I wrote long, shameful poems for, but folded them over in my notebook. I didn't know when I followed him a few weeks ago that I'd feel this way about him. A desire so strong it's eating me alive.

"Wait, Ben, what the fuck man. How do you know about my fucking grades, and the paper I wrote or who my father is?" Guy shoves me away from him.

"Your friend seems to be a little agitated, Benjamin. Are you still sure you want to wager his future at MIT on your ability to beat me at chess in six moves or less?" Uncle Olsen's eyes are gleaming. He thinks he's got me backed into a corner.

"You knew exactly what I was," I snap at Guy. "And yes, I'm going to kick your ass." I sit down at white. In my mind, I know every move Uncle Olsen is going to make. I look at him. I know this mood, it always lends to him playing fast and sloppy. And I'm prepared—maybe I've been playing online chess for a week with someone named GuysGun007 who taught me the Hippopotamus Defense. I'll make myself look vulnerable and stupid. Uncle Olsen will take the bait and I'll get that phone call for Guy. I chuckle, and I told Guy I wanted him to help me win—guess that was another one of the lies I tell myself.

But, before we can start, Guy grabs my arm. "We need to talk Ben." His grip is hard, unyielding. I welcome the pain—it triggers something dark inside of me. I let him pull me up from the chair and out into the hallway. Uncle Olsen is laughing in the background.

"Do you want the call to MIT or not?" I pull my arm out of his grasp.

"You're fucked up man," Guy says, his voice low and raspy. He looks at me with those eyes, they are filled with rage and desire. I don't know if it's actual desire for me, or lust for the game we are playing with Uncle Olsen and each other. But, I don't have time to figure him out right now. I only have time to win this match. I look at my watch.

"I told you, I have OCD. I'm fucking obsessive. I followed you that day and couldn't get you out of my mind. I searched online—it didn't really take much to figure out who you were. Since your dad is a Senator and you've been published. You're brilliant and I can't stop man, I want—" I pause. I see him balling up his fists. Yep, Street Screamer Guy is about to punch me.

But then Guy takes a deep breath and lets his shoulders and fists relax.

Our eyes lock. I don't look away, my body is urging me forward.

"Look Ben, you think it's easy being me? I'm fucking mental and it's really hard for me to meet people who might get me. But, I have boundaries bro. If you want to know the real me, you have to respect me. After this shit with your Uncle, I'm leaving for some air," he says. He's so close to me now, I could taste him if I wanted to. And I really fucking want to. I tap on my leg and Guy reaches over and laces his fingers through mine to settle my vibrations. "But, I'm gonna call you tonight, so we can laugh about the look in your Uncle's eye after you beat his sorry ass."

I smile and lean my head in, Guy leans his in too and we rest forehead to forehead for a few seconds. Our skin, hot and sticky. I catch myself before I lean in to kiss him. "Yeah, that

180

sounds good," I whisper. Every atom in me is now focused on one thing and one thing only. Beating Uncle Olsen so I can talk to Guy on the phone tonight and hear his laughter. Maybe I'll record our conversation so I can listen to it over and over. I'll imagine all the things Guy and I will do. I'll write devious stories about our college years, after I apply and get accepted at MIT. I'll draw pictures of what our apartment looks like. And write hot nasty poems about what we do behind closed doors. My body aches.

I don't even remember going back into the Library.
I don't remember beating Uncle Olsen.

I look at my watch. Guy should be calling any second.

Paranoia

by Rodaina Yasser
Third Place

It smelled like rotten eggs in here. Like a hundred rotten eggs all brought together. Whenever I smell something bad, it takes me a few minutes to get used to it. But now... it's been exactly fourteen days and I could still smell it. The strong stench of rotting flesh. I took a deep breath through my mouth and gagged. When I opened my mouth, I could taste the smell. I hadn't cried once since it happened. I hadn't talked to anyone. At first, I didn't know if he was dead or just sleeping. So I called for him, '*dad, are you awake?*', I'd asked. '*Dad*', I'd said again. He didn't even stir. I walked outside his room and sat in the living room.

A day went by. Then another, and another. He never woke up. With every passing day, thoughts screamed louder in my mind. With every minute I counted on the clock, the feeling that I was lost intensified. Not once had I imagined anything like this would happen. The shock of seeing my father's lifeless body lying in bed kept me from acting. It blinded me from believing it. He was surely asleep. Just asleep.

The smell started on the fourth day. I'd walked up the stairs again, opened his bedroom door and had to swallow back my vomit. His skin was a greenish colour and drool spilled from the corner of his mouth. Yellowish liquid dampened the mattress beneath him. I was thankful, though, that his eyes were closed.

I didn't cry. I didn't actually do anything. I didn't fall to my knees and weep. I didn't feel sad. I didn't feel the sorrow of his death. I didn't feel anything. I covered my nose and mouth with the sleeve of my shirt and walked over to the window by his bed, I opened it. Then I checked every other window in our house and opened them all, hoping the smell would fade away with the wind. I shut his door and went back to the living room. I sat on the couch and curled my knees up to my chest and just sat there.

I'd been sitting on the couch ever since.

I tried to think about anything that would distract me. To erase the image of his body from my mind, but nothing came to mind. I wasn't prepared for this. I'd never thought about this day and what I would do had it come. The first few days after I found him, I was numb. Completely numb. My mind was numb. My body was numb. I didn't sleep. And then, questions sprang in my mind, thoughts I'd never considered before, the worst fears I'd ever had grew until they consumed me. I knew I was supposed to be grieving. But the only thing I was thinking about was what I was going to do now.

On the last four of the past fourteen days, the panic started to settle in. I remember my father's words about decomposition, he'd told me about all its stages during one of our science lessons. We were studying animal's decomposition but he told me that humans also smell if they haven't been found for several days. I knew the smell would travel with the wind until it couldn't anymore. Our house stood alone, away from the other houses and away from people. Father always told me it was better to stay away.

But what if the smell was stronger than the wind, what if it travelled as far as the other houses. In our science lesson, dad didn't tell me how far the smell goes.

I hugged my knees closer to my chest as my eyes found the puddle of vomit on the floor. Every time I saw it, my stomach flipped and I tasted bile at the back of my throat. But I couldn't move away. I couldn't move from the couch. I didn't dare move around the house without my dad. What would I do without him now? Where would I go? I could just stay here forever. On this couch. I'm sure the smell would go away. Even if it didn't, it was better than risking anybody finding us. My father kept us away from everyone for a reason, he always told me. I ought not leave the house, whatever happened. He never told me exactly why we had to stay in but he always warned me about the world outside. About people and their cruelty.

And that's why my heart nearly jumped out of my chest when I heard it. The doorbell. The sound was so unfamiliar. So scary. I never even noticed we had a doorbell.

What if they're here to take me away? What about everything my father warned me about?

I pressed myself further against the back of the couch. The doorbell rang once again, filling the house with its sound, echoing across the walls, and growing a greater fear in my chest. I didn't move. Once it rang for the third time, my body began to rock back and forth. I couldn't control my breathing. I couldn't control my fear. They were probably here to take me away. They probably want to hurt me.

I heard a loud thud, followed by footsteps. More than one pair of feet, they headed towards me. I buried my head in my knees and the rocking didn't stop. The footsteps began to slow down, and then one after the other, they stopped. Only the sound of shuffling could be heard.

184

"Miss?" I heard the voice and flinched. It was strange. Unfamiliar. I've never heard anyone's voice but my father's, and my mother's when I was younger. The voice repeated, "Miss, can you hear me?"

I wanted to remove my head from my knees, I wanted to look at the man speaking. But I couldn't. Something stopped me. Doubts and bad thoughts, images of my mother crying ran through my mind.

"Miss, I need to know if you're okay." He spoke again. "We got a call about a really bad smell. Do you live alone?"

No, no, no, they'd found out. They were going to take me away. I slowly lifted my head and my eyes fell on the man closest to me. Without knowing it, I was flinching away from him. I let my eyes stroll around the living room. Two other men, all dressed in blue uniforms stood behind the one close to me, both grimacing and covering their noses.

"How old are you, dear?"

He tried to make eye contact with me but I looked away. I saw him gagging a little as I turned my head.

"You don't look okay. Can you tell me your name at least? I'm here to help you."

His voice sounded nice enough. "Emma. I'm sixteen."

"Who do you live with, Emma?"

"My..." I couldn't say it. I don't live with him anymore, "I live with my father."

"Is he here right now?"

My eyes lingered towards the stairs. "He's dead."

The clock ticked above me. *Tick, tock,* again, and again. I counted sixty of them–seven times. I blocked out every other sound except the ticking of the clock; the only familiar sound in the room. I looked around, taking in every aspect of the room. How different it was, compared to the comfort of my house. A strange feeling got mixed up with my fear, curiosity. I've always wondered what the outside world looked like, if everything looked the same as our house.

My hands shook as I tried to grab the glass of water in front of me. One of the police officers who took me from home told me to drink it and I also had to eat the apple next to it. He apologised for not having proper food but told me I had to eat it. I didn't trust him. I didn't trust anyone. The glass trembled in my grasp. I stared at the glass until I'd counted another sixty ticks before putting it back on the table. I'd been sitting in that chair for eight and a half minutes and I already wanted to leave.

I jumped when the door to the office opened and looked up. I wanted to go back to the safety of home. It's ironic really, when I was a little girl, all I remembered was wanting to leave the house to play outside and meet other kids. But as I grew older and as I heard more of my father's warning, I started to dread the day I stepped across the front door. Now, I'm finally and after sixteen years, outside. I just want this to be over so I can go back and never leave again.

"Emma," the man said and took a seat in the chair opposite of me. "You didn't eat. Or drink the water."

I didn't say anything. He sighed.

"Emma, you need to eat something. You haven't eaten anything in days, have you?" He asked. I just shook my head. "Well, it's important that you eat this apple. And drink the water. I'll see if I can get you anything else to eat."

Not one word came out of me. My hands shook harder.

"I'm sorry about your father." The policeman said. I doubted he was sorry. Why would he be? He didn't kill him, illness did. "Do you have any other family?"

I shook my head again.

"Is that why you didn't call anyone when you found him?"

I found my voice, fighting the instinct to remain silent. "Yes. I don't know anyone but him."

"I see. That's a horrible sight for a daughter to find her father like that. I'm sure you were in shock, that's why you didn't call us."

No, I didn't call the police because I didn't want them to take me away from the only place I've ever known.

"What school do you go to? I didn't find your records in any nearby school."

I wanted to ask him why he searched my name in schools but I'm scared to voice the question. I'm scared he'd find it challenging. "I was homeschooled by my father."

He gave out a hum and nodded to himself. Something about him didn't sit right with me, the way he leaned back, crossed one leg over the other, and narrowed his eyes at me. But who am I to judge? I only ever talked to my father and didn't know how people interact with each other. While I've heard my father speaking on his phone before, he always yelled, hung up, let out an exasperated sigh, and found me watching him from the doorway. He'd complain about the stupidity of people and tell me how he wanted to keep me safe from their brutality.

"It's always better to stay away from people, Emma." He used to say. *"You'll think you know someone... but then they'll just*

186

sell you out for money, for anything." He'd tell me after he hung up the phone.

"What are you going to do with me now?" I allowed my eyes to lift up to those of the policeman.

He looked at me and frowned. "Emma, do you think we're keeping you here because you did something?"

I shrugged.

"You're still a minor. Do you know the process we go through in situations like this?" He asked. I shook my head. "Okay, there are some steps that we need to take before you can settle in. The court's going to decide on your guardian. Usually it's a family member or someone a deceased parent named in their will. Given that you're sixteen, you're not a little kid, the court will likely give you a say in who you stay with."

"I want to stay at my house." I said in a small voice. "I have no remaining family. None that I know, anyway. I want to go back home."

He sighed, leaned forward, then pursed his lips. "I'm really sorry this is happening to you," he said. And then he was gone and I was left alone again, the ticking of the clock filling the room once more.

Uneasiness, it's all I felt as I was led to the common area. I could hear my heartbeat banging in my chest; the sound was dull and strong. My fingers fiddled with each other, I tried to stop but the apprehension was too strong. I felt people's eyes on me. I heard their thoughts from the look in their eyes.

You can't trust anyone. My father's voice rang in my head.

Turns out, my father didn't write a will. I had no remaining family from my father's side, only my mother's side; all of whom I had never met. I didn't even know they existed until the policeman told me.

But of course, they didn't want to take in a girl they'd never met. The police didn't tell me exactly what they said, but I heard the word *lunatic* come up in conversation with one of his colleagues.

So here I was in an orphanage at sixteen years old–a group home for orphans, so they'd called it. When I arrived, an old woman led me through the hallway. Her steps were too fast for my liking and I practically ran after her. I didn't get why she was in a hurry, I wasn't going anywhere. I was trapped in a place I didn't know.

She stopped abruptly and I almost ran into her back. She turned and faced me, her eyes ran down my body with what looked like contempt. I felt the tug in my stomach and started fiddling with my fingers.

"My name is Katherine Smith, I am the caregiver in charge of this section," she said, eyeing my hands. "Right now, we're going into the common area, you'll be able to meet the other kids soon, they usually come around this time." My fingers stop moving under her gaze. "Everyone here is just like you, you should be able to fit in."

As she spoke, I could only concentrate on the way her eyes kept sizing me up as if I was a threat to this place.

In reality, I'm the one that should be wary of them. Nothing about the way she looked or spoke made me feel safe.

I gave a forced nod and followed her into the room. The second I stepped inside, my knees started to shake and I found it hard to breathe. Twelve pairs of eyes with different expressions were fixed on me.

I heard a voice in my head, *"Escape, now. Run".* I recognized it–the voice of my father. Yet, I froze to my spot. I wanted to speak, maybe even smile at everyone. Maybe they weren't as bad as dad had made them out to be and deserved a second chance.

"Never trust anyone but yourself," The voice continued. All at once, his stories about the people outside our house came back to me. I opened my mouth but nothing came out. And nothing came in. I couldn't breathe. Suddenly my hand was clutching at my chest and I fell to my knees.

I heard the wheezing of my lungs and I saw the kids gathered around me. My eyes started to burn and I started to see everything blurry.

"Breathe, Emma." My father's voice echoed in my head again. *"In, and out, Emma, it's easy."*

I tried. It's not that easy, dad. In, and out. I breathed until I couldn't hear my wheezing anymore and my vision cleared. Once I was able to breathe again, everyone went back to their previous positions. Some sitting together and talking. Some were playing. Some were arguing.

Only one kid remained. As she stood over me, I noticed she was tall and big as I looked up at her from the ground. The look on her face was what I imagined the one my father always warned me from looked like.

"Weirdo." She spat, turned and walked away. I looked for the lady that brought me here, Katherine Smith. She wasn't around, she'd left already and I was alone, sitting by the wall with my knees hugged close to my chest. All the while thinking of how life could move so fast, how this all felt like a bad dream.

188

A week passed. I still hadn't spoken to anyone and very few tried to talk to me. Every time someone tried, my father's voice told me to be careful. Most of the kids started to call me a *freak*.

Most of the time, I sat in the back of the room, hidden from the mean eyes of the other kids. That was until someone found me in the back and sat next to me. A boy that looked to be around my age. I'd noticed him staring at me more than once before.

"Hi." He said. I didn't look at him. "My name's Miles. I know yours is Emma."

I tilted my head to the side and saw a smile on his face. It didn't look mean nor did it look deceiving, it was just a smile. I tried to believe that he was just nice. I tried to push my father's voice to the back of my mind and give Miles a chance. I wanted to try. But every doubt I had about him and about everyone else was awakened whenever someone talked to me. Whenever someone even looked at me.

"I'm sixteen, just like you," he continued, "my mother gave me up because she couldn't handle me, she said I was too much to deal with, and my father died before I could meet him. I bet he couldn't handle *her*." His face contorted in a bitter smile.

"I didn't ask you." I found myself saying. I found myself feeling more protected like that. But the way his smile fell away made feel an unfamiliar feeling, like I wanted to erase what I'd just said.

"Don't let your guard down, Emma". I heard his voice again. *"That's how they manipulate you."* That's how Miles was manipulating me, by making me feel safe at first. Just like the person my father yelled at on the phone, before he'd told me never to trust anyone.

"I know you're scared. I'm trying to make you feel more welcomed here–more at home." Miles said. There was a kind of warmth about his voice.

I lifted my head to look at him. "This isn't home."

He smiled, but this smile looked sad. "I know." He said, paused for a moment, then spoke again. "So, how'd you end up here?"

"My father died."

"And your mother?"

My mother. I gazed into the distance and lost focus of my surroundings. An image formed itself in front of me. A young woman with strawberry blonde hair–like mine–and freckles that dotted her cheeks and the bridge of her nose. Her bright green eyes, so vivid like the colour of fresh grass. She looked so full of life, yet something in her eyes was broken. She danced around the

189

house and sang with a beautiful voice. Suddenly, a tear dropped from her eye.

"Emma?"

I snapped out of my trance. The picture of my broken mother faded away. I looked at Miles, feeling my own eyes burning. I hadn't thought about my mother in years. I'd started to forget the features of her face. But I held onto her eyes and her beautiful voice. "My mother died when I was little."

Miles opened his mouth, about to say something, but I got up and sat on the other side of the room.

I jolted up in bed, breathing heavily with sweat dripping down my back. I didn't feel safe sleeping in a room with three other girls. I didn't feel safe sleeping in a bed that wasn't mine, in a place that wasn't my house. I remember when I'd look out the window from my room and freak out when I'd see someone walking by and look up at our house. I remember how I'd wonder if I'd make it out there. And now I'm out there.

I sat in bed, curled up against the wall, until morning came and Katherine Smith came to take us to breakfast.

Miles sat next to me again. He was smiling. The same smile from yesterday. I didn't know what he was up to. Why would he be nice when everyone else was calling me a freak?

"Good morning."

I gave him a smile that I'm sure came out as a grimace. He looked away and dug into his eggs. I tried to ignore the feeling that people were watching me. That they were talking about me. 'Weirdo', I heard from the far end of the table. I didn't look. 'Crazy mother' I heard again. This time I turned, the group of girls at the end of the table were whispering together and sparing glances in my direction. I tried to pretend they weren't talking about me, then when I turned away from them, I saw Miles looking at me weirdly. His green eyes were fixed on mine and his eyebrows were furrowed. I noticed the freckles on his cheeks for the first time. They gave him a younger look. My mother's face appeared in my head again, how her freckles always gave her a younger look.

"They'll get tired of it."

"What?"

His smile returned. "They'll tire from talking about you at some point. Don't listen to them."

I looked at those girls again. They were huddled together at the end of the table and whispering. Miles He spoke again. "I've known them since we were kids. They used to talk about me."

"Why?"

190

"Mostly because my mother abandoned me, but they like to talk about anyone." He shrugged. "Why do they talk about you?"

"Because they think I'm crazy. I've never left the house, but I'm not crazy, I just feel…" My voice trailed off. I didn't know why I was talking to him, why I was telling him how I was feeling and defending myself.

"What do you feel?"

"I feel… scared. Paranoid."

"I was scared, too."

In the common area, one of the girls approached me. "I heard your father locked you in the house and didn't allow you to leave for years. Is that true?"

I ignored her, like Miles told me to.

"I heard he used to lock your mother, too, until she went crazy."

I looked at her and stood up. "Don't you dare talk about my mother." I said then stormed away from her and headed to my room, wishing I had a better comeback. I didn't want to hang in the common area. I didn't want to see anyone. I wanted to go back home and never leave. My father was right, people were cruel. He was right to keep me inside all these years. I used to hate him at first. Until I saw why he did it. I saw that he was protecting me. He wanted to keep me safe from life's brutality. The same brutality that killed my mother, when she left the house and came back changed. When she thought it was best to take her life.

With the image of my mother in my mind, I snuck out of my room and to the drug storage room I knew was around the corner at the end of the hallway. I walked, seeing nothing but my mother. Her smile was gone. The green of her eyes were dull. Her skin was pale.

I don't feel alive. I left my soul back home when they took me away. And I intended to go back.

I opened the door and found what I had been looking for. I remembered the name of the drug, the shape of the bottle. My mother was sick of staying inside. My father let her out. He was only trying to protect her, like he was protecting me. But she didn't know that. She came back. I still see her. On the bathroom floor, with the empty bottle next to her lifeless body. The same bottle in my hand right now.

I walked back to my room and sat on my bed. How could I live like this any longer? Feeling scared every time someone looked at me and living in fear of what they said or how they would hurt me. I opened the bottle. I could see my father's body on his bed. Nearly a month after it happened, it hit me that he was dead. I closed my eyes when I felt tears coming and began swallowing the pills One after the other. Tears fell down my cheeks. The bottle had completely emptied by the time I started to sob. It slipped through my fingers and I heard it hit the floor. I fell back onto the bed and let the darkness consume me. Finally feeling joy at regaining my soul.

Are You Sure?

by Amber Felt
Fourth Place

Mia raised the shot glass and nodded to the two strangers across the bar. She tipped her head back and downed the golden liquid in a quick burning swallow.

"Woo!" she hollered, banging the glass down on the pine.

"Mia, slow down," Amy said.

"I've had one drink so far, relax." She smiled at the cuter of the two and he winked back at her. "Besides, it's rude to not accept a free drink."

"We have to get up early for work tomorrow. Just think about that before you get too crazy."

The bartender stepped in front of them blocking Mia's view. He refilled the shot glass. "Another tequila from the two gentlemen over there," he gestured with the bottle as he walked back toward the register.

"I'm not going to go crazy." Mia drank the second shot.

Amy shook her head and turned around, resting her back up against the bar. A flash under Mia's shirt caught her attention. She reached down and lifted the crimson polyester up an inch exposing a glittering belt looped through her jeans.

"Is that new?"

"Yeah, isn't it gorgeous? I was on my way to lunch and it sparkled at me from the window at Binzo's. I just had to have it."

Amy dropped the cloth and it fell over the gaudy accessory. "I thought you maxed out your credit cards?"

She waved her off. "It's fine. I have money in the bank."

"Mia! Our rent is due next week. Are you going to have your half this time?"

"It'll be fine," she repeated.

"It's not fine," Amy scolded. "I can't keep bailing you out. You need to think before you do things. For longer than a few seconds!"

"I made my bonus today. I'll have more than enough. Okay? Now relax. Lighten up a little. You need to *stop* thinking so much."

Amy scowled.

"Did you get that look from my mother?"

"Did you ever think maybe it's an expression you have a knack for invoking?"

"Smile and pull that stick out of your ass. Heads up."

Amy glanced over her shoulder. The two men were approaching. Her scowl deepened.

"Hi, ladies," the blonde, stocky man said.

"Hi," Mia's voice deepened as she dragged the word out slow and smooth. She looked sideways through slowly batting lashes at his dark, muscular companion.

"Our friend's band is playing up the road. Would you like to join us there?" the blonde continued.

"No, thank you," Amy said quickly.

"Oh, live a little," Mia said. "We'd love to."

The men grinned. "Excellent," the blonde said, and they turned and made their way toward the door through the dim, crowded room.

Amy protested as Mia began to follow. "Where are you going? Are you crazy?"

"This place is lame. I love live music. Let's go!"

"No way."

"Please. Pretty please. With a cherry on top." She curled her bottom lip under and wiggled it.

Mia had been making the same pleading pout face since elementary school. Amy's jaw muscles relaxed slightly. She sighed.

"Mia, I don't want to. What place are they even talking about? And what if the band sucks? What if they're murders? What if—"

"Amy, come on now. They are just two cute guys who want to go hang out at some other bar. There's no harm in that." She made her way toward the exit without waiting for her friend to object again.

Amy trailed along behind her.

Outside under the darkening spring sky, the girls huddled closer together. They made their way through the lively cluster of smokers milling about the patio. The men were waiting at the edge of the parking lot. Mia ignored the goosebumps forming on her forearms and thrust her chin out into the chilly breeze.

"Can we give you a ride?" The blonde asked.

"Absolutely not," Amy almost yelled.

He put his hands up defensively. "Okay, okay. I just thought you might like to see our new car. We just bought it today. We've been trying to show it off." He pointed toward the back of the lot. "It's a Ferrari."

Mia whistled. "Sexy!" She started walking in the direction of the red vehicle parked several rows back.

"What are you doing?" Amy grabbed her shoulder.

"I just want to see it," she tucked her arm under her own and tugged her along. "Then we'll drive over ourselves."

Amy rolled her eyes but walked along with her friend and the two strangers.

Mia walked carefree over the blacktop, in and out of the bright white lights shining from overhead.

The blonde bent down and reached for his shoe. "Sorry, just a second," he said.

There was a sliding sound behind the group. Amy glanced over and saw the side door of a van opening and a man emerging. She opened her mouth but no sound came out. She tightened her grip on Mia's arm. Mia glanced over just as the dark haired man came up behind her and covered her mouth before she could make a sound. The blonde man grabbed Amy, shoving a rag in her mouth. They dragged the girls toward the van as the third man approached.

Mia stared into her friend's bulging, terror filled eyes. The blonde man and the man from the van began hoisting Amy up through the door. Mia was panic stricken for only a moment. Then she began biting at the dark haired man's hand. She couldn't sink her teeth into flesh, they kept sliding down and smacking into each other. She wriggled and writhed. She planted her feet and pushed, attempting to jump up and down. She arched her back against her assailant. He struggled to hold on to her and keep her mouth firmly covered. Finally, she threw a heel back as hard as she could, landing a solid blow. His hand slipped an inch and Mia screamed an ear splitting screech.

Thundering footsteps ricocheted through the parking lot as the crowd of smokers rushed toward the commotion.

Mia's mouth was covered again after only an instant. She continued to buck and twist as the dark haired man pulled her towards the open van door. The blonde grabbed ahold of her and the two lifted.

"Hey, what's going on over there?" Several smokers were racing over to them.

Mia kicked forward this time, connecting with the blonde's testicles.

He doubled over, letting go of her.

The dark haired man flung her to the ground and wrenched open the passenger door of the van. He slid into the seat as the van engine turned over.

Mia jumped up and reached into the van. She grabbed Amy's hand as the blonde crawled in through the open door. She pulled her friend toward her. The blonde grabbed a hold of her ankle.

The van began backing up rapidly as a few of the smokers arrived and grabbed hold of Amy too. The blonde surrendered, letting go of her petrified body. She fell out of the van and thumped on the ground as Mia and the smokers were thrown backward from the sudden velocity.

The van tires screeched as it began lurching forward. Amy lay in shock on the pavement. Mia screamed "Amy!" as the back passenger tire ran over her friend.

When Amy was finally released from the hospital, Mia was entrusted with her care. She pushed her friend's wheelchair down the hall and toward the elevators. Both her legs were wrapped in thick white casts. They waited for the doors to open in silence. They rode the elevator in silence. Mia wheeled her out into the parking lot in silence.

Mia was elated that her biweekly visits to the cold, sick halls of the downtown medical center were finally over. She looked forward to helping Amy heal at home and hoped to heal their relationship as well. The two hadn't spoken much. Amy had been heavily sedated at first. Over time, she had stopped looking at Mia when she'd come in and sit down. Didn't say hello. Didn't say goodbye when she would finally stand up and leave.

Amy's parents had visited at first, but they lived thousands of miles away. Mia had assured them she would take care of Amy and they had flown back to their jobs, mortgage and other bills.

Now Mia helped Amy into the passenger seat, folded up her wheelchair and placed it into the trunk. They began the drive to their apartment in silence.

At one particularly long traffic light, Mia broke the silence.

"Amy, I am really sorry about what happened." She turned to her friend, but Amy stared straight ahead out the window. "I feel terrible that you were injured, but at least we're both alive. At least we... got away."

Amy said nothing.

"There's nothing else we could have done."

"Are you sure?" Amy finally looked at Mia with eyes squinted, head slightly cocked.

"What do you mean? We fought back. We escaped."

"We could have avoided the whole ordeal! If you would just *think* before you do things!"

The light turned green and Mia focused on driving. She welcomed the excuse to not respond.

"If that didn't wake you up, what's it going to take? Does something terrible have to happen to *you* to make you change? You should've been the one who got run over. This should be you," she gestured at her lame legs. "You should have pins and rods and pain—"

Mia pulled into their driveway and put the car in park. Her heart ached for her friend. She swallowed hard.

"I'm sorry," said Amy. "I don't wish anyone this much pain. I just worry about you. If you don't start showing a little restraint, something bad *will* happen to you."

"I know, Amy. I know. I'll work on it."

"You know," Amy continued as Mia helped get her in her wheelchair. "I started talking to someone while I was in recovery. A therapist. Might be something you should consider."

"A therapist? Amy, really. So I'm a little impulsive sometimes. I really don't think that warrants counseling."

"We could have been raped. Murdered! And you still don't think it's a problem?"

Mia's chest tightened for a moment. She couldn't handle the thought of losing her best friend. But she didn't lose her. She did what she had to to save her. Her Dad's face flashed through her mind. If only her mother had let Mia go with him that day, maybe she could have saved him. She had wanted to ride on the back of his big new motorcycle so badly. But her mother wouldn't hear of it. Maybe Mia would've seen the car that hit him, maybe she could have warned him.

"*Or maybe you would've died too,*" her mother always said.

She shook the thoughts away, forcing herself to focus on the moment at hand. She opened their front door and wheeled Amy through.

"What would it help to talk to a therapist?"

"You'd be surprised. Having someone to hold you accountable for your actions... help you see what it is you're doing... It's eye opening."

Mia was about to change the subject when she pushed Amy into the living room. She was shocked to see her mother sitting on the couch.

"What are you doing here?" Mia asked.

"It's nice to see you too sweetheart."

Mia rolled her eyes. She crossed her arms and leaned up against the door frame.

Her mother stood up and approached Amy with outstretched arms.

"How are you, you poor thing?" She bent over and wrapped her arms around Amy and the back of the chair, squeezing her shoulders and the hard plastic.

"I'm ok. I mean, I've been better," they chuckled. "But I'll be ok."

"Mom, what are you doing here?" Mia asked again.

"I just thought I'd come stay for a while. Help Amy out."

"Stay? No, Mom really—"

"That would be wonderful." Amy cut her off. "Especially while Mia is at work. I could really use the extra help."

Mia sighed. She couldn't begrudge her friend the assistance. But she felt like a child again with her mother butting in and trying to run her life.

"Where is your car, Mom?"

"I parked on the street. I didn't want to take your spot."

No, just my space. She huffed. "Fine, Mom. You win." She walked into the room and sat in the recliner in front of the window.

"Win? Honey, there is no 'winning' here. I'm just cleaning up your mess. Like I have had to do your whole life."

"Oh, here we go."

Amy spun her wheels, rolling herself into the middle of the room. "Stop now. Please? I've just gotten home after a very, *very* long time. And I would just like a little peace."

Mia's mother sat back down on the couch. "Of course, hon. Whatever you need."

"Humph!"

"Mia," Amy admonished. "Your mom is here to help us both really."

"That's right," her mother agreed. "She's always been stubborn," she said to Amy. "But she's gotten worse as she's gotten older. She's really just a big child. No self-restraint. No control." She turned toward Mia. "When are you going to start being more responsible? When will you learn to practice a little delayed gratification?"

"What I do is none of your business. I'm a grown woman!"

"Then start acting like one!"

"I am fully capable of taking care of myself. Obviously, I think things through when it's important."

"Are you sure?" Amy asked.

Mia whipped her head toward Amy. "What is this, an intervention?"

"We just care about you Mia," Amy said.

Mia threw her hands up. "I can't believe this." She stood up and stormed out of the house.

Mia sat near the edge of the water. A few families were spread out on the beach, but it was fairly quiet. The sun was setting to her left. The air was warm though the gentle breeze bit at her cheeks. She stared out into the orange streaked surf. Kicking her shoes off in front of her, she absentmindedly dug her heels into the sand and scrunched her toes.

I am not that *bad*, she thought to herself. *So I buy things I don't need. And occasionally drink too much. Who doesn't? I deliberate serious matters.*

She watched the pink tipped orange waves sloppily sliding left and right as they bobbed closer to the shore.

Don't I…?

She tried to think of any big decisions she made in her life. Her job, her living arrangement. Everything seemed to just fall into place. She hadn't needed to think about it. She was always in the right place at the right time.

Besides, she justified to herself, *nothing bad has happened, so what's the big deal? Well… besides almost getting kidnapped.*

She understood the gravity of that situation, but she failed to understand her mother and her friend's reaction.

They act like that was all my fault. I would've done things differently if I had known what was going to happen. But they are overreacting. There's nothing wrong with me.

Visions of past lovers danced by in the sparkling water. Tom, and Derek, and Donavon. At first she smiled. Thinking of how nice it had been to be courted. And the pleasant times they had. Then her back tensed and she grimaced.

She remembered the doctor's office and the shame she felt, though she told herself not to be embarrassed, and the relief of a prescription. She remembered staring at a pink line for 10 minutes straight praying a second line didn't appear. She remembered the phone call she received that prompted the next trip to the doctor. Remembered the terror she felt when she thought for sure the result was positive. And relief again when there was no death sentence.

Yet she still made the same mistakes.

I guess I could say no a little more often. To a lot of things. Or just… wait.

She thought about the shoes she bought the day before.

But no, you can't wait in life. The things you want will be gone. You have to strike while the iron's hot!

She thought about her father. He had always been so happy and carefree.

He didn't stop to think about possible consequences, he just did whatever he wanted. He loved life.

"Maybe you would've died too," her mother's words echoed in her mind.

She thought about Amy. What happened was awful, but no one could have known that was going to happen.

"*Are you sure?*" Amy's words rang out in her mind.

She groaned and slid her feet back into her shoes. Then she folded up her chair and headed back to her car, back to the apartment.

Her mother and Amy hadn't moved since she left. They were still sitting together in the living room. She sat back down in the recliner without saying a word.

After a few moments, Amy spoke. "Tell her," she said to Mia's mother.

"Tell me what?"

Her mother hesitated.

"It's important that you tell her the truth," Amy urged.

"Mom?"

"A car didn't hit your father," she finally blurted out.

"What?"

"He wasn't hit by a car. He—"

Amy nodded encouragingly.

"He got stopped at the Court Street drawbridge. The... the witnesses said he pulled up just as the lights were flashing and the gate came down. And he... he gunned it! He purposely sped toward the opening bridge. He was trying to jump it, Mia."

Mia sat speechless.

"He didn't make it."

"Why didn't you ever tell me?"

"I didn't want you to be angry. And hurt. Like I am. The idiot. The damned fool! How could he do this to us? How could he be so *stupid*?"

Mia pictured her father, hair blowing in the wind, speeding up the ramped bridge, huge smile on his face.

"Do you still think it would have been any different if you had been with him?" her mother asked. "No. He would've taken you along with him. Just like you and poor Amy here."

Mia didn't know what to say.

"Just talk to someone," Amy pleaded. "It's been really helpful for me. It might really work for you too."

"Ok, fine," Mia said. "I'll talk to someone."

"Great," Amy's smile beamed. "You can set something up when you take me to my next appointment."

Mia stumbled into the apartment. Amy was sitting at the kitchen table alone.

"Hey, you're home late," she said. "I've been waiting to hear how your appointment went today."

"Oh, it was ok, I guess. He wants me to write down every decision I make each day and how long I thought about it." She opened the fridge and started rummaging around inside.

"So, how's that going?" Amy asked.

"I didn't have anything to write down yet," Mia said, unwrapping a string cheese and biting it.

"Mia…?"

"Hmmm?"

"You just decided to eat cheese."

She was confused for a minute. Then she laughed. "That's silly. I'm not writing down every little thing."

Amy bit her lip. Then she said softly, "and I'm pretty sure you made the decision to drive home when you probably shouldn't have."

Mia spit the cheese out on the ground. "There. I won't eat the cheese. Happy? I won't do anything without chronicling it first." She threw the rest of the cheese in the garbage as she left the kitchen.

The next day at work, Mia's boss called her into his office and asked her to take on a new project.

Mia immediately responded "yes," but then she backtracked for a second. "Actually, I – uh—need to think about that and get back to you."

"Are you feeling ok?" he asked. "You have been dying to be the lead on a big assignment."

"I know, but—it's just that—I –" she watched impatience creep over his face. "Yes! Of course I want it," she laughed. "Thank you!"

"I need you to fly to Toronto next week to prepare for the kickoff meeting."

"Oh… Toronto?"

"Is that a problem?"

"No. No, sir. No problem at all. Thank you for trusting me with such a big account."

I guess I better write that down. I thought about it… some.

Her therapist was not impressed. They met for the second time the day before her flight.

"You only wrote down a handful of things. For a full 7 days, these are all the decisions you faced? Not to mention, you are caring for an injured friend and you agreed to go out of town?"

"Well, my mother is helping…too."

"Mm-hmm," he scribbled notes on his pad.

"How does your friend feel about it?"

"I—uh—I don't know. Fine, I guess."

"Fine, you 'guess?' How do you think she might feel about it? Had you considered her feelings at all while making your decision?"

"No. I didn't think about Amy. I thought about what a great opportunity this was for my career. I didn't make a rash decision without considering the consequences. This is a good thing for me."

Mia couldn't believe how he twisted things around. She wasn't a bad friend. She needed to prioritize her career too.

"Alright. How about the things you haven't written down?"

"What?"

"Have you had any alcohol this week? Have you driven drunk? Have you had unprotected sex? Have you—"

"Look, I don't need to be chastised – I get that enough from my mother."

"Mia, I am not here to judge. Just to help. You won't see any progress unless you are completely honest. With me *and* yourself."

Mia thought about Amy. About her pleas to stay at that first bar, to not walk through the parking lot, to think about things before jumping in with both feet. She felt Amy's arm constricting her own, pictured her bulging eyes, a strange man's hand clamped over her mouth. She watched the van crushing her legs.

She imagined her father smiling as he leapt to his death.

"Ok, I did realize I made too hasty of a decision, but it was too late. Amy deserves to have me around to help her since it's my fault she's hurt in the first place, but I couldn't say no after I agreed or my boss would never give me another project like this."

Mia inhaled deeply and then looked down at her shoes as she exhaled.

"And yes," she said keeping her gaze down. "I've done all those things you asked about."

"Good. Very good Mia. This week, please write *everything* down. And make an effort to think – really think - about every single decision you make. No matter how small it may seem."

She agreed and left.

She arrived at her first appointment after she returned from her trip carrying a notepad. She had dark circles under bloodshot eyes. Her skin was pale, and her lips were chapped and cracked.

202

Her therapist greeted her in his usual warm way and motioned for her to sit in the chair across from his.

"How was your trip?" he began.

A tear slid out of her unblinking eye.

"I—have – a problem," she choked out.

She flipped open her notepad. Every line was filled in. Each line ended with a thick black 0 traced again and again.

"I can't wait," she said. "Even when I tell myself to think before I act, I *still* answer almost immediately. It's painful to physically force myself to wait and think. Look at this." She pointed halfway down the second page. "When I had to eat dinner my first night at the hotel, I told myself, *you are going to think about what to eat for 15 minutes*. 15 minutes! That's it. I couldn't do it! My brain felt squeezed. I tried to mentally catalog options and it was like my brain was vomiting. The weight built up and my head got heavy and I sank to the ground. Every few seconds, I would drift to thoughts of other things. I would force my brain to stop. Stop! Think about dinner! And it pounded back at me. I sat there for two minutes before giving up and saying this is stupid I'll just eat pizza."

"Now, Mia, you shouldn't—"

"It gets worse! Much, much worse. I thought, well, maybe I just really wanted pizza. I thought, this was just a dumb decision to focus on. So I got a great idea. I thought, I will put myself in a situation where I know I shouldn't do something. And see if I can not give into my whims."

"Mia, you need to follow my program. I just asked you to—"

"I went to the casino."

Her therapist sat back in his chair and crossed one leg over the other.

"I spent thousands of dollars. Thousands of dollars I don't have. What is wrong with me?"

"Well now, gambling, and addiction in general, that's something else entirely."

"I don't have a gambling problem. Well, maybe. But it's like I have an *everything* problem! I got propositioned. I couldn't even believe it. Maybe they prey on women alone at a casino, I don't know. I didn't even think male prostitutes were real. I—I said yes. He was one of the most handsome men I had ever seen in my life. At the time, it just seemed like an experience one doesn't have often. I felt like... I felt like I would regret missing out if I didn't do it."

"If you didn't sleep with a prostitute?"

"I don't know how to explain it. It's the same whether it's dinner or going to a casino or having sex with a stranger. Something seems like fun or it's something I want and I just—I just don't think. No matter how much I write down in this little notebook. No matter how much I realize I have a problem, I just can't stop myself."

"Realizing you have a problem is an important step."

"It's awful!" Mia shouted violently. "I didn't have a care in the world before. Now, I think about what I've done and realize the terrible things that could have happened. But I still don't think about these things beforehand. It's only after the fact. And they're haunting me!"

Her therapist paused for a moment. "There is an experimental treatment I can perform. It would essentially rewire your brain to always contemplate each decision before making your choice."

"You can do that?"

"Yes. Is that something you would be interested in?"

"Absolutely! Sign me up!"

"Are you sure?"

"Yes, I'm sure."

Her mother gave her a ride the day of the treatment. She was thrilled Mia was undergoing a 'positive change.' She was groggy afterward, and her mother ushered her home and put her to bed.

The next day Mia woke up for work and was struck with the crippling inability to make even the smallest decisions. She stood at her closet trying to choose an outfit to wear.

What if it's chilly? I can't wear a skirt. What if it rains? I can't wear white.

Amy knocked at her door. "Mia? Would you like some coffee?"

"I don't know," Mia responded. "If I don't have coffee, I will probably get a headache. But If I do have coffee, it might ruin my appetite. If I don't eat breakfast, then I'll be hungry before lunch. Then my stomach might grumble and everyone will think I have gas. But if I do drink coffee then I will have to go to the bathroom and I don't have time now because I am running so late."

Amy opened the door and rolled in.

"Are you alright? Hey, you're not even dressed yet. You are going to be late. You better hurry."

"I can't leave if I'm going to be late. I will run right into traffic. Traffic is the most dangerous time of the day to be on the

204

road. What if I get into an accident? I better just stay home. But if I stay home, I am going to lose my job! I can't lose my job!"

"You need to see your therapist," Amy said. "I'll call him. And I'll call work."

"No, I can't call in. I'll lose my job."

"Don't worry. I'll tell them you're sick."

"What if they find out I lied? What if—"

"Lay down!" Amy ordered. "I will tell your therapist it is an emergency and to please come here to see you."

Mia's head was spinning. She began to get nauseous. She laid down on top of her covers and let Amy take care of her.

The next knock on her door was her therapist.

"Come in," she said.

"How's the treatment going?" he asked approaching the bed.

Mia's mother and Amy hung back in the hallway.

"It's terrible!" Mia howled. "I can't do anything. I can't even function. I'm going to lose my job. I'm going to lose everything. How will I ever even leave this room? That treatment ruined my life!"

"Are you sure?" he asked.

"What do you mean, am I sure? I'm an agoraphobic basket case! And it's all because of the treatment!"

"Are you sure?"

"Why do you keep asking me that?" Mia sat up in her bed and stared at her therapist.

He stood silent, waiting for her to calm down and think.

"Oh my God," she finally said. "I did it again."

He nodded.

"I agreed to this treatment without ever once considering what might happen."

He nodded again.

Mia began sobbing. "What do I do now?"

"It's ok," he said soothingly. "We can reverse the treatment."

"You can?" she sniffled.

"Yes. I think it was a great learning experience, don't you? And with some time and effort, you and I can make great progress in curbing your impulsiveness."

"Are you sure?" Mia asked cautiously.

He nodded.

Her mother and Amy looked at each other and smiled.

The Pineapple Queen

by Kate MacGuire
Fifth Place

Annie hit the snooze feature on her alarm and snuggled deeper into Michael's arms. He responded by kissing the nape of her neck and growling, "Screw that alarm. Let's play hooky."

What a brilliant idea. One more hour of delicious sleep, then breakfast at The Happy Hen followed by who knows what. It would be such a welcome break from the whirlwind her life had become.

She shifted in his arms to face him. "Sorry, baby. I meet my new client today." After three years as an account executive at the Meyers and Bristol Public Relations Agency, she was finally being trusted with her own client account.

"Nervous?"

She groaned. "Not even close. How 'bout total stress case? Panic-stricken? Dazed and confused?"

He gave her a wise smile and kissed her on the nose. "You're overthinking it. You earned this a year ago. You were just too shy to ask."

She settled back in for another snuggle but then sat bolt upright. "Oh, crap! I almost forgot. I'm meeting with my mom and the wedding planner today."

He frowned in sympathy. "You poor thing. Sure you don't want to elope?"

"I just wanna get hitched and have a shing-ding. Don't know why we have to worry about linen tablecloths and bridesmaid dresses and all that. But my mom's already dropped ten thousand in non-refundable deposits, so I guess we're in it now." She leaned over for a kiss. "Besides, this is my one chance to see you wearing something other than scrubs."

"Anything other than scrubs is highly overrated."

She smiled and slugged him on the arm. "It's the least you can do since I'll be wearing ten pounds of tulle and lace if my mom gets her way."

"Well, tulle or tuxedos, I don't really care. All I want is to make sure the band gets booked for our reception. You did that, right?

Thankfully her snoozed alarm went off just then, giving her an excuse to roll away. The Roving Roosters was Michael's college band, before he took on the demanding schedule of medical school then surgical residency. The rest of the band stuck together and managed to get booked for small local events, like street festivals and bar mitzvahs.

"Um, not yet," she hedged, searching for the slippers under her bed. "Found them!" she popped up from under the bed, fuzzy bunny slippers in hand. He didn't smile back. "Oh baby, don't worry. I've just been busy, that's all. I'll call them first thing when I get to the office. Okay?"

He pushed himself up and off the bed, turning his back to her. "I'm starting to think you don't want them to play our reception."

Her heart sank. "No, that's not it" she reassured him. "I love The Roving Roosters!" And that was true. Michael's old bandmates were a great group of guys who had stuck together through job changes, marriages, and kids. Sure, they had some rhythm problems and the occasional screeching off-note, but Annie didn't care. Imperfection was the spice of life...for some people. Definitely not her mother, who thought Annie was crazy for even considering hiring an amateur band for a reception with over three hundred guests.

Michael didn't look convinced. She crawled over the bed to him and planted a firm, no-nonsense kiss on his pouty, perfect lips. "The band is great. And so are you. I'll book them today." She held up two fingers in the sign of a solemn scout oath.

A little smile played at the corner of his lips. "I've never bedded a scout before."

She waggled her finger as a warning. "I've got to be at work in an hour!"

He leaned in with a wolfish grin. "Oh, that's plenty of time."

She found her mother at her usual table - small and discreet, just past the maitre d's station, where she could see and be seen by everyone who entered. Midway through her fifties, Annie's mother was slim and stunning in a black crepe dress with a mink stole.

"Darling!" Her mother angled her cheek for a kiss. "I thought you were coming right from work."

Annie took the chair opposite of her mother. "I did."

Annie endured the head-to-toe assessment of her taupe leggings, white blouse, and tweed jacket. Her mother raised an eyebrow to Louise, the wedding planner. "Annie, you must remember. We dress for the job we *want,* not the one we have."

Annie pressed her lips together lest she say something hurtful that would cause her mother to punish her with icy silence for two weeks. There was no point in reminding her mother that

208

her PR agency catered to the sports and fitness industry. At her office, a client's team jersey was considered dressing up. Annie ordered her usual lunch--a spinach-strawberry salad with iced tea --and braced herself for an hour of wedding madness.

Louise patted Annie's hand. "Annie," she said, drawling the vowels like diamonds. "Your mother and I have been discussing the centerpieces for the reception. I have some ideas that I think you'll love."

Her mother clasped her hands under her chin. "Orchids, darling. Only white orchids will do."

Louise smiled indulgently. "Oh, Laura. You just have the best taste." *And the fattest checkbook.*

Annie thumbed through the galley of choices the planner had assembled in a tanned leather binder. The first choice was white orchids in glass vases, with lemon yellow tablecloths, striped linen napkins, and a spray of baby's breath on every napkin ring. "Pretty, " Annie said. "Very spring-ey."

Louise practically purred as she pointed out the other choices. Annie thumbed past the roses, lilies of the valley, and the hydrangeas, then frowned. "I don't see the wildflower options.' She had emailed the planner a half dozen wildflower arrangements that she thought would be perfect for her reception.

When the planner gave her mother The Look, Annie knew her ideas had been nixed before they could take root. "Well, your mother thought…" There it was again, that sinking sensation in the pit of Annie's stomach that signaled she was outsmarted, outgunned, and outrun. *Tiger mom* didn't begin to describe the depth of her mother's commitment once she took an interest in Annie's life.

"Oh, Annie, honestly. Wildflowers? Like the ones at the grocery store? Why on earth would you want to sully an otherwise perfect wedding with a half-baked whim for...*weeds?*"

Annie frowned. The pictures she sent didn't seem common at all. And they weren't a whim. Her earliest memories were walking the countryside beyond her grandmother's tiny stone home, gathering wildflowers, seed pods, and wild herbs into a worn wicker basket. There was always a mason jar of flowers and greens on the kitchen table. The rest were dried, crushed, and stored to be used later in her grandmother's mysterious collection of dried tea tinctures and sweet biscuits. It thrilled Annie to think of her grandmother at the reception. How pleased and comforted she would feel, surrounded by the same simple gifts of nature that she had so freely shared with Annie.

The planner was discreet but helpful. "I think what Annie is going for is maybe something a bit less formal, yes?"

Annie nodded but that was only half the story. She wanted her guests to feel the way her grandmother always made her feel. Welcome and wanted just as she was. Impressing others was her mother's forte, not Grandma Bessie's.

"Let's take another look". The planner flipped through the portfolio, making suggestions about how to pair roses with something more understated. Annie looked helplessly back and forth between the flowers. They were all so pretty. Her mother's frown made the stakes known. It was white orchids or a two-week icy treatment.

"I just... I don't know..." Michael wouldn't care about the flowers either way. But she had really wanted to include her grandmother's taste for the simple pleasures in life. Trying to explain this to her mother was futile. She considered her own mother a little "daft" and not to be taken seriously.. She closed the book and sighed. "Let me think about it."

The planner was perfect and professional, as if that was the best choice in the world. "Of course, dear. You just let me know."

Her mother rolled her eyes and finished off her wine spritzer. Annie wondered if her mother planned to return to her office at the city's History museum, or if it would be another "work from home" afternoon.

"All right," the planner said. "Next item on the agenda. Music. Now, I've booked the string quartet for the church. That's going to be so lovely. And for your wedding reception, your mother had the *brilliant* idea of booking a swing band. Oh Lousie, how charming."

Annie looked back and forth helplessly. "Wait, what? No one's mentioned a swing band."

Her mother's grip was surprisingly strong. "Oh Annie, darling - I attended Mitchell's eldest daughter's wedding last summer. They booked a swing band and it was simply delightful. We can hire dance instructors to teach guests ballroom dancing basics. It will be so fun. You'll see."

"No, Mother. Michael wants to book The Roving Roosters. I promised!"

"Good grief, not this band nonsense again." Louise rubbed her temple as if a fierce headache was coming on. "Annie, you simply can't have a second-rate--and I'm being rather generous there--garage band for your wedding reception. This isn't some dorm room party with pizza and cheap beer!"

"Mother! This is important to Michael!"

Louise groaned. "I love Michael, you know that. But he's a *guy*. And guys can't be entrusted with decisions like this. This is the first event you and Michael are hosting as a married couple. It sets a bar, darling. It establishes your reputation in society."

Annie always thought her mother missed her era. She would have been so much happier, and more effective, as the mother in Edwardian society. She would be at her best negotiating, strategizing, and maneuvering her daughter into the most advantageous marriage possible."

"Mother! I'm not worried about 'society.' I just want to have a nice, meaningful wedding." Actually, she just wanted to get hitched and have a shing-ding. "Is that so much to ask?"

The wedding planner intervened again. "Annie, I understand this is your special day. But, I think you should rethink the band. I've listened to the track you sent me. And I read their reviews. They are… um…. mediocre. At best."

"So?" Desperation tightened her throat and made her feel nauseous. Flowers were one thing. Michael's one wedding request was something else.

"Well, you're going to have a lot of people there." The planner leaned in for the kill. "Have you thought about the reaction if the band flops? Your friends and guests will laugh at them. AT you." She leaned back in her chair and folded her arms over her chest. "And at Michael."

Her mother finished the job. "In some ways, Annie. You owe it to Michael NOT to book the band. In the end, this could look very bad for him."

Annie's mouth opened and closed like a fish out of water. Were they right? She thought back to all the shows and events that she and Michael had attended. Small little gigs at offroad taverns or street festivals. Sure, she and Michael loved the guys and knew all their songs by heart. But were they blinded? Like new parents who could see nothing but a miracle in their tiny baby? The thought of Michael feeling humiliated or embarrassed killed her.

"I don't know," she said. Michael had trusted her to plan the wedding any way she liked. This was the only request he had - how could she say no? "I need to think about it. Maybe we'll go with the big band." She shook her head in frustration. "Maybe. I'll let you know."

The planner nodded her head, professional and composed. "Of course, dear."

Annie let herself into Michael's apartment. He was in the kitchen, cooking something on the stove, his back to her. She hung up her coat, tossed her purse on the couch, and slipped out of her boots.

"I love my new client," she called to the kitchen, stretching out on the couch. "But I hate my account executive!" All day long her assistant had undercut her at every opportunity. Talking over her in the meeting and pointing out the flaws in Annie's ideas. "Little Miss Sure of Herself just jumps right in and tells my $100K client that they just *have* to be on Tik-Tok. Where's her data? What does she know about a return on investment? I hardly think my new client wants to market to thirteen-year-olds with a ten dollar allowance." She sighed heavily, then realized Michael was still at the stove, stirring away. "I'm sorry babe. I'm just babbling away over here. How was your day?"

"Fine."

All her alarms went off. Michael was never just "fine." He was *awesome* or *exhausted* or *totally bummed out*. Never just fine. "What's for dinner?"

"Soup."

Annie frowned and headed to the kitchen. Michael wore a cable knit sweater over jeans, his feet bare. She hugged him from behind, pressing her cheek to his back. "What's wrong, baby?"

He didn't answer, just kept stirring. A can of Campbell's Thick n' Hearty beef stew was next to the stove. Just one can.

"Do you want me to make a salad? Or some bruschetta?"

Michael's sigh was heavy and hard. "I ran into Jerry today." *Clink, clink, clink.* Spoon against saucepan.

She cocked her head... Jerry, Jerry. Oh, right. The band's drummer. Her chest tightened with dread. "Oh?"

"I told him how stoked I was that they were going to play our wedding."

Annie bit her lip. "Yeah, so I was going to talk to you about that." It would be a lie to say she'd forgotten to call the band. She thought about them all the time. She'd even picked up the phone a half dozen times. But she was stopped every time by the image the planner had planted in her mind: the band failing, guests laughing, and Michael feeling humiliated.

"They said they never heard from you."

"I know. I just... the planner thought maybe a swing band would be like, super fun!"

"I don't want a swing band."

"But it *could* be fun." She mimed dancing the jitterbug but it didn't make him smile. "Look, I just think we should think about all the possibilities, right? I mean, The Roving Roosters are awesome. *I* love them. *You* love them. But maybe our guests would want something... different. I mean, this is the first social event we're hosting as a married couple, right? Like, this is sort of, setting the social tone for our whole marriage."

212

He frowned. "Annie, what happened to *we're gettin' hitched and havin' a shing-ding*?"

She scratched her cheek and looked out the window for inspiration. All she could see was inky black darkness. "I just don't want to make a mistake, that's all."

"How could booking the band I want be a mistake?"

"But what if…" She braced herself. "They're...not...good?"

He looked up sharply. "They're not some glossy perfect-for-print bland band that aims for the lowest common denominator. But that's what makes them real. Like us." He turned back to the soup. "Or so I thought."

"I know. It's just…."

He shook his head and scraped at the soup some more. "It's just that you're trying to make everyone happy."

For one stupid moment, she thought he understood. "Right! I just want everyone to be happy." But the expression on his face said he was anything but. "I'm sorry. I guess the wedding planner and my mom got in my head. Let's book the band. It will be fine."

His eyes darkened. "It's too late, Annie."

"What? No, it's not. The wedding is still two months away."

"They're booked."

"For what? A bar mitzvah? Tell them to cancel. We'll pay double." Oh, her mother would love that idea.

"They're booked for a two week statewide tour. They got signed up with some kind of product launch for a new healthy, herbal soda."

"What? That's great! That's like… a big deal for them."

"Yeah." With a violent tilt, he dumped soup in his bowl, splashing broth and veggies all over the counter. "It's great."

He grabbed his bowl and headed for the table. If she wanted what little soup was left in the pan, she'd have to serve herself. Instead, she headed for the table, sitting opposite of him.

"So, I guess that settles that. All we have to decide is if we want to go with the swing band or… something else?"

"No, Annie. We have other decisions to make." He stopped trying to ignore her and faced her head on. "Like whether this is even a good idea."

Her heart made a sharp descent to her belly. "What are you talking about?"

"You. Me. Us. This wedding."

"Michael," she shook her head hard, willing him to stop speaking. "Don't say that."

He stared down into his soup, as if life answers could be found there. "If I don't say it now, then when? Ten years from now,

213

when we've intertwined our lives? When we have kids who count on us? When it's too late for us to choose a different path?"

Annie reached for his hand, desperate to feel his fingers curl into hers. His quick withdrawal made her breath hitch in her throat.

"Annie, I love you more than anything in the world. And I know you love me too. But will you fight for me? Like I fight for you? Because if you can't.... If you're going to throw me under the bus to make other people happy..." He looked up from the soup, his eyes dark pools of brooding brown. "Then what are we doing here?"

Annie's thumb found a hangnail on her ring finger. She fiddled with it until it twanged with pain. "I'm sorry, Michael. If it were up to me, I would have booked the band the day you asked me. It's just..."

His brow furrowed. "What do you mean *if it were up to me?* It's our wedding, isn't it?"

"Yes, but..." She moved from the hangnail to her engagement ring, twisting it in nervous circles. "My mom just...has ideas that are hard to change."

Michael shook his head. "Annie, don't you understand?" His spoon hovered in the air, making the beef and carrot tremble. "You'll never be able to fight for me--*for us*--until you learn to fight for yourself."

She drove home as a winter thunderstorm split the sky in two. Her windshield wipers fought to keep the glass clear. It was a relief to make it home in one piece. Even more to find Grandma Bessie in the kitchen, brewing a pot of tea. Annie gave her a sad kiss on the cheek.

"Rough day at work, dear?"

"Among other things." She reached for a cloth napkin her mother kept neatly rolled and stacked on the kitchen table and set it under the cup of tea Grandma Bessie gave her. With little prompting, Annie spilled the stresses of the day. A nasty co-worker gunning for her job. Planning a wedding. And disappointing the man she loved most in the world. Grandma Bessie listened and nodded, her face a map of life experience and age, but her eyes as vivid blue and energetic as ever. "I don't know, Grandma Bessie. I just want to make the right decisions. But no matter what I do, someone is unhappy."

"Decisions are like stones on a cobbled path, dear. Keep the destination in mind and your path will be straight."

Well, that didn't make a lot of sense. All she needed to know was how to fix things with Michael and keep her mother off her back. "Thanks anyway, Grandma."

Bessie gave her a knowing look. "Still not clear, no?"

"I know you're trying to help."

Bessie got up, humming to herself. She went to the cupboard where she kept her teas. She rummaged about until she found a purple and gold tin with an image of a pineapple. She pried open the tin with her bony hands and offered two tiny biscuits.

Annie took them reluctantly, wondering how long they'd been stuck in that cabinet. She set them on the edge of her tea saucer.

"Eat, eat," she encouraged. "They'll do you some good."

Annie *was* hungry, considering there was no soup to be had at Michael's place. Old biscuits couldn't kill you, right? At worst, she'd get food poisoning, entitling her to a day off from her hyper co-worker. She nibbled the edge and was surprised to taste the distinct sweet and sour tones of pineapple. "Mmm, these are good. I've never had a pineapple cookie before."

Bessie gave her a matter-of-fact nod. "Be a pineapple queen, sweetie. Stand tall, wear a crown, stay sweet on the inside."

Poor Grandma Bessie was getting a little fuzzy in her old age. But sharing biscuits with someone who loved her was a decent way to end a bad day.

The next morning, Annie woke a full hour before her alarm went off. She felt strangely energetic as she showered and dressed for the day. So energetic, in fact, that she bounded down the stairs two at a time, landing with a thud in the kitchen.

"Heavens, Annie!" Her mother straightened the pages of her newspaper. "Is a herd of elephants descending upon us?"

"Sorry, mother." *No, you're not.* Whoa, where did that thought come from? Before she could think about it too deeply, she found herself invading the cake dolly where Grandma Bessie kept her stash of donuts. Annie selected two, a cake donut to dunk in her coffee and a glazed one for the office.

"Annie," her mother scolded. "You can't be serious. Not with a dress fitting this week. Here, I'll make you a kale-blueberry smoothie."

Maybe a kale-blueberry smoothie was a good idea. More nutritious, good for the skin. *Kale-blueberry smoothies are disgusting. I want this.* Annie watched in wonder as her hands dunked the cake donut in the coffee, then smashed half the donut

215

in her mouth. *See? That was delicious. Don't wedding dresses have stretchy waistbands?* No, they totally do not. What on earth was going on in her head? She was no stranger to hearing from her conscience, but this didn't sound like her conscience. It sounded like the pushy toll booth worker who took her change on the New Jersey expressway.

Her mother shook her head over the crumbs tumbling down Annie's shirt. "We'll chalk it up to PMS. All right, about the photographer…"

An image popped in her head. Rachel Stewart was a classmate from college. She was a photography student and they had worked on a few student public relations projects. The last Annie heard, Rachel was offering onsite photography for corporate events, weddings, and family portraits. Maybe she could send her mom a link to Rachel's work, to get her warmed up to the idea. *Eff that, Annie. You want Rachel Stewart? I'll get you Rachel Stewart.* "I'll send the planner Rachel Stewart's contact information."

Her mother arched one eyebrow, clearly as surprised with Annie's behavior as Annie was. "Who on earth is Rachel Stewart?"

Your daughter's wedding photographer, that's who. Annie stooped to give her mother a kiss on the cheek before anything else could fly out of her mouth. "See you later, Ma."

"But.. Annie… you can't just…"

Oh yeah, old lady? Just watch her.

Annie gathered her briefcase and purse then hurried to the safety of her car. Once she was inside, doors locked, she looked in the rearview mirror. "What the hell is going on?"

With what?

"Me! You! Us! Why are you here, in my head? Making me talk like…"

Like what, Annie?

"I don't know. Rude. Pushy. Demanding."

Where I come from, you're just sayin' what you want. What's so wrong with that?

Annie stared around helplessly. The neighborhood seemed perfectly normal. Mr. Cranswick was watering his roses by hand. He caught her eye and waved. She waved back, hoping he hadn't seen the craziness of her talking to herself in the mirror. "There's nothing wrong, I guess. But...who are you? Why are you in my head?"

Because I am you. Just... the Pineapple Queen version.

Annie felt confused. Where had she heard that before? Oh yes, last night. With her grandmother. Her lips tightened with suspicion.

You can deal with her later. Let's get to work. I have a fresh can of whoopass for that co-worker of yours.

Annie hesitated, imagining Lucy's face when she met The Pineapple Queen. "Okay, then," she said, pressing the ignition button. "Let's go."

Annie turned off her office light and locked the door. She felt weary all over, but in a good-made-the-most-of-the-day kind of way.

You were pretty hot today.

No, her Pineapple Queen alter-ego was pretty hot. But it was fun to come along for the ride. Speaking her mind and telling her client exactly what he needed to get a good return on his investment had resulted in the client increasing their budget by $20K. She could do a lot of good for his public image with a bigger budget.

And the look on Lucy's face when you told her Tik-Tok was for amateurs…

"Yeah, that was pretty satisfying. But throwing my coat and purse on her desk…"

Too much?

"Definitely. Only Meryl Streep can pull that off."

Fair enough.

The staccato clip of her heels against concrete echoed against the parking garage walls. Annie reshouldered her briefcase. She had a lot of extra work ahead to hit a home run on this PR campaign.

One more stop, sugar.

"He doesn't want to see me. He's not returning my text or calls."

If Mohammed won't go to the mountain, the mountain must go to Mohammed.

"Are you going to give me a real choice?"

Nope, probably not.

So that's how Annie found herself climbing the three flights of stairs to Michael's apartment. It was late, he could be working, this was probably a waste of time.

So, you leave him a note. You tell him what you want. Your heart's deepest desires.

Annie searched her heart. All she wanted was Michael back in her life, giving her nose-boop kisses and canned beef stew.

That's where your stone path must lead.

She raised her hand to knock but the door opened before she made contact.

"Hey."

He's been waiting for you, Annie.

Maybe that was true. Maybe not. The trash bag in his hand kind of implied otherwise. Did this Pineapple Queen really know what she was doing? Maybe it was time for Annie to take things over. They would sit down, make a pot of coffee, talk things out. Surely she could help him see what she was thinking... what she was trying to do...

Oh, to hell with that.

Annie felt herself almost pushed from behind, right into Michael. Hard enough to make Michael stumble a bit and drop the trash bag. When he regained his balance, she slid one hand behind his head, finding the nape of his neck.

Where's the road going to lead, Annie? What's your final destination?

In her mind's eye, she could see it as plain as day. Michael and her at the beach, living in a stone cottage just like her grandma's. It would be warm and welcoming, not impressive at all. Wildflowers everywhere, gathered from their walks in the woods behind the beach. Gathered and dried and put into teas and potpourri satchels. No swing bands or linen napkins... just the two of them. There was only one direction she wanted to go and that was towards Michael and their future together.

Take the first step then.

So, she did. She pulled him to her, closing her eyes at the last minute. Her lips found his, navigating by heat rather than sight. She nibbled over his lips until she felt him relax and open to her. You are my destination, she breathed into the kiss. No more cul de sacs or U-turns. Just the shortest, fast route to you. "Let's elope," she breathed when they broke off the kiss.

He shook his head. "Don't you want a full wedding? The dress and bridesmaids? Swing bands and custom wedding cakes?"

"No," she half-pouted. "I want donuts and stretchy pants and you."

He shook his head. "Well, that made no sense at all. Except the last part. That sounded pretty good to me."

When she came home the next morning, Grandma Bessie was waiting with a fresh box of donuts and a pot of herbal tea. "Good evening, I take it?" she said, stirring some sugar into Annie's tea.

"Mm-hmm," Annie said, watching her like a hawk. "Somehow I think you know all about it. You and your pineapple cookies."

218

Bessie scooped a tremendous spoonful of sugar in her tea. "Mmm, maybe I do. Maybe I don't." She hobbled to the tea cabinet and rummaged until she found a small bag of seeds. She dropped two into Annie's tea followed by a brisk stir.

"What are those?"

"Just a little something to go with the pineapple biscuits. Restores balance, if you know what I mean."

Annie felt a moment of panic. She *liked* this new alter-ego, even if it made her feel a little schizophrenic at times. She didn't want to go back to the old Annie, trying to please everyone until no one was satisfied. Especially her.

As if reading her mind, Bessie patted her hand. "The sass goes, but the Queen stays."

Annie nodded and took her first sip of tea. Whatever those seeds were, they left behind notes of lemon and ginger. She suddenly had an image of her and Michael at the courthouse, the judge asking if she took this man to be her lawful husband.

Damn straight I do, the real Annie said. *Damn straight.*

Event 5
It's A Disaster!

Life gave us lemons and now citrus is taking over the world. For this Event, unlikely heroes step up to save humanity from something so ridiculously over the top, all you can do is laugh.

Core Concepts: backstory, tropes

For Want of Conversation

by MM Schreier
First Place

Granny Kerson puttered around her kitchen making breakfast. One poached egg on a slice of multigrain toast. Same thing she had every Sunday. The rest of the week she made do with a bowl of plain oatmeal. She used to have bacon and grapefruit and flaky, buttery chocolate-filled croissants, but her appetite just hadn't been the same since Alfred passed away. Besides, it was no fun making fancy meals for one, or sitting in silence, eating alone. Her husband had been an excellent conversationalist.

She huffed as someone outside honked. Twitching the kitchen curtain aside, she saw the new neighbors—she could never remember their names—bundling their children into their car. Granny frowned. Where were they off to at this hour? They weren't really the churchgoing sort of family.

The neighbor-wife kept stealing anxious glances at the sky as her husband shoved a couple of suitcases in the trunk. Ah, vacation then. Granny hoped for their sake they weren't headed to the beach. It was dimmer out than usual for this hour, probably a storm coming. She didn't search the sky for thunderheads; looking up made her vertigo act up. No sense wasting the day stretched out on the couch to check for a storm she didn't really care about. With her arthritic knees, it wasn't like she had a hike up Kilimanjaro planned. Even a short jaunt around the block started up the aches and pains.

The tea kettle whistled, and Granny smoothed the drapes back in place. Grabbing her 'World's Best Grandmother' mug, she filled the tea ball with loose leaf darjeeling. Her son, Jacob, had gotten her the strainer and showed her how to make tea by the cup. Not quite as good as brewing it by the pot, but far better than those nasty tea bags full of powder pretending to be tea.

A nostalgic smile drifted across her face. Jacob had always been a fussy boy. Fastidious about his appearance. No mud pies or frogs in his pockets for him. He had been happier with his nose in a book than playing ball with the wild, tousle-haired pack of neighborhood boys.

The smile faded. Granny tried to love her son's wife, like a good mother should, but the tart wanted a bigger life than the 'burbs of Buffalo offered and had dragged Jacob away to the West coast. She kept him and the grandkids so busy there was barely any time for a little old lady, alone in a decaying old cape with a rotting porch and an overgrown lawn.

Granny huffed. Maybe she'd just give them a ring. She glanced at the clock. It was only five in the morning in California. She picked up the phone. One of the great things about getting old—she could pretend that she'd confused the time zones. She might wake them, but at least she could guarantee they'd be at home.

She pressed *speed dial one*, and waited for the phone to start ringing. Instead, a tinny voice droned in her ear, "We're sorry. All circuits are busy. Please try your call again later." She grumbled as she replaced the receiver. So much for modern technology making life easier. Texting and email and social media. It was supposed to connect her to the world at the touch of a button. So how come she felt more isolated than ever?

With a sigh she sat down to her breakfast. The egg was cold and the tea over brewed. She ate it anyway. Living on a fixed income, she couldn't afford to be wasteful.

After clearing away the dishes, she flicked on the television. It was too early in the day for her stories, but there was usually some interesting cooking show to watch. She especially liked those two stout ladies on the BBC who made everything with lard. Granny tuned in, not for the recipes—everyone knew that English food was terribly bland—but because those old broads were sassy. They didn't wait around, hoping someone would call or visit. No, they hopped on their motorcycle, sidecar and all, and toured the countryside.

Granny smirked. Ah, to be a young whippersnapper in her seventies again.

She flipped through the channels. News. News. News. Every station was playing some special report. Granny glanced around for her glasses before remembering they were on a chain around her neck. Another thoughtful gift from Jacob. A visit would be nicer though. She shrugged, perched the glasses on the bridge of her nose, and narrowed her eyes at the broadcast.

"...appeared in the sky shortly after daybreak this morning. At this time there has been no contact with the spaceship but..."

Granny shook her head. Her hearing aid must be on the fritz. Spaceship? She turned up the volume on the TV.

"...extraterrestrials appear hostile in nature as all investigatory missions have been shot down by some sort of energy beam. I repeat: Earth is under attack!"

Granny rolled her eyes and clicked the remote. The screen went dark. Another one of those ridiculous, sensational hoaxes.

224

She never did have much patience for science fiction. Alfred, now, he had loved a good space opera—what was that one with the robots and the big hairy wooshie? She rubbed her eyes and glanced at his threadbare recliner. Three years empty, and she still wasn't cried out. Silly old fool.

Sniffling, she headed to the bathroom to double check her hair in the mirror. Sundays at 9:30 the church's meal delivery people arrived with their casseroles and crocks of soup. Granny felt bad taking the food; she never ate it. The chest freezer in the basement was stuffed full with dozens of prepared meals. Still, she looked forward to the delivery every week. It was nice to have a visitor. Even if they never stayed more than a minute or two.

Satisfied she looked her best, albeit wrinkled and skinny, she went into the parlor to wait. And wait. She frowned. They'd never been late before. Perhaps she had the time wrong. Granny checked the schedule. 9:30 on Sundays, just like she thought. She was old and a tad hard of hearing, not senile.

Grouchy, she stood up to go check the front step. Maybe they were in a hurry and just left it there? As she opened the door the chain rattled against the frame; she never used it anymore. She had nothing to steal, and navigating the hook was a challenge with her rheumatism.

No delivery.

Granny turned, but then paused. The hairs on the back of her neck stood on end. She looked up and down the street. Even for a Sunday, it seemed too quiet. No traffic. None of the neighborhood kids riding their bikes. Even Mrs. Gladstone's pampered Shih Tzu had stopped its never-ending barking.

Just as she was about to go back inside, something on the sidewalk caught her eye. An odd shimmering form, like a mirage, had appeared. Granny pushed her glasses up her nose and watched, curiosity getting the best of her.

The mirage solidified into a grey-faced man with enormous round eyes. His limbs seemed too long for his body, stretched like over-pulled taffy.

She blinked. Where the heck had he come from?

The stranger pressed a device on his wrist, and spoke in a rapid-fire string of clicks and whistles.

For the second time that day, Granny wondered if her hearing aids needed fixing. Maybe it was time to change the battery. She clucked her tongue.

As if drawn to the noise, the man turned and fixed his gaze on her. Oversized eyes whirled as he studied her.

"Halloo, there young man!" Granny waved. "Come over here, mister. Don't you know it's impolite to stare?"

The man flickered and reappeared in front of her. "Halloo there. Impolite to stare." He cocked his head as he repeated the words with exaggerated slowness.

"Are you lost?" Granny was certain the young man was an out-of-towner, based on his strange coveralls. "Are you here visiting someone?" She glanced at the neighbors' empty driveways. "I'm not sure anyone is at home."

"Yes, visiting. Assimilating." His voice sounded clipped, the words rattling out in a harsh staccato.

Ah, not just an out-of-towner, but a foreigner at that. "Well, as I said, no one's home. Why don't you come inside and I'll fix you a cup of tea while you wait."

Not taking no for an answer, Granny took the man by the arm and bustled him into the house. His skin felt scaly under her fingertips. "You know, dear. I have an excellent eczema lotion that just works wonders. You should definitely give it a try." She patted his forearm.

The man opened his mouth. "Take me to your lea—"

"Come into the kitchen, sweetheart, and I'll put on the kettle, then you can tell me all about it."

Granny pushed him into the chair at the head of the table. A twang went through her. Alfred used to read his newspaper there every morning. She shook off the memory, determined to be a good host. In an odd way, the visitor reminded her of her late husband, both bald as a pingpong ball.

She bustled around, measuring dried leaves into her favorite blue willow teapot. Only the best for visitors. With a glance at the man's ashen face, she added another heaping spoonful of tea. "A nice cup of English breakfast tea will fix you right up."

Granny kept up a stream of chatter as the tea steeped. She arranged a few cookies on a plate, hoping they weren't stale. "You know, these used to be Jacob's favorite. His wife doesn't let him eat processed sugar anymore, though. I say, a few sweets now and then never hurt anybody."

The man opened his mouth, showing a row of snaggly, chipped teeth. "I've come to negotiate your surren—"

"I don't want to embarrass you, my dear, but speaking of sugar, maybe you've had a little too much." She moved the plate out of his reach. "I could recommend an excellent dentist. Of course, my late husband, Alfred, was even better, but he sold his practice to a nice young man over a decade ago." She smiled and proudly tapped her own teeth, still bright white and even. "All real, you know. No falsies like a lot of people my age."

226

Granny poured the tea and set a mug in front of the stranger. "Here you go. Guaranteed to put a little color in your cheeks!"

He started to speak, but she made a *drink up* motion with her hands. She lifted her own mug to her lips and he hesitantly followed suit. The warmth from the mug seeped into her fingers as she drank.

The man took a swallow and started coughing, tea spraying everywhere.

Granny sprang out of her seat, as fast as an old lady could spring, her maternal instincts kicking into overdrive. "Hands over your head!"

She grabbed his long-fingered hands and threw them into the air, thumping him on the back for good measure. He choked and wheezed.

"How dare…" Cough, hack. "Poison…" Sniffle, cough.

Granny barreled over him. "I'm so sorry, sweetheart. I should have told you it was hot!" She mopped up the mess. "Jacob always used to drink too fast as well."

With a wistful smile she went out to the living room and pulled a heavy photo album off the shelf. The man was still spluttering when she returned. She plunked the book on the table and started turning pages.

Granny prattled on recounting stories of Jacob's first day of school and Alfred's annual fishing trip on Lake Erie. "He never did catch anything. Honestly, between you and I, it felt like an excuse to go boating and drink beers on the water. Only a couple, mind you, Alfred was a cautious man. Never drove impaired." She shook a stern finger at her visitor.

He shifted in his seat, eyes wide. Granny patted him on the hand. "Not much of a conversationalist, are you dearie? But you're an excellent listener." She pushed the cookie plate back across the table. "Go ahead, have one."

He glanced at his undrunk cup of tea, then back at the cookies. Face a little greyer, he pushed back his chair.

"Are you leaving so soon?" Granny pouted.

He gnashed his teeth. Backing away, he kept a wary eye on the teacup before slipping out the front door.

Limping after him, Granny looked up and down the street. The stranger was nowhere to be seen, only a fading shimmer remained on the sidewalk. How did he keep doing that, coming and going so quickly? Must be those long legs.

With a contented sigh, she closed the door and went to tidy up the tea things. It had been so nice to have a bit of company, even if the boy had been a tad odd. Teapot tucked away and mugs washed, Granny went to lie down for a quick nap. All that conversating had taken the energy right out of her.

Some time later, the phone rang, jerking her out of a sound sleep. She stood, knees creaking. "Hold your horses, will you?" She shuffled out to the kitchen and grabbed the phone. "Hello? Gertrude Kerson speaking."

"Mom! Are you all right?" The voice at the end of the line sounded breathless.

"Jacob, darling! I tried calling you this morning, but the lines were acting funny. And why wouldn't I be all right?" Such a worry-wart, her son.

"Don't you pay attention to the news? There was an alien spaceship hovering right over Buffalo this morning! They say we were being invaded, but then for absolutely no reason, the ship flew off. Last I heard it was headed out of the solar system at top speed."

Granny snorted. "Oh, Jacob. Don't be silly. There's no such thing as aliens. You and your father…" She shook her head ruefully.

"Mom, I'm telling—"

"You know, darling. It's past time you brought my grandkids for a visit." She brushed cookie crumbs off the table. "Speaking of visitors, let me tell you all about the nice young man I met today."

Light years away, in sector Alpha Forty-Two, Greblok tapped out their brief for the Council. The blue-green planet, third from its sun, had initially seemed full of potential. Early reports had mentioned a low-tech, low-intellect, primate population that would have made an excellent slave pool.

Greblok swallowed, throat still raw from the poisonous beverage and ears ringing. They considered, then typed in an addendum to the report: "Even elderly specimens are excessively hostile. Not worth the effort of assimilation." They pressed send, then entered coordinates in the nav system for a newly discovered gas giant with an avian race worth investigating. Even better, they were thought to be telepathic communicators. Greblok smiled. It would take almost a standard revolution to get there, but they could really use some quiet time.

PB&J Heroes
by Allison Rott
Second Place

"C-C-Cal-Calvin!" Laura yelled. Her panic did nothing for the splitting headache and body pains that left me unresponsive to her first scream. "C-Cal-Calvin!" She tried again, her hands shaking me.

I blinked my eyes open. Laura was looking down at me, brown eyes leaking tears, nose dripping, cute little round face scrunched up in the worst ugly cry I've ever seen. Beyond her head, and her black hair falling over her shoulders in waves, was the blue ceiling.

You'd think a blue ceiling would be indicative of where I was lying on the floor, but that wasn't the case on Blue Adventure Isle. Everything was blue here: furniture, rides, buildings, uniforms, souvenirs, and the food.

"Can you move?" Laura sniffed, her stuttering falling out of focus while I tried to remember why I ended up on the floor. Slowly I managed to push myself up to a seated position, getting a better look around the room.

The fridge, the scattered and shattered plates, bread, and couch reminded me where I was and what I had been doing. I had been in the break room making peanut butter and blueberry jam sandwiches for the other employees who didn't want to eat at any of the food stalls around the island.

"Ugh." I groaned. Everything hurt, probably because the building had been shaking and the only way I could keep my balance is on a bike so I was knocking into everything. I'm pretty sure I was the one who flung the plates off the counter.

"Thank goodness." She mumbled.

"Is the earthquake over?" I reached up to rub my head, pausing when I realized my hand was covered in blue peanut butter.

"I think so." She said. Laura stood, her knees shaking under the edge of her cargo shorts. She moved to the window, black hair swaying. "But... something else is happening out there." Her thin arms gripped the bottom of the window and she pushed it open, and now I could hear the screams. Distinct words weren't making it to us, out here at the administrative building's break room, but Laura was right.

Those weren't the screams of guests getting thrills from the rides.

"Um, Laura," I said. I was looking at the door to the break room staring at the viscous bright green goo leaking in the gap. Part of me was grateful to see a color other than blue in the nearly three months of working here as a water boy and lunch maker for employees. "There is ooze." Every other part of me was worried about the goo.

"Well that's bad." She crouched next to me.

"Nothing in the employee handbook emergency section said anything about ooze!" I hissed.

"Don't yell at me." She grumbled. Arms crossing over her chest, blueberry jam stains on her clothes and skin, she shrunk away from me. Her body shook with sobs. "I just w-wanted to work with kids and b-ecause of my st-stutter they put me in the mascot c-costume!"

"Laura-"

"And now everything is worse!"

"Laura-"

"And you're mad at me-"

"I'm not mad at you!" I screamed. She hiccupped and buried her head in her knees. "I'm sorry for yelling." I knew she wasn't good with confrontation. "I'm not mad at you." She continued to cry. It was the time I accused her of taking my chair at the employee training meeting all over again. Sobbing and stuttering her explanation of me misreading the seating chart.

"I, uh," she gasped. "I know."

"Okay. Let's try to get out of here." I groaned as I pushed myself up to my feet. I walked to the window, letting Laura sniffle her composure back as I looked out. It wasn't a huge drop to the ground, and despite the screaming coming from the attraction-filled side of the island, rides suitable for all ages, the surrounding trees looked calm.

When I looked up, towards the top of the roller coaster and the giant swing that I would stare at multiple times a day, they weren't there. I remembered first seeing them from the ship, awed once more at the crazy idea to spend work at a summer resort on an island. "Laura," I waved a hand at her. "You have got to see this."

The large umbrella-like top of the swing ride was off the pole, the long chains and swing bottoms moving and walking the top around. I felt Laura's warmth press into my side, her hand gripping mine. The giant swing's top was swishing as it moved. Rarely would we see one of the navy, sky, or royal blue chairs over

230

the tops of the trees before it was lowered once more to the ground.

"What the-"

Now the trees were shaking, ones closer and closer. There was a screech, not a human sound, but metal scraping.

"Move!" I dragged Laura away from the window with me, tripping over the mess. We ended up in a heap on the ground next to the couch as the wall with the window was smashed in with a piece of blue track from the newest world's tallest coaster, Screaming Deamon.

"D-did the p-park come to life?" Laura whispered.

"Seems like it." I groaned. Laura was half on me, she was tiny, barely five feet, and maybe one hundred pounds soaking wet. I wasn't groaning from her weight, but groaning about the situation. The metal screeching was closer now. "We gotta get out of here." I pushed Laura off and we struggled to get to our feet, shaking off drywall dust, some blue from the paint and white. We looked at the door, and the ooze.

"Don't like that." She mumbled.

"Yeah." We turned and climbed onto the track, looking out and seeing it was connected to more tracks, some trees knocked out of the way, leading towards the park. "Use the track to get out the window?" The track shuddered, knocking me right back over, cutting my knee on a bolt.

"Calvin!" She grabbed my shirt and yanked me off, as the coaster cars came and screeched to a stop just at the end of the track. The neon paint job, eyes and horns on the front car, and a spiked tail on the back, black designs on the blue cars, moved. The eyes looked over, the horns wiggled like eyebrows, and the tail twitched. The track was shuddering some more, metal screeching, and it was moving, retracting towards the back end of the coaster car.

"To the ooze!" I hated it. Stumbling over the broken plates and the overturned furniture towards the bright, possibly glowing, substance. But it had to be better than getting run over or crushed by a roller coaster come to life.

Laura was the one to pull the door open, and the goo rushed over our feet. It seeped into my socks, and my feet burned. We ran down the hall, through the strange goo. My foot hit an uneven part in the floor, and I crashed face first into it. Everything burned now, an alcoholic burn in my mouth with a strong taste of fermented fish. The splash next to me told me I hadn't let go of Laura when I fell, rather dragged her down with me.

She was up faster, spitting and coughing while she pulled with all her strength at my arm. The blue walls and floor were shaking again, and we started hearing more crashing down around us as the track started rebuilding through the building.

The handbook may not have said anything about ooze, but there were pages on the evacuation protocol. The evacuation point was the docks at the midpoint of the island.

We stumbled our way outside. Glancing back at the building for a moment we saw the track winding its way in and out of the building. Then we heard the rushing of the car as it followed the track to the top, the building collapsing in a heap.

Laura and I ran. We saw plenty more cracks in the ground, lots more ooze glowing where the fissures occurred. Our hands were still locked as our feet pounded the blue painted pavement path weaving between trees. It should have been easier to run than the windy hiking trails, but I managed to stumble on every other crack, dragging Laura down with me. I gave her an opportunity to let go and run ahead without me, but her fingers only clutched mine tighter as she pulled me to my feet.

She may have an issue with stuttering, but she was always nice. After upsetting her during orientation, I found her during free time to apologize. She was sitting in the corner of the outdoor theater, holding a packet of information about Blau, the blue cat mascot she would be this summer. She forgave me and turned back to her papers. When I made a joke about everything being blue, she chuckled.

"I k-know right?" She stared at me with wide eyes for a moment. When I didn't react to her stutter, she continued. "I'm n-not sure having *everything* b-b-blue is as c-calming as the website claims."

"Exactly!" I laughed. It was the beginning of friendship between the weirdest employees here.

Blue Adventure Isle wasn't a big island, but it felt like forever to get halfway across. The sun was still out, so it really wasn't that long. We saw guests and employees alike mingling on the docks and beach, panicked voices from nearly everyone.

One thing was clear, the boats the entertainment group owned for a purpose such as this, in all its sky blue glory, were useless, half sunk in the shallow water near the docks. People looked at us and the panic over the boats stopped and new whispers began. We were the only ones half coated in green.

Laura started pulling me towards a collection of nearby employees, including the head honcho, a tall bearded man who was scowling right now. "Houston," I called out to him, "we have a big, big problem." The retired principal had never laughed at that joke, and his head whipped over to me, first his scowl deepening, but after a brief moment, he just sighed.

232

"We have many problems." He grumbled. "But at least we have another two survivors." He nodded to Laura and I.

"Do you know what happened?" I asked. "How did the rides come to life?"

"Kid," I was not a kid (well, almost), but Houston addressed everyone like that, must be a manly fifty-something thing. "From what Lucy over there can piece together on the bursts of radio signal she can get," Lucy was perched on the top of the tallest of the half sunken ships, climbing gear rigged up and a few employees with the safety ropes, "turns out this island used to have nuclear power plants on it. Destroyed by some storms, the previous owners just buried everything. Now, decades later," He pointed to the green soaking into Laura and I's clothes, "the contaminated water is being regurgitated back up like acid reflux."

"You're telling me," I tugged at my soaked polo, "Laura and I, are coated in radioactive island vomit!"

The whispers finally stopped, all eyes, even Lucy's over at us. "Yeah." Houston dragged out the words. "Maybe you two should get out of those."

Laura and I stripped behind separate rocks, extra clothes from unclaimed baggage for some reason being stored on the ships, and were given to us. It was the first time I wasn't wearing blue since I arrived. A green muscle shirt, not that I had muscles to show, and black basketball shorts. Laura was given a purple strapless sundress. It was the first time I saw her curves accented, and she kept crossing her arms over her chest and hiding behind me.

"So, how are you two feeling?" Houston insisted we sit down at the makeshift campfire. The beach stretched out into the darkness, all the survivors in the circle of light, or hovering on the edge. It seemed the screaming was over, just the strange mechanical sounds from the other side of the island.

"I feel okay." I was exhausted, but that had to be normal, running for your life should do that to you. From our vantage point it looked like the swing ride and the roller coaster were focusing on destroying the buildings, hopefully they wouldn't come to the beach.

"Tired." Laura mumbled. She pulled herself closer to me, ducking her face behind my shoulder.

"What's the plan now Houston?" I asked.

"Lucy and a few other techies managed to send an SOS, but who knows if anyone is going to send help. Or when."

"We're doomed." Laura mumbled.

My stomach growled. I didn't bother asking, and no one offered anything to eat. Food was going to be tightly rationed,

233

whatever emergency supplies we could get off the ships. "Couldn't have waited until after lunch."

Gritty sand was stuck to my hands, so I tried to rub it away. It wasn't going anywhere, and it was...

"Calvin," Houston blinked, "your hands." I looked down. My hands were sticky, covered in sand and... and... carefully I used one hand to scrape the layer of sand and some of the thick sticky substance off. Blue peanut butter. I watched my hand secrete another layer of blue peanut butter.

"Um." Laura held up her hands, fingers hanging down, and dripping from the tips of her fingers, were thick globs of blueberry jam. "This is gross."

"Well," Houston pressed his lips together for a moment, "maybe you two will solve our food problem." And then he burst out laughing.

"Would this stuff even be edible?" It was blue, but so was the ingredients I had been making the sandwiches out of. "I mean, wouldn't it be radioactive?" Houston shrugged. I stared at my hand, the one that didn't have a palm full of sand anymore. Considering I had been drenched in ooze, a little more radioactive activity shouldn't hurt. I licked my palm. It was thick, it was sticky, and it tasted exactly like the blue peanut butter I had been eating all summer. I had to smack my tongue against the roof of my mouth to get all the peanut butter down. "Tastes normal."

"Really, you had to just... lick your hand?" Houston rolled his eyes. "Do you expect everyone to lick your palms?"

"No?" I said what I'm sure he wanted me to say. "I can scrape my palms onto bread, or plates, or... their hands?" I nudged Laura's arm and when she looked over at me I tilted my head back.

"Uh."

"Jam me." I wiggled and got my head under her outstretched hands, opening my mouth and sticking out my tongue like I was trying to catch a snowflake.

"At least you aren't licking me." She mumbled as a glob of jam from her middle finger landed on my tongue. It slid down to the back of my throat and I swallowed.

"That tastes normal too."

"Well I'm glad it tastes normal to you, though you might just be radioactive freaks."

"Thanks Houston." I grumbled. "No peanut butter for you." He didn't take me seriously, just telling Laura and I to figure out a way to stop secreting the insides of America's favorite sandwich (at least before peanut allergies gripped the nation).

234

Laura figured out pretty quickly that keeping her hands closed stopped the globs of jam from dripping out of her fingers. That trick didn't work for me. Peanut butter seeped out from between my fingers.

"You know," I told Laura after scraping some built up peanut butter on a large rock. "When my mother said she was worried I'd become a fat, food-stain-and-crumb-covered, lazy, couch surfer if I didn't build a work ethic, I don't think anyone expected the stickiest food to be leaking from my palms."

She giggled, the tiny smile lingering for a moment before she glanced out towards the slow moving machines in the distance. I turned as well, spotting the bright blue movement easily against the darkening sky. The coaster was currently looping its track around the top of the swing machine.

"It's only a matter of time, isn't it?" She whispered. I'm not sure if she didn't stutter, or if I was getting better at ignoring it.

"Probably." Of course the rides would come after us. Now that they've smashed every building on the island, all us survivors were clustered together, with nowhere to run.

"Hey guys." Lucy came over, face and legs a deep red. "We got confirmation of rescue coming, but it will be two days. The nearest islands also suffered from the earthquake so rescue boats are way further out."

"Do you think they'll ignore us for two days?" I pointed to the quiet whirring rides as another pile of peanut butter sloughed off my hand at Lucy's feet.

"No idea. Person on the other end of the radio, he thinks the original owners of the islands, the ones who built the nuclear power plants, mistreated the native people, and got most of them killed when the plants failed."

"So, the local legends of angry spirits waiting for the perfect time to strike isn't just a gimmick for the haunted house?"

"Guess not." Lucy shrugged. "It would explain the machines coming to life."

It made sense, in a crazy way. Like it made sense that Laura could secrete jam because she had splotches of it on her clothes and skin when she fell into the ooze. And my hands had been sticky with peanut butter, obviously having touched the incomplete sandwiches during the initial earthquake.

"Oh, and Houston is going to set up a night watch schedule, so let's go." Lucy walked away without even making sure we would follow, but that was just Lucy.

"I guess we are still working." I grumbled. "Since radioactivity, rides coming to life, and new food producing abilities aren't anywhere in the contract section on being able to stop working before the end of summer."

"Come on." Laura grabbed my sticky hand. "Maybe Houston had a plan to deal with the rides."

Houston may have been the man who solved the great water bottle shortage two weeks into summer, and the great power outage at four weeks, rumored to stop bullies in their tracks with just a look, but nope, he didn't have a plan to combat the rides coming to life week ten of our summer contracts.

I'm not sure any of the grumbling surrounding Houston's admission to not knowing what to do was actually all that serious. How does one prepare for the inevitable machines powered by nuclear waste and angry spirits uprising against the species of their creators? Like I said, it's not covered in the employee handbook, of which I'm sure Houston had memorized after working here twelve consecutive summers.

When no one actually decided to start a mutiny while Houston let us comprehend his lack of knowledge, he gave out the schedule of the night watch and told everyone else to try to get some sleep.

"Hey," I approached Houston as he and Lucy settled down on the edge of the campfire light to take first watch. "Um, you didn't give Laura or I any watch shifts." And this was the guy who rotated me through every job Blue Zone offered before admitting I was too clumsy to properly pull my weight, and if I wasn't making the bare minimum wage he said he would've docked my pay.

"I know." Houston sighed and rubbed his temples. "Don't rub it into the others taking extra. But as much as it pains me to admit, you and Laura are our best bet for survival, so you need to be well rested."

I snorted. Then started laughing, even grabbing at my stomach as I doubled over laughing. My shirt was going to be sticky now, but maybe I should just get used to being sticky, since I had yet to be able to stop the slow secretion of peanut butter.

"Yeah," Houston brought out his famous off duty sarcastic voice, "real awesome that our survival may rest in the sticky hands of the clumsiest seventeen year old alive and the shy introvert mess because they can now make a sandwich needing only bread supplied to them."

It sank in then. If rescue didn't get here before the rides decided to finish the rest of us off, we were doomed.

Laura was sitting on the opposite far end of the circle of light, her back towards everyone. She was curled up, arms wrapped around her knees when I sat down next to her.

236

"What do we do Calvin?" Her voice was shaky and thin, a string about to break. "I'm scared." And then it snapped, and she was sobbing into her knees again.

I certainly didn't know what to do. There was nothing I could say to reassure Laura that wasn't a lie, and what the hell could peanut butter and jam do against living machines.

"I wish I knew." I had to say something. She cried harder and threw her arms around me, sobbing into my shoulder now. I wished she wasn't crying, but somewhere between the craziness, it wasn't all terrible. Laura's arms around me felt warm. I had been amazed at her determination not to leave me behind, despite my clumsiness slowing us down. I had always been impressed at how she handled children as a mascot without words. And even being sweaty and red faced at the end of her shifts, she was always smiling.

I fell into an uneasy sleep, Laura nestled up against me, literally crying herself to sleep. While I couldn't say for sure, I doubted any of the other survivors got much sleep either.

Morning came and the one bright side the rising sun showed us was the coaster and the swings were still just hanging out together on the park side of the island.

Houston divided some of the emergency cracker rations and Laura and I helped make them little sandwiches. Peanut butter and jam crackers were a better way to start using our rations than the crackers alone. Well, everyone except Ricky. The smallest of the child survivors, he was also unfortunately allergic to peanut butter. Laura gave him lots of extra jam. Ricky's mother didn't stop glaring at me through the whole meal. Like I chose to leak a deadly allergen from my hands without any control over it.

Laura at least was able to stop the jam flow, me, I just kept leaving globs of the blue goo anywhere I went. Some of the kids, not Ricky, started using the peanut butter mixed with sand to build elaborate castles, animals, people, and they even started building a wall between our beach and the strip of trees keeping the park and the administrative buildings separate.

No one wanted to crush the kids' dreams. If the ants didn't eat the wall, peanut butter and sand weren't going to be enough to protect us.

"Calvin and Laura come here!" Houston called from the boat we managed to get a radio signal from. He was leaning against the lower railing, lower because the boat was tilted, with another man next to him. "This is Bobby." He nodded to the shorter, pudgier, and more balding man. "He's a mechanical engineer, and he might have an idea to stop those." He said. Then nodded towards the metal scraping that was so constant now, I almost forgot about it.

I looked over my shoulder to see that the coaster had moved closer to us, circling a group of trees while the swing ride lumbered after it. A big glob of peanut butter made a splat sound on the deck; I thought it summed up my thoughts nicely on the matter.

"I was hoping they'd just run out of power," Bobby's voice was the most nasally monotone I had ever heard. "But since that doesn't look like it will happen anytime soon..." Another glob of peanut butter hit the deck. "Our best bet might be you two," Bobby nodded to me and Laura, who by now had half hidden herself behind me again. "Gumming up the works."

"What?" I thought I knew what he meant, but I asked for two reasons, one, I really wanted to make sure I heard him right, and two, if I did, not only would it mean Laura and I facing the rides in order to stop them with our strange new abilities, it also meant he was missing a perfect pun opportunity and I wanted to see if he would rectify it.

"Seizing up the gears." Bobby clarified. When neither myself nor Laura made any acknowledgement of understanding what he was saying, Bobby continued. "Breaking the mechanical movement. Sticking the moving parts. Um," Bobby ran a hand over his almost hairless head.

"Oh," I tried to snap my fingers, but the only sound I ended up making was another two squelches of the smaller chunks of peanut butter hitting the deck. "You mean jamming up the works?" Houston put his palm across his face. Bobby blinked, sniffed, and then sighed the kind of disappointed sigh I was used to hearing from my parents whenever I brought home a bad grade or broke something from being clumsy, both frequent occurrences.

"D-do you really think it will work?" Laura stood besides me now, one hand gripping my wrist.

"Well..." Bobby dragged out the word until Houston cut him off.

"It might be our only hope." I felt Laura's arm shake my arm, another plop of peanut butter falling, this time onto my shoe.

"Well, it is certainly better than my plan."

"What is your plan?" Houston took the bait.

"Hoping at least one of the machines, or spirits possessing them, or whatever, is allergic to peanuts, or blueberries, or both." Houston didn't look like he was going to respond, but I heard an angry grunt from the dock. "No offense to Ricky or his mother!" I called out. That earned me a little giggle from Laura, and her fingers loosening a little around my wrist.

238

"But first," Houston rolled his eyes, "You two, go see Lucy about those cuts and scrapes we can see now in the light of day. Did you fall through a thistle patch or something?" I shook my head. I hadn't seen any thistles on the island. Just the usual of running into trees, branches, bushes, and falling onto roots and rocks. And since, in the moment, Laura and I had been fleeing hand-in-hand, I dragged her into, through, and onto most of the same stuff.

The stinging of the cuts hadn't bothered me, seeing as I usually had a plethora of small injuries just like them from day to day movements that don't go quite right. Besides the daily bruises and scrapes from walking around, I've sprained my wrist, twisted both ankles and burned my fingers seven times. All in two months working here. Since these new scrapes hadn't been bleeding a lot, I had ignored them. I guess Houston didn't want to send injured kids out to face giant machines bent on destroying us.

Laura sat with me, humming and rubbing her arms with her closed fists. She didn't have nearly as many scrapes as I did, though I had a feeling she wouldn't have any if I wasn't as unsteady as a toddler trying to learn how to walk with skates on. Lucy did as I asked, though she sent up an eyebrow at the small cuts. I didn't know what to say about that, clearly she thought it a waste of the first aid kits we were able to scrounge up from the boats, some of the only things not blue on this entire island, but one of the first things we learned here was Houston's word was final.

With that done, Laura and I trudged back up to Houston waiting at the edge of the forest now, near a bit of a dirt trail that I was familiar with. It was part of the web that connected the entire island. I used the dirt trails to avoid the heavily trafficked paved walkways when riding the bike with a cooler in the wagon around to drop off water for employees at the strategic locations, also known as the other scattered break rooms.

Mack came down the path, pushing the bike I used, wagon and cooler still attached. "Excellent," Houston grinned. "Are there still waters in there?" Mack was broad, had a square jaw, skin the color of wet sand, not quite seven feet tall, and a very quiet guy. The strong and silent type. A nod was all he gave, and honestly had he said anything I would have been more terrified. Now why couldn't he have fallen into the ooze? Maybe he would have gotten super strength.

"We'll be taking the cooler, Laura, you can ride in the cart. Calvin, you ride better than you run, so..."

"I get it." I sighed. "We don't get a cool superhero car, plane, boat, or submarine," I gestured to the bike as peanut butter dripped from my fingers. "We get a bike with a wagon."

"Cart." Houston corrected.

"Whatever." I tilted my neck from side to side, until I heard a nice pop. Some of the tension gone, I was as ready as I could ever be. "Come on Laura." I looked over at her, and her eyes were already filled with tears. "I promise I won't crash the bike." It didn't seem to calm her as much as I hoped, but she climbed into the wagon, wrapping her arms around her knees.

"You know," Houston put a hand on my shoulder, "I wouldn't ask you to do this if-"

"If it wasn't our only hope." I sighed. For a moment the only sounds were the mechanical whirrings of the rides slowly making their way towards us. Maybe they knew we had nowhere left to run.

"Good luck kids." The gruff, no nonsense man squeezed my shoulder before stepping back and saluting us. My stomach twisted into a billion knots knowing we might not come back, nor be able to stop the machines. Bad odds never stopped me before, at least in every video game I ever played and impromptu off road bike races with people more experienced than me. These odds weren't going to be enough to stop me this time either.

Sitting and pedaling was natural, and Laura weighed about as much as an empty cooler at the end of my shift, so everything was going smoothly. No matter how many bumps the bike took, or how tight or odd the turns were, I always had complete control of the bike in a way I didn't have over my own body.

"You know," I said loudly, maybe too loud considering we were heading towards a dangerous enemy and likely demise, but I needed to make sure Laura could hear me over the wind as I picked up speed. "When my parents insisted I get a summer job this year, I tried to convince them to let me see if I had a chance in a career in BMX racing."

"I wanted to teach a children's art class," Laura responded, "but at the park districts and libraries I applied, no one looked past my stutter." If she was stuttering now, the wind was whipping it away, or maybe there was something about going to face the seemingly impossible that made speaking not so scary anymore.

I left a trail of peanut butter along the edges of the dirt path. It was still just constantly dripping from my hands, but at this point there was no reason to try to stop it.

Even though I had a few chances to turn onto pavement, I stuck to the dirt, winding my way far around where the roller coaster was whirring in circles, and circling back to approach the swing ride from behind. Not that it had a clear front or behind. The top dome part was just sections of light and dark blue, striped like a circus tent. The same colors alternated were the swings, or legs now.

"How are we supposed to stop that?" She grumbled. "Most of the actual mechanics are in the post it left behind." I slowed by moving the handlebars back and forth in tight zig zags as we approached the walking mushroom top.

"We stop the legs I guess. If I get enough peanut butter on the hinges for the chains at the top, maybe it won't be able to move."

"You try to climb it and it won't even have to shake you off before you fall to your death." She hissed.

"What if..." I glanced back at her, nodding towards her white knuckle fists, "you make it slip first?" She looked at me, looked at my hands, and looked at me again.

"Think you c-can weave between the legs without getting stepped on?"

"If you think you can leave enough jam behind to make it lose its footing."

"Only one way to find out." She pushed herself to her knees, holding one fist over either side of the wagon. I gripped the handlebars, leaned forward, lifted my butt off the seat, and cranked the bike into high gear. It wasn't just the ride's swing legs I had to maneuver around, this area was also littered with smashed food stalls and strewn about food, broken benches, railings, and fissures where the ooze probably had seeped up. And there were bodies, the people not so lucky. It would have been too much to think about, to truly absorb then. Instead my mind turned the dead people into mannequins for my sanity.

I'm not sure how many times I circled the ride, doing my best to avoid sending the bike wheels out from under me when getting back around to the blue jam trail Laura was leaving. Left and right, sometimes having to come to the inside of the ride in the open part where the legs couldn't reach, because somehow it was aware there was something it wanted to smash moving around between its legs.

The blue trail became thick blue lines, then rings, before the plastic started to lose its grip on the pavement. "Calvin!" Laura screamed at the same time I heard it, multiple plastic pieces scraping the pavement and multiple chains rattling as they became loose. I whipped the bike around, barely able to pull the wheels back upright from jam collecting on them and the ground. Laura grunted as she was knocked off balance in the cart, but I had to turn so we were moving away from where the giant thing was falling.

With a great big thud and a cracking noise it hit the ground. I braked, hard, Laura slamming into my back and nearly sending me over the handlebars. We turned and saw it had nearly broken in two from the impact, and everything about it was limp and lifeless.

"Guess I don't need to get the hinges sticky after all."

If we were going to celebrate, we couldn't because that's when the whirring of the coaster track was getting louder and we both flung ourselves away from the bike in order not to get impaled by it. Or run over by the coaster that was riding it.

The bike and wagon were not as lucky as us, smashed to bits. Laura was standing, shaking, as the coaster's painted on eyes turned towards her, and the track behind it started retracting towards it. I ran forward and placed my hands on the undersides of the round beams, following it back where it extended away from the cars.

Somehow, despite the ground being a littered battlefield, I only tripped twice. Most of the track was coated with peanut butter. "Laura, run!" I screamed as I ran out of track to make sticky, having no idea whether or not it would work. She did, bolting straight towards me as the coaster started making the whirring sound right before it would eject the track.

But even as Laura reached me, knocking me to the ground as she flung her arms around me, it just kept whirring. No track, just whirring. And lots of smoke, and finally, a small burst of flames from the underside of the coaster before it all collapsed in a heap.

"We did it!" Laura pulled me back up, both of our clothes coated in peanut butter and jam.

"Huh." I scratched my head, not caring that my blond hair was turning blue and sticky. "Guess we did."

Her hand slipped into mine, peanut butter and jam mingling between our skin as we slowly headed back. Whenever I tripped over something she would steady me, and then give me a bright smile.

My mind was still wrapping around everything as our feet sunk into the dry sand of the beach. We didn't even have to say anything before the celebratory cheers broke out. I tugged Laura closer as the group surrounded us.

"Well done kids." Houston's hand clapped my shoulder, giving me a shake and a crooked smile.

"Thanks." I grinned back, before meeting Laura's slowly growing smile. The children led a cheer, even Ricky and his mother throwing their hands in the air.

242

The good mood lasted well into the night as we celebrated the best we could with what we had. Lucy and Mack got a partially clear radio signal for music.

Laura and I reenacted the fight (mostly) for the kids, with dramatic flare of course. We took turns narrating, while she stuttered a few times, but after those brown eyes met mine, and a deep breath, she would collect herself. Her movements were graceful and natural in the sand circle we called a stage. I was my usual klutzy self, leaving droplets of peanut butter and landing in the sand breathless at the end of the celebration.

Laura flopped down with me again. We continued to talk as the night wore on. We weren't sure what we were going to do about our strange new powers, but that was a problem for another day.

Vlad & Johnny

by Ella Moon
Third Place
Content Warning: cult dynamics

"Look, I don't want no Dracula in my home."

Vlad grit his fangs and muttered, "*One* guy gets a book written about him. Johnny, would you just let me inside?"

Johnny stared at him for a moment, probably questioning why he was snapping and standing like he was frozen in place. Vlad forced himself to breathe, pushing the tension out of his shoulders so he at least didn't *look* quite so much like he was looming, ready to strike. It apparently worked, because Johnny took a step back, wordlessly gesturing inside.

"You know that doesn't work for me," Vlad said, aware he was still snapping and too wound up to stop himself.

Johnny huffed out a breath. "Come inside, Vlads."

"*Thank* you," Vlad said, and finally stepped over the perimeter.

"And what brings you to this here humble abode?" Johnny asked, turning his back on Vlad to take the three steps to his kitchen.

Vlad had never actually been here before, and Johnny wasn't kidding about the humble part. His brother and Vlad's sister, Suzie, had bought a nice big house out in the suburbs after the wedding, but Johnny's architectural inclinations apparently bottomed out in a three-room walk-up which altogether looked like a strong wind might blow it over. It seemed at odds with Johnny himself, who had so many muscles built into his stocky frame that he probably would have been able to intimidate said wind into turning tail just by glaring at it.

Johnny glanced back over his shoulder, and Vlad realised that, trying to avoid the upcoming conversation, he'd probably been staring a little too long at the off-white walls and the faded brown couch visible off the other side of what barely passed as a hallway. He shut the front door behind him and followed Johnny into the kitchen, pushing the hood of his sweatshirt back off his head, then fidgeted uselessly, brushing the pads of his fingers back and forth against his nails.

"This is a little awkward," he started.

"Yah, no kidding," Johnny replied, propping a hip against the kitchen counter. "I got no problem talkin' with ya at family events or down at the store, but I wouldn't'a called us 'turning up in the middle of the afternoon' type friends. 'Specially not with the, what, the culture divide and all that."

Vlad elected not to bring up the time last Thanksgiving that Johnny had gotten extremely drunk and spent at least an hour with his head on Vlad's shoulder crying about his ex-boyfriend, which Vlad felt probably put them *past* the 'turning up in the middle of the afternoon' stage. He was, at least, correct that they weren't what one might call easy friends, which was indeed partially thanks to the 'culture divide'—more so to the fact that Johnny tended to (when sober) fastidiously avoid Vlad's touch and do his best to run away any time the conversation threatened to get deeper than 'hey, did ya see the Yankees game yesterday? Sucked, huh?', obviously still harbouring some of those long-engrained fears of vampires. Human media was lousy with them, which kinda brought Vlad back to the reason he'd come here.

"I need your help."

"And you got no-one else to go to?"

Vlad winced slightly. "Not really, no. Not that fulfills the necessary criteria."

"Those'd be?"

"Human, trusted, might say yes."

Johnny raised his eyebrows. "Well, now I gotta know."

Vlad took a deep breath, even though the oxygen was mostly unnecessary for him. Some things were more ritual than anything else. "I don't really know where to start with this."

"Beginning's the usual spot."

Vlad rolled his eyes, then turned around and began pacing back and forth across the shitty lino floor of the kitchen. "Okay, so, you know about hive mentality?"

"That's that thing with Dracs and privacy, ya?"

"Ya– uh, yes. Vampires in hives, which is most of us, are extremely unlikely to trust anyone outside the hive, and violating that privacy is- it's seen as something terrible, on a level with torture. But because I'm a loner, I don't have the same instincts about it."

Vlad paused, and Johnny said, "With ya so far, Vlads."

Scrubbing both hands through his short, wiry curls, which were already thoroughly messed up from having been hidden under his hood, Vlad sighed and said, "What I'm about to tell you cannot leave this room."

"What, I ain't allowed to take it into the living room?"

"Johnny, this is serious."

Johnny raised his hands in surrender. "Top secret, got it."

Vlad bit gently into his lower lip—last chance to back out, not bring a human in, go find some other solution that didn't involve- this. But there wasn't another solution, not a quick enough one, and however spiky Johnny could sometimes be around him, there really wasn't anyone else he'd trust with this. "There's a- a loner network, of sorts. Not like we have regular meetings or anything, but we're in contact. One of the things we're in contact *for* is... keeping an eye on the hives."

Johnny cracked a grin. "Like lotsa little beekeepers, huh?"

"*Johnny.*"

"A'right, a'right. Touchy tonight, huh, Vlads?"

"I have reason. Turning is coming up—the anniversary of the first recorded vampire creation, before we reproduced normally-"

"I do know all o' y'all's major holidays." Johnny looked mildly offended. "You're family."

"Right. Well, Turning's next week, and another loner heard whispers coming out of the Baltimore hive. It's the oldest hive in the US, and they've always been insular and secretive, even for a hive, but lately they've been... even more worrying. They've been having equipment delivered, and-"

"I don't gotta know the whole detective detail, do I?"

Vlad shook his head. "No. You don't. Point is, they're planning something for Turning. We don't know exactly what, but something bad. Something like all those vampire movies humans love making."

Johnny blinked at him for a moment, then said, "Well, that ain't good. Still don't know why you came to me, but. Can't you and the resta the loners deal with it, if it was such a big deal to tell me 'bout the network? Or ain't there some type of authorities you can take it to?"

"Not without telling them how I happened to come across such information, which runs far too high a risk of bringing the whole surveillance network crashing down. And like I said, there's not that many of us around. But maybe we could have dealt with it ourselves, if it was just that."

"There's more?"

"There's a human group. Anti-vampire extremists. They're based in New York, but they travelled to Baltimore a few days ago. No way they could have heard about whatever the Baltimore hive's doing—it barely got out to the loners—so they have to be planning something themselves. In the first place vampires settled in America, right before a major vampire holiday. You see why we're concerned."

Johnny huffed out a breath, leaning back onto his elbows. "Yah. Sounds like good grounds for mass extermination, vamps and humans both. Still not sure what I can do about it."

Vlad nodded slowly. "I'm the closest loner to Baltimore, apart from Suzie, and I don't want to involve her. You can come help me stop whatever it is they're both planning. See, I can get into the hive grounds, but I won't be able to get into wherever the humans are holed up. Not without being invited, and I can't see them doing that."

Johnny stared at him for a minute, then sniffed and straightened up off the counter, rubbing his big hands together. "So, just ta be clear, you're asking me, a plumber, to come take down not one but *two* extremist groups with you, a lab scientist, on no warning and with no backup."

"...Yes," Vlad admitted, wringing his hands.

Johnny watched him blankly for a moment longer, then broke into a huge grin. "So how're we getting to Baltimore, babes?"

"Thought you'd have some kinda magic Drac-type transportation," Johnny complained, vainly attempting to stretch his legs out and coming up against the inexorable barrier of the seat in front of him. They were the only ones on the very back seat of the Newark-Baltimore Greyhound, but it was still quite obviously too small a space to comfortably house Johnny. Vlad, on the other hand, was perfectly at home sitting in the opposite corner, back to the window and his legs stretched out along the seat.

"What, the Greybat line?" he retorted, and Johnny glanced sideways at him, a smile chasing across his face, dropping as quickly as it appeared.

"Oh, you're in a good mood now, huh?"

Vlad shrugged. It was slightly more tamped-down manic anxiety than 'good', but no reason for Johnny to know that. At least the nerves had switched into a state where he could return Johnny's banter like normal. No need to psych him out even more about this whole thing. "Well, we're on our way to doing something, but there's nothing I can do about it until we get close enough for my hearing to kick in."

"Yeah, 'bout that?"

"Super-hearing. Mine's particularly good. Once we're in Maryland, I should be able to tune into and locate both groups, and maybe, hopefully, figure out what they're doing. But we've got five hours to kill till then."

"Hmmph," Johnny replied. "Don't suppose you brought a pack of cards?"

"'Fraid not. How do you feel about I Spy?"

248

"Badly, Vlads. I feel badly about I Spy, 'specially with a guy who can see a mile further than me."

"It's called utilising your natural advantage."

"Yah, well, I ain't a fan of your 'natural advantages'."

Vlad managed to stop just short of waggling his eyebrows as he retorted, "That's just because I haven't used them to *your* advantage yet."

The waggle clearly came through anyway, because Johnny looked away again, cheeks tinged pink. It was adorably easy to make him blush, and Vlad would do it a lot more often if it weren't for actually, genuinely, trying his best to respect the fear-set boundaries Johnny usually drew around their interactions. Johnny grumbled something mostly unintelligible and very Jerseyian under his breath, then leant against the back window with his arms folded and said, "I'm going to sleep. Maybe you can function on twenty-minute batnaps every three days, but I wanna be well-rested before I gotta stop a mass extinction plot or two."

Vlad harrumphed lightly, both at the exaggeration—he needed at *least* an hour's sleep a day—and at being left without his main source of distraction and entertainment. When no response was forthcoming from Johnny, he gave up and slumped back into the corner, staring vacantly past Johnny out the side window and doing his best to zone out in preparation.

Johnny hadn't been lying about going to sleep, but he had clearly been underestimating his own ability to do so while sitting firmly upright. He'd been listing slowly sideways towards Vlad for the last fifteen minutes, and as amusing as it was to watch, Vlad didn't really think it'd put him in a good mood if he finally toppled over and woke up with his head hitting Vlad's lap. Vlad had kicked his shoes off and pushed them under the seat at least an hour ago, so he stretched out further and dug his toes into Johnny's thigh.

"Hhhrmmphhh?" Johnny said.

"Extremely cogent commentary," Vlad told him, and he lurched back upright, eyes blinking open.

"Vlad?" he asked in apparent confusion, then looked around, shook his head, and sniffed loudly. "Right."

"You know," Vlad said lazily, "for a guy who claims to be scared of vampires, you sure went to sleep easy around one."

"When did I ever claim that?" Johnny retorted defensively.

Vlad tilted his head to the side. "Well, never, I guess. I'm used to reading the signs, though."

"You ever seen me look 'fraid round your sister?" Johnny said, then made a huffing noise and clammed up, like he'd just betrayed something he'd never meant to. Vlad frowned curiously at him, but that was apparently all he was saying on the matter. Vlad hadn't seen that, as it happened, but then it stood to reason that he'd make more of an effort to hide it at family events around Suzie, his brother's wife, than he would around Vlad when they met in the streets. There wasn't much else reason for him to always avoid Vlad and duck away as soon as he possibly could, given that they actually got on anywhere from reasonably to terrifically well whenever circumstances conspired to force them into conversation.

"Okay," Vlad accepted for now. "If you wanna go back to sleep, I'd suggest leaning against the window. You were getting a distinct angle to you that way."

"Nah, I'm awake now. How long we got to go?"

"Couple hours."

Johnny sighed. "You got anything other than I Spy in your bag of tricks?"

"I'd offer to turn into a bat, but it's still light out."

"Thought that was a myth."

Vlad widened his eyes at Johnny, leaning towards him and baring his fangs slightly. "Vere are no myfzzz," he proclaimed with an exaggerated lisp.

Johnny huffed out a laugh and punched Vlad's calf. "Would ya stop?"

"Never," Vlad promised, leaning back. "I'll tell you who *is* scared of us, is your aunt. Do you remember how drunk she got at the wedding?"

Laughing, Johnny threw his head back against the seat. "Oh, poor Aunt Viv. Pretty sure that was her worst nightmare."

"When Suzie threw the bouquet and she actually leapt *out* of the way?"

"Oh, lord!"

"All I'm saying is, y'know, eels don't actually have blood but they *do* have nerves, so-" Vlad cut himself off with a sharp intake of breath, and Johnny leant towards him slightly.

"Whaddisit?"

Vlad lifted a finger to his lips, and searched for the familiar voice that had just brushed the edge of his hearing. He hadn't realised how close they'd gotten to Baltimore, too caught up in the ridiculous conversations he and Johnny had been having and how much he'd enjoyed watching him loosen up without getting drunk and morose. But that had been the hive leader, and Johnny had spoken too quickly for Vlad to get a fix on what she'd been saying or where she was.

250

Snatches of conversation from random Baltimoreans drifted past as Vlad sifted rapidly through voices, attempting to recapture her.

"Ready-"

He clenched a fist, digging nails into his palm, and focused, focused, focused.

"The machine will be ready for Turning?" she said, and whatever poor crony she was speaking to replied,

"Yes, Ms. Anna, the nighttime machine is almost prepared-"

And he'd been focusing too hard on the words, because suddenly he was hearing someone else, a man, close to the hive but not so close as to be in the same building-

"The daytime machine'll be ready for their big ritual day. That'll drive 'em back where they-"

Vlad snapped out of it, back to the bus, where he'd at some point swung his legs around so he was sitting upright. Johnny had a hand on his shoulder, leaning towards him with a concerned expression. "Vlad. You okay? Talk to me, Vlads."

Vlad took a shuddering breath and turned into Johnny, letting him slip his arm awkwardly around Vlad's back and hold him in place. Turned out those big muscles were good for more than just the potentially violent pursuits Vlad had recruited them for.

"You okay, Vlad?" Johnny repeated, his voice rumbling through his chest and against Vlad's side. "You're turned even paler than usual, you're almost white."

"I know what they're planning," Vlad said, and forced himself upright, away from Johnny's arms. And chest. And still very sweetly worried face. "Both of them."

"But that's in*sane*!" Johnny exclaimed. "Either o' those things'll kill everyone, sooner or later!"

"Yes, well, rest assured in the fact that you're smarter than two extremist groups combined," Vlad told him, some equanimity restored.

"I..." Johnny trailed off and shook his head. "You got a plan to stop 'em?"

"Yeah. We find them, and we stop them." Vlad was saved from any follow-up questions by the bus gently rolling to a stop. "Let's go."

Johnny was keeping pace with Vlad along yet another side street when he finally asked, "You sure you know where you're takin' us?"

"Yes," Vlad answered shortly. He'd tuned in to check a couple of times, but even that was unnecessary, really. He'd know the way to this particular hive building blindfolded and headphoned.

Another few minutes of silent walking, and they were there. Vlad pulled them to a stop, holding out an arm to block Johnny. Johnny halted just behind it, and looked over at the nondescript side door, two small steps up from the concrete ground of the alley. "This is it?" he said doubtfully.

"What, you wanna march in through the front door?" Vlad asked. "We might have to go that route with the humans, but I can guide us through here, and maybe we can get in and out without having to confront anyone." Please, lord.

"A'right, a'right. Lead the way."

With a deep breath—rituals, rituals—Vlad reached for the door. In exactly the kind of arrogant move he would have expected from the Baltimore hive, it wasn't even locked. Then again, the thought of anyone breaking into the Baltimore hive building was absurd, so maybe it wasn't so arrogant after all.

It opened onto what passed for a hive pantry, exactly as Vlad had known it would. His spatial awareness magnified by the adrenaline running through him, he felt Johnny flinch behind him at the sight of the blood bags hanging along the icy walls. Of course, the most he'd ever seen was Vlad and Suzie's fridges. Humans always reacted badly to this idea. "You know it's all animal or synthetic," Vlad hissed. He hoped it was, at least. "Come on."

"It's-" Johnny gulped, then shut the door and moved up next to Vlad with surprisingly quiet steps. "Yeah. Yeah. Okay."

Vlad nodded sharply and strode across the freezer, Johnny following behind him.

The building was just as much of a maze as Vlad remembered it to be, but with the map in Vlad's head, that actually worked to their advantage. Mazes were very hard to patrol, and it took until they were almost at the third dining room—the one Vlad had identified as most likely having been converted to house the machine he'd heard them talking about—before they encountered anyone. Focused on checking his suspicions about the dining room and listening for Anna and just trying to get out of here, Vlad didn't hear him until it was too late, and a small wiry man with glasses, staring at the ground and apparently lost in thought, almost ran into the two of them. He looked up with a surprised, "Oh!", then squinted at Vlad.

Vlad gave him a polite smile.

252

He opened his mouth, said, "Aren't you-?", and was interrupted by Johnny punching him in the jaw. His head jerked to the side, got a shocked little 'o' expression, and promptly followed his body down to the floor.

Johnny looked over at Vlad, who smiled gratefully at him. "Thanks."

"What was he sayin'?"

Vlad waved a hand. "Probably 'aren't you human?'"

"Sure looked like it was directed at you," Johnny muttered, but followed Vlad as he stepped over the prone vampire and continued on.

"Maybe '-a loner'."

"...Maybe."

"Here," Vlad announced, and pulled the third dining room door open without fanfare, before Johnny could get any further with questions.

What was on the other side was enough to shut them both up. Vlad retained just enough presence of mind to pull Johnny inside with him and shut the door behind them, then stood still with Johnny, staring at it.

The only thing that had been retained from the original dining room was the large oak table in the middle of the room. The walls had been stripped bare and hung with white tarps, and a seemingly random combination of beakers and mechanical parts and tools lined the mantelpieces, but the main event was taking up the entire table. A welded-together compendium of glass and sleek metal parts, it bore the energy of a Ferrari that had been taken apart and then reassembled by someone who had never seen a car in their life. On closer inspection, everything seemed to be connected to everything else, but at first glance one got the distinct impression that tubes were haphazardly sticking out everywhere, ready to start spewing the powder inside them all over the room. One large spout came out the top, the only apparent opening. Tracing down from it, using the fear lurking in the back of his mind as a knife to sharpen his focus, Vlad realised that one of the round glass chambers he'd assumed was filled with grey powder was-something else. The powder was moving, seemingly autonomously. He took a few steps closer, scanning rapidly across the device, cataloguing the colour, viscosity, opacity of the five or six separate liquids and powders scattered across chambers along the bottom of the device, all below the moving grey creatures.

Behind him, Johnny said doubtfully, "*That* monster's meant to put out the sun?"

"No, I don't think so," Vlad muttered.

"You were wrong about the endless nighttime plot?"

"No." That had definitely been what he'd heard. No more sun, no more humans, just vampire-friendly night forever. "No, it's just got other means to do it." He gestured vaguely at the creatures. "Those are nanites."

"Li'l baby robots?"

"Essentially, yeah. I just…" He counted along the liquids, muttering chemical names under his breath for a minute before he spoke up again. "They're gonna fire them up, use them to block out the sun. I'm just trying to figure exactly how they're planning to get them into atmosphere."

Besides him, Johnny cocked his head to the side, then looked up at the ceiling. "No way they can do that from here, eh? There's got to be at least three floors above us."

"Good- good point. They're going to have to take it out somewhere."

Johnny raised his eyebrows. "Can't do that inconspicuous-like. Not with something this big."

"So," Vlad said, half his brain still running through chemical reactions. "If we sabotage it without them realising… they should be discovered by someone else when they take it out, at least when it fails to work. Oh! The methyl acid over there has to react with the ethyl-hydroxide, oxidise the aluminium powder, meet the air, electrify-"

"Ya gotta dumb this down for me, Vlads."

Vlad blinked and shook his head, then pointed along the device as he explained, "Uh, that fluid has to get into that chamber along with the powder from up here, and then come out of this tube. But short of smashing it all, I don't know how to-"

"Ah," Johnny waved a hand. "Leave that one to me, babes. That's just plumbing. You watch the door." He grabbed one of the tools off the mantelpiece, and turned his attention to the device.

"I-" Vlad blinked again. "Okay, I'll watch the door."

This seemed way too easy. Anxiety ran its fingers over his neck and back, unease sitting heavy in his gut. But he dutifully stood guard by the door, watching the continually empty corridor as Johnny did whatever he was doing to the tune of occasional clattering and light cursing. The machine really must have been fully prepared, if they'd left it all alone down here, waiting for the Turning. Thank the lord for superstitions—if they hadn't been waiting for an appropriate date to deploy it… Vlad didn't even want to think about it.

It only took Johnny about ten minutes before he replaced the tool on the mantelpiece with a quiet thud and came up behind Vlad, tapping him on the shoulder. "All done, Vlads. That thing's gonna go off with a fizzle and a pop and absolutely nothin' else."

254

Vlad heaved a sigh of relief. "Okay. Let's go."

"You got a lock on the humans?" Johnny asked as they walked back out.

"Think so. They're not far." They turned the corner just past where they'd knocked out the little vampire, who was still lying prone in the corridor, and Vlad stopped, Johnny almost running into him. "Wait. We should do something with him, or they'll know we've been here."

"Point," Johnny said, and they both turned around.

Vlad rounded the corner first, and froze a second later.

Johnny actually ran into him this time, sending him swaying forward before Johnny grabbed his arm and pulled him back onto his centre of balance.

"Vlad," proclaimed the woman now standing over the prone vampire, jet-black hair curling down against jet-black skin, staring at them coldly from jet-black eyes.

Even without taking his eyes off her, Vlad could feel Johnny beside him glancing quickly back and forth between them. "You know her?" he whispered quietly. Not quiet enough, of course, because she switched her gaze to him, drew herself up, and replied for Vlad, who had yet to swallow past the dryness in his throat.

"I *birthed* him, human."

"What?"

"Hello, Anna," Vlad managed, with, he thought, the admirable appearance of calm.

"You won't even call me mother?"

"We're well past that, Anna."

Johnny had apparently drawn the obvious conclusions, and was staying silent, stock-still just behind Vlad's left shoulder.

"I knew you and your sister had turned from us. I didn't realise you'd turned *to* them."

Johnny stiffened behind Vlad, who said, the deliberate calm in his voice approaching monotone levels, "We didn't turn to anyone. We left because we saw the path you were headed down. And haven't we been proven right?"

Anna watched him, unblinking. "You really thought I wouldn't hear that you were here? You *got* your hearing from me, little one. You won't stop us."

Johnny leant forward as if he was about to speak, and Vlad kicked him in the ankle as Anna continued, "You may have abused your family birthright to enter here, but you will go no further. What you have done to Kristopher is the only damage you will inflict here today."

Vlad sniffed, holding her gaze even as his pulse raced and pounded in his ears and his thoughts raced after it. She thought they were coming this way down the corridor, she didn't know they'd got to the machine. His hearing had always been better than hers—she mustn't have heard what they were saying, just Vlad's voice. They could still pull this off, if only- if only she kept some maternal instinct. He should never have brought Johnny inside here, the power she had as hive leader could easily wipe out both of them if she wanted to. He knew that, he should have known she'd find them but he'd- he'd gotten cocky. Maybe that was a family trait after all.

Anna never bothered with things like breathing, any more than was necessary. When she stood still, she was like a statue, carved out of black marble. She was statuesque now, and Vlad did his best to match her, but knew his own breathing gave him away. Despite his tensing, trying to restrain it, he knew it was elevated to the point of visibility. Only the briefest flash of disgust preceded her next, invisibly fast movement.

Vlad blinked, and she was directly in front of them. The three inches of height she held on him drew themselves out as she loomed over him, lips parted slightly. Vlad's focus was so spent on keeping his gaze upon her fangs, waiting for the strike, that it wasn't until Johnny started to move around him and he went to throw an arm out that he realised Anna was gripping his wrist, fixing him in place, sense memory and fear paralysing him. Desperate to keep Johnny from intervening, images of his death at Anna's hand already looping through his brain, Vlad managed to drag his feet into movement. He stepped sideways, further into Anna's grip. Placing himself firmly between the hive leader and Johnny's new position, hoping he'd get the message.

Vlad's free hand was trembling, the glint of Anna's fangs filling his field of vision. But this was his fight. He still held the slimmest hope Anna would spare him, and he would not have Johnny killing himself for Vlad's sake. She would have no qualms about *his* death.

Slowly, steeling himself, Vlad dragged his gaze up to Anna's night-dark eyes. He swallowed dryly as he was hit by the careless regard in them. It was the way one might look at a vaguely irritating insect, and it only deepened as they made eye contact and she saw the fear in Vlad's. She curled her lip slightly, scornfully, then released Vlad's wrist with a push.

"Go," she said coldly. "I will not kill you or your foolish human tonight – he will not survive long past Turning, in any case. But rest assured, little one – if ever I hear you or your sister step foot in my city again, our affiliation will not be near enough to save you."

Barely retaining outward control, Vlad tipped his head in acknowledgement, long-engrained instinct leading him to bare his neck to her. Then he turned, grabbed Johnny's arm, and pulled both of them out of there as fast as he could go.

After all that, sabotaging the human machine was somewhat of an anti-climax. Johnny said nothing about Anna the entire time there, said almost nothing to Vlad at all. Vlad tracked the humans to an abandoned warehouse two streets away and Johnny dispensed of the sole guard with a very efficient chokehold. While the hive had been awake, the late hour meant that the humans had left their warehouse otherwise empty— insofar as Vlad could tell from peering through the doorway he couldn't cross, they'd gotten nanites from the same source as the hive, only these ones were programmed to reflect sunlight continuously across the entire planet, effectively driving all vampires underground. Johnny sabotaged their only slightly tidier-looking machine the same way, and they stole the guard's wallet on the way out, leaving him hopefully believing himself the victim of a random and oddly smooth-run robbery from two men who clearly had no idea what they were dealing with.

Johnny didn't speak, apart from a few necessary clarifications, until they were back at the bus station. And Vlad wasn't going to force him to. This had been exactly the reason he'd hoped so fervently to avoid meeting anyone inside the hive. His and Suzie's self-enforced exile from the Baltimore hive was an open secret amongst the vampire community, but she'd never told her husband and Vlad had never wanted to bring it into her human family—especially not under these circumstances. It was more than that gnawing at him, though—there was a guilt more specific to him, and to Johnny, even though he'd technically told no lies. Everything he'd said to Johnny, from the moment he'd knocked on his door, was the truth—he had only left out his own additional reasons for wanting to do this himself.

When they were finally on the bus, due to ride through the night and arrive at Newark the next morning, Vlad ventured, "I think that went well. All things considered."

They were once again on the far back seat, but while Johnny had resumed his previous corner, he was slouched down into it, and Vlad had curled himself up in the opposite corner, legs tucked under him. The vibrations as the bus began to drive away ran through his back, half-pressed against the cold metal.

"What'd she mean, you got in by your family birthright?" Johnny asked, and Vlad blinked. That hadn't been the question he was expecting.

"Uh, the invitation rule is void for family homes. The metaphysical definition of family can be a bit shaky, but I suppose tonight proved it definitely applies to blood family, no matter how you feel about each other."

Johnny crossed his arms. "But it doesn't recognise family by marriage?"

Where the hell Johnny's mind was going was a complete mystery to Vlad, even more so than usual. "It recognises partnerhoods, as long they've been in existence long enough."

"But you couldn't get into my home. Does it only apply to the partners themselves?"

Oh. "Oh. Uh…"

Johnny looked over at Vlad properly, raising his eyebrows. Vlad sighed. "No. I could've just walked in. If you'll recall, I thought you were scared of me. I didn't want to- I thought it might help you feel safer."

"I ain't scared of you," Johnny reminded him. "Your mama, on the other hand."

Vlad winced. "Please don't call her that. Please don't tell Suzie you know."

"What happened?"

That was the question he *had* been expecting, and the one he was more prepared to answer. "Like I told Anna. We realised the direction the hive was going. We- I never thought they'd do something like this, but we were adults, and we saw… the propaganda. The refusal to allow any interaction with humans, the insistence that we weren't just different but better, that all humans just wanted to erase us. Not all hives are like that," he rushed to add. "Most aren't, same as most humans aren't. But moving hives isn't really something you do, so Suzie and I took loner status and got the hell out."

"Suzie-" Johnny muttered. "Is she named after her? Suzanna?"

Vlad nodded.

"What about your father?"

"Oh, he was there. Somewhere in the depths of the hive, probably. But Anna is the leader."

Johnny jerked his head back towards Vlad. "You mean, she was the *hive* leader?"

"Yes."

"Doesn't that make you, I dunno, some kinda hive royalty? Wait, don't that mean she could've killed us easy as blinkin'?"

258

The energy finally drained out of Vlad at that, leaving him in a rush that left him slumped into his corner. "Yes," he repeated simply, and was surprised when Johnny's gaze turned soft, sympathetic without being pitying.

"Leaving musta been terrifying."

"Yes."

"Going back musta been worse."

Vlad managed to raise his head at that, meeting Johnny's gaze. "Yeah," he agreed, equally soft, and Johnny uncoiled himself, half-standing and awkwardly side-stepping across to Vlad's corner, ducked down to keep his head from hitting the ceiling. Vlad watched him come silently, until he sat down again right next to Vlad and lifted his arm. Vlad watched his face for a moment, then took the offered comfort and scooted over enough to rest his head on Johnny's shoulder. "You're not afraid of me, are you?" he murmured into the well-worn flannel under his face. Johnny didn't respond, just rested his arm over Vlad's shoulders. "You're afraid of your feelings."

Johnny tensed, but didn't pull away or say anything further.

"It's okay," Vlad said. "We'll talk about it when I wake up." As he drifted into exhausted sleep, he summoned enough of the last dregs of his energy to add, "Me too."

Turning Day came and went with no more drama than a brief fight over who got which leftovers and Suzie's laughing admittance that she'd just been waiting to see how long it would take Vlad and Johnny to figure it out. It wasn't until Vlad and Johnny were back on a bus, this one for a much shorter ride home into the city, that Vlad got the chance to check the news for the first time in hours.

The newscaster was finishing up a story about council elections as he pulled it up on his phone, then she paused and looked at something above the camera. "The major news for tonight," she said, and if he'd been breathing, he would have held his breath.

The screen flipped to film footage, and he slumped back into the seat, relief filling him. He bumped his thigh against Johnny's, and when Johnny looked over and made a questioning noise, nodded down at the phone.

On screen, a very disgruntled Anna, hidden under a floor-length black cape, and a burly clean-shaven man, presumably the leader of the endless daytime squad, were being led away in handcuffs as the newscaster coolly, quietly narrated, "Today, on the important vampire holiday of the Turning, not one but *two* groups, one vampire and one human, were apprehended when mysterious, presumed explosive devices they had brought into Baltimore's public parks apparently failed to go off. The vampire group appears to be affiliated with the historic Baltimore hive, while the human group has been linked to several prior anti-vampiric attacks. Authorities are investigating further, and we will keep you updated as this story progresses."

Johnny huffed out a breath and slung an arm over Vlad's shoulders, pulling him closer. "We did it, huh?"

"Yeah," Vlad agreed, nodding. "Lab scientist and a plumber. Foiled two doomsday plots and took down two extremist groups in the process."

The newscaster was still talking, sports scores or some inconsequential cat-stuck-in-a-tree story, and Johnny reached out and muted it, gently taking the phone out of Vlad's hand. "You did it," he said. "She ain't hurting no-one no more."

As streetlights blurred past outside, with the kind of warm exhaustion that could only come from overeating at a family holiday settled into his bones and Johnny's arm firm around him, those words finally sank in. She wasn't hurting anyone anymore. Vlad nodded again, slowly.

Johnny dropped a soft kiss into Vlad's curls, then asked, "Hey, was your sister bettin' on us?" Vlad was laughing quietly as the bus rolled on into the night.

Whether We Weather the Weather
by Teague LaBrosse
Fourth Place

"Hell in Manhattan today," The news anchor's voice echoes through the vast marble lobby, "as self-proclaimed super villain, The Pouting Prince, terrorizes the city." Shelby rushes in from the pouring rain. Her dark hair sticking to her face. "His flying weather machine has created floods, blizzards, and fires; destroying the Upper West Side." She hurries up to the front desk, the wet slaps of her feet announce her presence. "As his rampage continues uninterrupted we are all left to wonder," She rests against the desk, out of breath, "Where is *Hero Man*?"

"Can we turn this thing off please?" She asks the desk clerk as she sets her wet bags on the floor. The clerk, Robert, looks up at her scrunching his brow.

"Forgot your umbrella?"

"No, Robert. It was supposed to be sunny today."

"Clearly mother nature didn't get the memo." He jokes lightly.

"You haven't even been listening to this!" She half yells, switching off the radio, "It's a *villain* with a *weather machine*. So I need to get upstairs!... Is there any mail?"

Robert looks at her unimpressed, folding his arms. "I don't appreciate you yelling at me," He says the way a disappointed mother might to her teenage daughter. Shelby groans, really playing into her role as the daughter, as she rolls her eyes and throws her head back to look at the impossibly high ceiling.

"Fine. You're right, Robert. I'm sorry I yelled... *Does he have any mail*?" She looks back down at him, he is smirking confidently.

"Yes. Let me grab it for you," He says with a full smile, walking into the also-too-large mailroom to the left of the lobby.

The sounds of heavy rain hitting the large windows marries nicely with the sound of the impressive waterfall feature adjacent to the front desk. The several fireplaces around the lobby are electric so they don't add to the soundscape, which Shelby thinks is a shame. Although they do add a warmth to this cold lobby that the artfully defused white lights do not.

Robert comes back from the mailroom pulling a luggage cart with six full mailboxes stacked on top of each other.

"Oh that's a lot less than usual."

"Yeah the post office burnt down this morning, so."

"Right, the fire storms."

"At least the rain put out the fires!"

Shelby sighs, "Thank you, Robert." He smiles and nods at her, as she pulls the mail to the elevators past the mailroom and one of the several fireplaces. There are no buttons for the elevators, just a single touch screen with a scanner below it. Shelby pulls the ID card attached to her hip, up to the scanner. The screen lights up revealing a number pad as she lets go of the card allowing it to snap back into place. She hits 6-5 into the keypad.

"Retina scan required for floor 65" the feminine elevator voice says.

Shelby leans over and opens her eyes wide as if she were trying to make them pop out of her head by willpower alone. The red light scans up and down her corneas, giving a *DING* as the doors finally open. She pulls the heavy trolley onto the elevator, her other bags awkwardly hitting her knees as she goes. Coming to a grunting stop, she takes a deep breath in. Still drenched from the rain, the damp thud of water dripping on the elevator floor taps on her nerves. She lets out a sigh allowing the weight of her head to drop against the elevator wall, as she ascends to a job she's wildly underpaid for; personal assistant to *Hero Man*.

The doors open with a chime revealing an expansive open concept luxury loft. Shelby lugs the cart into the apartment.

"Will you please just try it on?" Hero Man's stylist pleads from across the room.

"No!" Hero Man sobs, "I'm not doing anymore press, Cinema!" He is curled up on the long sofa, wearing his royal blue full body super suit with red and gold details. His cape tangled up underneath his perfectly sculpted body, and the Super Alliance crest shines on his shoulder with each movement. *Has he not changed since his mission last week?* Shelby wonders.

"Oh good you're here!" Cinema says turning to Shelby, "You need to deal with him. He's being more impossible than normal." His fashionably gaunt face twists as he looks her up and down with his judgemental golden brown eyes. "But maybe dry off first."

"We have bigger problems," Shelby says walking past Cinema.

"Girl, at least grab a towel!"

She turns with a huff grabbing a fresh towel from the linen closet by the bathroom. As she closes the cabinet she sees the stocky form of the chef, Pepper, rushing towards her. Pepper's round face is flush and dewy.

"Oh good you're here!" Pepper says, "He's being more infuriating than usual. He won't eat anything but ice cream!" She proclaims as if it is the greatest sin he could possibly commit.

"Okay I hear you both, but-"

"But? He's been wearing his super suit for a *week*! I need him to take it off so I can wash it. And so he can wash himself before I puke from the smell alone!" Cinema rants.

"Right, but there's-"

"Shelby, he isn't eating! He's going to die from starvation-If he was a normal human his body would have gone into shock already!"

"Guys there's a super villain attacking the Upper West Side as we speak!" Shelby half yells.

"*WELL,*" Cinema throws his perfectly manicured hands up, "go get him off the couch!"

Shelby groans in frustration, stripping off her blazer as she throws the towel around her neck, marching over to Hero Man. His back is to them as he's curled in the fetal position scrolling through his phone. Various empty ice cream tubs and spoons are littered around him like bones in a sad vulture's nest. Standing over him she can see his graying scruff has overtaken his usually clean shaven face.

"Hero Man, you need to get up now," She demands, taking the role of the mother this time.

"NO. They all said I'm the worst super! If that's how they feel, then they don't get me!" He whines at her in a broken voice.

"Who said that?"

"The internet troll people, Jenna!"

"My name is Shelby."

"They all hate me and I hate them back!"

"Okay, *Dick,*" He flinches at the use of his government name, "you need to get up now!"

"SHUT UP MEGAN!"

"IT'S SHELBY!"

"DON'T SCREAM AT ME!"

"*Aaaaaaaah!*" She screams, making claw hands at his back. Taking a forceful breath in, she violently recoils her hands into trembling fists. Then breaths out with a slight growl turning around to her colleagues, who step back at the sudden action. "Team meeting. Kitchen. Now." She says, and they obey.

The kitchen is clean and glamorous, like one a celebrity chef from the Food Network might have. They circle around the granite island, leaning in close.

"There is a villain with a weather machine who has already wrecked part of Manhattan and is heading this way quickly." Shelby fills them in, "How do we get him out there to fight?"

"We don't," Cinema shrugs, "I can't even get him to change, no way he's going to save the city."

"Well, what about the other supers?" Pepper asks, "Can't they help?"

"No, because they're all *dead*, remember?" Shelby says.

"All of them?"

"Yes!" Cinema says, looking completely defeated. Pepper, on the other hand, has never been one to quit so easily.

"It can't be all of them!" She demands.

"It can, and it is. They're all dead, Pepper!" Shelby says.

"*Leg-Pop-Off Man*?"

"Trampled to death."

"*Anything-Eater Gal*?"

"Eaten alive."

"*Memory Lad*?"

"You know... I can't remember."

"But he's for sure dead," Cinema interjects.

"Definitely dead." Shelby agrees.

"So that means?..."

"Yup. He's the only one left..."

"We're so fucked." Pepper says, finally giving into defeat.

"That's why I've been so busy lately, cataloging all the powerful super tools that have been left to him, in the vault." Shelby says like she's reliving a traumatic memory.

"Wait," Pepper perks up, "Didn't some of the supers get their powers directly from their magical super hero items?"

"Sure," Cinema says, "That's how they got away with such horrendous color schemes."

"Well then why don't we-?"

"No!" Shelby interrupts her, "Absolutely not."

"Wait what?" Cinema asks.

"Please Shelby," Pepper grabs her hands, "It's perfect! We can stop him!"

"Oh." Cinema realizes, then frowns, "*Oh.*"

"Shelby, is this how you want to die?" Pepper asks, "Soaking wet, trying to get this hopeless oaf off the couch to fight?" The trio looks over to the blue mass that is Hero Man on the couch.

"*Veronica*!" He cries to Shelby, "I can't reach the *remote*!" His finger is tapping the remote that he could reach if he extended his arm all the way.

"No," She says, turning back to Pepper, "I don't want to die like this."

"Alright then, it's settled."

The vault is immaculately organized. Swords and battle axes hang proudly on the walls, closest color organized holding full outfit, boxes and shelves neatly arranged, and absolutely everything is labeled. Cinema and Pepper are in awe as they look around.

"Jesus Christ, Shelb," Pepper mumbles.

"This is so sexy," Cinema says with a chest full of pride.

Shelby, knowing she's done well, wears a confident smirk as she pulls out a box labeled *The Pal Patrol: Power Rings.* The other two huddle in close as she opens the box revealing a rainbow of metallic glowing rings.

"No. Way." Cinema says, his eyes almost glowing as bright as the rings.

"What are these?" Pepper asks, leaning in closely to read the labels under each ring, "Flight, Invisibility, Fire?"

"They're power rings," Shelby says smiling down on her color coded babies, "and I've finally collected them all."

"Collected?" Cinema frowns at her.

"You're right, I'm sorry. Hero Man finally *inherited* all of them."

"You're a sick ticket."

"Point is," She snaps, "The rings will give you whatever power that's associated with them. Heat-Vision, Teleportation, the works."

"Good, 'cause you know I hate losing," Cinema smirks.

"We are gonna be so O.P!" Pepper reaches for the rings only to be smacked away by Shelby. "Ouch, hey!" She whines, holding her own hand close to her chest.

"You can't wear more than one!" She explains, "That's how like a third of them died!"

"Oh shit."

"Yeah. So, let's choose carefully," She says looking up to them with a smirk, "Then let's go kick that prince's ass right out of the sky."

The screams can barely be heard over the raging storm in the heart of Hell's Kitchen. The Pouting Prince, vicious and beautiful, looks like a sorrowful romantic era painting attacking from the sky. He rides upon a luminescent cloud, shifting from red to blue to purple, and on and on, through a rainbow of colors. A control panel elevated from the cloud stands in front of him. Tears stream down his youthful yet perfectly sculpted face, looking like a living marble statue, as he screams into a microphone, "If I can't have happiness, then no one can!" Pulling a lever down, lighting strikes from the cloud into a nearby bar, setting it ablaze.

Running out of the subway in monochromatic suits, in a style akin to Hero Man's, are Shelby, Cinema, and Pepper. Each with elbow length caplets, light yet sturdy armor, and sleek form fitting masks. Luckily for them, Cinema often used them as test subjects for his super-design-work, so not only are their hero suits functional, but they're fashionable as well.

Half the people in this neighborhood run past them down the stairs, the other half scatter in every direction like cockroaches in the light. The trio look horrified at the Prince, his purple cape blowing in the wind.

"Well well well, what do we have here?" The Prince says turning his attention to the orange, gold, and teal figures standing below him, "A litter of half-baked-supers? How pathetic."

"We've come to stop you, and your *rain* of terror!" Shelby yells in her most heroic voice.

"Oh? And how are you planning to do that?"

"With the power of-" She hypes herself in her orange super suit, as she lifts a minivan above her head with one hand, "*Strength!*"

Pepper runs up the side of a building in a teal flash, flipping off the side, landing in a power stance, "*Speed!*"

"Aaaand," Cinema throws gold glitter above his head to match his suit, "*FRIENDSHIP!*"

The two women stop and look at him in disbelief, so does the Prince.

"Really, Cinema?" Shelby barks, "You picked the ring of *Friendship*?!"

"Uh, yeah," Cinema says like it was the only obvious choice, "I need to be able to befriend the winning side if things go south."

"Oh my god we're so fucked," Pepper says.

"Yes you are!" The prince yells, running his hand against the control panel causing fire to rain from the cloud. He laughs maniacally, watching Shelby dive roll out of the way, Pepper run to safety, and Cinema just scream and duck behind the nearest car.

Shelby quickly lifts the car Cinema is cowering behind and hurles it at the weather machine. The Prince navigates it like a champ, dodging the car without hesitation.

Pepper runs up the side of a nearby building, jumping off the side, fist first into the Pouting Prince's face, nearly knocking him off the cloud.

266

"Nice shot, Pepper!" Shelby shouts.

"It's going to take more than a little punch to stop me!" The Prince says, rubbing his jaw.

"That cape looks *stunning* on you!" Cinema shouts, his ring glowing gold. The Prince just looks at him, considering the small flamboyant man. "Purple is really your color!"

"Uh. Th-thank you?-" *PUNCH*, Pepper gets him from the other side.

"Nice distraction, Cinema!" Shelby says.

"Woah!" Cinema looks almost embarrassed, "That wasn't a distraction! I really meant it. You look great!"

"You mean it?" The Prince says into his mic.

"Absolutely!" Cinema shouts reassuringly.

"That really means a lot. I wasn't-" *CRASH,* Shelby sinks a car into the side of the weather machine. "No! That is it!" The Prince shouts, button smashing his control panel.

A small tornado grows out of the side of the cloud, quickly increasing in size as it races towards Shelby. She throws a car that gets spun around and thrown back at her, barely missing the top of her head. Looking to her left then right she hurries to a city bus, lifting it with more effort than anything she's thrown before, but still manages to make it soar through the sky.

Three times its original size the tornado easily redirects the bus hitting Shelby off of her feet into a stone building. From underneath the bus Shelby's orange ring glows as she throws it off of her. Standing with a wobble, Shelby goes down hard.

The Prince, already having turned his attention to Pepper, ducks out of the way of her third attack. As she lands in the street below, he pushes several buttons and an icy fog emits from the machine. The streets around her freeze over.

"Ha! Like a little ice is going to stop me!" Pepper boasts, her ring glowing, she runs all of two steps slipping, swiftly landing on her face, knocking her out cold.

"I think it worked quite *icely* if I do say so myself!" He cackles.

"Honestly?" Cinema says, hands on his hips, ring glowing, "That was so impressive."

"Oh come on now," The Pouting Prince says sheepishly, "it wasn't all that."

"No I mean it! You stopped the strength *and* speed rings like it was nothing!"

"I mean," He's blushing, his hand rubbing the back of his neck, "I did defeat most of the original Pal Patrol."

"Look at me," Cinema says smiling, "Not even surprised! Not. Even. Surprised. You are a really competent villain." The Prince chuckles bashfully.

"Well my father wouldn't think so."

"Oh girl, what's the tea? Is dear old papa the reason you're doing this?" His ring is glowing.

The multicolor cloud descends from the sky, dissipating to reveal the full machine underneath as it powers down. "Ermmm, I guess?" He says leaning on the powerless switches.

"Needed some attention?" Cinema asks warmly. The Prince tilts his head, raising his eyebrows in a way that says, *you're not wrong,* "I get it. I do some crazy shit when I'm feeling ignored."

"Really?" He perks up, with a new glimmer in his eyes.

"Oh God yeah!" Cinema's ring is lighting up half his body, "What did you expect to come from this though?"

The Prince groans, "I don't know! I hoped he'd at least be willing to come fight me himself."

"Wait!" Cinema says, jaw dropped, "Your dad is *Hero Man?!*" The Prince's eyes roll with a smirk, and he sheepishly nods. "Oh-Em-Gee! Why didn't you tell me?"

"It's kinda weird," He chuckles, *"Argh! I'm gonna destroy the city 'cause my neglectful father is Hero Man!* Like it's just... I don't know!"

"Prince," Cinema says dead serious, "I work for Hero Man."

"Shut up, you do not!"

"Bible," He says, placing one hand over his heart and the other in the air like he's being sworn into the presidency.

"What are the odds?"

"What are the odds?!" Cinema echoes, "Tell you what," He has a huge smile on his face and his ring is absolutely radiating, "You and I are gonna go to his loft, *right now*, and let him know what a great son he's missing out on."

"I don't know..." He's smiling back at Cinema.

"No, I insist! We must. The look on his ice cream covered face will be too good!"

The prince giggles and nods, hopping down from the weather machine, "Okay, yeah let's do it!"

"Brilliant! We can figure out what to say on our way over."

The two walk arm and arm down the devastated street, as Shelby and Pepper slowly regain consciousness.

"Cinema?" Shelby calls dazed and confused, "What are you doing?"

Cinema turns over his shoulder, "I'm taking my new *friend* to see Hero Man!" Her eyes widen, shocked back into consciousness, "Do you mind taking the trash out?" He jerks his head towards the weather machine with a wink. Then he turns back to the Pouting Prince, gossiping like a couple of school girls all while his ring continues to glow.

The Bear Whisperer

by Kate MacGuire
Fifth Place (Tied)

Natalie smiled as she dodged kids playing tag while she restocked the buffet table. The Appleton Inn had never been so busy. For the first time since the logging mill shut down, all her rooms were booked. This was also the first time she had catered an event for over a hundred guests. Some were curious locals but most were out-of-town visitors who had booked reservations for Ursaville, Alaska's first-ever eco-tourism business.

It was late afternoon. The cool nip in the air hinted at the season's first frost. Beyond the back deck of the Victorian style inn, Natalie could overhear Chet Jackson, the town's mayor, being interviewed by a journalist who traveled in from Anchorage for the big event. Natalie had no doubt that Chet was in his element. Getting attention and making money were Chet's favorite pastimes.

The journalist smiled at the camera. "Good evening, Anchorage. This is Lacey Smith on location in Ursaville, Alaska. Never heard of Ursaville? Don't feel bad. It's a tiny town off Blue Water Bay that less than a thousand people call home."

Natalie rolled her eyes as she swapped empty glass pitchers for new ones full of ice and lemonade.

"But Ursaville is following the playbook of some of Alaska's bigger cities, like Anchorage and Juneau. I'm here today with Chet Jackson, the town's mayor, to learn more about the new business venture that he's betting will put Ursaville on the map." She stepped back so the videographer could pan a large tour bus behind her. The bus has been professionally wrapped with images of large grizzly bears poised beside a river, their mouths open as a salmon hovered tantalizingly out of reach. "The Bear Bus, Ursaville, AK" was stenciled on the bus in black lettering the same height as a small child.

"Thank you, Lacey," the mayor said. "Ursaville has always prided itself on being a humble, industrious town. But thanks to environmentalists who care more about beetles than hard-working Americans, the logging industry can no longer sustain this town." Natalie dawdled a bit, even though she knew Chet's schpiel by heart. "Ursaville sits in the heart of wildlands where a third of Alaska's native brown bear population roam. Knowing how people treasure these wild animals, we decided to build an industry around them."

The journalist looked like she had somewhere better to be. "So, what exactly is The Bear Bus, Mayor Jackson?"

"The Bear Bus is a luxury charter bus equipped with every modern amenity. We can now take visitors from all over the world directly into the heart of bear country. Now people can observe bears in their natural habitat. Much like going to the zoo but so much more personal and authentic."

The journalist smiled. "And the bears don't mind?"

The mayor belched a hearty, forced laugh. "Oh, no. They love the attention."

"Excuse me, sir." A little girl in a ponytail, wearing overalls and a flowered shirt, tugged on his shirt. "Will I see a bear, sir?" Natalie melted at the expression of pure innocence on the girl's face.

The mayor eyed the camera, then dropped to his knee. With exaggerated gentleness, he asked, "What is your name, sweetie?"

"Aim-eeeee."

"Well, Amy," he said, patting her on the shoulder. "I can personally guarantee that you will see a bear on the tour. Would you like to stand next to one and get your picture taken?"

Amy's parents glanced at each other with indulgent, surprised smiles.

"Yay!" Amy jumped up and down, clapping her hands.

The journalist turned back to the camera with a practiced smile. "Well, there you have it, Anchorage. Just another small Alaskan town using their imagination to make life more…bear-able!"

The mayor struggled back to his feet and asked for a wet wipe. Natalie handed him the wet rag she stowed in her apron for emergencies.

"Why are kids so damn sticky?" he muttered, scrubbing his fingers.

"Mighty big promises you're making there, Mayor." Natalie was startled to hear Rick's voice. He was a young, quiet biologist who had moved to Anchorage three years ago to study how climate change was affecting Ursaville's vulnerable wildlife. Rick sat hunched over his lemonade, as if protecting it from attack.

Chet's lip curled with undisguised disdain. "Oh, I intend to keep them, Dr. Peta."

Natalie rolled her eyes again at the stupid nickname. It was payback for Rick's research that led the EPA to shut down

Chet's favorite fishing spots to protect an endangered mouse species.

Rick chuckled, unperturbed at Chet's dig. "At least I'm not taking hordes of innocent people and all of their snacks and cameras into the heart of bear country."

Chet gave him a haughty stare. "I had a lawyer create a proper release of liability!"

Rick snorted his disgust. "It's been three years since we've had a bear attack. Are you mad, Chet? These bears have already lost 40% of their habitat due to human activity. They're fighting for dwindling resources and now you're going to take a busload of city slickers into the heart of their den?"

The mayor rubbed his thumb and index finger together. "You hear that, Rick? It's the bear sound of the world's tiniest violin. 'Cause that's how much I care about a bunch of bears who do *nothing* to sustain this community." Chet smoothed his hair. "Now, if you'll excuse me, I have some work to do to support my community."

Chet and Rick stalked off in opposite directions. Natalie watched Rick limp away, using a cane for balance while she fingered the bear tooth that dangled from her woven leather bracelet. Her stomach lurched with anxiety, thinking of the night her fiance made this for her. It was the night before they were scheduled to be air-taxied from his remote camp site where he was cataloging bears as part of his Ph.D research. Daniel had braided strips of dried leather together, then added a tooth they had found on the banks of the river where the bears caught their salmon. She'd never been one to even camp, let alone hang out with bears all summer. But Daniel had gently coaxed her past her fears of latte-free zones and things that slither and bit.

The party was winding down. It was time to clear the buffet table and set out coffee and dessert. As she moved back and forth, she noticed a boy chasing two screaming girls. "Grr, grr," he play-growled in his best imitation of a bear. "I'm going to eat you up."

Natalie paused, her hand covering her racing heart. Dear god, what about these children? The mayor had advertised all over the lower 48 and through Canada, pitching The Bear Bus as a family-friendly attraction to attract waves of tourists to their tiny town in his latest get-rich-quick scheme that might also keep the town afloat. With a clatter, she dropped the coffee cups and hurried out to where the mayor was sweet-talking some out-of-town visitors.

"A moment of your time?" Natalie walked a few feet away until they were close to the lattice fence that hid the inn's trash and recycling cans. A hint of rotting vegetables and soiled diapers wafted with the Alaskan fall breeze.

The mayor looked around furtively before tugging a cigarette pack from his jacket. He was under the mistaken notion that no one knew he smoked.

"Chet, you tell me right now... is this thing you're doing really safe?"

He squinted through the smoke. "'Course it is. Why wouldn't it be?"

Because it's your idea. "It just seems rushed, that's all."

The mayor took another deep drag then looked to the sky and its vast carpet of stars. "I've taken precautions."

"Like what?"

Chet threw his half-smoked cigarette to the ground and crushed it under the toe of his snakeskin boot. "Such as... none of your business. The good people of Ursaville trusted me with the town's future, so I guess you'll have to do the same."

"Chet, this isn't about you! There are children here, and innocent people spending their hard-earned money on something they think is safe."

"It is safe," he spat. "You're letting your..." He searched for the right word, "*...trauma* affects your judgment. I have taken extensive safety measures to make sure the bears are safe too."

Rick limped out of the shadows. "What do you mean you've made the bears safe too?"

The mayor's expression was pure contempt. "I don't have to explain myself to you people." He indicated the inn's outdoor space, filled with tourists and townspeople. "Look at all these out-of-towners spending money here. Tilly's been so busy she had to hire two more waitresses. Paul's doing extra fishing excursions and you," he confronted Natalie, "are doing a tidy little business this week, aren't you?" The mayor thumped his chest with a closed fist. "I did this for Ursaville. Not you," he stabbed Rick in the chest with his meaty finger. "Or you." He looked at Natalie with hooded eyes, shaking his head in disappointment. "Honestly, Natalie. Your lack of faith is so hurtful... after everything this town has done for you."

Rick stepped in front of Natalie. "Dammit, Chet. That damn bus is like a food truck for bears, delivering all the calories they need to make it through the winter."

Chet didn't respond. Instead, his gaze focused beyond Rick to the party behind him. Natalie slowly turned to follow his gaze. The party had come to a screeching halt. No talking, laughing, or socializing. Instead, all eyes were on the three of them.

274

Chet glared at Rick, then arranged his face back into a reassuring smile. "Ha, Rick! That was a good one… a food truck for bears." Chet sauntered back to the group. Natalie overheard him telling one of her guests that Rick was an aspiring comic. "You should see him at open mic night at Louie's Bar & Grill. He's a hoot! For a biologist anyway."

Natalie felt something tapping her back. She looked down to see Amy with a small bear tucked under her arm.

"Atalee? I like bears. Bear like me?"

Natalie's heart squeezed at the little girl's worry. She gave the girl an impromptu hug. "Oh, Amy. You're so sweet, everyone likes you!"

Amy bit her lip, apparently unconvinced.

Natalie slid Daniel's bracelet from her wrist. She hadn't taken it off since the night Daniel gifted it to her with his proposal. The ring would come later, he promised, when they got back to town and could order a proper ring from Anchorage. Natalie tied the leather straps so they were snug around Amy's wrist. Amy played with the bear tooth charm. "Oof," she said.

"That's right. That's a bear tooth. It's a good luck charm that will keep you safe with the bears," Natalie said. She was just making this up on the spot, but maybe it was true. Maybe that explained why she had lived and Daniel had died.

Natalie wiped down the counters and prepped the coffee for the next morning. Her back ached from a long day of work, but that was a good problem to have. For once, her mortgage payment to the bank would be on time.

She was about to set the inn's alarm system when the phone rang. She picked it up quickly before it woke her guests.

The caller asked for the mayor. "I can't reach him on his cell phone or his office," the man explained in a clipped New England accent. "He gave this number as an alternative. It's quite urgent that I speak with him immediately."

"He's at the new Bear Bus Lodge. The cell phone reception is terrible. Can I take a message?"

The man introduced himself. He was a lawyer for Scents Unlimited. "Mr. Jackson purchased one of our products, The Bear Whisperer, last spring. I have a simple, urgent message. Can you relay it to him?"

"Of course." Natalie found a small pad of paper and pencil. "Go ahead."

"Tell Mr. Jackson to discontinue use of The Bear Whisperer immediately. He must receive this message before there is any interaction with the native bear population."

Natalie scratched the message on the pad. His urgent, almost frantic tone, was making the hairs on the back of her neck stand up.

Natalie gripped the phone. "Wait," she whispered. "What is The Bear Whisperer?"

The man hesitated. "Well, I suppose I can tell you that without violating confidentiality agreements. My client is a small start-up specializing in the science of pheromones. The company expanded their research into other applications. The Bear Whisperer is a patented diffusing system that disperses bonding pheromones to bears in the wild."

Natalie forced herself to loosen her grip on her pencil. "What do these pheromones do?"

"These are the same pheromones emitted by a mother bear when nursing her cubs. When concentrated and dispersed over many miles, the bears in the treatment zone become docile, content, and quite tolerant."

Natalie carefully put down her pencil lest she snap it in two with her tense fingers. "So why," she swallowed hard against her tight throat. "Are you leaving this message?"

The man hesitated. "I'm sorry, ma'am, but that information is sealed pursuant to a preliminary injunction."

Dread tightened Natalie's throat until she found it hard to breathe. "Sir, I have thirty families scheduled to head into the Alaskan forest tomorrow for a bear-watching tour. Are they in danger?"

The lawyer hesitated. "Ma'am, you do whatever you have to do to stop those people from getting within a mile of those bears. Do you understand?"

But he hung up before she could answer either way. Natalie paced the room, chewing on her thumbnail. What was she supposed to do? These people had traveled from all corners of the earth to have close encounters with *Ursus arctos*, the huge native population of brown bears that were part of Alaska's mystique.

She dialed Chet's cell phone, hoping against hope that the Verizon gods would grant her a connection. But no, her call rolled over into his voicemail. She couldn't imagine facing him alone when he returned that night, excited to launch The Bear Bus's inaugural tour. She needed back-up. There was only one person she could think of who could be that support.

She headed to the second floor and stopped outside of Room #8 and knocked gently, hoping Rick was still awake. But there was no answer. She tested the knob and found his room unlocked. Rick was propped up in bed, a binder leaning against his chest. His reading glasses were still propped at the end of his nose though his eyes were shut tight.

"Rick," she whispered.

He continued to snore lightly. He was handsome in that understated, rugged way that Natalie found irresistible. She never went for the metro-sexual types. Bare chested too, which made the scene even more forbidden and awkward. What if he liked to sleep in nude? She really should leave, save them both from embarrassment. Instead, she touched him lightly on the shoulder.

'I'm sorry," she said, averting her eyes. "I just really need to talk to you."

"It's fine." He sat up straight in bed, adjusting the covers. She got a glimpse of his green and plaid boxer shorts. Phew. "What's wrong?"

When she described the phone call, his expression went from curiosity to concern to anger. "Scents Unlimited?" he clarified. "Dammit. The E.U. has completely blocked them from patent applications. What has Chet gotten himself into?"

"Him and the thirty families who are ready to meet bears tomorrow."

His expression was deadly serious. "I'll see what I can find out about this Bear Whisperer device." He opened his laptop to get to work. "Oh, Natalie?" She stopped in the entry.. "I'm glad you woke me."

Natalie gave him a tentative, grateful smile. "Me too."

Late that night, when Natalie had just about scrubbed the color out of her granite countertops, she heard the rumble of Chet's old Ford 250 engine pull up to the inn.

"I'll handle this," Rick told Natalie.

Rick showed Chet everything he'd been able to find on the Web. The injunctions to stop distributing and marketing The Bear Whisperer. Rumors that the pheromones targeted the bear's limbic system, increasing aggression and territorial behavior. Rick's expression was sad as he navigated to a different screen. "Don't look, Natalie." But it was too late. The horrific image of the mauled Russian zookeeper was an instant trigger for an avalanche of memories. She closed her eyes, pushing away memories of Daniel's battered corpse dropped like a rag doll at the base of a white spruce tree.

"Chet." Natalie spoke with unusual sharpness. "You have to cancel this tour."

Chet swallowed hard, clearly affected by the images. "I just don't understand." He showed them pictures he had taken on his cell phone while checking on The Bear Bus Lodge where visitors would stay overnight. "I took these just a few hours ago."

Natalie thumbed through the images. A mother bear lay on her back under a tree, just ten feet from Chet as her cubs nursed. When Natalie opened the video clip, she gasped in horror. There was Scarface, so named for the eye scarred shut after a dominance fight. That was the bear that had harassed her and Daniel on their last research trip. The bear that had probably killed him while she waited in the Cessna for her fiance to return with a lost hat. But this bear was docile and calm, groaning with pleasure as Chet scratched him under the chin.

She handed the phone back to Chet, feeling nauseous at the video encounter with her nemesis. "It doesn't matter, Chet. You have to shut this thing down. Someone could get hurt."

For a moment, Natalie thought they had him. Who could argue with the Fish and Wildlife Service? Or those grisly images? But then Chet's jaw set in a familiar manner. He slammed Rick's laptop shut. "I don't care what you or that lawyer says. This is my town. Those bears are as friendly as Golden Retrievers."

Natalie touched his arm. He looked down as if she were made of acid. "Chet, please. The children…"

"Are going to have an amazing time." His expression was grim. "Besides, if things go badly, Scents Unlimited designed an app that can shut down The Bear Whisperer remotely. If things get weird, I'll shut it down. Okay?"

She shook her head. "No, Chet. Not okay!"

But he didn't hear her, because he was already out of the door and halfway up the stairs to his room.

Natalie looked back at Rick, her mouth opening and closing like a fish out of water. The thought of little Amy being anywhere near the bears that ripped Daniel apart was sending her over the edge.

Rick noticed her tears. Instantly he was on his feet, limping his way to her. He gathered her into his arms before she could protest. "Don't worry, Natalie. We'll find a way to stop him."

When her breathing was normal again, she brewed a pot of chamomile tea to steady their nerves. He added honey to his. "I'm sorry about those photos of the Russian zookeeper. I wasn't thinking."

"It's okay. I know you were just trying to get through to Chet."

Rick took a few sips of his tea, shifting awkwardly in his chair. He studied her face. "Do you want to talk about it?"

"Not really," she admitted honestly. But talking was a way of processing her trauma.

278

Rick listened patiently as she told him of Daniel. How his love for bears had led him out of New York and into a graduate Ph.D. program. His graduate thesis was studying how climate change affected resources for Alaska's brown bears. "I was terrified of wild animals and hotels that don't include hair dryers," she admitted with a smile. "But I felt safe with Daniel. He taught me how to avoid bears with bells and loud noises. How to set up our camp w/electric fencing and keep food in bear proof boxes. But over time, as he got to know the bears, he kind of..." She searched for the right word. "Changed."

Rick nodded without judgement. "Started thinking of them as friends, rather than wild creatures?"

"Yes, exactly." She'd never really discussed this with anyone before. "He had the craziest ideas, really. That he could sing the bears into a peaceful state. And that they would be insulted if he carried bear spray or electrocuted them with fencing."

"That happens sometimes when people spend more time in the wild than with people."

She sighed. "I told him that was my last trip with him. If he wasn't going to take basic precautions for our safety, then I didn't want to go. We fought terribly the night before we were scheduled for pick-up. But it seemed like I got through to him." She took a sip of her now-cold tea.

Rick's voice was persistent but kind. "What happened to Daniel?"

She set her mug down. "We were all boarded on Steve's Cessna to leave camp and head back to Ursaville. Then he remembered he'd left his favorite hat behind. He refused the can of bear spray Steve offered him, saying he'd be back before a bear even knew he was there. We waited and waited." She closed her eyes and shook off the images of Daniel's remains. "After he died, I was alone in the world. Ursaville took me under their wing." She felt self-conscious about talking about herself so much. "Enough about me. What about you?"

"Well, you know I'm a biologist with the U.S. Fish and..."

She shook her head. "Not the boring stuff." She indicated the cane leaning on the wall next to him. "That."

Rick pulled up his pants so she could see his leg. Or rather, what remained of his leg. The calf muscle was missing, leaving a gnarled, uneven bone behind. It was healed but grisly. "I understand how Daniel could put himself in a bad situation. I did the same, back when I was a student volunteering in bear counts as part of my graduate work. My ego got in the way and next thing I knew, I had a bad encounter with one of my 'nice' bears." He dropped the pant leg and slid his leg back under the table.

Natalie looked down at her empty tea cup. "What are we going to do about Chet?"

Rick bit his lip. "If we freak out and shut this tour down without proof, Ursaville will never recover. It'll be just another boom-and-bust town."

Natalie was aghast. "You can't be serious."

"But we're going too, Natalie. We'll be right there the whole time, ready to shut this operation down at the first sign of trouble." Seeing her expression, he laced his fingers through hers. A rush of electric energy zipped through her body, setting every nerve fiber on alert. She felt Rick's finger under her chin, guiding her face closer. "Trust me," he said. Then his lips were on hers, warm and gentle, her first kiss since Daniel died three years ago. For a moment, the people, the bears, her grief all faded into the background. All she could feel was his warm invitation. All she could taste was honey.

Late that night, Natalie woke up feeling dazed and disoriented. Where was she? It took her a moment to reorient. She was in Room #8. With a snoring, naked man. There was no point to regretting what she
}had done. Daniel had been gone for three years. She would never "get over him" in a way that made sense. But she could take the memory of Daniel's love into the future, whatever that might be.

There it was again. The sound that woke her up. A rhythmic abrasive sound, like a tree branch rubbing against the house in the wind. But all the trees had been trimmed that spring. And it wasn't a windy night.

She got up and found her clothes in the dark. Rick was still sleeping, snoring lightly and curled in a ball. She contemplated waking him but decided against it. Managing the creaks and groans of this old Victorian was her job.

She stopped in the hallway, trying to identify the source of the sound. Downstairs, for sure. She turned on the hallway light and headed downstairs. She checked all the windows in the living room and hallway as she passed. Everything seemed shut tight. The laundry room and bathrooms were quiet, but she checked the pipes all the same.

She stood in the kitchen, cocked her head, trying to pinpoint the source. It seemed to be from the back of the house, where the backdoor and cellar was. *Scratch, scratch, scratch.* Whatever was making that sound was deliberate, not random like a tree branch and the wind.

She made her way down the hallway to the glass-paned back door. Maybe she was wrong about the wind. There was definitely movement out there. Her feet seemed to slow with every step. Something about that movement out there seemed wrong.

As she approached the back door, she held her breath. The scratching sound stopped. Slowly, she reached for the wall switch that would turn on the back deck's light. *Click.* The lights illuminated the source of the scratching. Her initial "awww" feeling was soon followed by sheer dread.

A brown bear cub was at her back door, reared up on his hind legs. He looked up with chocolate brown eyes. Good grief but he was cute. A perfect miniature version of the bears that roamed the woods beyond her cottage. But baby bears never traveled alone. They always had a mother nearby.

Natalie glanced furtively from side to side. No mother in sight. "Go away, little bear," she said to the cub still scratching at the door. "Shoo. Go find your mother." Maybe it was best if she turned off the lights and went away. Bored, the baby bear might find his way back to his mama.

But movement beyond the shadow's of the porch light caught her attention. She hated to turn the floodlights on because they might wake up guests with north-facing windows. Her hand reached and hovered. Was she being ridiculous? Living with bears was part of the deal in Ursaville. They came into town sometimes, looking for unsecured trash or feral cats. But still. She had a hotel full of guests, didn't she? She'd flip it on, really fast, just to reassure herself.

Natalie didn't understand the shifting sea of brown that lay beyond her porch. It made no sense, until part of that blanket of brown lifted its head and caught her gaze. Dear god, it was a bear, and not just one. Dozens and dozens of bears, maybe a hundred, spread out over her lawn, snuffling and huffing, swiping at each other from time to time. She'd never seen so many bears in one place... *her* place.

The bear that caught her gaze looked down to the cub at her door. Even at this distance, Natalie could see its pupils dilate. The bear broke off from the others, loping her way, huffing all the while. This was the mother that Natalie feared, charging right for her door. With a tremendous scream-growl and a thud, the bear hurled itself against the door, her face filling the glass so that Natalie could see the long thread of saliva hanging from her chin and sheer rage in her eyes.

Natalie involuntarily screamed and jumped backwards, losing her footing and landing on her butt. By some miracle, the door held fast against the bear's assault. Natalie's scream seemed to enrage the mother. She reared back and charged the door again and again. Natalie felt frozen by the horror of it. Watching the door bow under the pressure of the grizzly was enough to break her stupor. She scrambled to her feet and started for the stairs but was stopped by the solid wall of flannel-covered chest.

"What's going on?" Rick sounded as frantic as she felt.

She pointed with a trembling finger at the back door. The mother had attracted other bears to the porch, their faces filling the glass inset of the back door. One of them was almost comical as he studied the door, looking for vulnerabilities.

"Bears, Rick. Hundreds of bears."

He looked doubtful at her claim of "hundreds." but then they heard shattering glass in the kitchen. Rick pulled her up. They ran to the kitchen where a gray-muzzled bear was reaching for the bananas she kept on the counter.

"Come with me." Rick yanked her arm for good measure as he ran-limped with his cane. They checked the perimeter of the downstairs. Floodlights illuminated hundreds of bears swarming the inn's property.

Natalie felt panic overtake her body. "Rick, what the hell are we going to do?"

From overhead, they could hear footsteps and voices. *What's going on down there?*

Rick looked at her, wide-eyed. "Get everyone downstairs now."

Natalie led the crowd of confused and now frightened guests downstairs. Bears were fighting with each other to get access to the broken windows, growling and mouthing each other for space and resources. Rick was quizzing Bob, the charter bus driver, on how many rounds of ammunition he had for his shotgun. Only twelve.

Rick's gaze shifted to the living room window. "We got a lot more than twelve bears out there."

Natalie could hardly hear Rick's voice over the howling and growling of the bears. The overpowering odor of musk and rotten carrion from the bear's breath was making her queasy. She spotted Chet, huddled in the middle of the frightened guests.

"You!" she cried. "This is your fault!"

"We don't have time for this," Rick said. "Chet, turn off that damn Bear Whisperer. The pheromones are driving the bears crazy."

Chet fumbled with his phone. "It's not working. The app is dead."

Rick rolled his eyes. "Figures. The company probably shut down everything when they got their first subpoena. Where is this damn machine anyway?"

"The east fire watch tower."

282

Another crashing window, this time from the laundry room. There was a terrible groaning sound overhead.

"Bears are on the roof," Rick said grimly. "We don't have much time."

Natalie's gaze fell on Amy who was watching her intently. She couldn't let Amy suffer the same fate that Daniel did. Thoughts of Daniel rose to mind and his crazy ideas about bears.

She looked at Rick. "Please don't think I'm crazy, but I have an idea. Daniel swore he could soothe the bears with singing." She bit her lip.

If Rick thought she was crazy, he hid it well. "Go on."

"If we get everyone singing in the living room, maybe it will draw enough bears so I can run to the Jeep. I'll drive to the fire watch tower and disengage The Bear Whisperer."

His gaze was steady. "I'm coming with you."

"You can't." She smiled and indicated his cane. "Take everyone to the cellar. It's the safest place."

Rick drew her into his arms. "It's too dangerous."

She looked up, then kissed him hard. Kissed him for Daniel and everyone who'd ever been afraid of bears. "It's our only chance, Rick."

He nodded once, accepting their fate. Then he turned to the people and whistled to get their attention. "I'm going to ask you to do something. If you want to live to see daybreak, you're going to do this without any questions, 'k?"

Natalie followed the group to the living room. All eyes were on her. She took a deep breath and sang the first line, then the second. As people recognized the song and its lyrics, they slowly joined her until they were all singing *Take Me Home, Country Roads* at the top of their lungs. Rick ran from window to window, watching what the bears did. He gave Natalie an enthusiastic thumbs-up.

"It's safe to go," Rick mouthed.

She nodded and told the group to keep singing. Crap, she was still in her nightwear. Tiny shorts and a tank with no bra. There wasn't enough time to change. She would just have to grab shoes from the hallway closet and go. But the only shoes she could find were a pair of black, sparkly stilettos. She swore under her breath and slipped them on.

Natalie grabbed a flashlight and a granola bar from the kitchen, then headed for the back door. A quick check from the safety of the hallway confirmed that the coast was clear. Just as she was about to leave, someone pushed her from behind and snatched the keys from her hand. "What the hell?" she cried out.

It was the mayor, streaking past her, keys jangling in his hand. Before she could stop him, he jumped in the jeep and peeled away, leaving a spray of gravel and dust in his wake. *Unfuckingbelievable.* At least she had The Bear Bus.

She slowed and parked in front of the tower, then ran for the tower. The ascending stairs were blocked off by a chain link fence and padlock. She had no choice but to climb the metal scaffolding to the tower. She wrapped her hands around the first metal rail and pulled herself up. *Left hand, right hand, left foot, right foot.* Over and over, slowly making progress up the tower. Even though she knew better, she looked down at one point and nearly lost her balance, the tower's cold steel railing slipping under her five inch stilettos. She quickly regained her balance and took a deep breath.

At last, she made it to the tower. But there was nothing inside the office that looked like a pheromone dispersal device. She'd come all this way, climbing a tower in skimpy clothes and ridiculous high heels. What was the point?

But then it occurred to her. A machine that disperses pheromones should be outside, right? She headed back out the door, walking the slatted catwalk that surrounded the tower's office, yanking her shoe out when the heel got stuck between the slats. And then she saw it. A small box that looked a whole lot like an outdoor speaker system, except for the words "Bear Whisperer" stenciled in white.

She reached up and yanked the box down. She would find a way to disable this box, even if it meant smashing it to smithereens with a sledgehammer. But thankfully, a simple on-off switch at the back settled the matter.

She was about to head downstairs when she heard the tower's scaffolding groan and creak. She stopped and cocked her head. What the hell was that? If she was lucky, it was just the tower shifting in response to the winds that sometimes kicked up off the bay. But if she wasn't lucky…

She risked a peek over the railing. A giant brown bear looked up at the same time, meeting her gaze. A giant brown bear with one eye sealed shut by scar tissue. *No.* She squeezed her eyes shut, willing her fears away. It couldn't be. But more groans and creaks made her eyes fly open, confirming her worst fears. It was Scarface, the bear that had killed her fiancé three years ago. Now he had his sights set on her.

She had a minute, maybe two, before the bear cleared the railing and joined her on the tower's catwalk. She looked around for a weapon. All she could find was an expired fire extinguisher. As she braced herself for the fight, she realized how ridiculous this was. There was no way she would defeat a thousand pound grizzly with a flimsy little fire extinguisher. The best she could hope for was spraying him in the face with the powdery white spray, blinding the one good eye he still had, and using the time to shimmy down the tower to the bus. *Creak, groan, creak, groan*...the smell of rotten carrion got closer and closer. She forced deep breaths and tried to remember the words to *Take Me Home, Country Roads*, but honestly, remembering her own name seemed beyond her capacity at the moment.

Any doubts she had about the bear's intentions were vanquished with the terrible growl he uttered as he cleared the rail. She took a few steps back but she couldn't go too far or the spray would be ineffective. She took a deep breath and waited, one step closer, another step.

Finally he was in range. He reared up on his hind legs, making his already impressive body even more terrifying. She screamed and unleashed the fire retardant, aiming for his eyes, nose and mouth. He roared in protest, then dropped to all fours to rub his muzzle against his forearms. She emptied the rest of the canister for good measure then turned to run, wanting to take full advantage of his incapacity to get away. But as she ran away, she felt his massive paw swipe at her back legs, ripping the flesh open, and knocking her off her feet. She flipped on her back and the bear was almost on her. Apparently the fire retardant didn't have as much of an effect on angry bears as she hoped. She crab-walked backwards on her hands and feet, feeling his hot, musky breath on her chest and face. Is this what Daniel felt in his last minutes?

When her back hit the railing of the fire tower's deck, she knew she was out of options. She closed her eyes and looked away. *Please let this be over fast.*

And then, inexplicably, the sound of a shotgun so close it made her ears ring. For a moment she was dazed, confused, deaf. With a tremendous groan, the bear collapsed on her legs, pinning her in place. She froze in place, having no clue what was going on. If a bear didn't kill her today, she might just die from a heart attack.

She was dimly aware of movement in her peripheral vision. Another bear? Perhaps. It didn't matter. She was spent to the core and had nothing left to fight with. Exhausted, and drained, she turned her head to find Rick kneeling at her side, shotgun in hand. His face was earnest and by all appearances, he was shouting at her. But she couldn't hear anything above the ringing in her ears. All she could do was clutch for him, demand that he wrap her up in his arms, bury her into his flannel and not let her go until the darkness had passed.

Martin and the Viral Video

by Charlie Rogers
Fifth Place (Tied)

The three monks, who were not really monks at all but liked the sound of that title, gathered on the rooftop of the old Ex-Lax building. Paul and Mary held hands in breathless anticipation as Peter peered through a pair of binoculars he'd picked up from a clearance bin at TJ Maxx.

"I see him," Peter cried. "The chosen one!"

"The one who'll save us all," Paul whispered, reverent.

"What?" Peter turned to his companions.

"He said, 'the one who'll save us all,'" Mary said, pointing towards the apartment window they'd been spying on a moment before. "As it was prophesied."

"Oh, I thought you said something else," Peter said. He noticed a fleck of something in Mary's hair, and plucked it out. It smelled of banana. He popped it into his mouth and confirmed that it was, in fact, a small chunk of banana.

"Nope, just prophesy stuff," Paul said.

"Okay, cool," Peter replied, and returned to his binoculars.

Across the street, oblivious to the people spying on him through cheap binoculars, Martin struggled with his dance routine.

"Left arm forward, right arm forward. Hip wiggle. Ugh. Theo, why is this so hard?"

Theo, who was a cat, did not respond, gazing past him towards the kitchen.

Martin approached the full-length mirror he'd propped against the exposed brick of the living room wall. "You're talented. You can do this!"

His reflection didn't seem convinced.

He cued up the music and returned to his starting stance. The beat kicked in and he let it move through him. He thrust his left arm forward, then his right. But as he began to wiggle his hips, one of his feet shifted the throw rug underneath him, causing him to lurch forward, crashing into a heap on the floor.

"I can't do this," Martin moaned. "I'll never go viral."

Theo, still a cat, offered no reaction.

The monks remained vigilant on their rooftop perch.

"What's he doing?" Paul asked, excited.

"Dancing in his underwear," Peter replied.

"Perhaps dancing is his superpower," Mary said.

"Wait, he's vanished!"

"Perhaps vanishing is his superpower?" Mary offered.

"Is it too soon, I wonder," Paul asked, stepping away to adopt a thoughtful pose on the edge of the Ex-Lax building, "to tell him of his destiny?"

"Later," Mary suggested. "I'm kinda hungry."

Across town, in an unassuming coffee shop with a corporate mandate to be as unassuming as possible, a woman ordered her favorite drink.

"Triple caramel latte," she said to the bleary-eyed barista. "Extra foam. Extra shot of caramel. Extra shot of espresso. Two stevia..."

"This is ridiculous," Simon seethed to his seventeen-year old niece as they waited for their turn to order.

"Calm down, Uncle Simon," Althea said. "We're next."

"I cannot calm down."

"...did you get the extra shot of caramel? Make it two shots. Almond milk foam and soy foam, pre-mixed..."

Simon tapped the woman on the shoulder and thrust his cellphone into her face. "Excuse me, ma'am. Please watch this video of a human child playing with a puppy."

"What? Oh - that's adorable." The woman's eyes glassed over.

"Now go sit over there."

The woman did as commanded.

"See?" Simon turned to Althea. "My plan works. Anyone who views this video will instantly be completely in thrall to my every whim."

"I don't know why you're explaining your plan to me," Althea said. "I wrote the mind control code and embedded it into that video, which I also shot. It's my brother Jydn and our chihuahua Mister Dinguswingus."

"I'm sorry, what's your brother's name again?"

"He's your nephew." Althea scrunched up her face. "His name is Jydn. Mom says that vowels are a tool of the patriarchy."

"I'm sure she does. And you have a puppy there as well as a newborn?"

"It's a lot," Althea said.

"May I take your order?" the barista asked.

"Oh, yes," Simon replied. "But first, watch this video."

288

"Look at this video," the woman from the coffee shop said to the man locking up his bicycle outside the shop. "It's so cute."

"Look at this video," that man said to the Dominican nanny pushing a triple-wide stroller.

"It's so cute," the nanny told the yoga instructors gathered outside the gym.

"Look at this video," one of the yoga instructors told her celebrity client who showed up seven minutes early.

"It's so cute," the celebrity told her manager via text message.

"Look at this video." The manager sent a group text to all her talent.

"It's so cute," a struggling actor showed the video to the man next to him on the subway.

"Look at this video," the subway man shoved the video in the faces of everyone else on the train.

"It's so cute," they replied in unison.

Martin's phone dinged as the beat was about to kick in.

"What's that?" he wondered aloud. "Maybe it's about my pizza?"

He paused the music and picked up his phone, reading aloud. "'Look at this video, it's so cute.' No! I don't have time to watch other people's viral videos, I have my own to create!"

He hurled the phone at the sofa, where it bounced onto the floor, startling Theo.

"Or maybe I should? For research? What do you think, Theo?"

Theo licked his left front paw.

"You're right, maybe I should."

But his trip across the room to retrieve his phone was interrupted by the door buzzer.

"Oh! My pizza!" He grabbed his keys and dashed out the door, forgetting that he wasn't dressed.

As he bolted down flight after flight of stairs, a crotchety old woman's voice called out, "Put some pants on, you freak!"

"Quit staring through your peephole, Mrs. Kostapopolis," he called back as he rounded the corner to the last set of steps.

Once downstairs, he threw open the front door to find… it was not his pizza delivery after all.

Three strangers waited on the sidewalk. Two men and a woman, all middle-aged with graying temples and paunches, all in ill-fitting t-shirts and ill-advised sweatpants, all stood with their mouths agape.

"He's a hottie," the taller of the two men said. "You didn't mention that."

"Much better close-up," the other man said.

"Without pants," the first man said.

"I did tell you that part," the shorter man said.

"Shut up," the woman said, shoving both her companions in opposite directions.

"You're not my pizza," Martin said.

"Give me your purse," Simon said to the zombified woman as she passed them on the sidewalk.

"Of course, Master," the woman replied, and handed him her knockoff handbag.

"Now go away," Simon added, admiring the sequined pocketbook.

"Why'd you do that?" Althea asked, as the woman wandered away. "That doesn't go with anything you own."

"You're a smart girl," Simon said, tossing the purse in a trash can.

"I know. I literally wrote the code you're using to mind control people."

A young man in a tanktop and basketball shorts approached them, his phone outstretched in their direction. "Look at this video."

"Shoo," Simon said.

"Yes, Master," the man replied, his face expressionless.

"Finally," Simon cackled, pressing the tips of his fingers together in true supervillain fashion, "after years of being picked on and picked last for kickball--"

"Are you playing a lot of kickball these days, Uncle Simon?" Althea's eyes rolled up hard enough that it hurt.

"Maybe I would! You, there!" He pointed at a zombified construction worker staring at a pylon. "Let's play kickball."

"Yes, Master," the man replied, unmoving.

Simon turned to Althea. "Do you remember how to play kickball?"

"I'm what, now?" Martin asked the strangers, back in his apartment.

"The Chosen One," all three replied. "Jinx!" They burst out laughing.

After a brief bout of hysterics, the one named Peter composed himself. "I'd like to tell you a story. Do you know what 'me too' means?"

290

"You mean like when a woman publicly acknowledges she's been sexually assaulted?"

"No! Err, yes, it does mean that now. But decades ago, it held another meaning."

"I think I wanna put some pants or something on." Martin looked to Theo for backup, but Theo was a cat.

"Please don't," Paul said.

(Later Paul would confess that he wasn't even gay, he was just so taken with the sight of The Chosen One's near-naked flesh that he started to drool. That and the fact he hadn't seen another human being in a state of undress, save his own horrifying reflection, in many, many years.)

(Later still, Paul would confess that he was maybe bisexual but didn't want to make a big deal about it.)

Peter puffed out his chest and began to recount a tale as old as time, dating back to at least 1996.

"There was a service at the dawn of the public internet," he said. "It was affectionately known as AOL, which stood for America, On Line. I think. Anyway, the original AOL was a closed system in which AOL users could only interact with other AOL users in chat rooms and through an arcane system known as IMing. Much like the DMs of today."

"It was a magical time," Mary added.

"When the floodgates to the internet were opened, and AOL users were let loose, like wild, caged animals, they did not understand many of the traditions of the internet. So they would become well-known for responding 'me too' to a message board thread… without quoting the original message."

"What does this have to do with anything?" Martin asked. He was growing frustrated with his visitors and their inscrutable ways. Also, he wondered what had become of his pizza and acknowledged that hunger was making him cranky.

"It was in this long-gone era that my compatriots and I came upon a prophet. His name was ALANIS16, and he foretold many future events. He warned us of the overhyped danger of Y2K, and that the Catwoman movie with Halle Berry would suck really bad."

"Did he predict 9/11?"

"DO NOT QUESTION THE PROPHET!" Peter bellowed.

"Oddly, no," Mary said.

"He vanished after a short while, most likely because he'd used up his free minutes, but not before we'd recorded his many wisdoms."

"That led us to you," Paul said, stepping closer to Martin, who inched away.

"The prophet spoke of a grave threat that would arise in the distant future, a terrible virus that could devastate mankind."

"Like the pandemic?"

"Not the stupid pandemic. Something much, much worse. But amid the despair, he also told us someone would be chosen to battle the virus, alone, our Chosen One, who would reside at 452 Atlantic Ave, apartment 3F."

"That's me," Martin sighed.

"We've traveled a great distance to meet you," Mary said.

"We came all the way from Stuyvesant town," Peter added.

"That's like twenty minutes away." Martin again looked to Theo, who stared at a wall.

"Twenty-five!"

"We had to take two different subways," Paul offered.

The front door buzzed.

"Finally, my pizza!"

"I'll get it," Peter said. "I'm wearing pants."

"Look at this video," the delivery guy said and shoved his phone in Peter's face.

On the screen a tiny brown chihuahua pranced around a toddler's face while the toddler giggled. It was the cutest thing Peter had ever seen. He needed to show his friends.

"World domination is so much better than I expected," Simon shouted as he and his niece walked down the promenade in Brooklyn Heights.

"It's not exactly the world, yet," Althea sighed.

"Give it time." He stopped a zombified man shuffling past them. "You, give me your shorts."

"Of course, Master," the man replied.

"And, you, I want that shirt."

"Oh, no," Althea muttered.

"Now, you six, form a privacy circle around me!"

"Of course, Master," they intoned.

A moment later, Simon emerged from the circle wearing a neon green spaghetti-tank tucked into wrinkled beige cargo shorts. "What do you think? I went to the gym twice this month and I think it's time I start showing off a bit."

Althea covered her eyes and shook her head. She was beginning to question the wisdom of handing her uncle the keys to world domination.

"It's so cute," Peter said, thrusting his wallet at his friends.

292

"I have the same one," Paul said. "We got them on clearance at TJ Maxx."

"Look at this video," Peter said.

"What video?" Martin asked. "That's not a phone."

"He doesn't have a cell phone," Mary said. "Worries about 6G or something. Something's wrong with him."

"Look at this video," Peter repeated, a bit more desperate, shoving the wallet in Martin's face. "It's so cute."

Mary gasped. "Our virus… the one we've come to prevent. It's a video. And poor Peter's seen it."

"I was practicing for a viral video when you guys arrived," Martin offered.

"That's the answer," Mary said. "Maybe."

In Prospect Park, Simon stood before a crowd of thousands of people, possibly tens of thousands.

"My parents always knew I would be evil," he shouted into a megaphone he'd picked up off a zombified cop. "Or else why would they have named me Simon?"

The crowd stood in rapt attention.

Althea sat in the shade off to the side, scrolling through her social media feed. It wasn't very active now that everyone had been enthralled to her uncle's every whim.

"Bullied as a child, I dreamed one day of ruling the world," Simon continued. "There was this one time in high school that Adam Canfield called me a loser and stole my bowtie on the school bus and I vowed to get revenge. Adam, are you out there?"

In the distance, a hand rose.

"Hey, Adam, good to see you. You look terrible."

He then sprinted over to where his niece sat.

"Okay," he said to her. "It's time to do the thing we talked about."

"No," she said. "I refuse."

"Come on Allie, please?"

"Absolutely not."

"I'll buy you an ice cream?"

"From who?"

"Please?"

"I am not playing the Macarena song on my phone for you to lead the world's largest flash mob. It'll mess up my song recs."

"Fine. You know what? I don't need you." He returned to his spot at the head of the crowd. "Hello again good people, my unwilling slaves. Does anyone have Gangnam Style on their phone?"

"Ugh," Althea muttered.

"One more time," Mary said.

"I can't," Martin said. "I'm tired. I'm hungry. You guys ate most of my pizza. This is too much for me. I didn't ask to be the Chosen One or whatever. Saving the world is a lot of responsibility."

"We can take a break, I guess," Paul said, taking a seat next to Martin on the couch.

Martin let his head rest on Paul's shoulder.

(Later, Paul would admit that at the moment, he knew he was, in fact, gay, and finally, after decades of lying to himself, okay with admitting the truth.)

"I've always wanted to be a performer. I moved to the city six months ago with big dreams of breaking into Broadway," Martin sighed. "It's been my dream my whole life, and I've been working towards it since I was a kid in Ohio. I worked three jobs all through high school, saving every penny, so I could come to New York and live my dream."

"I guess they don't know you're the Chosen One," Paul said.

"I can't even get an audition anywhere. I'm too old, too young, too tall, too short. So I thought, maybe I could do some videos, maybe I'd go viral? I did some comedy, first-person POV ones - nothing. I got a stranger to film me doing workouts in Central Park. Nothing. I'm running out of talents. So I thought I'd try dancing. I suck at it."

"I'm not good at anything either," Paul said.

"Guys? I don't mean to rush you, but--" Mary gestured towards Peter.

"Look at this video," Peter said, struggling against the bungee cords binding him as he lay in the corner of the room.

"You're right." Martin stood. "I need to do this. It's getting bad out there."

Out on the street, cars had stopped in the middle of the road. A smattering of random people did the Gangnam Style dance to no music, surprisingly well.

"I've got an idea," Martin said. "I've been doing this all wrong."

Althea snuck away from the crowd somewhere between the seventh and eight iteration of the song, and wandered mostly-deserted streets. This was a disaster.

She'd been mad that Mister Dinguswingus had chewed up one of her favorite sneakers and that her vowel-less brother was getting all her mother's attention. She'd announced she was going into the city to see her uncle and her mother had barely noticed. So when Uncle Simon had said he wanted to conquer the world, she'd shrugged and offered her help.

Now all she wanted was to go back home and flop on her bed, maybe play a bit with her little brother or that scamp of a puppy. But the trains weren't running and for all she knew, her mother was one of the zombies in the crowd.

Her phone dinged. Finally, some social media activity.

It was a video of a goofy-looking guy dancing, without music, in his underwear.

"Oh," she said, to no one.

"Look at this video, it's so cute," Peter said after viewing Martin's dance video.

"It didn't work." Martin collapsed onto his couch once more, tears forming at the corners of his eyes.

Paul took the seat next to him and took Martin's hand. "It was just our first try. We'll get it."

"You're sweet," Martin said. "But I'm a failure. I'm not the chosen one. I'm just a loser."

"Look at this video, it's so cute," Peter said again.

Mary sat on the floor in the opposite corner, petting Theo, who tolerated her presence. She and her friends had spent most of their lives preparing for this moment, even if they'd never really known what they were preparing for. She couldn't give up now. And she couldn't give up on Peter. He'd always been their leader, because, well, she wasn't sure why. But now everything depended on her.

"Look at this video, it's so cute."

Mary stood up. "No. This might be a cliche rooted in toxic masculinity, but failure is not an option. Paul, quit swooning over Martin and focus. And Martin, quit moping and put on your big boy pants. Not literally, because I think the underwear is a good angle. We'll figure this out if we put our heads together."

"She's right," Paul said, standing. "Definitely don't put pants on."

"Look at this video, it's so ridiculous."

"Okay," Martin said, standing as well. "We can -- wait -- did you hear what Peter just said?"

"Wait!" Simon cried. "Where is everyone going?"

A construction worker who'd been happily blasting Gangnam Style from his phone approached him. "Look at this video."

A young man appeared on the screen, his wide eyes both fearful and resolute. The camera panned back to reveal him dressed in tighty-whities and he immediately began gyrating with the most white-boy moves Simon had ever seen. He tripped over his shuffling feet but immediately got back up and resumed dancing. Then the camera panned away, showing a cat licking its hind legs on a windowsill, and behind the cat a sign read "EX-LAX BUILDING."

"That's ridiculous," Simon said.

"You're ridiculous," the construction worker said, and punched Simon in the stomach.

"You can't do that!" Simon cried. "You're my slaves!"

"Not anymore." A shirtless bodybuilder stood above him. "And I want my shirt back."

"You're in big trouble," Althea's mother said, greeting her at the door. She held Jydn in one arm and Mister Dinguswingus in the other.

"I know," Althea said, and leaned in to give her little brother a kiss.

"So what happens now?" Martin asked.

The four of them all looked at each other, uncertain who should speak or what to say.

"I guess we go back home," Mary said. "Peter's back to himself and everything's returned to normal."

"And you're getting tons of media requests and social media followers," Paul added, "so… you'll probably forget all about us."

"No way," Martin said. "Especially you, Paul."

Paul blushed so hard he turned purple.

"I still feel a little off," Peter said. "Or maybe I'm just hungry?"

"That's what we should do! Pizza!" Martin exclaimed.

Theo looked up from his perch. He was a cat, but he knew what that word meant. Scraps of meat and cheese for him. He leapt towards the others, rubbing against their legs.

"It's decided. Pizza with my new best friends!"

Theo purred. He knew that he was, in fact, the chosen one, born of a great destiny to combat a coming evil. A true threat. These humans would be useful in assisting him, when the time came.

Judges' Choice

Each portion, the judges read hundreds of amazing stories. After careful consideration, they choose one piece as the collective favorite to exemplify the best, most enjoyable read overall.

The Judges' Choice has no judgement criteria, no boundaries, and every submission is eligible.

The Lightkeeper's Daughter
by Frances Turner
Judges' Choice

Standing high on the landscape, I was put here to guide the men of the sea, with my light, through the darkness. In the beginning, men lived within my walls. We shared a responsibility to keep the mariners safe and the waters free of wreckage. But through the ticking of time, no lasting bonds were formed, and I didn't know love.

Until there was Rose. The child whose wide eyes were the pale colour of a sun-stripped sky. Our first encounter was on a bright summer's day when her father, Walter, and her mother, Alice, shared a picnic on a blanket overlooking the ocean. They talked about jobs and opportunities while Rose lay on her back, chewing with the tiniest teeth on a small wooden toy.

Her skin was unblemished, untouched as yet by the years already etched into her father's face and her mother's sighs.

Rose blinked as she looked to the clouds, playing peek-a-boo with the sun. Little wisps of her dark brown hair blew in the breeze. Her eyes darted about as she watched birds fly overhead and the rotation of my lamp as it went round. She cried when they picked her up to go home.

A few months later, they moved in and Walter settled into his job, tending my oil-lamps, making sure my light flashed bright. The family warmed my soul as their fires glowed in the winters and their chatter and song filled the fresh air in spring.

When Rose first started to walk, I watched as she gathered sticks in the patches of green grass and the plants that clung to the cliffs.

When she'd grown taller than her father's knee, I watched her draw animals in the dirt and listened to her tell stories, in her sing-song voice, to the dolls she perched on the ledge at my base.

And when she was as high as her father's waist, I watched as Walter and Rose tramped down the hillside to the ocean. They talked of birds and tides and dolphins and boys. They inspected shells on the beach and every time they climbed back up the hill, Rose would lay one or two of her small treasures on the earth at my base.

One stormy afternoon, when she'd grown as high as her mother's shoulders, she asked her father if she could help him paint my skin. As she started to climb the ladder, her foot slipped, and she fell sideways. I felt a thud as her head smacked against my foundations. She lay motionless, her eyes closed. Walter rushed over and knelt at her side, trembling, his eyes wide. I stood helpless, watching them both, beginning to understand fear. Walter lifted her limp arm and placed his shaking fingers on her wrist. It seemed as if my light turned a full rotation before Walter finally let out a deep breath and offered a thank you to his god.

He jumped to his feet, and sweeping Rose up in his arms, he called out to Alice, "Hospital!"

Alice burst out the front door, and I watched as she ran alongside Walter as he hurried up the trail with Rose cradled to his chest. I had never seen Walter drive away so fast. With every hour that passed, the sea churned. My gears stiffened and the frigid air stung my walls.

When morning finally broke, the sun rose over calmer seas.

Mother, father and daughter returned in the afternoon. Rose rested in bed, her head wrapped in a bandage, while Walter and Alice sat up into the wee hours of the night, talking about options and schools and life in the city.

Walter said, "We nearly lost her. This remote peninsula is no place for a nearly teenaged girl to grow up." The next day, Walter made a call that sent them all away.

The sea turned grey. The water seemed lifeless, and my soul's inner light faded.

Within months, my oil lamps were replaced with generators and the lightkeepers only came infrequently for an hour at a time. Once cared for with human touch, I was eventually monitored and managed by a machine in a city more than a hundred kilometres away.

And then, many years later, Rose returned on a spring morning, hand in hand with a boy. She led the boy along the trail towards my lookout. I smiled inside as I listened to their gentle laughter. Her face was light and soft, her complexion remained unscarred. She patted my skin as they walked past. My light flickered, and a spark re-ignited in my soul.

She led the boy down the hill towards the beach where she and her father had ventured together when she was young. The boy wrapped her in his arms as they huddled together in the crisp morning air, watching an orange and purple horizon

300

transform to a yellow, then blue sky. The wind carried their whispers back up the hill. They talked of studies and travels and all their wishes and dreams. I sensed their hearts beating in rhythm with time.

At the top of the hill, Rose stopped by my side and stood still.

My mind flooded with memories of her childhood.

As she turned to go, Rose knelt and placed a shell on the earth at my base.

Many seasons passed before Rose returned. The light that had shone, dimmed again to an ember.

It was Mitchell—the boy, now grown into a man—who I caught sight of first. Holding Rose's hand, he led her along the trail before she suddenly let go and took off in a sprint towards me. He raced to catch up.

My skin tingled at her touch as she sat down, breathless and smiling, on the ledge where she used to perch her dolls.

Mitchell knelt down on his knee and pulled out a small box from his pocket. As he opened the box, he asked Rose a question. She sprung from her seat, straight into his arms. After a long kiss, he placed the ring on her third finger and they stood watching the ocean, holding each other tight.

They were halfway down the trail when Rose stopped to pick a flower. She patted Mitchell on the arm and he stood waiting while she raced back with my gift and her smile.

"I didn't forget you," she said.

Another year later, on a sunny day, when the grass was bright green and dotted with summer buds, they arrived at the top of the trail. Mitchell stepped out of a car, dressed in a black suit with a white shirt. He held the door open, and holding her hand, he helped Rose emerge from their car into the afternoon light. She wore a flowing white dress and a gossamer veil. Mitchell scooped her up in his arms and carried her up to my point.

They stood there beside me, their eyes sparkling like the sun, and the wild sea at their backs as a man clicked his camera. Her veil wafted in a light breeze, her cheeks glowed pink, and her red lips framed a wide smile that radiated like the bright beams I threw out to the stars in the ink of night.

Once the camera stopped clicking, Mitchell and Rose stood quietly, hand in hand, watching the sea. When they turned to go, she pulled a flower out of her bouquet and placed it lovingly on the earth at my base.

When they returned two summers later, Rose had a bump on her belly, which she rubbed with her hand. They sat on a blanket, nibbling at sandwiches, as they watched a flock of mutton-birds feed on a shoal of fish out in the sea. They talked of names and houses, and held each other close as the gulls cawed overhead and a southerly wind swirled about them. The air was charged, and the sun peaked through the clouds as if to say hello. As they gathered their picnic to go, Rose hunted in the grass and found me a shell.

Mitchell chuckled and asked her why.

Her response was swift, "I've just always thought that if I leave a gift, it means I'll always be able to return."

The next time Rose and Mitchell came, a child ran ahead of them on the trail. As they grew closer to me, Rose lifted the little girl into her arms and placed her on Mitchell's shoulders. I watched as the three of them made their way down to the spot where Rose and her father used to sit and listen to the roar of the sea. The waves pummeled those rocks that day, as if putting on a blistering show for the newcomer. As they climbed up the hill, Rose helped her young one find shells and flowers. They stopped by my side and Rose spoke to me like I was her friend. She introduced me to her little girl, Rachel, and Rachel to me, before they laid those flowers and shells in the shape of a heart at my base.

Each summer I watched as Rachel grew taller, looking more like her mother with every passing year. Yet it seemed the only thing that changed about Rose was the way she wore her hair.

Then came the summer when Rachel scrambled down the hillside for a walk on the beach while Rose and Mitchell sat on their blanket overlooking the cliff. They talked about Rachel leaving for university and Mitchell's new job and their new home in a new city, far away.

As Mitchell and Rachel packed away the picnic and headed towards their car, Rose stayed a while with me. She sat on my ledge, looking out towards the sea. The air felt thick with memories. When she stood to go, she kissed her fingertips and pressed them against my skin.

It was years and years before I saw them again. Distant machines kept me going. My mariner's beam stayed bright, but the flicker inside me had nearly blown out.

302

Then one winter's day, when the winds were strong and the nights were long, Rose and Rachel appeared on the horizon. Rachel looked towards me while Rose bowed her head. Rachel looped her arm around her mother and they walked slowly down the track and up the hill to my side. As they came closer, I could see Rose's hair streaked with silver, and the lines on her forehead matched the deep cracks in my skin.

Rose carried a copper vessel in her hands and, it seemed, an emptiness in her heart. She sat on the ledge at my base, placing the vessel in her lap. She sang a quiet song with a melancholy tempo and a crack in her voice. In the place where Mitchell had knelt all those years ago, Rose stood and kissed the side of the vessel and hugged it tight. Then, with Rachel's arm draped around her shoulders, she stepped towards the cliff's edge, lifted the lid and turned the vessel on its side. A heavy cloud poured out and took flight on a sudden gust of cold winter air. We three watched the cloud sail towards the ocean on the wings of the wind. Rose's sorrow sank deep into the earth by my base.

Years passed.

Then, not long ago, Rachel and Rose appeared again on a breezy summer day. Rose's face was pale and her body looked thin. Her head was covered in a scarf.

Rachel wore a wide-brimmed hat and a large belly.

Neither of them attempted the path, but they looked toward me and I returned their gaze before Rose turned her face toward the sun. Then, grabbing Rachel's arm for support, Rose shuffled the few steps to the railing at the cliff's edge.

When Rose tore the scarf off her bare head and let the scarf fly away, my foundations shook at the sight of her frailty.

I threw love into the wind. Rose shivered.

Rachel wrapped a shawl around her mother's shoulders and helped her back to the car.

Storms pummeled the coast for months. My skin blistered as I was thrashed by gales and rain. And then, with the last quarter moon, the wild weather faded to calm.

This morning, the sun got up early. A rare pod of dolphins is playing in the waters. When they flip and dive, I understand again what joy looks like.

Sunlight bounces off the white flowers on the cliffs below, and the sandy ribbon trail to the carpark glints with a shimmer. I rest my eyes on the golden path, hoping once again to see my darling Rose.

My gears skip a beat when I see Rachel starting down the trail, carrying a small baby in her arms. But Rachel's pace is heavy and her head hangs low. As she grows near, I see her dab a tissue at the corners of her red-rimmed eyes. She stops, standing in almost the exact spot where Rose first lay on a blanket all those years ago. Rachel pulls that same blanket out of her bag and lays it carefully on the grass. She kneels and lays her baby down.

Through quivering lips, she says to her child, "Oh Helena, other than in your grandfather's arms, this is where you Gran most loved to be."

The child's eyes are as pale as the sun-stripped sky, and little wisps of her dark brown hair blow in the gentle breeze.

I watch as Rachel pulls a wooden box out of her bag. A flower is carved into the top, like the flower Rose gave me on her wedding day. Rachel gently strokes the box and kisses the lid. When the lid is opened and the box is tipped, a sudden gust of air lifts Rose. She drifts like a cloud on the wings of the wind.

Standing high on the landscape, I look up to the sky, then out across the horizon. Rose dances on the sea-swells and I see her soft features in the clouds. My soul shines with this final gift.

Rose. Returned.

The Authors

John Adams
John Adams (he/him/his) writes about teenage detectives, robo-butlers, and cursed cowboys. His favorite genre is one he's coined "absurdist speculative melodrama" – meaning "monsters being monstrous, aliens being alien, and humans being all too painfully human." His short stories have been published by Australian Writers' Centre, *Dream of Shadows, Intrinsick, Metaphorosis,* and *Paper Butterfly*. His plays have been selected for productions and readings by theatrical organizations like the William Inge Theater Festival, Whim Productions, the Barn Players, and the Midwest Dramatists Conference. He performs across the U.S. with That's No Movie, a multi-genre improv team.
Web: https://johnamusesnoone.com
Twitter: @JohnAmusesNoOne

Calen Bender
Calen Bender is a young aspiring author living in the Seattle area. He hopes to use his stories to help people by creating worlds where they can step away from the stresses and doubts of the real world and find peace, excitement, catharsis, and companionship.

Maria L. Berg
Maria L. Berg received her M.S. in biopsychology from the University of New Orleans with an emphasis in visual perception and memory in human subjects, and did a practicum with NASA at the Michoud facility, programming data into MatLab. She is an active member of Pacific Northwest Writers Association (PNWA) and the Academy of American Poets. Her short fiction has appeared in "Five on the Fifth," "Writer Shed Stories," "The Evening Theatre," and America's Emerging Fantasy Writers: Pacific Region, among others.

Sarah Connell
Sarah Connell is the author of the trilogy, Project Awakening, and her latest flash fiction piece, Longshot, won a place in the magazine *Beyond Words*. She has completed thesis work on Francophone literature in Alsace and worked on ranches on the outskirts of Yellowstone.

Fiona Donaldson
Fiona is a motorbike-riding, crochet-loving, tea-drinking English language teacher who has never written a short story before, but

enjoys writing far too many words during NaNoWriMo every year.

Sean Fallon
Sean Fallon lives in Melbourne, Australia, and currently writes for Film Inquiry, the movie and TV criticism website. His fiction writing has been featured in *The Big Issue* and *Reader's Digest* as well as on numerous websites and anthologies.

Amber Felt
Amber Felt lives with her husband, 4 children, and 2 cats outside of Buffalo, NY. Writing is her passion and her "hobbies" include software engineering and pursuing a PhD in computer and information sciences.

Lisa Fox
Lisa Fox is a pharmaceutical market researcher by day and fiction writer by night. She thrives in the chaos of everyday suburban life, residing in New Jersey (USA) with her husband, two sons, and their couch-dwelling golden retriever. Her work has been featured in *Metaphorosis, New Myths, Luna Station Quarterly, Brilliant Flash Fiction,* and *Defenestration*, among others. She won the 2018 NYC Midnight Short Screenplay competition and in 2020 had short fiction nominated for the Pushcart Prize and Best Small Fictions.

Bridget Haug
Bridget Haug plays with words at the edge of the world. Born and raised in France, she lives in New Zealand where she sometimes sits down to write the stories lurking in her brain. She's an emerging writer whose work has appeared or is forthcoming in *MetaStellar* and *42 Stories Anthology*.

EJ Howler
Growing up on a steady diet of plucky teen adventure stories, my dream has always been to add to the market stories that I wish I had growing up. When not writing, I still like to keep my hands busy with a crocheting project, or our rambunctious kitten.

Jayne Hunter
Jayne Hunter is a writer, equestrian, and mother. She has too many pets and not enough time to write but she won't stop trying. She is at work on a novel.

Teague LaBrosse

Teague LaBrosse (she/he) is from a small desert town in California, where the imagination runs wild for no reason other than shear boredom. Having since moved to Hollywood CA and now New York City, he is creatively inspired by all the ways the weird intersect with the mundane. This passion increased reading the works of Eugene Ionesco as well as other absurdist and nonlinear play writes. Striving to be a writer and actor in the entertainment industry, Teague cannot deny her passion for storytelling in any form!

Kate MacGuire

In a family of doctors and engineers, Kate MacGuire is the black sheep writer of escapist fiction. She received the Swarthout Award for short fiction and placed third (flash prose) in the 2020 Women's National Book Association contest. She lives in North Carolina with family and loves the beaches and Farmer's Market! Drop by www.katemacguire.com for updates and stories.

Ella Moon

Ella Moon is actually three writers stacked on top of each other wearing a trenchcoat. The one on top writes specfic and romance, the one in the middle writes literary drama, and the one on the bottom spends most of its time making outlandish quantities of tea and trying to convince the other two that they don't really need to be writing right this moment. Together, they have stories in publications including *72 Hours of Insanity vols. 7 & 9*, Red Penguin's *A Heart Full of Love*, Murderous Ink Press's *Cosy Nostra*, and online at *Little Old Lady Comedy* and *Defenestration*. One or the other of them can usually be found ignoring the advice of the other two and buying more books and/or mugs and/or sweaters.

M. Ong

Ong was born somewhere in Canada where they spent late nights writing instead of doing their math homework. Currently attending university, they escaped the tight grasp of engineering and is finally chasing their passion for writing. When they are not writing, you can find them laying somewhere thinking about ideas or wondering where they left their phone.

S.E. Reed

S.E. Reed grew up believing in magic. She was taught every fairytale was real, palm readings were gospel and that ghosts lurked in that space between twilight & dawn... Surrounded by the shimmer of Evergreen trees in the mossy Seattle suburb of Lake Stevens, Washington, S.E. stitched costumes for the school play, edited the yearbook and wrote politically charged poetry for the student literary magazine. S.E. Reed, her husband and their 3 children currently live in Boca Raton, FL and spend their time swimming, searching for buried pirate treasure, and living their most magical lives.

Charlie Rogers

Charlie Rogers is a writer, photographer and amateur hermit who lives in New York City with the ghosts of some cats. His short fiction has appeared in *Intrinsick, Pif Magazine*, and the TL;DR anthologies *Endless Pictures* and *Hope*.

Allison Rott

Allison Rott lives in Illinois, a train ride away from the Windy City. It is the perfect length ride to catch up on her reading or let her daydreams work on stories. A voracious reader from her own childhood she has never lost her love of stories or the many many ways of telling them. She has stories in three anthologies, "The Lingering Rift" in *Foxtales 4*, "Feeding the Universe" in *72 Hours of Insanity, vol. 7* and "Pocket Watch Problems" in *On Time*.

Arden Ruth

Arden Ruth is a paralegal by day, fantasy author by night. When she isn't diving into worlds of magic and mythical creatures, you can find her eating her way through all the tacos in town. Arden serves as the Executive Editor at YeahWrite and is currently working on the first novel of her upcoming Hybrid trilogy. She lives in Seattle, Washington with her husband and two fur-babies. To read more of her stories, visit her website at www.ardenruth.com.

Jason Ryder

A father who writes when he can. It has always been my dream to write and be published.

MM Schreier

MM Schreier is a classically trained vocalist who took up writing as therapy for a mid-life crisis. Whether contemporary or speculative fiction, favorite stories are dark and rich in sensory details. Weird twists abound—fiction with just enough truth thrown in to make folks question. Or perhaps that's non-fiction that's somehow gotten twisted up in imagination. A firm believer that people are not

always exclusively right- or left-brained, in addition to creative pursuits, Schreier manages a robotics company and tutors maths and science to at-risk youth. When spare time allows or inspiration is needed, Schreier can be found hiking or snowshoeing in the Green Mountains of Vermont with a spoiled Labrador Retriever. Follow at: mmschreier.com
Twitter: @NoD1v1ng

EJ Sidle
EJ likes to write stories about magic and monsters. She shares her house with a freeloading canine who kindly offers moral support while she edits. Besides writing, EJ enjoys comics, cacti, and classic rock. Also coffee. Come say hi on Twitter @sidle_by

Frances Turner
Judges' Choice!
Born in Washington, DC, raised in Maryland, and a member of the Menominee Indian Tribe of Wisconsin, Frances is also part French, Lithuanian and Polish. She loves travelling and photography. After a life-changing walk on the Milford Track in 1992, she's now lived half of her 56 years in Aotearoa (New Zealand). While she considers Kate and Alex - her two strong, confident and independent daughters – to be her greatest legacy, she's also been a management consultant, founded a dance company, run several arts organisations, serves on boards and raised millions for charities. She was supposed to travel the world in 2020, but the universe had other ideas. She loves escaping into books of all genres and plunging herself into the combined thrill of emotional anarchy and sheer joy that comes with writing creative fiction and non-fiction.

Rodaina Yasser
I am a dentist from Cairo, Egypt. I love writing more than I love my job. I haven't published anything before, but I have participated in challenges and contests. I have also worked in freelance writing.

The Judges

Ashley Barnhill
While some writers dreamt of creating famed works of literature at a very young age, my same dream started sometime in middle school. Needless to say, I wasn't ahead of the game like others, but I'm glad I'm in it now. I put my first foot forward by dabbling in poetry, but now I'm trying to work on my prose in preparation for writing better short stories and later novels.

Jake Berry
Hello! My name is Jake and I am a University of Maryland alum with a bachelor's degree in English. I have been a reader as long as I can remember, and began writing my own short stories from as far back as 6 years old. I adore any sort of literature or narrative in any medium, whether it be novels, films, or video games. In my spare time I like to lift weights, play video games, read, and take photographs (usually of my dog Penny).

Veronica Cashman
I am an English graduate with years of experience with creative writing, though I am always looking to expand my knowledge. I am working to expand my experience with the world and become an editor with a publishing company.

Vincent Chow
Vincent is an undergrad student at Washington University in St. Louis majoring in English and Computer Science. He was born in Toronto, but grew up in Cincinnati, Ohio. He is an aspiring writer, D&D geek, and likes to travel and hike.

Melissa Conney
Melissa Conney lives in Westchester, New York. She graduated from Drew University, where she majored in English with a creative writing concentration and minored in Political Science. She was Associate Editor, Chief Poetry Editor, and Copy and Format Editor of *Chaleur Press* in 2019. She was Prose Editor and Public Relations Manager of *Insanity's Horse*, an art and literature magazine at Drew University, in the Fall of 2020 and the Spring of 2021 semesters.

Joley Costa
Joley is a 19-year-old research and writing enthusiast and proud redhead, currently pursuing a bachelor's in Arts & Literature at

Minerva Schools at KGI. She's passionate about the intersection of writing, education, and social justice. Her favorite authors include J.M. Coetzee, Haruki Murakami, and Virginia Woolf.

Taelor Daugherty
Taelor Daugherty is a rising senior at Agnes Scott College. She is an English Literature major with interests in writing for novels, film, and television.

Carla Dominguez
Carla recently completed her BA in English Creative Writing from California State University of San Bernardino. In her free time she enjoys reading, writing, listening to music, and watching movies/TV shows. Now that she is out of college she hopes to start a career in publishing and is extremely excited to be a part of The Writer's Workout.

Chad Dyer
My name is Chadwick, but you can call me Chad. I'm a Senior at University of Georgia, majoring in Journalism. A used book store is my happy place. There, you can find me hunting for classic Science Fiction and Fantasy books to find inspiration for my own writing. I hope to help other writers with their work so they can feel confident and prepared!

Emma Foster
Emma Foster is a recent college graduate planning on attending graduate school next year. She is currently gaining experience in editing and publishing while she works on the five different majors projects she always has at any given time.

Kathryn Garcia
My name is Kathryn Garcia and I was born and raised in Houston, TX but I am currently attending Washburn University in Topeka, KS. I am majoring in English and minoring in Religious Studies. I have a dog named Racer who is so silly and cute you wouldn't believe she's thirteen years old.

Aryk Greenawalt
Aryk Greenawalt is a nonbinary writer with a passion for middle grade fiction and poetry. Their writing has appeared in *Rattle*, the *Rising Phoenix Review*, and *Riggwelter*, among others. They will begin their MA in Creative Writing at Bath Spa University this fall.

Phoenix Grubbs

Hello! I'm Phoenix Grubbs. I use they/them pronouns and am going into my third year at Michigan State University. I plan to double major in English with a Creative Writing focus and Professional and Public Writing. I love reading, writing, drawing, and learning.

Sofia Leggett

I am a student from Tennessee currently enrolled as a creative writing major at Agnes Scott College. I have loved reading and writing my whole life and greatly enjoy the opportunity to learn and experience both in this internship! In my free time I like to play music, read, and play with my dogs.

Brandon Lovinger

Brandon Lovinger is a student at the University of South Florida. He is currently majoring in English with a concentration in Creative Writing and is an aspiring screenplay writer.

Thảo Mạc

Thảo Mạc
Intern
Ludwig-Maximilian-Universität

Sydney Macias

Sydney Macias is a practicing novel writer whose interests take form in speculative settings. Her work explores large casts of morally ambiguous characters dealing with themes of grief, identity and power. Originally from Los Angeles County, she sought to experience real seasons and get her Bachelor of Fine Arts with an Emphasis in Writing from the School of the Art Institute of Chicago. Her work is influenced by X-men comics, young adult science fiction and fantasy novels.

Olivia McCrackin

My name is Olivia McCrackin. I am a third-year student at the University of Denver. I major in French and International Studies with a minor in Political Science.

Skyler Melnick

Skyler Melnick graduated from the University of Southern California in May, with a B.A. in Narrative Studies. She's delighted to be involved in The Writer's Workout, to continue cultivating a space for fellow writers to be creative, challenged, and part of a community.

Shala Morgan
I've had a love for writing ever since I was a little girl. I love making people laugh, something that's been helpful in my career as a RN. This past year I re-discovered my passion for writing, and my humorous side has been eager to be expressed. In addition to writing, I love spending time with my husband and my dog, reading, and playing video games.

Lauren Nee
Lauren Nee is currently studying psychology and creative writing at Susquehanna University. She lives in Freehold, New Jersey with her parents, her younger sister, her dog (JoJo), and her cat (Duke). Lauren loves to read and write fiction, and you can most often find her doing so with a cup of tea in hand. She hopes to become a published author in the future so that she can continue to share her love for storytelling with others.

Cayla Newnan
Cayla Newnan has been passionate about writing ever since she tried to write a rip-off of *The Baby Sitter's Club* at age 10. She is a rising fourth year student at the University of California, Riverside, where she is studying Media and Cultural Studies and Creative Writing and is a member of the University Honors program. Cayla's work has been published in *Ramblr* and *Harness* magazines, and she is currently working on a long-form contemporary fiction piece for her senior Capstone project.

Lindsey Odorizzi
Lindsey is a rising junior at Brandeis University double majoring in English and Creative Writing. She's been obsessed with reading and writing from a young age, and wants to pursue a career in the publishing industry when she graduates. Her favorite book series is either Percy Jackson or Chaos Walking, which is funny because she's more of a realistic fiction writer. In her free time, you can usually find her watching marvel movies or crocheting.

Jennifer Osuna
Walking in Another's Shoes: Writing is all about the different perspectives of our characters. Tell us a story in the point of view from an unlikely source.

316

Elizabeth Price

Elizabeth Price is a rising senior studying History and Russian Language at Dickinson College. She has always loved writing and telling stories, whether it is on the page, on the stage, or anywhere else in between. She loves reading, and oftentimes prioritizes finishing one last chapter before moving on to things that need to be accomplished in a day. Her favorite authors are V.E Schwab and Kendare Blake, but she also has a soft spot for autobiographies (a personal recommendation would be "A Long Walk to Freedom" by Nelson Mandela). She is currently splitting her time between Denver, Colorado, and Carlisle, Pennsylvania, but her absolute favorite place to be is outside in the sun, no matter what state she's calling home.

Lexie Price

Lexie Price is a 21 year old undergraduate Creative Writing student hailing from Fayetteville, Arkansas. She loves fluffy animals, can be easily bribed with chocolate milk, and is deeply humbled to be able to work with and learn from so many different creative minds.

Layna Putterman

Layna Putterman is a student at Vassar College and an avid reader, who plans on majoring in English. They are an aspiring librarian and author. They have written many short stories, one of which has received a gold key and silver medal from the Scholastic Art and Writing Awards. Currently they are working on a novel.

Nadia Ramdhanie

Aspiring to work in the publishing world as an editor to help rising authors achieve their dreams while also learning more about people and the world through reading.

Emilio Ramos

My name is Emilio Ramos. I am a retired veteran of the United States Marine Corps who is studying communications and creative writing at Mount Mercy University in Iowa. My life revolves around reading, writing, and my two dogs. I aspire to one day be a published author of fiction.

Christina Roffe

Hello! My name is Chrissy Roffe, and I am an avid fan of writing for many different audiences and forms of media, including journalism, books, and video games! I have written many kinds of articles, ranging from news pieces to opinion pieces on my favorite games. My free time consists mostly of discovering new video games that spark my creative interest, learning new dance choreographies to my favorite K-pop songs, and watching YouTube.

Alexandra Salyer
Alexandra Salyer is a judge for this year's Writer's Games and an undergraduate student at Dartmouth interested in English and creative writing. She loves reading and writing with a particular affinity for fantasy, historical fiction, and realistic fiction. She also loves being outdoors and going on walks with her two dogs.

Chelsea Scarberry
A Kent State student currently studying Digital Media Production and Creative Writing. Loves reading, writing, and watching TV (anything with a supernatural element or horror in it). When she's not doing any of those things she's bound to be drawing or cuddling with her cats.

Mary Kate Sheppard
Hey all! My name is Mary Kate Sheppard and I'm an English Creative Writing major at the University of Tennessee at Chattanooga. I love to read but if I'm not nose deep in a good book, you can find me writing stories, hiking, or spending time with my four-legged partner in crime, Dutton.

Kahlo Smith
Kahlo Smith is a writer, editor, and hobbyist Saber fencer living in Santa Cruz, California. When she isn't baking or gardening, she likes to spend her free time chasing cryptids through the woods.

Corey Sobell
Corey Sobell is a rising fourth year at Elon University where he majors in film and English and minors in criminal justice. Corey has written a variety of genres throughout his writing journey. One of his favorites is short stories (fiction and nonfiction), which is why he's excited to intern for The Writer's Workout. Outside of writing, Corey enjoys singing, hiking, and of course, reading.

The Writer's Workout is a registered 501(c)(3) nonprofit organization.

Mission:
The Writer's Workout strives to provide a motivating atmosphere that fosters self-growth and development through encouraging language and education. We want to help you be a better writer.

WW appreciates your support!

www.writersworkout.net